KINGDOM OF RUNES

OATH TAKER

AUDREY GREY

For Amanda Steele,
who believed in this story from the beginning
and makes me laugh every single day.

SOLISSIA

THE
MOTHER'S
SEA

COURT
OF
NINE

THE
GREAT
STEPPES

ASHARI

KINGDOM
OF
ICE

ISLE
OF
MIST

DRAGON-T
STRAIT

THE FLOATING
CITY OF
TYR

MORGANI
ISLANDS

ASGARD

GUL
THRE

FEYRA'S
SPEAR

THE
DESERT OF
BALDR

THE
SELKIE
SEA

DROTH

EYIA

BAY OF
SHADOWS

DARKLING
BAY

SPIREFALL
CASTLE

SHADOW KINGDOM

THE
RUINLANDS

CRED TREE
OF LIFE

FEYRA'S
TEMPLE

THE
WITCHWOOD

BLOOD BONE
MOUNTAINS

E SUN COURT

GLITTERING
SEA

KINDOM OF
VERDURE

THE BANE

DEVOURER'S
CAMP

FENDIER

MANASSES

DEAD MAN'S STRAIT

ASHIVIER

PERTH

FALLEN KINGDOM
OF LORWYNFELL

THE
EENS

MUIRWOOD
FOREST

CROMWELL

UNE
EN
EE

RUNE
WALL

KINGDOM OF
PENRYTH

VENASSIAN
OCEAN

VESERACK

THE MORTAL LANDS

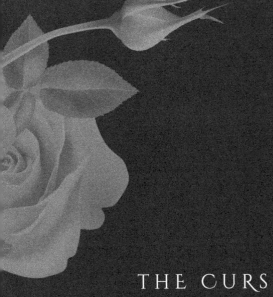

THE CURSEPRICE

Forged in heartbreak, set in bone, cast in blood, carved in stone.
A thousand years will my curse reign, unless I have these six things:

The tears of a fairy from a wood so deep.
The fig of a vorgrath from his mate's keep.
The scale of a selkie burnished gold.
The bone of a wood witch a century old.
The midnight sliver of a Shade Queen's horn.
The sacrifice of two lovers torn.

ONE

Haven Ashwood had a horrible habit of flirting with death. Take tonight, for instance. One slip from the giant ash tree she was climbing, one rotten branch or slick patch of bark, and she would plummet a hundred feet to the mossy ground, her bones splintering to shards.

It would take weeks—maybe months—for anyone to discover her broken body.

She grinned darkly at the thought as she shimmied farther up the ancient tree, the assortment of blades strapped to her baldric and leather belt knocking against the soft trunk.

Death by falling. Not how she envisioned going out, but also not terribly surprising when one insisted on climbing dead trees.

Shivering, she wrapped her cloak tighter around her body as she inched toward the end of a wobbling limb. Freezing to death wasn't any better, but ever since the Curse had reached the outer wall, the warm Penrythian nights had turned cold and harsh.

Prince Bellamy Boteler's Royal Companion Guard dies of a broken neck and frostbite on the morning of the prince's Runeday.

Bell would never forgive her for dying so stupidly. Which is why he had absolutely no idea where she was tonight—or where she came most nights she couldn't sleep.

If he knew she snuck into woods infested with Shadowlings, well, he'd probably kill her himself.

"I'm not scared of you," she taunted the creatures, leaping to the next tree. Her cloak flapped out behind her, the floppy hat she wore threatening to break free as she scrambled for a foothold.

"Apologies," she murmured to the tree, patting a knobby portion of the trunk that resembled an eye.

Legend claimed that the trees were soldiers from the fallen kingdom of Lorwynfell fleeing the Curse, turned at the very gates of Penryth. Haven wasn't prone to superstitious talk, but the weeping moans and cries that came from the massive trees were so heartbreaking, so human, that she found herself talking to them sometimes.

Tonight, though, the cries were deeper, more insistent. As if the trees were actually trying to tell her something.

Don't be silly.

The new branch bowed beneath her weight. She flung out her arms for balance, tightening her core as adrenaline prickled her half-frozen flesh. A quick glance down sent a fresh wave of fire racing along her nerves. The drop was at least seven stories high.

Yes, look down, Ashwood. Wonderful idea.

More rotten branches followed. Each one dipping from her weight and sending a burst of bark raining to the ground.

Her breath spilled out white and thick. She followed it up into the triangle of sky between the gnarled and bent limbs where the full moon sat fat and heavy—a sure sign the Shade Lord's monsters were coming out to play soon.

Despite what Bell's father, King Horace, promised his subjects, she knew the hills teemed with the creatures. Watching. Testing. Waiting for the day the runespell cast deep into the great wall would weaken.

Her lips puckered to the side. As long as she stayed high in the trees, she was safe. Unless Shadowlings had recently acquired the skill of climbing.

Sucking in her bottom lip, she leapt to a higher branch, grasping for a handhold. Brittle bark crumbled beneath her palms and sprinkled over her cheeks. Her fingers were numb, her lips and cheeks frozen.

Nearly there.

She scanned the rolling hills of Penryth far below. A thick blanket of fog hung heavy over the land, swelling the valleys and clumping in the woods. The air was moist and moldy, shot through with the faint scent of bergamot, cinnamon, and blood.

A prickle of dread formed between her shoulder blades. Tonight was a Devouring, the magick-laden mist that descended over the countryside. It came randomly, with no rhyme or reason, no pattern that she could tell.

Some said the Curse had to feed on mortal souls to grow stronger. Others said it was slowly stripping the land of its magick.

All Haven knew was once the sun chased away the heavy mist, the land was strewn with villagers left either insane or dead.

"Great night for a forest excursion, Ashwood," she muttered, picking up her pace.

Her fingers slipped beneath her ruby-red cloak, stroking the runestone sewn into its silk lining. The magick inside that one gem supposedly protected her from the Curse's dark magick, but the stone had never been tested.

Hopefully, tonight would be no different.

A low snarl rang from the valley, muffled by the trees.

"Hello," she murmured, rubbing a thumb over the smooth hilt of her runesword, heavy against her hip. "I know you're here."

From the time she was a little girl, she'd heard songs and stories about the Shadowlings, the creatures that appeared in the magick hour during full moons, devouring children and light magick before disappearing back into the mist.

The songs also told of the Lord of the Netherworld nearby. As master of all dark creatures, myth said it was he who followed them into the woods at night.

Doubtful. She'd killed dozens of Shadowlings and never once had she run across a Shade Lord.

Although she'd never been in the forest right before a Devouring either . . .

Shaking her head, she leapt onto the final tree that held her treasure, her excitement washing away her fears.

Let this Noctis Shade Lord come. She would be more than happy to introduce him to the sleek bow and iron-tipped arrows strapped to her back. Or the four blades dripping from her person, each one coated with a different runepoison.

Haunting groans whispered through the treetops. She needed to hurry.

Her hat nearly slipped off as she adjusted her position, allowing cold air to slither along the nape of her neck. A sharp limb tore at her cheek.

Shielding her face, she pressed herself deep into the nest of foliage.

There. Just below a crooked branch, the stars wavered inside their indigo patch of sky.

"Gotcha." But it wasn't until the invisible runebag she'd tied to the branch nearly a decade ago was nestled in her palm that she felt relief, the tightness in her shoulders easing.

She hardly remembered climbing the ancient ash back then, or carving the protection rune into the gray trunk afterward, a way to both safeguard her treasure and find it later. Not that it needed much protection here.

At the time, she planned to escape King Horace and use the runestones to buy her way across the sea. All her hopes and dreams for finding answers about the family and home she'd been stolen from rested in the bag hanging from her hand.

Another groan drifted through the stillness, its humanlike timbre scraping down her spine and reminding Haven why even the poachers refused to enter Muirwood Forest.

Ignoring her growing unease, she focused on the prize in hand. As soon as she untied the invisible ribbon, the spell released its hold and the faded-green purse formed. Other than three superficial scratches against the leather, the bag appeared untouched.

Thank you, creepy, haunted forest.

She calmed her breathing and slipped a hand inside. The moment her fingertips brushed the velvet cloth surrounding each runestone, a sweet feeling rose in her chest until she could almost taste her need for them. To touch them. Hold them.

Possess them.

Once it had been her habit to roll the polished runestones through her fingers, delighting in the feel of their smooth bodies. Their roiling power seeded deep inside, begging for release.

Once she would have never parted from them.

But these were different times, and she pushed the emotion away, ignoring the pull of the stones. Each one called to her in its own special way. Out of the twenty stones, eight came from the Nine Mortal Houses.

Only the Halvorshyrd Rune was missing—the rarest runestone of them all. In fact, as long as she'd hunted runestones in the crumbling cities of the Bane, no one had ever produced a true Halvorshyrd Rune.

She sighed through her teeth as she felt Bell's stone against her fingertips.

His was the smallest. A flat, murky opal, cracked and dull from age, it wasn't the prettiest of the stones, nor the smoothest. Most would have passed it over for the stunning runestone made of pure amber, or the large, egg-shaped stone with the elegant House Bolevick Rune carved deep into its jade surface.

But the shiniest stones were usually the least powerful.

Pocketing Bell's runestone, she knotted the ribbon, the purse disappearing in her hands again. The runes could have bought her freedom long ago—and more.

So much more.

The branch above her swayed as she rehung her invisible treasure.

Once the stones were safely in place, she ran a finger over the black dahlia pinned to the top of her baldric, circling the insignia that marked her as the prince's companion guard.

Loyalty to Bell is more important than freedom. Remember that.

She repeated the speech as she carefully began shimmying down the tree. By now, the words were practically a mantra. Countless nights she'd talked herself out of leaving, the oath she swore to Bell like a chain wrapped around her neck.

Her promise to serve him was stronger than the homesickness, agony, and loneliness that carved an ever-growing hole inside her chest. To know where she came from, who her people were.

To know where she belonged . . . if anywhere.

Exhaling, she shut out her thoughts and prepared to navigate a tricky section of the tree. The trunk was too thick to scale down and the branches too thin to safely hold.

Before she could find a way down, a scream tore through the woods. She froze, straining to hear above the groaning sound of the forest as the wind tugged at her hat, whipping the branches back and forth in the air and churning the mist below into a frenzied mass of ivory.

The fine hairs on the back of her neck lifted one by one.

Steady now. Fear swirled through her, heady and potent. The trick was accepting the emotion and letting it pass through her.

She waited until the fear abated before nocking the red arrow tipped with jessamine.

No, not strong enough.

Replacing it with the oleander-soaked green arrow, she released a breath and squinted down at the forest floor, searching for the slightest movement within the mist.

"Come out, come out, wherever you are," she breathed.

A twig snapped below.

Her chest tightened until it ached. Pressing into the tree's trunk for steadiness, she whipped right and left, breaking a workable space for her bow in the tangled wall of branches. Then she pulled the bowstring taut and waited.

Snuffling noises filled the silence, the same sound the king's hunting dogs made when they were on a scent.

Usually when she came to these woods to hunt, she ensured she was downwind. But tonight . . . tonight she'd been impatient to find Bell's present. She'd been distracted.

An unforgivable sin in the night forest.

Wafts of mist rolled back as two hulking forms appeared. The lead beast had the girth of a bull and was tall enough to scrape its back down the lowest branch of her tree. Long, black fur jutted from its body in tufts. The scent of wet dog and raw meat, similar to the smells from the butcher shop near the market, invaded her nose and made her gag.

The monster gaped up at her with eyes like hot coals. An unearthly noise—part shriek, part whine—shot from its parted jaws, the moonlight refracting off jagged rows of white teeth.

The tree shook as the beast lifted on its hind legs and rested a huge paw on the trunk. Its black claws sunk deep into the bark, and the tree shivered and moaned.

The second creature was gliding quietly through the mist, stealthy and cat-like despite the bulky muscles straining beneath its pelt.

Images from the bound parchment in Bell's beloved library called *Beasts of the Netherworld* came to mind. But the terrifying, bull-like beasts weren't catalogued inside the stiff, yellowed pages of text.

An unnatural scream pierced the quiet. Her mouth went cotton-dry, the bow wobbling in her hands.

She didn't need a book to tell her the arrow was worthless. Even if the iron tip managed to pierce the thick armor of fur, the runepoison couldn't take down something this large.

Still, she pointed at the creature's face—its right eye, to be exact—and prepared to fight, if necessary.

Suddenly, the beast slammed the tree with its two huge, black paws, hitting it over and over. The impact rattled her bones.

The monsters were trying to knock her down.

She hugged the tree trunk for support, scraping her cheek against the rough bark as she struggled to hold her weapon, but the arrow slipped from her fingers and plunged into the fog below.

All at once, the shaking stopped. The air went quiet. Even the trees quit weeping.

She plucked another arrow from her quiver, her labored breath cutting the silence. Both creatures were sitting, their long, black-spotted tongues hanging from their panting mouths. Each sported triangular ears that were pinned back flat against their thick skulls.

They watched her quietly, the only sound a low whining.

The air was frigid; each breath was like swallowing shards of glass. She cried out as shadows fluttered through the air—*ravens,* hundreds of them, screeching and cawing as they alighted in the trees.

Where had they come from?

Before Haven could answer that question, her world boiled down to one sensation: a presence. At the same time, fear swirled in her veins, a deep, primal terror she'd never felt before.

Instead of passing through her, the fear grew stronger, *stronger.*

Until it threatened to paralyze her.

The thick branch she stood on quivered with the weight of something—something heavy enough to depress the branch several feet.

She held her breath, sure the branch would snap, but thank the Shadeling it just bent low and then held.

Gathering her courage, she pivoted to face it. Whatever *it* was. A shimmering outline wavered the air, but when she squinted to focus on the distortion, it shifted just slightly—as if taunting her.

She squinted and was rewarded with what appeared to be the long limbed shape of a . . . man. Then the distortion once again transformed, rolling in and out of her vision.

Just like she'd done a hundred times before, she exhaled, releasing her terror to the wind.

Every Shadowling could die if one knew where and how to strike. Whatever this was, she hadn't had time to discover its vulnerabilities, so she defaulted to her failsafe.

An arrow pointed at where she guessed its wicked heart to be.

"I see you," she hissed. The beasts below snarled as she pulled the bowstring taut. "Show yourself, Shadowling."

Her heart hammered against her sternum as the silence stretched into a minute. Maybe she was hallucinating. Perhaps—perhaps the Devouring had found a way past the runestone protecting her. Perhaps the twisted magick had taken her mind.

Only one way to find out. Grinning like a madwoman, she uttered a prayer and released the arrow.

TWO

The familiar twang of the bowstring struck a chord of pleasure inside her chest. The arrow shot straight at the distortion, iron tip glittering—and froze midair.

Fluttering emanated from the arrow, its shaft shrinking into a dark ball. Black feathers sprouted from the mass. But it wasn't until the arrow tip morphed into a curved beak and claws appeared that Haven understood what she was seeing.

Her arrow had transformed into a . . . raven.

The arrow-raven cawed twice, soared into the air, and then landed on what she guessed was the thing's shoulder.

Not thing. Shadowling. Which meant she could kill it.

Yet she was starting to doubt. Never had a Shadowling performed magick before.

And the ravens? Ravens were harbingers of powerful magick and evil.

Gritting her teeth, she reached for her last poisoned arrow. Just

11

before her fingers pinched the weapon's shaft, there was a *hiss*. The smooth cherry wood bow inside her fingers became warm and squirmy as a light-green snake appeared, its white underbelly slick like carved ivory. A pink, forked tongue tasted the air.

Impossible.

She threw the serpent down, more from shock than fear, and watched it slither toward the distortion . . . now a very visible, very *real*, man.

Even casually crouched on one knee, he was towering, his tousled hair the color of bleached bone, his skin pale and luminescent as the moon. Thickset black horns crowned his head, so dark they swallowed the light. They rose just above his temples and spiraled gently to follow the curve of his skull.

But her attention snagged on his pale-silver eyes set wide and deep below two onyx slashes of eyebrows. A ring of yellow glowed bright around his crystalline irises, and she found herself drawn to the light the way a lost hunter would be drawn to the warm glare of a campfire.

Somewhere deep down she understood two contrasting truths. First, he was the most beautiful and the most terrifying man Haven had ever seen. And second, he wasn't a man at all.

He was something *else*.

In fact, she would have been less horrified if he bore fur and claws and rows of pointy teeth. Then his physical appearance would match the terror swarming through the hollow of her bones like fire ants, urging her to run.

To hide.

Still, beneath her fear, Haven felt curious, a trait that would someday be the death of her—just hopefully not today. "What are you?"

"Not a Shadowling, Little Beastie." His voice was a haunting lullaby, the sound of raven wings and snake tongues and the wind howling through dead winter leaves. "Now," he continued softly, his gaze sliding to her hair. "What might you be?"

Shivering, she ran a hand over her head, expecting the hat that covered her hair. But it must have fallen off when the beasts below were rattling the tree, and her fingers snagged in the tangled nest of rose-gold hair wrangled into a bun at the base of her neck. In most lighting her locks appeared an odd, dusky pink.

Straightening to project a courage she didn't feel, she met his strange eyes and said, "I'm Haven Ashwood, Royal Companion Guard to Prince Bellamy Boteler."

"Indeed." His head ticked languidly to the side as he studied her, an animalistic movement. His nose was straight, refined, his lips the only soft part of his face. "And are you not afraid of me, Haven Ashwood, Royal Companion Guard to Prince Bellamy Boteler?"

Her chest tightened, his voice calling to some dark, ancient part of her. "Should I be?"

His lips lifted in an opulent grin. She flinched, expecting fangs, but instead a row-full of straight, ivory teeth greeted her.

"I came here looking for the mortal who's been killing my creatures," he said. "Do you know anything about that, Little Beastie?"

My creatures. That meant . . . her mouth went dry at the implication. A Shade Lord.

"Yes," he breathed, his voice unnaturally smooth, hypnotic. "And not just any royal Shade Lord. The Lord of the Netherworld. Of all the beasts in the land."

His lulling voice shivered with pride, and she almost said, *Good for you.*

But then he was inches away—when had he moved?—his

bright, yellow-ringed eyes emanating like the runestones above. Up this close, she could make out the elongated pupils slashed through his irises, more oval than round.

"Now you know what I am," he purred, "but I still don't know what you are."

Bark scraped her shoulder blades as she pressed into the tree, trying to create space between them. She was feeling more and more like a hare caught in one of the king's traps. "I'm just a mortal. Why do you care?"

"A passing amusement. Besides, it's only civil to learn about the thing you plan to feast on."

Her stomach clenched. Rumors that the Noctis race drank the blood of mortals had swirled through the castle for as long as Haven could remember, but she had never believed them . . . until now.

A gasp escaped her lips as his face pressed close to hers, his cool breath sliding over her cheeks and conjuring deep, wracking shivers through her torso.

His mouth paused over her neck, and she stopped breathing.

"Are you afraid?" he asked.

"No," she lied, lifting her chin even as her knees threatened to give out.

"Your scent says otherwise."

Slowly, he inhaled, running his nose along her collarbone and up her neck—

"I killed your creatures," she said, her voice wavering as she tried to pull his attention away from the artery throbbing just below her jaw. "I hunted them, snared them, and killed them for sport."

His head snapped up to level with hers and angled to the side, a quick, predatory movement that turned her veins to ice.

He blinked once, twice. Slow, lazy, curious blinks. She had

the misfortune of noticing his eyelashes were thick and charcoal-colored, rimming his strange eyes like the liner the courtiers used.

Then he laughed. "What a strange Beastie you are. No fun at all. But as much as I admire your courage, I'm afraid you're boring me. Now, please scream."

It was a command laced with magick.

A tingle pulsed behind her eyes. She tried to fight the order, but a scream formed inside her chest, adrenaline searing her veins as her heart bucked wildly.

For the briefest of seconds, she was terrified.

But another emotion rose to the surface. Anger. He was in her head, uninvited.

Using her rage, she drove the planted emotion from her mind until darkness gave way to light, and she was back in control of her mind.

She glared at him, fiercely proud, as she swallowed down the scream he desired.

"I'll never scream for you," she said, her voice stronger than she felt.

The corners of the Shade Lord's lips puckered as his curious smile returned. Dark talons slid from his fingers.

He traced one sharp claw across her jawline. "Hmm. That was . . . unexpected."

In the instant it took for him to blink, she had her favorite elk horn dagger in her hand. The next second it was dragging across his chest.

Why wasn't he reacting? He held perfectly still, his head bent as he watched the blade carve across his chest. His lips were parted slightly, a curious look lifting one corner of his lips.

Before he *could* react, she lunged for a branch five feet to her left. The moment her feet hit the limb, she leapt again, dropping from branch to branch until her boots hit soft, leaf-carpeted ground.

The beasts snarled as she rolled over her shoulder to break her fall. But they made no move to attack as she popped to her feet in a dead sprint, moldy leaves and moss tangled in her hair.

Mist rippled out from her cloak, the dark magick inside the gauzy fog stroking her legs and arms. The prodding turned to clawing as the darkness looked for a way around her runestone's protection.

Crap, crap, crap, crap—

An ungodly noise filled the forest as the ravens poured from the trees, screeching. Their feathered wings beat against her cheeks. Their claws scraped against her skin. The trees howled and groaned.

She focused on her footfalls, the mist swirling into an angry sea around her, her breath coming in and out strangled and hot.

The beasts roared again, their growls echoing through the woods. *Faster!* She pelted through curtains of low-hanging moss and hurdled fallen trees. But she felt caught in a nightmare where no matter how hard she ran, invisible quicksand sucked at her legs and tangled her feet.

Where are they? She swung her head left and right, searching for the Shade Lord and his monsters. Branches tore at her cloak and face, and she whacked at the crooked limbs with her blade, imagining they were the Shade Lord's claws.

Her pulse thrummed in her ears. She knew these woods. Knew which trail led to the wall and which ones led to the deep ravines that would break her bones. Any other day she could navigate them with her eyes closed.

Now, though, her vision tunneled, her brain went cloudy with fear, and all she saw was a gray labyrinth of trees. Trees and darkness and fog.

Fog that hid monsters.

A fallen cedar appeared inside the mist and she leaped over it, batting away a raven raking her eyes.

What are you doing, idiot?

Running was pointless, stupid even; she was wasting energy that she would need to fight. Yet the panic inside wouldn't let her stop. Her thoughts whirled like the mist, her legs pounding the earth in cadence with her ragged breath and frenzied heart.

She'd stabbed a Shade Lord. He knew she was responsible for his Shadowling's deaths.

Runes, she'd *stabbed* a Shade Lord!

Not a Shadowling. Not a common Noctis. But a Shade Lord, the most dangerous and powerful kind of Noctis. Unfortunately for her, this particular Shade Lord was also the dark ruler of the Netherworld, and husband of the Shade Queen's daughter—if the myths and Bell's tomes were to be believed.

The opalescent runewall rose through the trees, moonlight glimmering off its surface.

"Thank the Goddess," she rasped as she clawed her way up the steep hill to the runewall. Clenching the blade between her teeth, she scaled the pale stones, her hands tangling in the morning glories and jasmine that blanketed the wall.

As her fingers scraped over the rough stone, bright-orange runes briefly flickered to life, fading back into the stone just as quickly.

An earthy flavor tingled over her tongue, rich and coppery, with the slightest hint of licorice.

But it wasn't until she scrambled over the top and paused to catch her breath that the whisper of cinnamon hit, and she realized what she tasted.

No. Unease twisted her gut, and she held up the dagger, bile burning her throat. Thick black blood coated the edge of her blade. The blood of the Shade Lord imbued with dark magick.

Her tongue throbbed and ached, a cool, fluttery sensation spreading from the lips and working its way down her throat and into her belly, a swarm of frost-winged butterflies.

She leapt from the wall and landed hard on the dewy lawn, trying to ignore the cold knot between her shoulder blades as she hurried back to the castle, the sound of the ravens' caws following her through the garden.

Haven always trusted her instincts above all else, and now they were telling her she had done something irrevocably stupid. She could almost feel the world shift slightly, as if her actions had changed the future somehow.

Goddess Above, what had she done?

THREE

Archeron Halfbane watched Prince Bellamy Boteler's Companion Guard cross the yard and enter the garden trail, her boots quiet against the rock path that wound through the moonberry trees.

The girl moved with a quiet, sanguine grace few mortals possessed, her sharp gaze flicking over the landscape in practiced sweeps. The obscenely large floppy hat she normally wore was gone, exposing the strange hair she kept knotted and hidden under caps and scarves and hoods.

Beneath the moonlight, her hair appeared ashy-blonde, tinged with just the whisper of rose. But during the day, the few strands that escaped her hat were bright rose-gold, the color of the winter orchids that grew along the terraces of Effendier.

Tilting his face to the stars, Archeron sniffed the air, a low growl rumbling in his chest.

Why would she cross the wall tonight when it was obvious a

19

Noctis was around?

It was beyond him how she'd stayed alive this long, the little fool. For a mortal, she had the Goddess's blessing and the Shadeling's luck.

As she slipped by him, blind to his presence, he sunk into the shadows of a marble archway. Mortals—even well trained ones— barely noticed the world around them. They were slow and weak, their magick useless.

The few Royal mortals that could access the Nihl had to rely upon runes, and even then, their attempts to harness the Nihl were clumsy and uninspired at best.

Out of sheer boredom, Archeron trailed the girl for a spell, slipping easily in and out of the shadows. He'd watched her many nights darting through the gardens and crossing the wall. She almost always came back smelling of Shadowling blood and grinning like a mortal fool.

But now, her shoulders were tight, and instead of taking time to inspect the night blooming star flowers, which seemed to fascinate her to no end, or play in the several fountains that dotted the gardens—a childlike habit that amused him—she scampered across the courtyard and disappeared inside the city gates.

Archeron rolled his shoulders. Where was the longbow usually strapped to her back? Or the soft rattle of arrows inside her quiver only he could hear?

Pulling more air into his nose, he picked out the faint but pungent tinge of fear in her scent, intertwined with her usual smell of sweat and the jasmine soap she favored.

He hadn't thought to study the expression on her face; unlike his race, the Solis, mortals had trouble managing their emotions. Instead of learning to control them, they tried to mask their feelings behind an absurd mask.

Years of this had taught Archeron to overlook mortal features altogether, and most of the time he could gather what he needed from their gestures and voices alone.

And yet . . . had her cheeks been paler than normal? And her lips had been frowning. At least, more so than usual.

Archeron snarled. *A mortal problem, not yours,* he reminded himself. He came to the gardens to forget about the people of this court, not worry about the missing weapons and tight shoulders of a fool who tempted death every night.

The Prince's Companion Guard was an annoyance, a slip of a girl darting among the blood roses and disrupting his solitude. For the entirety of his enslavement to this realm, while the mortals chased their silly dreams in their beds, the garden after sundown had been his alone.

Still, as much as he resented the intrusion, he also found himself hoping she made it back from her nightly hunts.

Which, somehow, the little fool always managed to do.

Once, driven by boredom and curiosity, he crossed the wall to watch her. She slayed two Vultax that night, no small feat for a mortal girl. An Effendier Sun Queen would have made it look prettier, but they'd been trained from birth in the art of warfare, and every act of violence was transformed into a languid dance one could hardly look away from, even the victim.

In this blasted Netherworld of a kingdom, mortals insisted their women stayed weak as lambs, without proper weapons or skills to survive alone.

A rare grin found his face. King Horace would have a fit if he knew the Companion Guard to his eldest son was entering Muirwood Forest and slaughtering Shadowlings at night.

Perhaps that's why Archeron no longer bristled quite so much at the girl's presence. Why he whispered a small thanks to the

Goddess every time she came back alive. She was a passing distraction in his immortal existence, a reminder of the fierce warrior Sun Queens of his homeland. That was all.

But if she truly survived a Noctis tonight, then a part of him was glad.

Archeron plucked a moonberry from the short, bell-shaped tree by the fountain and then popped the tart berry into his mouth.

If he were in Effendier, he would've had to climb to the highest branches to find any left, but they had no effect on mortals so the firm, amethyst berries went untouched by everyone but him. They also made a potent tea, but he wasn't interested in tea.

Not tonight. Not for the past countless years of servitude to this incompetent king.

Warmth spread inside his chest as sour juice rolled over his tongue. He sighed, leaning against the tree.

For a breath, he could see the white shores and pounding turquoise waves of his homeland. Could smell the air perfumed with the wild orchids and tiny nightblood roses that tangled along the rocky paths leading to the sea, mixed with the salty essence of the water.

For a bittersweet moment, he was free.

But then the effect wore off and he was back in Penryth, stuck in a mortal realm that stank of sweat and death, chained to a mortal king whom he could kill with a thought but was instead forced to carry out his every cruel whim.

Archeron Halfbane, bastard son of the Effendier Sun Sovereign, was a slave.

Damn the law of the Shadeling and Goddess. If he could, he would've ripped his own heart out years ago rather than feel the agony and longing he felt for Effendier.

Archeron stripped another berry from the heart-shaped, golden leaves and crunched the fruit between his teeth until he was back on those rocky shores, a thousand miles from the cursed land of mortals.

Lost in his waking dream, he swore someday he would find a way back to his homeland, whatever the cost.

FOUR

The Shade Lord's blood tingled and burned on the tip of Haven's tongue, and no amount of wiping her mouth on her sleeve or spitting could erase it. Down the hall, two giggling ladies-in-waiting stared at her longer than was polite, so she bared her teeth and spit near their shiny, fashionable boots.

That sent them scurrying off like empty-headed mice, and a weary smile stretched across her lips.

By the Shadeling's horns! She couldn't wait for this day to end, and it wasn't even dawn yet. She paused by an open window, candles flickering from the ledge.

Centuries before, runelight filled these halls. Gifted from the Solis, the eternal light was supposed to last forever.

That was before the Curse, though. Its greedy, dark magick feasting on all the light magick until there was hardly a grain of it left anywhere.

A distant scream drew her attention to Muirwood Forest, and

a chill wracked her chest.

Even now, she could feel the Noctis's scalding gaze.

Had the Shade Lord and his beasts found more prey? She bit her lip. The Shadowlings could have easily caught her.

And the Shade Lord could've stopped her in the tree if he'd *wanted* to. Could have frozen her dagger before it ever dared kiss his chest, or turned the blade into a frog, a mouse, or a toadstool. Anything he wanted.

Why did he let her go?

The question tugged at her. She held up the elk-horn dagger, its ivory handle smooth from use, and frowned. The blade was clean—she'd smeared the syrupy blood on the wet grass—but still, she couldn't get rid of the feeling that she should bury the knife deep into the earth and forget about it.

Wasn't there supposed to be strong magick in a high-ranking Noctis's blood?

And if he truly were the Lord of the Netherworld . . .

Stop it. She was safe now inside the wall. And maybe the blood hadn't actually touched her tongue. Maybe it didn't contain the dark magick that devoured everything in its path.

Maybe. She despised the word.

Haven released a breath and focused on the pale runewall that protected Penryth, slithering all the way from the western coast of Eritrayia to the far east.

A shudder skittered down her spine. If the monsters broke through the wall and invaded, the last of the protected southern cities would fall in a day. With the mortal lords drained of rune magick and the Solis hiding across the Glittering Sea, they were defenseless against the monstrous Noctis and the Curse.

Don't think like that. The wall was forged in the sacred moonstone of the Goddess, the magick impregnating the stone cast by Solis and meant to last a thousand years.

Those same spells permeated the castle, whispering of long ago when famed Solis warriors roamed Fenwick and Penryth found favor with the Sun Sovereign of Effendier.

No Shade Lord, however powerful, would be crossing the wall tonight.

She yawned. Already the air shivered pink with the promise of dawn. *Another sleepless night in the books.* Her sleepy gaze slid over the royal gardens that speckled the grounds, flanked by trellises of climbing roses, lush green hedges, and weeping willow trees.

Ribbons and streamers of every color hung from the delicate branches, their bronze bells chiming softly, and lanterns twinkled like the stars above. It had taken weeks for the servants to hang them all.

Today was Bell's day, and Shadeling be damned if she would let that horned monster ruin it.

Pushing the memory of the night's events away, she hurried to the armory and talked Master Lorain out of a fine yew wood longbow and four sleek arrows. All it took was a few coins and a smile. Usually.

Sometimes the battle-scarred armorer would lecture her on the importance of safeguarding the king's property, but always under his wine-soaked breath, as if even he were a little bit afraid of her.

Most of the kingdom was wary when it came to Haven, a fact she'd grown used to. She could tell by the way the courtiers averted their gazes and attendants scuttled past her in the hallways. Even the servants avoided her when they could, and not just because she was good with a blade—which she was.

She was a female, trained in the fighting arts. Instead of jewelry, she dripped steel. Instead of satin gowns, she donned worn leather scabbards and baldrics. And instead of wearing her tresses elaborately coiffed like a peacock's tail feathers, she preferred a dusty old trader's hat.

Women here were expected to flaunt bright, unnatural colors. But other than the ruby cloak Bell had gifted her, or the riotous rose-toned hair the Goddess saw fit to give her, she preferred the muted colors of nature.

Haven was different, and in mortal Penryth, there was nothing more terrifying than that.

Despite the early hour, Fenwick castle was alive with servants and guests. Haven drew up her hood, slinking by the perfumed nobles from the surrounding estates.

Runes, she missed her hat. If she had time today, she would go searching for it.

The castle residents were used to the way she dressed, but outsiders made a habit of staring at the leather pants that clung to her long legs, and the corset-less tunic that swung from her athletic shoulders.

And when they saw her hair . . .

Which is why she made sure they didn't. Better they think she's a boy than gawk at the unnatural color.

As Guard Companion to Prince Bellamy, Haven was given some leeway in her attire. Still, she was expected to carry the Boteler standard in her mannerisms and dress.

But she couldn't climb trees in a gown or nock an arrow with the silly deerskin gloves popular with the courtiers.

She rolled her eyes as a noblewoman with a painted face and a sharp nose frowned at her. Like most mortal women with means, the noblewoman's hair was braided, powdered, bejeweled, and piled high atop her head.

But it wasn't her garish hairstyle Haven found implausible. It was the poor woman's breasts, which were squeezed into two pale, pillowy mounds atop her chest.

Goddess Above, how was she supposed to kill Shadowlings with her breasts squished and a petticoat tangled around her legs?

Haven slipped inside the dust-trap she called a chamber, eyeing the dirty clothes strewn across the unmade bed. She'd spell a goat for a few hours of sleep, but there just wasn't time.

Sighing, she set to work washing the dust from her boots and face with a cold washrag. Her lady's maid, Demelza, appeared seemingly out of thin air, as was her habit.

She immediately started clucking over her charge, muttering prayers to the Goddess under her breath.

"No sleep again, m'lady?" Demelza asked, her guttural northern accent grating Haven's ears and making the question sound more like an accusation.

Demelza was from some Curse-fallen kingdom near the Bane, the name of which Haven could never quite pronounce.

Stout and slightly hunched, Demelza had a sun-weathered face and thin lips prone to frowning. Sandy, gray-shot curls tangled wildly around her head—the only part of Demelza that wasn't neat.

"There's no rest for the brave, Demelza," Haven teased.

"'Tis demons," Demelza muttered beneath her breath.

Haven sighed. "They're called nightmares, Demelza. Don't you have those where you're from?"

Although Haven very much doubted Demelza's nightmares—or anyone else's, for that matter—were like hers. But her lady's maid just clucked her tongue.

After cataloguing Haven's many faults—impossible hair, dirty nails, callused hands—they fought over Haven changing for Runeday.

As usual, she won the battle of wills, keeping the same pants and tunic but capitulating to the Boteler standard, a black dahlia, pinned to her breast.

Demelza's constant frown deepened into a scowl when Haven fashioned another silk scarf to cover her hair. Haven frowned back at her sour maid, daring her to argue.

At least this scarf was festive and clean, embroidered in a pattern of gold dahlias to match Haven's pin.

Her knot of hair beneath the scarf, on the other hand, was loose and sloppy, still dusted with twigs and bark and dirt.

But she was in a hurry to find Bell before the ceremony, when the king would steal the prince from her for the day, and the forest offerings would have to stay.

Leaning down—her lady's maid was nearly a foot shorter than Haven—she kissed Demelza's craggy cheek and went in search of the prince. Right before Haven ducked out the door, she caught a rare smile creep across Demelza's face.

Bell's chamber was two halls down, but he wouldn't be inside, not at this hour. When her head was usually just hitting the pillow, Bell's was blinking sleepily at the pages of a book. The musty bouquet of old manuscripts and dust calling him from slumber like the stout whiff of black Penrythian coffee did her a few hours later.

She hurried to find him, the scents of savory meats and pies wafting through the corridors making her belly rumble.

The cooks had worked all night for Bell's celebration, and the prospect of endless pastries and gluttony without guilt should have lifted her spirits. The food and runegames would last for weeks, filling the pockets and bellies of the villagers.

It was a time for celebration—something the kingdom desperately needed.

Yet, as she slipped through the heavy oak doors leading to the library, the excitement she felt was eclipsed by a growing pit in her stomach, made worse by the lingering taste of the Shade Lord's blood.

Nothing's wrong. You're going to celebrate Bell's birthday, probably get drunk and fat, and then wake up tomorrow with a headache and the reality that all is fine.

But she couldn't help feeling she was on the precipice of . . . something. And that even the slightest of winds could blow her—and everything she loved—into the abyss.

FIVE

The library was a three-story circular room covered floor to ceiling with books, so many it would take her years to count them all. Sunlight from the domed glass ceiling warmed her cheek, her boots treading quietly over the worn Ashari rug covering the wooden floor as she wound through the smattering of desks. Dust whorled in the spears of light trickling from above.

She found Bell on the second story balcony, curled up in a moth-chewed quilt, his dark, tight curls teased atop his head and his face obscured by a giant, leather-bound book. His reedy arms trembled beneath the book's heft.

Whatever cold shadow had fallen over her this morning lifted at the sight of her best friend. His skin was the same coloring as the smoky quartz walls in the grand ballroom, a stunning mixture of his father's ivory tones and his mother's ebony color.

It was as if the Goddess had chosen the best parts of both parents, bestowing him with the king's wide eyes, the color of the palest-blue topaz, and his mother's fine nose and lips.

As Haven neared, the runestone seemed to heat up in her pocket, and hesitation made her pause.

Would Bell like his present?

A thousand shiny baubles from all over the kingdom already swelled the throne room, tributes for Prince Bell on his Runeday. The clothiers would present him with fine tunics laced with gold and boots made from calf leather. The merchants would heap his ceremonial runethrone with gold and silver.

And the king, who had already given him a sleek, long-necked stallion with a mane twined in silver, would publicly show off his wealth by gifting his eldest son rare spices and bulbs from across the sea.

For a prince who had everything, a small runestone from his guard companion and best friend was unimpressive. Also completely and utterly inappropriate, considering the penalty for trading runestones was death.

Her lips drew into a smile. Bell would love it.

Lost inside his tome, Bell didn't notice her until she slipped beside him on the threadbare rug, wiggling her feet under the quilt. She plucked the last two biscuits from the discarded tin plate by his knee and wolfed them down.

"Easy there, Piglet." Dropping his book, he tugged her into a fierce embrace before pulling back to look her over. "I'm not even going to ask where you were again, and assume, since you just devoured my old biscuits, you're well."

Haven clicked her tongue, talking through her mouthful. "Course . . . I am."

"I saw the mist from my window. It was the Devouring, wasn't it?"

On my Runeday, his voice implied. She could read him as easily as he read his books.

"I wouldn't worry about that. It was long overdue, anyway." She gathered her sketchpad and the tin containing her charcoals, carefully setting them on the floor. "Wait, you actually pulled your nose out of something as riveting as"—she lifted up the book cover—"*Histories of the Nine Mortal Houses?*"

"Funny, Haven Ashwood. You know, you should try it sometime."

"Boring myself to tears?"

"Learning about things that *aren't* trying to kill you." He closed the book. "I was brushing up on the history of my ancestors' Runedays, all forty-seven of them."

Her heart skipped a beat. "You shouldn't—"

"It's okay." He grinned, his blue eyes sparkling. "The last Boteler who displayed lightcasting abilities on their Runeday was my great-grandfather. The rest were barren. I think I'm safe. Although, it's too bad I don't have my mother's rune history."

"There's nothing in the library about the House of Ashiviere?" Technically, Ashiviere wasn't a House but a small kingdom northwest of Penryth, seceded from one of the Nine Houses centuries past. Bell's mother was the last of King Ashiviere's line.

When she died, the kingdom broke apart. Now warring tribes ruled it.

"No. I've looked everywhere." He rubbed his knuckles over his sternum, a habit whenever he spoke about his mother. Through the partially open collar of his tunic, she could just barely make out his sword-shaped birthmark. It was faint, the shade of watered down coffee.

His mother had a similar birthmark, as did his older brother and the rest of the Ashiviere line, apparently.

"Well, I wouldn't worry about it," Haven assured him, resting the book on top of a pile of tomes.

But the statement stuck in her throat.

There was so much about his mother's history they would never know. King Horace refused to talk about her or her family, and even though Bell's grandfather was still alive somewhere, the king had never offered him safe haven or allowed anyone to mention him in the king's presence.

"Not that I wouldn't love to be the first Boteler in almost ninety years to possess magick . . . even if that meant the Shade Queen could claim me."

Haven shivered. "Bell, don't tease about such things."

"Why? The king would have to be proud of me then."

The king. Not Father. The bitterness in his voice made her cringe. "Bell, if the . . . your *father* had any sense, he would be proud of you regardless. I know I am. But don't think about him. It's your Runeday, Prince Bellamy Boteler. Enjoy it."

Bell sighed. "You're right. I'm going to hide out here and read until they tear me away, and then I'm going to put on something dashing, stuff myself on iced raisin cakes, and woo the kingdom with my good looks and unfailing charm."

"So basically it's like every day."

Bell's fine shoulders lifted in a shrug. "Pretty much."

Haven elbowed his ribs. "And as your dedicated Companion Guard, I will force down all the cakes and custard I can handle to save you from looking like a glutton."

"You would do that in the service of your Crown Prince?"

"I'm dedicated like that."

"Huh. And what if I asked you to change into something that doesn't look like it's been dragged through the forest and used to clean out the stables?"

Haven groaned, running a finger over her lovingly worn, knee-high boots. "You sound like Demelza."

"Oh, Demelza, Demelza. She should be paid double."

She snorted. "Triple. Poor woman thinks I'm haunted by demons. She prays under her breath in between our arguments."

Bell's smile faltered. "Still having nightmares?"

The concern in his voice made her cringe, and she forced out a grin. "You know Demelza. She sees Netherworld wraiths everywhere."

"That she does." The tension in Bell's face eased as he stood, his blanket dropping to the ground in an explosion of dust.

Once another ancient book was chosen, they settled back on the floor against a row of texts dedicated to Runemagick, the only section Haven had any interest in.

But Bell loved the histories of Eritrayia, especially the fables, and she watched as he carefully selected an earmarked chapter from The *Book of the Fallen.*

She knew the exact story he would read before he even opened his mouth.

"In the beginning," Bell said in his gentle, singsong voice, "there was Freya from the land of the Sun, and Odin from the dark Netherworld. They met during a full harvest moon in the land of mortals between their two worlds, and despite their many differences, they fell in love . . . Are you listening, Haven?"

"Uh huh," she mumbled as she opened her sketchpad and began drawing the Shade Lord and his beasts.

Although she could never sit still long enough to read, she often lost herself in Bell's voice, the stories tumbling from his lips as real as if the fables' inhabitants had been painted on canvas.

Now, as her fingers traced the outline of the Noctis's sharp, ivory cheeks and fluttered back and forth to recreate the deep shadows around the eyes, calm washed over her.

As Bell's best friend, she was tutored alongside him. The teacher, a haughty, fine-boned Veserackian scholar from across the mountains, decided almost immediately she was hopeless. Nothing could keep her still long enough to listen to his lectures or sit down for those long, boring tests.

Sketching somehow focused her immense energy while allowing her to listen. If not for that miraculous discovery, she'd still be an illiterate street rat.

Bell's melodic voice called her back. This particular tale was her favorite. In her mind Odin appeared, dark and solemn, as he spied the lovely, fierce Freya for the first time. Unable to bear children as mortals do, they used their vast magick and the bones of every animal, including mortals, to create two separate races.

Their children were wild and beautiful. The Noctis took after their father, with wings full of inky-black feathers, claws like raptors, and broad onyx horns. A full-grown male Noctis could reach seven-feet tall, their muscular bodies large and menacing, while a female Noctis was usually slimmer and sleeker—though no less menacing.

The Solis were tall and golden like the setting sun, with eyes like jewels and hair like spun gold, same as their mother. They most resembled the mortals, a fact that caused bitter jealousy in the Noctis. Just like their darker brethren, the Solis made mortals like Haven look tiny.

At least, all according to the stories told about them from years past.

Bell turned the page, dragging Haven from her thoughts. Her chest tightened as she glanced at the illustration on the second page.

"The Shadow War," she breathed, her voice equal parts awe and terror.

A ribbon of jealousy clenched her heart. No mortal could

have created such a perfect rendering of colors and light; the delicate features of the figures on the page took skill learned over centuries, well past a mortal's lifespan, and some part of her raged at the thought she would never be able to create something so beautiful or exquisite with her short, mortal fingers.

"Do you think Freya regretted giving us Runemagick and starting the war?" Bell mused, running a finger over the outspread wing of a Noctis bent over the fallen body of his brother, a dying Solis.

Haven shook her head. Odin had been furious when the Goddess gifted the Mortal Houses with the Nine Runes, and the love they shared turned to bitter hatred.

Odin gathered his Noctis children and waged a war against the Solis and his estranged lover, Freya, invoking ancient dark magick and awakening something evil.

"The war probably would've happened anyway," Haven offered. "The Noctis and the Solis will never share the same realm in peace."

The priests claimed the Noctis' dark magick made them tricksters prone to jealousy and rage. That they would always hate the Solis.

Which was why, when the Noctis lost the Shadow War, they'd been sent back to the Netherworld and the veil between their world and the mortal world sealed tight.

"They say Odin went mad with rage and grief," Bell added, his tone an unnerving mix of reverence and fear. "That his dark magick turned on him, twisting his heart until he transformed into the . . . Shadeling."

The word Shadeling came out a whisper, and Bell involuntarily flinched, his eyes squeezing tight.

It was said the terrifying God could hear every time someone said his name. Which seemed odd considering his name was infused into countless common phrases.

"Is it bad that I feel sorry for the Noctis?" Bell asked, biting his lip. "They were banished from their home into the Netherworld and tortured by a monster. And they just look so . . . well, forlorn, with their sad droopy wings and frowns."

Haven snorted. Only Bell could feel sorry for the Noctis. "You've only seen them in illustrations. They might be perfectly happy being monsters."

"I doubt that." His voice grew wistful. "Even monsters have souls. Like that creature you're drawing there." His gaze flicked to her sketch. "There's a sadness behind those handsome eyes."

She glanced down at her partial drawing of the beasts from the woods, a large blank spot where the Shade Lord's body should be. His face though, had been drawn in perfect detail, right down to the striations in his strange, glowing irises and the silvery bands in his onyx horns.

"His eyes don't look sad to me," she muttered, cringing as the Shade Lord seemed to sneer at her in amusement. She covered the sharp, too-real face with her charcoal-smudged hand. "Besides, he's not real."

Bell just stared at her with that dopey smile.

Biting her lip, she regarded her best friend, the boy she was sworn to protect with her life. Often, she wondered how someone as good as Bell could have come from someone like King Horace.

But the prince's kind heart was both a blessing and a curse. Someday, Bell would be King of Penryth, the largest and most valuable kingdom in the mortal lands.

Rulers here had to be cunning and ruthless to survive. And Bell was neither of those things.

That's why he had her.

She shuffled her sketchpad on her lap, prepared to rip out the page, crumple it, and forget the Shade Lord forever. But her gaze snagged on the hollows below his cheeks and shifted upward to those vibrant, otherworldly eyes.

Inexplicably, he seemed tied to the shadow of foreboding that hung over today. As if his presence had shifted something inside her, cracks forming in the delicate sense of security she clung to in Penryth.

Bell cleared his throat. "One more story?"

But she couldn't look away from the Noctis beneath her fingertips . . .

"Haven?"

Releasing a ragged breath, she tore her gaze from the monster on her page and flashed Bell an apologetic smile. Already, the restless stirrings she could never quite escape were calling her to uncoil. To move. To do anything but sit and think.

There was only so much her sketchpad could do to muffle those impulses.

Plus, she needed to map out Bell's activities for the day and then check the areas he would visit, ensuring nothing was out of the ordinary and that he could travel safely. With villagers from the nearby kingdoms journeying for days to attend, the crowds would be huge.

"Bell, I can't." She slipped her charcoal-smudged hand over his, dropping the velvet-wrapped runestone into his palm. "But . . . I got you something."

As soon as she removed her hand and he saw the scarlet cloth, his eyes lit up. "Haven Ashwood, did you get me a present?"

"You only turn seventeen once. Open it."

He lifted the cloth to his ear and shook it. "Let me guess, it's a puppy."

"*Open it!*"

With a dramatic flourish, he revealed the runestone. It shimmered in the soft light, radiating a silvery fire from within. The rune came to life beneath his gentle touch, a delicate orange line swirling and moving in time with his heartbeat.

Bell's breath hissed between his teeth. "Nethergates! This is . . . this is real, isn't it?"

"Well, I didn't get it at Gilly's booth in the market."

"It's warm." His mouth stretched in a wide grin as he held the stone up between two fingers. "What House Rune is this?"

"Volantis."

"Volantis? That's a . . . that's a . . ."

"Protection Rune." The stone sparkled, and Haven laughed. "It likes you."

Any other mortal would have scoffed at her suggestion that the runestone had feelings. Even Damius, the rune-hunting Devourer she'd spent years working and training under would've said she was crazy to suggest the stones were anything but instruments.

Still, when Haven held the runestones, she could feel *something*. A connection, an emotion, as if an invisible thread ran from the stone connecting her to the Nihl—which was, for her, impossible.

But not for Bell. Not with his royal blood, imbued with the magick of his ancestors. There hadn't been a royal lightcaster of the Nine in years, but that didn't mean it wasn't down there somewhere.

"Between your thoroughly armed presence and the longevity runestone I'll receive today," Bell chided, "I don't think I'm in need of any more protection."

"You never can be too careful."

Bell closed the stone up in its cloth and slipped it into his pocket. "I just hope you didn't go through too much trouble to get this."

"None," she lied, standing up. "Now you'll be doubly protected even when I'm not there. In fact, you'll live to such an old age you'll beg to be put out of your misery."

What she didn't tell him was that, while technically the House Volantis Rune was a protection rune, the runestone in Bell's pocket wasn't from the Nine Mortal Houses.

It was a powerrune, forbidden for mortals.

Which in her experience made it all the more powerful . . . and deadly, if caught with it.

According to the Goddess's law, the Nine Mortal House Runes were reserved for nobles descended from one of the nine humans first given magick. But there were thousands of runes, most stronger than the ones allowed the Mortal Houses.

Of course, there were hundreds of fake runes too. But Haven was the only one in Damius's crew who could spot the rare, forbidden runes that were off limits to mortals.

On the black market, the stones were worth a small fortune; if she were ever caught with them, they were worthy of death.

But why should the Solis have all the fun?

There was a loud crack as the doors to the library slammed open and someone entered, their steps echoing over the wood floor like the blows of a mallet.

The king's mistress was a sharp, bony woman who hid her thin lips and sagging skin with an array of pigments, silks, and jewels, but her most stunning possession was a curtain of marigold hair that cascaded nearly to her waist. Little diamond-studded dahlia barrettes winked from her tresses and drew the eye.

At the sound of Cressida's stabbing gait, Bell's shoulders sagged into his light frame. He quickly slunk down the spiral staircase to meet her, seeming to shrink a little more with each step.

Haven was about to follow when she glanced over the page the book had opened to when it fell from Bell's lap. A pale woman covered in a headdress of black raven's feathers stared from the page, so real Haven felt the icy stare of her bruised-blue eyes prickle over her skin.

Just like the Shade Lord, a pair of onyx horns curled from her head. The name Queen Morgryth Malythean was printed at the bottom of the page in heavy, imposing font.

Haven shivered, a gust of cold air washing over her. The illustration began to move, shadows unspooling from her body and lifting off the page—

Haven snapped the book shut and tossed it between two runespell texts, the whisper of a name on her tongue.

Shade Queen. Curse Maker. Darkcaster. Ruler of the Netherworld and Queen of the Noctis.

Haven had never noticed the drawing before. *How was it not burned, anyway?*

Mortals were superstitious by nature, and most believed the Shade Queen could spy on them from any likeness of herself.

Silly, yet Haven felt the deepest urge to rip out the picture of the dark queen and toss it into the fire burning in the fireplace below.

Cressida's sharp voice dragged Haven back to reality. She loped down the stairs, her teeth clenched so tight they ached.

One hand gripped the hilt of her sword as an internal war waged within her mind, the practical side ordering the impulsive side not to murder the king's mistress right here in the library, if only for Bell's sake.

But in Haven's present mood, she couldn't promise anything.

SIX

Haven reached the bottom of the library stairs just in time to see the king's mistress towering over Bell, her ageless face—manipulated by magick, no doubt—twisted into a sneer.

"Bellamy," Cressida snapped in a voice like ripping fabric. "Why aren't you properly dressed and ready to meet our guests?"

Bell quickly bowed his head. "My apologies, Cress—"

"The Crown Prince does not apologize. Now stand up tall and *try* to look the part." Cressida brushed a lock of brassy hair off her shoulder, the jeweled dahlias pinned to the top of her head sparkling. "And do hurry. The king and Renk are hungry, and my hair won't keep much longer in this humidity."

Renk was Cressida's son and Bell's half-brother, and the only person Haven had ever gotten close to smothering in their sleep.

Bell sighed. "I'm sorry, Cressida. I wasn't thinking how my actions would affect you and Renk and . . . His Highness."

Haven's blood boiled in her veins, and the hand on her sword itched to wield it. Yet if she acted against Cressida now, it would only make Bell's life harder, so she cracked her neck and tried counting runes.

"Also," Cressida continued. "You should know we have guests at the table. King Thendryft and his daughter. Do try to look interested in her."

Bell's Adam's apple dropped low as he swallowed. "I told my father . . ."

"What?" Cressida lifted her drawn-on eyebrows. "You will marry her, Bellamy, for Penryth. I almost feel pity for the poor girl."

"I won't." But Bell's voice was soft, his eyes downcast.

Cressida clicked her tongue. "Selfish, selfish boy. Your mother should have taught you better. It's a shame she's not here today. Although perhaps that's a relief, considering the way you've turned out. The Goddess Above knows I've tried, but I can only do so much for a boy of *your* kind."

Mid-count, Haven grasped her sword and slipped it part-way from its sheath, the sound like a den of serpents hissing. Runes, she'd *tried* not to murder the woman.

Now it was time to let the steel talk.

Cressida flicked her cold gaze to Haven for the first time since entering. "Touch a hair on my head, girl, and yours will be rolling down the hill before you can blink. Or perhaps you'll be staked outside the walls and left for the Devouring."

A ribbon of dread unfurled inside her chest at the thought.

"Is that what happened to Master Grayson?" Haven asked, enjoying the way the skin at the corners of Cressida's eyes tightened with displeasure.

Years ago, near the end of the competition to become Bell's Guard Companion, Cressida had approached Haven and asked her to spy on the prince. In exchange for feeding Cressida important information, she would guarantee Haven the position.

Haven had said no, and not meekly.

Afterward, Cressida told Haven's mentor, Master Grayson, not to let Haven win.

In an act of defiance that humbled her to this day, her mentor still awarded her the position.

As punishment, he was cast outside the runewall. Haven never saw him again, but the memory of watching him disappear into the dark woods at dusk still haunted her.

Cressida grinned. "Be careful, girl. You are just as replaceable as that old fool was."

Turning on her heels, Cressida crossed the library, her long hair swaying behind her as she called over her shoulder to Haven, "What a shame you're not a boy. Even someone like you would make a more suitable prince than Bellamy, I fear."

The air lightened as soon as Cressida left. Bell seemed to grow a few inches taller. Haven unclenched her jaw and tried to keep her face neutral.

The last thing she wanted was for Bell to have to worry she would do something rash and stupid—which she almost had.

Bell studied the toes of his polished black boots. "Shadeling's shadow, she's horrible. I thought today would be different. I thought, because it was my Runeday . . . never mind. I might as well expect a scorpion not to strike."

"Maybe someday she'll strangle on that garish hair."

Bell managed a weak laugh.

But she knew there were no words she could say to comfort him. She tried and failed a hundred times before, each time only making things worse.

"You should leave me, Haven. Go somewhere exotic and

beautiful." There was a finality in Bell's voice that terrified her.

"Why would I ever do that?"

Bell met her gaze, his eyes shiny with unshed tears. "I'll be married soon, and everything will change—"

"I'm not leaving you."

He sighed. "You're my best friend, Haven. My person. But I don't think you were made to live in anyone's shadow—even a handsome prince like me. Someday you'll realize that and escape this prison."

"Never say that to me again," she snapped, letting her anger at Cressida get the better of her. "You're the only family I have, and I'm never leaving you. Got it, *droob*?"

One corner of his mouth shifted upward. "What the runes is a droob?"

"An idiot," she fibbed. She'd picked the word up from a Northern trader who taught her a few curse phrases of Solissian.

"Okay, now what does it really mean?"

She grinned wickedly. "Knob. Wanna hear another one? Rump falia."

He lifted an eyebrow.

"It means butt-face."

Bell laughed, but the sound was strangled and quickly morphed into a sob. Tears streamed down his face. Two fat, horrible tears that cruelly reminded Haven there were parts of Bell she couldn't heal, even with famous Solissian insults.

She let him cry for a while. Then she put a hand on his fine-boned shoulder, pouring all her emotions and words into that one touch. She was careful to keep her grip light instead of clenching in anger.

Each day, that vile witch seemed closer to crushing Bell's beautiful spirit, all because his dark skin reminded her of the woman the king would always love.

Above all things, Haven despised bullies. And Cressida was the biggest bully around.

"If I'd known how much you hated being called a knob," she teased, desperate to cheer him up, "I would have stuck with idiot."

"Maybe I am a knob, at least according to Cressida." When Bell glanced her way, the dark lashes framing his topaz-blue eyes were clumped, but the tears had stopped. "What if she's right, Haven? I'm not the prince the kingdom needs. I'm horrible with steel, even worse on a horse. I live inside these books, inside imaginary worlds where I can be anything I want. But as soon as I step outside the library, I'm a disappointment. I'm me, and everyone will see that today."

"Bell," she began, her voice thick with emotion, "you are better than any man or woman in this kingdom—"

"It doesn't matter," he muttered, rambling on as if he hadn't heard her. "It doesn't matter how many sword lessons they make me take, or how many councils I attend, I can't be the prince they *want*."

Haven realized she hadn't sheathed her sword. Slowly, she slid the steel back into its cage, fighting the helpless feeling that clumped behind her sternum and made her feel seconds away from puking.

She was Bell's protector, trained to guard him from every threat imaginable. Her entire existence was built on keeping him safe. But what good was she if she couldn't even protect him from his family?

Defending a body was easy; defending a heart was a lot trickier. If only there were a rune to protect Bell from heartbreak, she would scour the earth to find it.

Haven kissed Bell's high, tear-slick cheekbones with the promise of hurrying back so he wouldn't have to endure the runefeast alone. But her mind was still on that revolting woman.

One day, Goddess willing, she would help the king's mistress into an early grave.

SEVEN

The sun burned the tops of Haven's cheeks and fouled her mood as she surveyed the market inside the city walls. She could almost feel the smattering of freckles across her nose and cheeks darkening.

On instinct, she moved to lower the brim of her hat . . . only to remember she lost it earlier.

"Shadeling's luck," she muttered, nudging her roan mare, Lady Pearl, through the crowd.

It was said the Goddess watched over them during the day in the form of the fiery daystar, but as much as Haven loved the Goddess, she had no affection for the relentless Penrythian sun.

Ten minutes beneath its angry glare and already sweat drenched the back of her tunic and stung her eyes, a pink tinge coloring her pearly skin. Even the black-and-gold scarf covering her hair hung limp and wet across her skull.

Before her spread a sea of ruddy, sweat-sheened faces. The

city was unusually busy, bustling with visitors from neighboring kingdoms this side of the runewall.

Using gentle pressure, she guided Lady Pearl around a tent selling runed charms and worked to clear a path further north. Lady Pearl was a good, dependable girl, but the commotion of the city had her on edge.

"Good girl," Haven cooed, patting her sweat-damp neck.

From here the crowd was almost too thick to pass. She shielded her eyes with her hand and glanced around, trying to get a feel for the general mood of the city.

Penrythian banners proudly flew from the windows of the white townhomes flanking the square, heat trapping above their red-tiled roofs and shimmering the air. The smell of candied almonds and watered-down ale mixed with the hot air into a thick, syrupy drug that tugged on her eyelids.

The King's Road slithered just past the gates, hemmed in by rolling green-blue hills that stretched to the horizon. Behind the city, Fenwick Castle loomed atop a steep, rocky hill.

Tall as a mountain, the monolith spit green flames from its spires to announce the second Prince's Runeday, its ornate gables and impossibly tall turrets blotting out half the sky. Dark smoke dribbled from its many chimneys.

It was so easy to forget Prince Remy had come first. Eleven years Bell's elder, Remy died in the last battle of the Final War just before his twentieth summer.

Barely nine-years-old, she and Bell had been hidden at the king's summer palace, away from the fighting. It was right then, waiting in that humid palace huddled together in fear, that she decided she would enter the royal soldier's academy and win her spot as Bell's companion guard when she came of age.

The battle lasted two long, horrible months. And when it was over, there were no victors.

She could still smell Bell's vomit from the day he had to absorb two hard truths: His older brother had been killed, and Bell was now the Crown Prince and heir to the Penrythian throne.

Pulling herself from the bitter memory, she dug her heels into Lady Pearl's flank, prodding her through the stagnant crowd.

"Move!" she called, leaning forward and grabbing a fistful of Lady Pearl's snow-white mane as she skittered sideways. "Make room!"

People from the untouched kingdoms of the west thronged the King's Road, more than she would have thought possible, trampling the grass and defiling the air with the tang of unwashed bodies.

A scuffle broke out, and the crowd spilled down a hill, knocking over tents and makeshift market stalls selling fake runestones. She released a nervous breath, her palms itching.

They didn't have enough soldiers to control a crowd this size, and it would only get larger as the day wore on. In a few hours, Bell and his entourage would travel down this road on the way to the temple where he would receive his runerights.

A panicked feeling shot through her as the mob pressed on them from either side. She didn't do well in tight spaces.

Apparently, Lady Pearl felt the same. She nickered, her tail swishing anxiously back and forth. Haven yelled again to clear a path, but few people even glanced up at her.

The king's banner flying from her saddle, three black dahlias curving the jagged blade of a dagger, made no difference.

Clenching her thighs, Haven leaned forward and tugged on the reins. At the same time, she tapped Lady Pearl's flank with her toes. A cry went out from the masses as the horse reared, her long, graceful legs pawing the air.

With a space cleared, she guided Lady Pearl in a circle, carving out more space until her heart slowed to a calm tempo.

Now that Lady Pearl could actually move, Haven spurred her into a gallop toward the castle, her heart thumping to the sound of the horse's hooves tearing the earth.

If they weren't careful, Bell's Runeday would end in disaster.

Haven followed the tantalizing smells to the great hall where the runefeast was held for the nobles from the neighboring kingdoms. Of all the rooms inside Fenwick Castle, even the library, this was her favorite, and the only chamber that showed any hint of the queen's renowned taste.

Soaring vaulted ceilings of stained glass let in the sunlight, and crystal chandeliers threw sparkles around the room. Ivory panels gilded in silver and gold flanked the walls.

She trailed a finger over the hand-painted dahlias covering every inch of the columns as she passed, waving away the retinue of attendants flocking around her.

Her mouth watered as soon as she spied the meats and savory pies piled onto the first table. Another table heaped with silver trays of ripe, colorful fruits and berries, poached pears, stuffed olives and an assortment of cheeses. A third table was reserved for pastries.

She plucked three sticky buns from a platter; two went into parchment paper and then her pocket, one into her mouth. As she crossed the parquet floor with interlocking flowers and suns to the round table where the royal family sat, crumbs rained along her path.

A line of Royal Guards darkened the wall with their crisp green waistcoats and grim expressions. At first, the two men in the middle smirked at Haven, refusing her rightful place closest to Bell's chair.

All it took was the touch of her sword hilt and the *droobs* rushed to make room.

After that, she refused to acknowledge their presence, but a smug grin found her sticky lips; every guard here had met the end of her sword at one point or another.

To save their fragile egos, they spread rumors she used forbidden Runemagick and conjured Shade Lords to win. Only her close friendship to Bell kept her from hanging, but that only seemed to make them resent her *more*.

Leaning back against the wall, Haven wrinkled her nose at the foul scent of the tallow tapers along the wall.

How long had they been using elk fat?

She'd noticed small changes recently. Porridge five days for breakfast instead of two. Courtiers wearing last season's dresses. And some of her favorite spices, like saffron and sugar, were rationed until the food tasted like hog-slop.

The Curse had ground trade with the neighboring kingdoms to a near halt, meaning Haven would have to go without sugar in her tea and the halls would smell like burning lard.

She caught Bell's attention and beamed. His face brightened at the sight of her, and he straightened in his high-backed chair, the dahlia engraved into the wood behind his head nearly as large.

Poor Bell. He wore a too-big crown of tarnished gold that slid down to his thick black eyebrows, weighted with rubies and black pearls, and the stiff collar of his shirt scraped his chin every time he turned his head.

The heavy red cloak cascading down his slumped shoulders was fur-lined, and already, sweat beaded over his temples and brow.

He looked utterly miserable. Especially with King Horace on

the right, and Cressida and Renk on Bell's left. She imagined he'd look the same trapped in a room full of vipers.

At least there were others. Lord Thendryft from the next kingdom over sat directly across from Bell, along with the Lord's eldest daughter, Eleeza. The young princess had sleek dark hair, skin a shade richer and deeper than Bell's, and full, ruddy cheeks meant for smiling.

A chuckle erupted from the table as Lord Thendryft finished some tale Haven hadn't caught.

Bell was the only one at the table not laughing. His pale-blue eyes kept darting to Eleeza across the table, and he had scratched a red spot into his neck.

Rumors swirled that King Horace and Lord Thendryft had already arranged the marriage between Bell and Eleeza, and Cressida had all but confirmed it with her earlier taunts.

The princess gave Bell a shy smile, and his gaze collapsed to the uneaten pile of meat and figs on his plate.

"So, Prince Bellamy," Eleeza inquired softly. "Are you excited about receiving your runerights?"

"Excited?" he scoffed.

The table went quiet, and Haven barely kept her eyes from rolling. *Freya save us.* By the gleam in his eyes, he was about to make some smart remark, so she coughed, *loud.*

Flicking his gaze to her, Bell forced a tight smile. "Yes, Princess Thendryft, I am. How was your Runeday?"

Eleeza's face brightened. "I was nervous, of course. We've all heard the stories about what happens . . ." Her voice trailed away. "I mean, that won't be the case for you. Your family hasn't produced a lightcaster in half a century, at least."

Bell cleared his throat. "You're right, Princess. We have been magick-barren for over seventy-five years."

"*You're right, Princess,*" Renk whispered in a mocking, feminine tone. A cruel grin split his thick jaw.

At sixteen summers, he was already a foot taller than Bell, with a high forehead overhanging bird-like eyes and thin lips to match Cressida's. His lank marigold-yellow hair, also like his mother's, hung to his broad shoulders and needed a good washing.

Wiping his sleeve across his greasy face, Renk chuckled. "But it happened twenty years ago to Prince Cavalla, did it not? One second he's receiving his runestone and eating honey cakes, the next, the Shade Queen's monsters have him in their claws." He bit into a large, browned pheasant leg and continued without chewing. "I . . . bet . . . he never thought he had . . . magick, either."

Bell stiffened. Eleeza impressed Haven with a sharp look at Bell's half-brother.

Cressida cut her eyes at her son. "Chew before you speak, Renk."

Renk's throat bobbed as he swallowed his unchewed food. "I heard the Shade Queen's daughter drinks your blood first. Just sucks it right out of your veins." He uttered a high-pitched laugh. "But before that, she lets her monsters toy with you. Waits until the moon is full—"

"Enough talk of dark magick," the king said, picking at his teeth. He barely even spared a glance for the spoiled *droob* he called a son.

Haven glared at the king's bastard. She couldn't decide who she wanted to kill first: the mother or the son. They were equally repulsive, and she'd stayed up more than one night trying to determine how Cressida had won the king's heart after his first wife died giving birth to Bell.

King Horace had never married Cressida, a decision that probably kept the vile woman from poisoning Bell so Renk could ascend the throne.

Without the Boteler name, Renk stood little chance of ever ruling Penryth.

King Horace glanced at Bell with flat eyes and a distant smile. Like Bell, the king was slight of build, with thinning, wavy hair and Cupid's bow lips. But where Bell had kind eyes and a ready smile, the king was reserved and calculating.

And he could be cruel, too. Haven had seen him imprison peasants and merchants who couldn't come up with their tithes during the hard years after the runewall had been built.

Her mind wandered back to the day she met Bell, nine years ago. If not for Bell's intervention, the king would've had her flogged and sold to be a slave, or worse. There was always worse.

"So, Lady Ashwood," the king began, fixing his hooded eyes on her and interrupting her thoughts. "How is the King's Road?"

Haven released a breath, wishing the king didn't still unsettle her after all these years. "There are many here today for the celebration, My Grace, but—"

"Good." King Horace dismissed her with a stiff nod.

"But," Haven persisted carefully, "I fear there are too many to ensure Bell . . . Prince Bellamy's safety. As you know, the soldier's ranks are dwindling, and a crowd like this, I'd like to take the royal entourage on the private merchant's road instead."

In the ensuing silence, the only sound was the crackling of the fires. All eyes rested on her, the girl who interrupted the king. The king's thick, fawn eyebrows, shot through with gray, gathered together as his mouth tightened.

Renk's gold-gilded plate made a clattering noise as he dropped his pheasant leg and leaned back. "Father, why does Bell's He-She think she can dictate Runeday?"

Haven bristled. *Father?* That was reaching. Renk was a bastard not fit to use that word alongside Bell, and she fought down the urge to put an arrow through one of the beady eyes blinking from his swollen head.

"Renk, if only you could keep your mouth closed," Bell murmured. "You would actually look like you *belonged* at this table."

Something bitter and cold passed over Renk's face as he fixed Bell with a stare that promised he would pay for that insult later.

"Besides," Bell continued. "She's only trying to protect us."

"*She*? Are you sure about that?" Throwing a sloppy wink at Eleeza, Renk smirked. "Or maybe you are sure. Maybe she opened her legs and let you look."

Eleeza glared at Renk before catching Haven's eye. The girls shared a look, and Haven decided she liked Lady Thendryft.

"Enough vulgarities, Renk," the king said in that bored voice, barely glancing at his son.

"Yes," Cressida chided. "If we don't visit the temple soon, it will be too hot to bear. As far as the King's Road is concerned, the Botelers have traveled that path every Runeday for three hundred years, and I'm sure one ill-advised girl will not change that. Am I right, My King?"

King Horace nodded. "Of course, we'll still travel the King's Road. Archeron"—he waved his hand, gold and rubies flashing from his fat fingers—"come with us and make sure I arrive safely."

Haven swallowed as a tall, lithe man appeared by one of the columns. She hadn't noticed him before, a fact that irked her immensely. He glided to the table without seeming to move, and all the diners froze.

Everyone except Cressida, who turned to watch him with unabashed hunger.

"Yes, My Lord." His voice was like honey, smooth and sweet,

but an undercurrent of resentment tainted every eloquent word.

"Have you met my Sun Lord?" the King asked Lord Thendryft, his eyes gleaming with pride, as if the Solis was a prize hound to show off.

"A true Sun Lord?" Lord Thendryft murmured as he studied Archeron with newfound interest. "I did not know there were any left in the Mortal Lands."

Sun Lord. An incredibly powerful Solis from across the Glittering Sea, his title meant he was either tied to the Effendier Sovereign's royal line or so skilled in magick he had a place at her court.

Once, when the Solis were as plentiful as mortals in Eritrayia, with their own kingdoms and trade routes carved out here, a true Sun Lord wouldn't have been such a marvel.

She'd seen illustrations in the texts of luxurious, seven-day balls where Solis and mortals came together to celebrate the holy days of the Goddess and Shadeling and discuss trade.

But those days had long passed. Now, a Sun Lord was a novelty, a myth most only read about.

Haven had never spoken to the Sun Lord Archeron, but she had noticed him around court, always slipping through the shadows next to the king. She once heard a lady of the court whisper that Archeron Halfbane was bound to King Horace, a slave.

Of course, the woman also said other things about the Sun Lord that made Haven blush.

Not that Haven blamed her. Next to him, the nobility in their fine velvet brocade gowns and heavy jewelry looked like silly children dressed up in their parents' clothes, playing pretend.

Even in his simple black tunic, his honey-blond hair brushed back to pool inside his high collar, he oozed power and strength, commanding the attention of the entire room.

She sighed. Everything about him was youthful and alluring

and strong; his well-tailored clothes accentuated broad shoulders and muscled thighs, and his eyes . . . his eyes were the color of emeralds, sharpened with the solemn gaze of someone who had lived centuries, despite looking not much older than her.

The guests scraped back their chairs and stood, their curious glances clinging to Archeron as they exited. Cressida made a point to pass by him, running a hand over his shoulder as she did.

Archeron ignored them all, his chiseled face unreadable and attention fixed on some invisible spot on the wall.

Bell wore that same look a thousand times during sword lessons with Master Grayson, before his untimely demise.

Archeron Halfbane was *bored*.

Rolling her eyes, Haven snatched a few more pastries and then ran to catch up with Bell. Solis might be gorgeous, but they were also cowards who fled the mortal realm for their protected lands across the sea, leaving the mortals to fend off the Curse themselves.

In fact, the only Solis she'd ever met had stolen her from her family and sold her into slavery.

This Sun Lord, pretty as he was, would be no different.

EIGHT

Haven was the only person in the entourage not smiling. She stuck close to Bell, forcing Lady Pearl to practically brush against Bell's large chestnut stallion, his new birthday present. Sunlight rippled off the stallion's muscles as it turned repeatedly to nip her horse.

Haven frowned. The choice of mount was horrible for Bell; weighted down with his crown and heavy red cape, he could barely wrap his legs around the huge, ornate leather saddle, much less control a beast this size.

Especially when both his hands had to grip the worn pommel just to stay on, which meant he couldn't wave to the crowds gathered in the courtyard to watch him.

The stone keep rose to their left, the stables to their right. A path had been made between the lean-to market stalls, and the air filled with the tang of horse manure, hay, and the clean scent of the white rose petals that were strewn over the cobblestones.

Villagers cheered and threw rice grains at the group, the few wealthier merchants tossing wreaths of lilies and jasmine.

The king and his mistress headed the procession, with Bell in the middle beside Haven. Renk and the noble families followed behind. The hooves of their horses made hollow thuds against the wooden drawbridge and snowed dust into the mossy moat, sending little ripples across the water.

The road between the first gate and the last was small, but the crowd was manageable. The soldiers in the front of the procession kept the path clear, and slowly, the tension in her shoulders loosened.

Perhaps her worries were unfounded and she had been . . . wrong. Admittedly a rare occurrence, but everyone had to be wrong once in their life.

Feeling more relaxed than she had all morning, she eased back from Bell a few paces. The sun had a lulling effect, and her body soon fell into the gentle rhythm of her mare's gait. She even polished off a few pastries, licking the icing from her fingers, her eyes slits of pleasure.

Glancing behind her, she noticed Archeron on a pale-gray stallion two hands taller than Bell's beast. Solis typically rode the giant horses bred by the noble Sun Lords of Asharia. But Alpacian horses were as big as they were rare, and Haven had never seen one this close before.

Drawn by her curiosity, she slowed her mare to inspect the beautiful animal. Up close, it wasn't gray at all, but silver, shot through with tiny gold hairs making its coat and mane appear to sparkle. Delicate antlers of azerite sprouted from the beast's crown, hardly longer than her forearm.

The semi-translucent material was a mixture between platinum gold and opal, each gold band representing a year of the fabled creature's life.

Famous rings and necklaces had been crafted from azerite, and since trade had fallen off, the rare material was worth a small fortune. Cressida alone had at least three necklaces made of the stuff.

"He's beautiful," she remarked.

The Sun Lord stared straight ahead.

She cleared her throat. "Hey, Sun Lord. Do you speak?"

Nothing. Not a single flicker on his poreless, tawny face. The kind of face that didn't turn pink under the sun or suffer freckles.

"Magick got your tongue? Fine. But I need to know that you're ready in case the crowd gets out of hand. So, maybe just a nod of your head, or . . ."

"She." His emerald gaze flicked lazily to her, and he raised an eyebrow. "And you have icing on your lips."

"I'm sorry?"

"The horse. She's a female. And you need a napkin."

Haven clenched her thighs over her saddle to keep from spitting a biting remark and quickly wiped a sleeve over her lips. "Look, *Sun Lord*. Can I count on you if things turn bad?"

Instead of answering, he stared ahead, his sensual lips curved into a lazy smile as his eyes narrowed into green slits like a cat sunning itself.

"I should've known a Sun Lord wouldn't be up to fighting."

"I was ordered to get King Horace there safely, mortal," he said, still looking straight ahead with his bored expression. "Not his son."

"So, you would let an innocent boy be harmed?"

"That innocent boy will one day be a cruel, oath-breaking king just like his father. Why would I care to save him?"

She gritted her teeth. "You don't know him!"

For the first time since their conversation, he actually graced her with a long, probing look. Her cheeks bubbled with heat. But she matched his intense stare, drowning the urge to lick the stickiness from her lips.

She was grateful when he released her from his burning gaze and said, "All mortals are the same when they come into power."

"Then . . . then I order you to save the prince if something happens."

He chuckled. "I don't take orders from you, little fool. Now run along."

"Droob," she muttered under her breath, enjoying the tiny flicker of shock that rippled across his smug countenance.

Goddess Above, it took all her self-control to ride away instead of wiping that smirk off his face with one of her arrows. Everyone knew iron infused with raven's blood could pierce a Sun Lord's supposedly armored flesh.

According to the texts, three hundred years ago, ravens were plentiful in Penryth. But after the Curse fell over the land and the veil between worlds was ripped, the Shade Queen entered Eritrayia and all the ravens flocked north to her.

Haven reached back and ran a finger over the raven-feather fletching of her arrows. Most of the iron-tipped arrows in the armory were old, many relics of the last war, when the mortals of Penryth fought against the Solis.

It gave her immense pleasure to know that if needed, she could put an arrow in that arrogant bastard's heart.

"He's pretty," Bell said, shattering her thoughts.

Haven turned up her chin. "All Solis are pretty and equally worthless. I'd rather have his horse."

A faint laugh came from behind her.

Bell adjusted the crown on his head. Sweat darkened his temples and slicked his neck. Haven was roasting inside her green summer cape; she couldn't imagine how Bell felt beneath his fur-lined velvet cloak.

"I wonder," mused Bell, "what it'd be like to be so gorgeous that everyone was half in love with you."

"Annoying, that's what."

He gave a dramatic sigh. "I'd settle for one person to love me, you know, the way they do in the books. The way Odin loved Freya."

"And look how wonderful that turned out for them."

Bell shot her a *you're hopeless* look before adding, "It would still be worth it, I think."

Haven opened her mouth to protest—she loved him like that—but then she swallowed her words and slumped into her saddle. She cared for Bell as much as anyone could love a person, a *brother*, and she was fine without the other kind.

But she would never be enough for Bell. Neither would princess Eleeza, or any of the *princesses* his father mentioned over the years.

A prince, on the other hand . . .

They were nearing the last checkpoint. People milled on the other side of the gold-plated iron gate, so many it took the guards a few minutes to clear a path just to open the doors.

As soon as the grated doors creaked open, a thunderous roar cracked the air, and Bell's stallion startled. The beast nickered and whipped his massive head, stripping the reins from Bell's gloved fingers. Haven managed to capture the reins and calm him, but her heart was in her throat.

Nethergates, she hated being right sometimes.

The crowd was imposing, larger than before, the hills dark and shivering with masses of villagers from all over. Her mouth went dry; her palms itched. If something went wrong, her arrows and sword would be of little use on a crowd this big.

Haven's attention drifted to the throng of people. A plump woman broke through the line of soldiers, screaming for the prince.

One of the soldiers grabbed the woman before she could reach Bell. The distraction allowed two men to slip past the guards. Haven met the idiots as they stumbled toward Bell, barely able to stand.

Great, they're drunk.

She drew her sword and raised her eyebrows at them. *Really want to do this?*

That sent them careening back, although the *droobs* were too drunk to realize how lucky they were she hadn't run them through.

The gold handle of her sword was slick beneath her sweaty palms as she rested it on her lap. The sun's glare reflected inside the steel, and she shifted it, blinking. A trickle of sweat dribbled down her spine. There was no breeze to ease the scorching heat, and the crowd was growing restless.

Haven had been present ten summers ago for Remy Boteler's Runeday, and she couldn't remember the crowd being as hostile, or brazen.

In fact, Bell's older brother even walked his horse into the crowd at one point without incident, throwing silver coins. The villagers of Penryth believed the belongings of a noble on their Runeday held magick that would cure diseases and ward off evil.

Perhaps it was the Curse that made them so desperate to touch Bell now.

Or perhaps it was something else. A scrawny young girl stumbled from the crowd, but something about her choppy movements drew Haven's focus. The flesh sagged on the girls face, her eyes bulging black orbs about to burst from their sockets.

Pointing a crooked finger at the prince, the girl emitted a string of high-pitched cackles.

Runes! The girl was curse-sick. As Haven scanned the rest of the crowd and discovered more Curse-stricken villagers, a heavy sense of dread tightened her chest. These people were infected by dark magick, meaning they were unpredictable and dangerous.

"Curse-sick!" Haven shouted, trying to get the soldier's attention. "They're curse-sick!"

A curving stretch of forest spread out to her left, forcing the throng of packed villagers closer to the King's Road. A flash of silver drew her attention to the soldiers on the other side. They had drawn their steel and were driving back the onlookers.

A few villagers slipped through and began running toward the entourage. Haven weaved behind Bell to meet them, cursing as she spied their black eyes.

The lead soldiers holding the road open suddenly broke off and ran to help.

"No, idiots!" Haven yelled, waving her hand, trying to stop them. "Get back to the road!"

But it was too late. The crowd spilled into the road ahead of them. She whipped Lady Pearl to face behind, but the crowd cut that off as well.

They were trapped.

Everything slowed down. The empty space around her became a sea of curse-sick people clamoring to get to the prince. A woman broke from the crowd with her child and clutched Bell's cloak. Haven cringed at the child's mad eyes and gray skin.

Others followed, ripping at his boots, the white ribbons braided into his stallion's mane, anything they could grab.

Bell's stallion suddenly bolted, his ears flat against his head and eyes all white as he bucked and kicked at the crowd. Amazingly,

Bell managed to stay on. And then his stallion stopped and reared, legs pawing at the sun like some magnificent, wild beast.

In what felt like slow-motion, Bell lost his grip on the reins, fell backward into the crowd, and disappeared.

For a single heartbeat, Haven was paralyzed with fear for Bell. Someone shouted, "Get his crown!" and people crawled and fought to get to him.

They're going to tear him apart. Anger shot through her, breaking her trance.

Spurring Lady Pearl forward, Haven kicked at the crowd and swung her sword at countless figures, trampling bodies beneath her horse's hooves without a shred of remorse.

One thought blazed through her heart: Save the prince.

The crowd yawned open for her, revealing Bell on his knees, his cloak spread around him like blood. A thin man with a dirty beard had his fist in Bell's hair, trying to rip out a lock. Urging her horse even closer, she smashed her boot into the man's temple with a satisfying *crack.*

He crumpled as if a magick spell had suddenly liquefied his bones.

Bell glanced up, his eyes wide and darting. His crown was missing, and a small cut ran along the length of his cheek. "Haven!"

She reached down and helped him mount behind her, Lady Pearl shifting nervously under the weight.

Haven leaned forward and patted the horse's sweaty neck. "Good girl. Just a little more, I promise."

Haven wheeled her mare in a circle, trying to push back the crowd. But there were too many people, and once they saw the prince behind her, they were crazed, crawling over each other to get to him.

Her sword was heavy as she swung it, once, twice, until she stopped counting. The villagers near the front tried to jump back, yet the crowd pushed them forward. Closer.

Too close.

Haven's breaths came out loud and fast, and a quiet sort of panic had stripped her limbs of sensation. Her heart smashed against her sternum like some poor trapped creature.

In the back of her mind, she understood that if they got Bell off her horse, he wouldn't make it out again in one piece.

Glancing over her shoulder, she took in the crowd between them and the soldiers. The nobles and the king were packed into a tight circle, with Archeron tall and bright in the middle.

His bored expression hadn't changed, and she imagined lopping off his stupid head when this thing was done.

With a casual flick of his hand, he carved out space in the crowd as if an invisible sickle reaped them like stalks of wheat. A few more waves of his hand, and the road was clear.

Haven turned Lady Pearl again, her hindquarters knocking bodies back, but more took their place. Lady Pearl's ribs shuddered as she breathed, gummy froth lining her pink lips. With the combined weight of Bell and Haven, her mare was tiring twice as fast.

A frustrated growl roared from Haven's throat.

She wouldn't be able to hold them off much longer.

King Horace and Cressida were fleeing, his long black cloak trailing behind him. Haven hissed. If she were any closer, she would've put an arrow through his cowardly back.

She called out to the soldiers, but they only smirked at her and galloped after the king. They were finally getting their revenge for all those times she embarrassed them.

To their credit, Lord Thendryft and his daughter, Eleeza,

hesitated. They had a small retinue of soldiers, but anything would help . . .

Frowning, Lord Thendryft glanced their way before ordering his party to flee.

A string of curses erupted from her lips.

Archeron turned to follow, but then he paused, shook his head, and glanced her way.

For a moment, their eyes locked, and all she saw was him, this Sun Lord, this dark-hearted bastard who held Prince Bell's fate in the flick of a hand and yet was going to watch as the mob tore him to pieces.

She snarled at Archeron, sending every vile thought she could muster his way.

He sighed and lifted his hand.

There was a whoosh, and the crowd surrounding them flew backward ten feet; the air erupted with the scent of roses and dew-covered grass.

In shock, she sat open-mouthed for a heartbeat as the realization took hold. *He did it. The bastard actually did it!*

Before the mob could regroup, Haven kicked Lady Pearl into a hard gallop, and the sea of onlookers parted before her. She leaned forward and laid her head against Lady Pearl's soft mane, urging her faster, whispering praise and encouragement into her delicate, gray-tinged ears.

Bell's arms trembled around her waist, squeezing so hard she fought to breathe.

"Hold on, Bell!" she called.

Even after the mob fell away, they ran. Even when Lady Pearl's gallop turned into a jolting trot and Bell's grip weakened around her, they kept going until finally Lady Pearl slowed to a limping walk.

The hiss of Haven's blade returning to its sheath was a beautiful sound. Haven looked up and found a dense canopy of green leaves hiding the sun. The sudden shade felt wonderful on her skin, and she straightened, inhaling the earthy smells of the woods that flanked the northern side of Fenwick's sprawling estate.

She pushed deeper down the wide path.

They all required rest, especially Lady Pearl. Her white coat had turned gray with sweat, and air blew from her nostrils in loud puffs. Haven needed to check on Bell and make sure he wasn't hurt beyond a few scrapes and bruises.

Still, something nagged at her to keep going, and she scoured the black oaks and aspens forming a wall on either side. The woods were too quiet, the canopy of trees too still. A few dying leaves swirled into their path, but otherwise, it was as if the world had been frozen.

Where were the squirrels and birds? The white-tailed deer?

Haven slid from the saddle to the ground, her boots crunching against dry grass and leaves, and took the reins, pulling gently to move Lady Pearl faster. Her tail swished back and forth, and she pushed into a steady trot as Haven jogged beside her.

Something pale and mossy caught Haven's eye through the trees. The wall. They must be near the end of the woods. Her lips cracked into a grin and she almost yelled out to Bell, yet she halted, planting her feet into the forest floor.

Something was wrong.

A tall, branchy sycamore tree had fallen over the wall, creating a large hole—large enough for a Shadowling to enter.

Her body trembled as everything clicked into place. That's why the animals were gone and the woods were quiet.

"Shadowling!" Haven hissed, darting into a sprint and tugging Lady Pearl behind her just as a bird startled from the trees ahead.

Her gaze tracked the bird, and when she glanced back down the path, a large beast stood blocking their way.

"Sneaky little monster," Haven whispered as she scraped her sword from its sheath and prepared to fight.

She'd hunted, trapped, and snared all sorts of Shadowlings, but always on her terms, with a carefully laid out plan that didn't include the Crown Prince.

This time, Haven had gone from hunter to hunted.

NINE

Haven wasn't afraid to die—she had come to terms with that inevitability a long time ago—but Bell's death was different. She'd sworn to protect him, to give her life for his.

Now it was time to prove that.

Stepping in front of Lady Pearl, she slipped the second sword from its place between her shoulder blades, twirling the weapons in her hands; the habit steadied her.

Behind her, Lady Pearl nickered nervously, her hooves stamping the forest floor.

A snarl tore from the beast's chest. It was a Lorrack, and it was huge—easily the size of her mare—with a wolf's shaggy gray head and yellow eyes on a stag's lean, muscled torso. A full rack of sharp black horns nearly as tall as Haven sprouted from its massive head, and instead of hooves, it had the claws of a reptile.

Sharp teeth glistened from its maw as it inched closer with unnatural stealth.

"Bell," she whispered. "Turn Lady Pearl slowly, and when I say go, I want you to ride like the Netherworld out of here."

"No."

"Bell," she growled through clenched teeth, "I'll be distracted if you're here. Please."

The Lorrack was crouched down, creeping closer. Its wet black nose sniffed the air, and she could swear it's beastly eyes narrowed with hatred.

Any second it would pounce.

"Bell!"

The sound of Lady Pearl's hooves crunching the dirt as she turned eased the tightness in Haven's chest. She held onto the Shadowling's predatory gaze. The second she blinked or looked away was when it would move.

Taking a step to meet the Lorrack, Haven yelled, "Go!"

As soon as Lady Pearl took off, the beast whipped its enormous head to watch them, drawn by instinct to the movement. Its shaggy tail twitched, its hindquarters shuffling with energy.

The creature shot through the air after them in a flash of gray and brown. Spread out, it was massive, the muscles trembling beneath its thin stag's coat.

Haven lunged, drawing her sword across its white belly. After rolling over her shoulder, she popped back on her feet just as it hit the ground.

Snarling, the monster snapped at her and continued after Bell and Lady Pearl—as if it knew that was how to hurt her.

"Over here, you stupid creature!" Haven yelled, but it continued stalking them, its ears pinned back and tail twitching.

Panic tightened her chest. Bell didn't even have a blade to protect himself. Mid-sprint, she grasped her sword by the tip and flung it at the creature's loping body—but her blade missed, striking the earth right next to it.

Whipping its head back to growl, the Lorrack's black lips pulled into a jagged smile.

For half a second, desperation blinded Haven. She blinked just in time to see Lady Pearl turn and rear.

Then the beast was leaping, its maw wide and glistening. One of Lady Pearl's hooves cracked against its long jaw in a blow that would have stunned a wolf.

But this creature, this Shadowling, kept going.

Bell had fallen on his back, and he crabwalked toward the brush.

"Bell!" Haven screamed.

One hand gripped her bow, the other nocked an arrow and ripped back the bow string. But it was like a bad dream where her movements were slow and clunky, and the wolf's row of jagged yellow teeth descended on Bell—

A bright-orange explosion lit the forest, followed by a thunderous crack. The beast screeched and stumbled backward, flames roaring over its flesh.

Haven lowered her bow and watched in horror as it sank to the ground, slowly, so very slowly. It seemed to be shrinking and decomposing, its fur sloughing off. Its skin shriveling into a husk.

After what felt like several minutes, she blinked and the thing became an ashy, smoldering pile. Horrible black smoke drifted from the ash, tendrils of reddish-gold mist whirling around Bell in faint, shimmery loops before slowly fading.

Haven lunged toward Bell and threw her arms around his neck, something she hadn't done since they were eleven. His entire body shook, his panting breaths warming her cheeks as she oscillated between crushing him to her and looking him over.

"What happened?" she breathed, plucking the twigs and leaves from his ruffled hair. The scent of burned roses was overpowering.

The flames, the iridescent air, the smell—it had to be something to do with the beast. She couldn't let herself think otherwise. That Bell had performed magick. And their innocent joking about it earlier today suddenly felt not so innocent.

Not Bell. Goddess Above, please not Bell.

Yet there was no denying the magick. She could smell it, taste it, feel it. And there was no wishing it away.

"I . . . I . . . they're burning." He held up his trembling hands. "My hands are burning, Haven. I, I think I used Runemagick."

That word stopped the breath in her lungs and turned her stomach to stone. *Runemagick.* It was synonymous with the Shade Queen, with death.

Forcing shallow breaths into her lungs, she ran a finger over the fine ash pile beside him, sniffing it—as if that could tell her anything—and rubbing it between her fingers. Bits of ash caught in their clothes and hair.

"No. No . . . no. It can't be." Her throat ached. "You don't have your runestone yet."

But even as she said it, her mind flashed to the little runestone in his pocket.

The forbidden powerrune that was supposed to protect him.

The rune *she'd* given him.

Bell must have thought the same thing because he had it out. "Ah," he cried, quickly folding it back in its bright square of velvet. "It's . . . it's hot, too."

Hot. Which meant . . . blasted Shadeling Below, what had she done?

But Haven couldn't have known Bell would harbor trapped magick. Magick that had waited decades, perhaps centuries, to reappear inside the most unlikely host.

"He left me." Bell glanced over his shoulder, as if he could still see his father abandoning him to die. "He actually left me. I knew I wasn't his first choice as his successor, but I always thought somewhere deep down he must care about me." A bitter noise rasped from his throat. "Now I know that was a lie."

Haven hadn't cried in years. Not since the night she escaped her master, Damius, and promised herself she would never let anyone see her tears again. But for the first time since she'd made that promise, she came close to breaking it.

Scraping her forearm over her eyes, she released a craggy breath and stood.

She needed to think, to come up with a plan, and she couldn't do that if she was a mess—or if her thoughts were turning to murdering the royal family instead of escaping. "We have to get you out of here."

"What?" Bell met her stare, eyes wide and glazed. He stumbled to his feet. "Go where?"

"Anywhere. Across the sea to Solissia. Asharia, maybe, or Effendier. We just can't stay here. We have to assume the Shade Queen"—her breath quivered at the word—"The *Shade Queen* will have felt the magick and sent someone to find you."

She didn't tell him there was already a Shade Lord on the other side of the wall—which he could cross now to find Bell, according to the laws of the Curse.

Every noble child with Runemagick belonged to the Queen of the Noctis. Even the runewall couldn't keep her from entering and claiming Bell now that his magick declared itself. It would whisper across the wind and through the Netherworld like tugs on a spider's web, drawing the Shade Queen out of her lair.

Forcing any thought of the dark queen from her mind, Haven calmed Lady Pearl with soft words and smooth strokes across her neck. Pale horseflesh shivered beneath her hand, but Lady Pearl finally stopped kicking.

"Haven."

Bell's haunted tone of voice startled her, and Lady Pearl's ears flicked back as she whipped her head to glare at Bell.

"Haven, leave me."

"No." She grabbed his arm. "Don't say those words again."

"I'm already lost, Haven."

She shook her head, drawing Bell into her arms. He was shaking. "Stop. I'll figure something out. Okay?"

Nodding, he pulled back, his bright eyes wide. "I have to receive my runerights before we go."

"Now?"

"Imagine what will happen if I don't show. The king and his soldiers will come looking for us. They'll track us and drag me back—even with magick. *Especially* with magick."

"I won't let that happen, Bell."

"You don't know the king like I do. Now that his son is a lightcaster, I'm worth something to him." Bitterness tainted his voice. "And you, you'll be strung up and flogged for helping me. But if we wait until they're all pissed on cider, we might have days before he realizes I'm gone."

"Every minute longer here puts you in danger. Besides, the king will notice whenever you leave."

"Will he, though? The Goddess knows he's forgotten about me for weeks at a time." He dragged a hand through his hair. "Besides, we can't just run off into the wilderness with no supplies or plan. We need maps, food, water, weapons."

Everything he said was true. And yet everything inside her screamed to leave right now.

But maybe . . . maybe the ceremony would be quick. Maybe his extra rune would add another layer of protection from the

Shade Queen. Maybe it'd been so long without a noble lightcaster that the Shade Queen had forgotten the cruel Curseprice for the murder of her daughter at the hands of a mortal prince.

Maybe. There was that blasted word again.

"Okay," Haven said, even though the idea of staying in Penryth one second longer filled her bones with dread. "But we leave right after you receive your runestone."

Haven brushed her fingers over Lady Pearl one last time. Her skin had finally stopped trembling, and a wide blue eye rolled to the ash pile as she huffed from her pink nostrils and then stomped at it.

"I feel the same way," Haven whispered to her mare, helping Bell onto her back. His face was the color of old bone; he was probably half in shock.

Then again, so was she.

With every passing second they remained beneath the warm sun's kiss, Haven's racing pulse slowed, and the memory of the beast and Bell's Runemagick faded.

No—not Runemagick. They couldn't say for sure that's what it was.

Bell, too, seemed to relax now that the darkness of the woods was behind him, his cheeks regaining a bit of color. He even smiled when they passed the persimmon orchard, the amber and green leaves bright with pops of orange fruits and the air heady and thick with the scent of scattered persimmons rotting beneath the heat.

Despite everything, Haven's mouth watered. It seemed an inappropriate time to be hungry, but then, Haven was always hungry—and she hadn't had any real breakfast, just a few measly pastries. The next few minutes were spent dreaming about the foods she would pack before they fled.

But soon that led to the actual part where they had to escape.

The anxiety over being caught quickly gave in to nervous excitement. Now that she finally allowed herself to think it could happen, a bubble of hope swelled inside her chest.

For the first time in years, she felt light. As if a weight had lifted from her shoulders.

Nine years was a long time to spend in one place, but Penryth still wasn't her home. In the back of her brain, a small voice whispered the promise she'd made years ago: to find her way back to the family she was taken from.

Scraps of memory told her she was from across the sea in the realm of Solissia, but that was all she knew.

It would be enough. It had to be enough.

A grin spread across her face. She and Bell would find her home and her people together. And she could still fulfill the oath she made to Bell the day she became his Companion Guard, as well as the life debt she owed him.

The Royal Guards' yells shattered her thoughts; she hadn't even realized they were at the temple. A much friendlier crowd milled around the gold domed structure, quiet and calm as they waited for Bell with bowed heads.

Probably the merchant families; they would've been protected from the Devouring last night behind the runewall.

Haven stayed between Bell and the crowd as she and the prince climbed the wide marble and gold-flecked stairs leading up to the temple. It took everything she had not to curse the soldiers ahead for abandoning the prince.

"Cowards," she muttered, relishing the fact that they, too, would soon be a distant memory.

At over three hundred years old, the temple was ancient. Haven blinked at the imposing structure.

Sunlight caught in the silver and gold veining the pale marble. Red trumpet vine and lavender morning glories draped over the gilded roof, twisting around the twelve ivory columns. Foxglove and ivy covered the iron doors. The cloying scent of flowers filled her head and upset her too-empty stomach.

How in the Netherworld was the temple still standing? Runemagick had to be responsible. Perhaps in the vining flowers?

The texts said it was easier for a lightcaster to put longevity spells into vining plants than an entire building, which was why the runewall was covered in them as an added precaution.

She noticed more flowers twining over the windows and sprouting from cracks in the marble. Plucking a yellow jessamine flower from the arched doorway, she twirled the petals between her fingers.

And then it came to her: all the flowers were poisonous to some degree. And from her experience with the Shadowlings, she'd learned that flowers poisonous to mortals were thrice as deadly to Shadowlings.

Maybe the temple was covered in these vining flowers not to protect the building, but to protect the mortals inside during runerights. The thought sent a shiver scraping down her spine, and she plucked a few more petals before following the soldiers inside.

The temple was an octagon. Each wall displayed a scene from the Sacred Goddess's text, taken from the story of the House of Nine. The Boteler House mural spread over the back wall, an image of Bell's ancestor on his knees beneath the sacred runetree of life, the All-Giver.

Or, in Effendier, the Donatus Atrea.

A gray, smooth-barked tree sprouted from the middle of the

marble floor, mirroring the painted one on the temple walls. It was tall, its golden leaves nearly scraping the concave ceiling. Pearly-white dahlias the size of Haven's fist hung from the delicate branches, silver and pink veins running through the near-translucent petals.

Nine rows of pews took up either side of the room, filled with nobles impatiently fanning themselves. Once, each row held a different house from the Nine Mortal Houses, and their flower insignia was etched into each pew.

But now, with so many of the Houses having succumbed to the Curse, only a few actually held true nobles from the Nine. The rest were highborn mortals who had wrenched control of the remaining territories, claiming questionable lineage and even more questionable ties to magick.

As she hurried Bell down the aisle, her hunger turned into a dull headache. Expensive perfumes drenched the air, but it couldn't hide the smell of sour sweat from a long day's ride beneath the Penrythian sun.

Near the front, she spied the royal family sitting casually on the first pew with the black dahlia inside a circle, and she drowned the urge to punch the smirk from Renk's face.

Following his gaze, the king gave Bell a quick, impatient glance. His lips downturned at the image of his son, disheveled and sweat-stained, face ripe with fear.

Couldn't the king show a little relief that Bell was okay?

She dug her fingernails into her palms. In a few hours, she would never have to deal with this wretched family again.

The priest, a hunched figure draped in layers of dark muslin and reeking of rosewater, hobbled to Bell and led him to the front. Haven gave a quiet gasp as the priest faltered on the first step, but Bell took his arm and led him up to the dais.

Haven didn't see the Sun Lord until she was almost on top of him. He leaned casually against the wall, eating a persimmon with his eyes half closed. His golden skin and sun-drenched hair matched the painting of the Sun Lord behind him, handing the sacred flower to one of the House Nine families.

It was the sacred flower given to all Nine Houses, enhancing their magick and giving them the ability to access the Nihl and use the runestones.

Everyone possessed magick to some degree, but most mortal's magick was so weak, even with a strong runestone they could barely cast a spell or lift an object.

She blinked at the golden painting behind the Sun Lord. Goddess Above, it could be *him* for all she knew. Solis and Noctis lived longer lives than mortals, but the most powerful of their kind, the Sun Lords and Shade Lords, lived hundreds, sometimes thousands of years—at least, if she believed the ancient texts.

"You know," Archeron purred in his honey-sweet voice, "staring isn't polite, Mortal."

She bit her cheek to keep from taking the bait. She would stare all she wanted. Besides, he had to be used to it by now. You couldn't look that different, that . . . pretty without people staring.

"You know," she said, "if you want to justify your hatred of my kind by goading me into cruel words, you're wasting your time."

"I already have a reason to hate your kind." Venom laced his voice. "Now I'm simply trying to ward off a pest."

Pest? She rolled her eyes and focused back on the procession. Her palms itched, and she tapped her fingers against her thigh. The priest was prattling on and on, his slow, breathy voice interrupted by coughs and hacking.

She growled under her breath, praying to the Goddess he didn't keel over before it was done.

Every few seconds, her gaze flicked to the windows, checking for something out of the ordinary. Cold sweat rivered between her shoulder blades. This day was lasting an eternity.

"Worried about something?" the Sun Lord mused, light from the nearest window highlighting swirls of silver thread inside his tunic.

A few onlookers glanced over, ready to hush Haven and Archeron, but when they saw the Sun Lord they quickly looked away.

"Now who's staring?" she growled.

"I wasn't staring." He took another small bite of his persimmon. "Your energy is off." He sniffed the air. "And—why do I smell Runemagick?"

Her heart punched in her throat. "Maybe you smell yourself?"

"No. This was mortal Runemagick, and it was clumsy." He cut his hooded eyes at her. "That's why it smells singed."

"Stop talking. People are starting to stare."

"Your kind always stare at me. I'm used to it."

Peacock. Pursing her lips, she glanced at Bell. The priest was leading him to the tree to recreate Bell's ancestor receiving the sacred flower.

Blasted priest, move faster!

She swallowed down a scream as the priest slowly, slowly reached for a limp, low-hanging dahlia.

"And Horrigan from House Boteler . . ." the priest droned in his ancient voice, holding the stupid flower in his shaking hands, "was one of Nine to receive the sacred gift from Goddess Freya, readying his bloodline for the magick of the holy Nihl."

"C'mon," she growled, much louder than she'd intended, drawing disapproving glances from the king's mistress.

Archeron flitted his bored gaze over her. "In a hurry to be somewhere?"

She sneered at his too-pretty face. "Maybe I don't enjoy your presence."

"Doubtful."

A murmur rippled across the pews as Bell kneeled at the foot of the stairs. Haven found herself holding her breath. The priest clutched a black, pearl-inlaid box with dark roses swirling over the top.

The box squeaked open, and silence fell over the room.

She craned her neck to see inside the box. According to the texts, the desiccated bulb of the sacred flower Bell's ancestor consumed had been preserved inside the box; on every Boteler Runeday, a runestone appeared.

Haven bounced on her toes as the priest pulled out an onyx stone, pinching it between his gnarled, shaking fingers. Somehow, he managed to fasten it to a heavy iron chain.

Impatient as Haven was, her lips pulled back in a grin as Bell bowed his head and the priest draped the dark stone over his neck.

An orange mark flashed from the stone and disappeared, quick as a falling star.

Thank the Goddess, it was done.

Something—a flicker, a shadow—caught Haven's attention, and her body went taut as a bowstring. Archeron still wore his apathetic mask, but a muscle trembled in his strong jaw. And his arms, which had been laced tightly over his chest, had freed themselves and were now hovering over the steel at his lithe waist.

With a smooth, slow motion, she pulled out her bow and nocked an arrow, the raven's fletching tickling her cheek. She hadn't had time to apply the poison to the iron tips, so she reached for one of the flowers she'd placed in her belt—

But the delicate yellow petals withered and died inside her fingertips, crumbling to powdery gray ash. Outside the window, the other flowers suffered the same fate. The vines curled and twisted in on themselves as the flowers became cinders that blew away on the sudden, howling wind.

A rhythmic thudding drew her attention to the tree. The dahlias were dropping to the floor of the temple and bursting into flame. A woman on the end of the pew stood and pointed at the tree, her mouth hanging open.

All the leaves were shriveling into ash.

Before the woman could release her scream, the iron doors to the temple crashed open.

TEN

Of all the nightmares Haven had ever endured—and she'd experienced a lot—none were as horrifying as this.

Dark creatures scuttled over the tall ceiling and walls, their talons clicking against the marble. She fixed on the closest monster making its way across the ceiling. Splotched in raven's feathers and scaly dark skin, it had a hairless humanoid head, all-black eyes, and crooked, membranous wings tipped in talons.

Pointed ridges lifted from its back, and it took a moment to realize the bony protrusions were its spine pricking through its wax-paper skin.

Haven's arrow streaked through the air and hit the creature directly in the hunched back, sinking deep into the base of its neck. The creature screeched—an inhuman howl—and fell to the floor.

It writhed for a moment and then, impossibly, got to its feet.

Not so fast, dummy. She sent another arrow into the beast's wing, shredding it like paper . . . but the hideous thing snarled at her and kept going.

Nethergates! Her weapons were useless without poison.

"Bell!" she called, glancing over her shoulder at him.

A green wall of soldiers surrounded the prince, arrows whizzing from their crossbows. He was a statue of fear, his eyes twice their normal size. They shared a glance and she mouthed, *I'll fix this.*

But that seemed more and more impossible by the second.

Especially as countless creatures swarmed the temple, smashing to the ground in deafening thuds. The nobles scattered, their screams reverberating off the walls in a macabre symphony.

One beast severed a noble's head with a swipe of unnaturally long claws. Still gaping in a terrified howl that resembled a ghoulish grin, the head rolled down the aisle to rest against the stairs.

Haven's entire body went cold and numb, as if the blood inside her veins had simply evaporated.

She put an arrow into the offending creature's torso, but the blasted monster ripped the arrow out with its needle-like teeth, its slimy skin healing before her eyes.

Her vials of runepoison . . . No, there wasn't time to tip her arrows.

A figure blackened the doorway.

She nocked her last arrow and raised her bow, expecting the Shade Queen.

Instead, the Shade Lord from the forest sauntered in.

As opposed to last night's sleek hunter's tunic and cloak, he was decorated in the grand regalia of an otherworldly prince.

A jagged crown of onyx nestled between his horns, partially obscured by his artfully tousled moonstone-white hair. Oil-black armor highlighted his wide shoulders and tapered waist, so perfectly molded to his form it seemed a part of him.

Tiny steel daggers jutted from a high collar of sable and gold, and she wondered how they kept from pricking his sharp jawline.

But the most arresting part of his ensemble was a cape of raven feathers cascading down his back, each exquisite black plume flashing a different color depending on the light.

This was the Netherworld prince she'd heard horror stories about, the cruel, beautiful monster who stole mortal children and lurked inside nightmares.

As if he knew he was being appraised, his wings surged above his shoulders, an impressive tapestry of inky blues and blacks. The glossy feathers glinted and shimmered, his delicate wingtips nearly scraping the red pine beams arcing the ceiling.

Their eyes met. His bright and feral; hers wide with fury.

A tingling sensation ticked down each knob of her spine, forcing a puff of air from her lips.

Hello, Beastie, a voice teased inside her head. *Did you miss me?*

Her body went rigid at the intrusion; at the same time, she let the arrow fly, but it burst into a cloud of ash right before it hit the Shade Lord.

Instead of floating away, the soot of her former arrow maneuvered into the shape of a raven. It swooped over the ceiling in lazy, mocking circles, taunting her from above.

Nice try. His voice scraped down her shoulder blades and lodged in her core, each word piercing her walls and burrowing deeper into the places she kept hidden.

He held up a hand tipped with shiny black talons, and everything slowed to a stop. A sharp gasp escaped her throat. Monsters and nobles were frozen in place like nightmarish statues. A dark feather hung in the air.

One woman in a buttery-gold dress, her face paralyzed in terror, was suspended over the pew she'd been jumping over. Her dark-brown hair streaked behind her in horizontal layers.

But Haven was free. She patted her body for the rest of her weapons—only to find they were gone.

The Shade Lord glided up the aisle with preternatural grace, sliding through the bodies and stepping over the fallen, his steps too quiet. He ducked beneath the dying tree, his dark raven's-feather cloak slithering behind him like one of his creatures.

His eyes, now bright silver orbs in a bed of inky lashes and dark shadows, didn't leave Haven's. The citrine band around them flickered, and she half expected flames to erupt.

"No," she pleaded in a voice not her own. "Don't take him."

Still watching her, he lifted his hand toward Bell. The soldiers surrounding him crumpled to the ground like autumn leaves bursting in the wind.

Finally, the Shade Lord dragged his gaze from Haven to Bell, who was frozen, his mouth open mid-scream, eyes all white. They were riveted to the Shade Lord.

His lashes fluttered—he could see.

Which meant he was probably terrified.

Bastard! Haven lunged at the Shade Lord and was flung back, skidding across the floor into the wall. Darkness swallowed her vision. She blinked away the pain in her spine and head and tried again.

This time, he lifted his hand without even looking, and suddenly her body was locked into place, a hard, cold wall surrounding her—as if she were encased in ice.

Only her eyes and lips could move. Spewing a string of curses, she kept her gaze on the Shade Lord as he approached Bell. The Shade Lord paused at the second step, his chin tipped toward where the Sun Lord still casually leaned against the wall; a smile twitched the Shade Lord's lips.

"Archeron," the Shade Lord said, enunciating each syllable

with care. "I forgot you were still enslaved to the mortal king. How boring."

Archeron picked at his teeth with a dagger. "Stolas."

Haven could just barely wrench her head from its frozen position to watch them.

"Pleasant day for procuring a mortal for Morgryth. I didn't realize you and your gremwyrs were still bound to her. How *boring.*"

A raspy chuckle spilled from the Shade Lord Stolas's lips, his sharp Adam's apple bobbing up and down. "You know how demanding my wife's mother can be, especially without Ravenna to comfort her."

"Yes. I imagine your dear Ravenna is quite comforting to the mortal children she feasts on every full moon."

A muscle feathered in Stolas's sharp jaw. "I don't suppose you're going to try to stop me?"

Despite the pleasant, almost friendly way they spoke, their voices were hewn with disdain, and the air between the two immortals sparked with hatred that was impossible to ignore.

"As much fun as that would be, old friend," Archeron drawled in his honey-sweet voice, "we both know it's the Shade Queen's right to demand a Curseprice. But I might ask you to do something about your pets' stench."

"Speaking of pets," Stolas purred, his strange eyes drifting to Haven. "I find this one quite interesting. Is she yours?"

A long stretch of silence passed, Haven's heart throbbing against her ribcage the only sound.

"Mine?" Archeron countered, and she bristled at the amusement in his voice. "You know how I feel about mortals, Stolas. And this one is more annoying than most."

Haven would have hissed at the pretty bastard, if she could've moved her lips, but he must have grown tired of her cursing because suddenly she couldn't speak.

"Shame." Stolas rested the full weight of his feline stare on her. "They make the best lap dogs, dripping with terror and so very compliant. And when they become tiresome, they dispose of quite easily. A snap of their delicate spine usually does the trick."

Netherworld swine! She tried to scream it, tried to make her lips and tongue form the bitter words, but they remained lodged in her throat. He chuckled as she struggled against his power.

Unable to vent her anger, she poured her fury into her stare, burning him with it, wishing she could set him on fire the way Bell had his beast and watch him burst into flames. . .

A shock zipped through the air, and Stolas's eyes widened, just slightly. He cocked his head, rubbing the back of his neck.

What was that? It was so subtle she could've imagined it, but he'd definitely felt something. Hadn't he?

It was so hard to tell what was happening without being able to move.

Her lips were suddenly free, and she gathered all of her loathing into her voice. "Someday, I swear on the sacred Goddess, my blade will pierce your monstrous heart."

"Foolish Little Beastie," Stolas crooned, even as his eyes darkened to storm clouds. "Making promises you cannot keep."

"Watch me."

Stolas angled his head, one neat midnight eyebrow quirked. *How did I taste?* he whispered wordlessly into her mind.

Her heart raced at the memory, panic and loathing forming an ever-tightening band around her chest. She tried to wriggle, but her body was locked tight. Her mouth parted, but no words could describe her disgust and anger.

So she did the only thing she could do: she spat at the Shade Lord.

Stolas blinked in surprise, the shock quickly transforming into something darker. Rage shimmered beneath his pristine facade. The promise of a monster about to break free its chains.

Shivering, she somehow forced her chin a few millimeters higher and awaited his wrath with her eyes firmly shut.

Laughter filled her head. She snapped open her eyes to see his were dancing with amusement.

With a ruinous smile, he swiped a finger over his cheek and then slipped it into his mouth, and she had the bad luck of noticing how full his lips were as they closed around his finger.

Now I know what you taste like, he growled into her head, the sound both sultry and dangerous.

Heat surged and rippled across her flesh, his voice swirling inside her the way she imagined chiffon would feel against her bare skin.

Then he turned his attention to Bell. "Apologies, but the Shade Queen demands your magick, lightcaster."

She tried to scream but her vocal cords were once again bound, so she used her inner voice to shout, *Leave him alone!*

The Shade Lord ignored her, not even a flicker of reaction crossing his steely countenance. He had the look of predator wholly fixated on his prey.

Her throat tightened with panic. For the first time in her life, she was helpless, truly helpless, and she despised the feeling.

Agonizing memories flooded her brain. After the king's men caught her selling runestones, she was to be sold into servitude. Bell had been looking for a new saddle when he saw the slaver beating her. It was the day of his ninth birthday. He could've asked for anything, but despite her status as a foreigner and convict, despite the dirt caking her odd-colored shorn hair and the insults she hurled at anyone with a pulse, he had chosen her.

Her.

In return, Haven pledged her life to Prince Bellamy; now that oath was being broken, and there was nothing she could do.

Her lips yawned and, drawing up every single ounce of her willpower, words spewed out. Before she could think about the consequences, she made another oath. "I swear by the Goddess and the Shadeling, I'll break this damnable curse and save you, Bell."

If Bell heard her, she couldn't tell. Stolas whistled, and one of his beasts on the ceiling unfroze. With a screech, the gremwyr spread its eight-foot wings and shot toward the prince.

A shadow darkened his frozen face. He managed to blink and then the beast had him in its black claws and was rising, its bony wings beating the air and blowing back the noble's hair and cloaks.

Finally freed to move, Bell twisted and fought, his legs windmilling the air.

A single feather drifted to the marble floor, dark against the pure-white marble.

See you soon, Little Beastie, Stolas whispered.

Then they were gone.

Bell was gone.

Haven's insides were shattering into tiny shards. When the spell was lifted and she could move, she ran blindly through the stunned crowd. The sun burned her eyes. The air was choked with the scent of cinnamon and blood and dust.

She didn't stop until she found Lady Pearl and they were streaking back to the palace, the wind cleansing her hair and clothes of that awful smell.

Only then could she show her emotions.

Only then could she fall to pieces.

Except, as she replayed the events in her mind, the only thing she felt was anger, and by the time she reached the castle's shadow, a blistering rage had formed inside her.

Damn the king and the Shade Queen and the bastard Shade Lord. Damn the cowardly Sun Lord. Damn them all.

In the span of a minute, everything changed forever. But Haven Ashwood knew one thing for certain: she was going to get Bell back, even if she had to burn down the Netherworld to do it.

ELEVEN

Inside the city walls, Haven came close to violence more than once. Normally, she could ignore the peddlers with their oily smiles and lies, but she wasn't in the mood as she crossed the courtyards.

The revelers swelling the area were even worse. By their drunken cheering, they had no idea the prince had been taken.

Clenching her jaw, Haven snarled at the stocky man thrusting fake runestone bracelets into her path, the dyed beads rubbing color onto the man's sweaty palms.

"Some loverunes for you on this fine day, boy?" he called, confused by her clothes and hidden hair. "Get a girl in the sack first try. That's a promise."

Without slowing, she cut the bracelet with the small knife she'd nicked from a Drothian noble a few stalls back, bright beads scattering over the ground. As her blade finished its path, it nicked his purse too, dropping the soft leather pouch into her waiting palm.

It all happened in less than a second.

By the time he bellowed a string of obscenities at her, she'd slipped into the crowd and was gone.

She ended up tossing a few silver pennies to a young, shoeless girl with two wide-eyed children crawling in her lap. Something about their hungry eyes and hollow cheekbones reminded Haven of herself years ago—before Bell saved her.

No, don't think about him. Focus on gathering supplies and a map, and any texts that might be helpful.

Clearing her mind of emotion, she entered the castle and hurried to her chamber. Packing was easy; she only owned three tunics and two pairs of pants—one, she currently wore.

Her glass vials of poison were corked and clearly marked by the name of the flower, and they clanked as she gathered them. Four of her favorites—oleander, jessamine, wolfsbane, and nightshade—went into her pocket.

The rest were carefully wrapped in an embroidered yellow-and-blue silk handkerchief Bell had gotten her, before he realized she hated such gifts.

She found her sketchpad and pencils hidden beneath her mattress, along with the ornate sword Bell had custom made for her last year.

Unlike fabrics and perfumes, she absolutely approved of weapons as presents, which Bell soon learned.

Being friends with a prince had its perks.

Everything but the sword went into a dusty saddlebag and then onto her shoulder.

For a moment, the lightness of the bag startled her. Surely after nine years she had more belongings. Things that said something about her, that marked her life in some way.

But for the last nine years her life had been all about Bell, and there was no room for anything else.

Her mind went to the bag of runestones hanging from the dead tree. That and her sword were the only important things. The rest of her stuff was replaceable.

She examined the beautiful weapon, named Oathbearer to remind herself of her oath to Bell.

Inside its expertly forged steel, she saw Bell's face reflected back. His kind eyes. The wry curve of his lips before he said something humorous.

Now, of course, she had a new oath: to break the curse. But she didn't need a sword to remind her this time. The promise clanged through her, loud and unrelenting.

Her life from this moment forward was forfeit.

Haven silently ticked off what weapons she would need on the way to the armory. A dozen arrows and a leather quiver. A new hand-scraped ash bow. New daggers, three, at least. A girl could never have enough knives.

She grinned at the memory of a lovely pearl-handled dagger Master Lorain had shown off that morning.

She would need that too.

Visiting the armory was like attending a holy place, and Haven always gave a quick nod and a prayer to the warrioress, Freya, when entering.

The tang of polish, lemon oil, and old leather filled Haven with joy. Ignoring Master Lorain's protests, she helped herself to everything on her list, including two unused leather bracers that would protect her skin from chafing if she used her bow much— which she fully intended to do. Plus, there were slots to store her poisons for fast access.

The library was next. So far, Haven had managed not to think about Bell at all, but being in this place, surrounded by all the books Bell loved, threatened to destroy the walls she'd quickly erected as shields.

She could picture him this morning, rumpled and sleepy. She could hear his soft, lilting voice echoing off the high-ceiling.

Her throat tightened.

Was he scared? Hurt? Perhaps mad at her for not protecting him? She should have insisted they leave immediately. How could she have been so stupid?

Closing her eyes, she took a deep breath, her old master Damius's words steadying her: *Emotions are tools. Only feel them when they're useful.*

So she pushed the ache of Bell's absence down deep into the place where she buried all her raw feelings and pressed on.

Tucked into a tiny corner near the bottom of the stairs was a section dedicated to the Curse. Haven pulled out all the books, thumping them down on the rug, and sat on the floor, quickly sorting the ones she thought might be useful.

When she had four ancient leather tomes in front of her, she began flipping through the brittle yellow pages, muttering apologies under her breath each time she accidentally ripped one.

If Bell were here . . .

Stop. Her jaw locked, a cleansing breath hissing through her teeth, and she focused on the pages. It'd been so long since anyone had tried to break the Curse that Haven wasn't even sure how to go about it. But there had to be a way.

By the Goddess's Law, every curse had a Curseprice.

Haven scoured every book, every delicate page. Nothing. She did find a nice, detailed map of the entire mortal lands of Eritrayia.

Muttering another apology, she ripped the page out, folded it, and slipped the paper into her bag.

The next page told the tale of the Curse, although she didn't need to read it to remember. Everyone knew that a mortal prince killed the Shade Queen's only daughter, Ravenna.

In a mother's rage, the Shade Queen cast a dark Curse that tore the veil between the Netherworld and the mortal lands, ending a century of the Noctis' imprisonment and allowing the Shadowlings to re-enter their lands.

The story behind why the mortal prince killed Ravenna was not so clear. Some scholars claimed the prince broke off their engagement, killing Ravenna with grief.

But the tales Haven heard growing up were much darker and whispered of a northern prince who wanted to ascend to his House throne, but as the youngest brother of three, was last in line to succeed.

So, the youngest prince summoned Noctis to rid him of his brothers and father, but after Ravenna helped the youngest prince ascend the throne, she demanded to rule beside him as his queen.

On the day of their wedding, the prince poisoned Ravenna, and while she lay in a deep slumber, he cut out her heart . . .

Haven slammed the book shut, a cloud of dust stirring the air. Such stories were best left to the past. She needed to know how to break the Curse, not why it happened.

Chewing her bottom lip, she stood. She'd have to study the map later and see if perhaps it offered hints. But right now she needed to gather food for her trip.

After the library, Haven found a few loaves of hard bread and dried pork belly in the kitchen. Judging from the busy courtyard outside the open windows, most of the nobles and their families remained; the villagers must have fled after they heard the news, because uneaten food piled the counters and tables in the kitchen.

When one of the cooks stirring a pot of dark sauce noticed her, the damp-faced woman made the sign of the Two Gods, the Goddess, and the Shadeling—a tap between the eyes and a tap to the heart—and shook her head.

The gesture was supposed to represent Freya's throne in the Nihl, the mortal heaven above their world, and Odin's place in the Netherworld below, where he'd been imprisoned after the fall of the Noctis.

Apparently he'd grown so dark and twisted even the Shade Queen didn't want to release him after the Curse set them free.

Haven made her own sign of the Two Gods in thanks for that small miracle. Then she crossed the kitchen to leave.

Her plan was to head straight to retrieve her runebag, but when she noticed a servant girl fixing a tray full of buttery toasts and salted herring, little dishes of caviar brightening the mix, Haven followed the girl instead to the king's council room.

If the king had a plan, perhaps she could help.

And if he had information on how to break the Curse, even better.

TWELVE

As soon as the girl disappeared inside the chamber, Haven scampered up the stairwell a few corridors down and slipped inside an upstairs room that had once been an apartment for visiting Solis Royalty.

A curtainless window ran floor-to-ceiling, dull and dirty with age. Solis only slept a few hours a day, so there was no bed, only a plush ivory chaise lounge with tufted buttons and thick, azure-fringed pillows. The scent of dust and age told her no one had used this room in a while.

Falling to her knees and dragging a golden velvet stool out of the way, she said a small prayer to the Goddess that the hole was still here. Relief tumbled through her as she pulled the wooden peg from the baseboard and a slant of light appeared. Voices drifted from the hole.

Her lips pulled into a sly grin as she peered down into the king's council room. Perhaps King Horace had a plan, for once.

Perhaps he'd even prove his love for Bell.

She sighed, sending dust devils skittering along the baseboard, and focused on the long oval table the lords sat around below.

The first person she noticed was the Sun Lord. As if he truly were the sun, all the mortals caught in his orbit. Archeron leaned back in his chair, arms propped behind his head, his tall, lithe body making the chair he sat in look like a toy.

The smoothness of his tawny flesh contrasted against the pale, withered skin of the mortal lords all around him, and fostered the lie that he was the youngest—not the oldest being—in the room.

A smirk contorted his face, his lips twisted as if fighting back a laugh.

King Horace sat red faced at the head of the table, his rheumy blue eyes wide and his hair still disheveled from the temple. Kings from the surrounding, untouched lands rimmed the table.

The room trembled with their shouts as they talked at the same time, suggesting solutions:

A runespell to bring Bell back.

Bind the Shade Lord who took Prince Bellamy to the nobles using ancient runes none of them quite remembered.

Send yet another emissary to beseech the people of Solis for help.

Their obvious fear and lack of any real plan disgusted her. These were the last remaining mortal lords of Eritrayia and Bell's only hope. At one time, Bell had said kind words to every single lord at the table, making a point to learn their names and history to make them feel at ease whenever they visited.

He deserved so much more. Yet here they were, trying to impress one another with their stupidity. *Droobs!*

She could barely contain her sigh as Lord Grandbow, the bald king across from Archeron, thumped his hand on the table, his saggy neck trembling as he said, "A great injustice has been done today. We must gather our armies and march to the Ruinlands."

Lord Grandbow didn't *have* an army to offer. Neither did most of the others, not after the curse-sickness decimated the population outside the wall.

Haven shifted her gaze to Archeron. He was picking carefully at his fingernails with a gold-handled knife, the disgust on his face mirroring hers. At some point, his chest shook with laughter, although she was too far away to hear it.

"Speak, Sun Lord," one of the lords, a ruler from a kingdom she couldn't bother to recall, hissed.

Archeron flashed a saccharine grin. "I'm afraid my jokes won't be as clever as yours."

"You find our words humorous?" Lord Grandbow demanded, his eyes bulging from his fat head. *Runes, he was ugly.* Especially when contrasted with the Sun Lord's effortless, otherworldly beauty.

Archeron's gaze rolled heavenward, and his eyelids closed.

"Archeron."

The king's voice snapped Archeron's eyelids back open, although he continued staring at the hideous mural on the ceiling. Something dark seemed to pass between them, an invisible cord demanding his attention, perverting his will. Haven instinctually recoiled from it.

"Why didn't you save my son?"

Archeron thrust his gaze onto the king, and Haven took pleasure in the way King Horace flinched.

"You didn't ask me to," Archeron pointed out. "I believe your last binding command was to get you to the temple safely. The words, 'protect my son from the Lord of the Netherworld,' never left your lips."

The king cleared his throat and glanced around. Haven chuckled under her breath as his cheeks turned a bright shade of red.

"Obviously, I couldn't command you," the king gritted through clenched teeth, "because I was under that evil monster's spell."

Now it was Haven's turn to roll her eyes. *More like you were pissing your royal britches.*

"Ah." Archeron blinked lazily at the king. "That is . . . unfortunate."

The table erupted with voices as the lords began to argue again, trying to talk over one another, the sound adding to Haven's frustration. A sigh hissed through her teeth.

This was pointless, a waste of time.

The mortals were never going to do anything about Bell, just as they never did anything about the last hundred princes and princesses taken by the Shade Queen.

A younger lord with fine brown hair and a beaked nose cleared his throat until the room quieted. "What about breaking the Curse?"

The lords looked down at the scarred table stained with wine, studying the gold and silver jeweling their manicured fingers.

"I mean," the lord persisted, his voice raising a few octaves, "no kingdom has tried in at least twenty years—"

"Enough!" The king held up a hand. "Before the wall, when the kingdoms of Lorwynfell and Arlynia had yet to fall, and you were just a sparkle in your father's eye, every kingdom sent their best soldiers to the Ruinlands to break the Curse. Even the Sun Sovereign of Effendier sent her finest Sun Lord warriors."

The young lord frowned. "I've heard the story."

The king narrowed his eyes, running a finger over his collar.

"Then perhaps you should listen more carefully. The soldiers that went to the Ruinlands were never heard from again. Still, the kingdoms sent their best and bravest men every year to break the Curse. And every year, they never returned. Finally, the realm of Eritrayia managed to unite one army with the goal of marching to the Ruinlands and breaking the Shade Queen's Curse.

"It was a fine army, the best our world has ever seen. We soldered down all our iron and steel and had the Sun Lords rune the metal before making it into the most magnificent armor ever made. Then we lined up along the King's Road and watched this army with all of our sons march away on their fine horses with their fine armor. Mankind's greatest hope."

The young lord was holding his breath, and he leaned forward to rest on his elbows. "And?"

The king's grin was a horrible thing. "And not a single soldier ever returned."

Despite her disappointment, Haven almost felt sorry for the young lord as all the color blanched from his face and he managed to mutter some reply she couldn't hear.

"Besides," King Horace said, "no one seems to remember how to break the Curse. Only the wishes granted afterward. One wish for each Curse breaker—if you believe the tales. And knowing the wicked and cunning Noctis, I do not."

Wishes? Heart pounding, Haven pressed closer, struggling to hear above the laughter from the nobles.

They might not think such a thing was true, but why would the Shade Queen start rumors to encourage people to break the Curse when it benefitted her the most?

Abruptly, Archeron leaned his tall frame over the table, clasping his hands together, and met the king's gaze. "A shame, though. Imagine what a lightcasting Boteler could do. Imagine how the other lords here would envy your kingdom and its return to magick. With Prince Bellamy back, Penryth would be the most powerful kingdom in Eritrayia . . . if not for the Curse, of course."

Haven drew in a breath and strained to listen. Although what Archeron said was true—the mortal kingdoms once rose and fell by the power of their magick—he wouldn't take the effort or time to speak unless there was something in it for him.

He certainly didn't care about Bell's safety, or Penryth's return to power.

The king's eyes sharpened with interest. "Yes. Very right, Archeron. It is a shame. The Boteler bloodline has always produced the finest lightcasters. The *finest*."

The other lords nodded in agreement, muttering to themselves, but their faces couldn't hide their relief that, at least in their minds, Prince Bellamy would never come back, and Penryth would never be restored to its place as the most powerful kingdom.

Archeron kept his face placid and cool as he watched the king, but a vein popped in his neck.

What was his motive? Haven could almost see the king's shrewd mind turning furiously over and over behind his pale-blue eyes, his fingers pulling at the wispy hair trailing his weak chin.

Finally, a clever grin brightened the king's face, and he pounded the table until the other rulers stopped to listen. "I, King Horace, command my Sun Lord Archeron to travel to the Ruinlands and break the Curse. Bring back my splendid son with all his magick, Archeron, and I will reward you with gold and jewels like you've never seen before."

Archeron forced his face into a scowl, but a grin danced behind his frown. Leaning back again in his chair, he tilted his head up and locked eyes with her.

Runes! Haven jumped to her feet and slammed the stool back against the wall, not caring who heard.

Her heart hammered into her throat.

She should have been relieved the king was doing something to help Bell. But why did it have to be the arrogant Sun Lord? And how could the king of all of Penryth let himself be tricked in such a manner? The Solis didn't care a fig for gold and jewels.

There had to be another reason Archeron wanted to go.

Haven shifted the bag onto her right shoulder, the glass vials nestled inside tinkling softly, and rolled her shoulders. It wasn't her concern if King Horace was a damned fool.

She slipped out the door, turned to cross the hall, and froze.

Her shiny new scythes were drawn as she whipped around, golden sunlight curving inside their wicked blades. The Sun Lord tilted his head at her, his hands clasped behind his back. "Hello."

"Hello?" she snarled. "You sat there and watched the Shade Lord and his beasts take my friend, and that's what you say to me?"

His broad shoulders shrugged. "Yes, hello. It's the mortal greeting, and after all these years, I'm finally giving it a try."

"Damn you to the Netherworld," she hissed. "How's that for a greeting?"

"Better. More lively."

"You're a bastard!"

A grin split his face. "Most likely."

"And . . . and a coward."

As soon as Haven said it, something flickered inside his eyes that told her she'd gone too far.

For a stretched out second, he said nothing, the tendon in his broad jaw straining. Then he lifted a sharp, honey-gold eyebrow. "Be careful the words you spew; I've killed mortals for less." His gaze momentarily flicked to her weapons before sliding back to her face. "Now put those away."

Hardly daring to breathe, she slid her scythes into the scabbard at her waist. She felt naked without them in her hands . . . and the Sun Lord was so close, his warm, sweet breath caressing her cheeks, smelling of leather and nectar.

Runes, when had he approached her? She hissed at his unnatural ability to control space and time, to slip through the planes of this world unnoticed.

"If I'd known you were going to get close," she spat, "I wouldn't have sheathed my weapons."

His eyes hardly left hers as he cracked his neck. "A trick of the mind. You should pay better attention when a Solis is around. We don't play fair."

"Well, I'm paying attention now."

"Like you were when you met the Shade Lord?"

Her mouth went cotton-dry.

"Was it Stolas?" he continued in his honeyed voice, though his eyes darkened at the mention of the Shade Lord. "Why didn't he kill you, I wonder? It's not like him to show mercy."

Talking about the Shade Lord reminded Haven of Bell, and Bell reminded her that she was angry.

Pivoting on her feet, she marched to the corner at the end of the hall and turned—and came face to face with Archeron, grinning and leaning casually against the wall, studying his nails. "Has no one ever told you that leaving mid-conversation is rude?"

Her hand fell to the crossbow hooked to her belt. "What do you want, Sun Lord?"

"Well, I was coming to tell you goodbye"—his gaze slid over the weapons decorating her body—"but I have the sneaking suspicion we're going the same direction."

"I doubt we'll see each other again. I work alone."

The smooth, golden skin of his chest trembled as he laughed.

"And I don't work with mortals, so that's settled. However, I am curious how you plan to get there. Travel into the Ruinlands isn't cheap, and they don't take mortal currency."

An image of the runebag flashed through her mind—and yet, as soon as it did, she felt the urge to hide the thought and protect it. "I'll find a way."

Something in his face changed; it was smugger than usual, his lips curled at the sides. "I'm sure you will. I wish you the luck of the Shadeling, Little Mortal."

"And you—"

But he was already gone.

A tingle settled between her shoulder blades. Something spurred her into a run. Haven bolted down the castle halls, her feet quiet on the dark runners carpeting the halls.

Her chest hummed with nervous energy, a fear she couldn't quite articulate burning her tongue. With each step closer to the Muirwood, breathing became a bit harder. Until she was sprinting, her weapons clanking against each other and breath coming out in hard puffs.

She couldn't say what, but something was off, something was *wrong*.

Get the runebag.

She flew down the steps to the gardens, flanked with gentle folk and nobility. A woman yelled as Haven knocked over a servant carrying a tray full of sparkling cider, glass shattering across the pavement.

Ignoring the yells, she loped across the lawn and scrambled over the runewall, not caring who saw. Flowers ripped from their vines and snowed to the lawn below.

A blanket of moist heat fell over her as she entered the forest, her boots sinking into the mud and moss, the smells of earth, rotten wood, and mildew fogging her mind. Wiping sweat from her forehead, she fought her way through the brambles and underbrush to the huge tree that held her runebag and shimmied up the trunk.

Let it be here. Let it be here. Let it be here.

But as soon as she made it to the top of the tree and saw the branch where it had hung only this morning, her heart dropped into her stomach.

It was gone. Stolen. A string of curses ripped from her lips as she pictured the thief in her mind, his arrogant too-pretty face and jeweled eyes as she put an arrow through his callous heart and ended him.

Time to hunt a Sun Lord.

THIRTEEN

Haven trailed the Sun Lord through the dense tangle of Birchwood and firs making up Blackwood Forest, entertaining herself with all the ways she would punish him when she caught up.

An arrow to the heart . . . No, too quick.

An arrow through the throat. Better.

Two arrows, one for each fancy emerald eye.

Yes, that would make her immensely happy.

On and on she plotted her revenge, Lady Pearl swaying beneath her as they followed the faint turquoise ribbon wending through steep gullies and over shallow rivers.

Several times, the shimmering trail backtracked. He was using the mossy waters to obscure his horse's hoof prints.

The bastard thought a few streams would throw her off his scent.

True, his attempts to cover his trail might have slowed her down, if not for the tracking rune she'd carved into the leather runepurse for just such an occasion.

"Idiot!" she snarled. "Bet you didn't expect that from a lowly mortal."

Unused to such outbursts from her master, Lady Pearl flicked her ears back and whinnied low.

"Easy, girl," Haven soothed.

She ran her hand over the horse's neck, the velvety fur a balm to her rage. If not for her floppy hat—which she'd discovered near the tree she fought the Shade Lord in—and her faithful mare, Haven's mood would have been terrifying.

Although, currently, it was pretty dismal.

As if to prove that point, she flicked the rim of her hat and snarled . . .again.

Thieving jerk. How could she have let the Sun Lord invade her mind and steal her runestones? Any other mortal would have been utterly screwed.

Most people were clueless when it came to the runic arts. They didn't know the difference between mortalrunes—like the runestones given to the Nine Houses meant to unlock magickal powers—powerrunes, and mundane runemarks like the one she applied years ago to the purse.

More common than powerrunes, runemarks could be wielded by those with little magick in their veins . . . even mortals like her, if they took the intense training to learn the art.

This particular runemark left a path only she could see shimmering on Archeron's trail. He was good at hiding his tracks, but every mile or so, she caught trace of the pretty bastard in the form of a broken leaf or a moss-scraped log.

Locking her teeth, she spurred Lady Pearl over a dead oak, sharp limbs scratching at her face and ripping the fabric of her cloak. She'd been following the Sun Lord half the day through gorges, deep valleys, and dense woods, through swollen, moist heat, and swarms of gnats that stuck in her mouth and eyes.

Netherfire! It was hot, and she was famished. Could the blasted Solis not take a break?

Dappled sunlight filtered down from the trees and scorched her arms. After pausing by a sluggish stream to let Lady Pearl drink, Haven pulled out her map, straightening the scroll so that Penryth unfurled over her thighs. With her pointer finger, she traced north past the runewall, up through countless Curse-stricken lands and over the fallen Kingdom of Lorwynfell.

She halted over the Bane, the tip of her finger seemingly frozen over that wicked land and its inhabitants.

Damius. Her breath hitched as dark memories began to slide from their carefully constructed cage.

Cold moisture pricked her palms as the name of her captor, the man who haunted her dreams, began to echo inside her skull.

A bead of sweat dropped to the map, smudging the fine lines of ink over one of the cursed cities. Pushing the nightmarish memories aside, she quickly rolled up the parchment and urged Lady Pearl through the river, sighing as cool droplets of water splashed onto her legs.

No reason to worry about the Bane just yet—or the terrible things that came with it.

The sun's glare softened, and the forest gave way to rolling hills and shimmering lakes.

Night seemed to fall all at once, and Haven allowed Lady Pearl a short break before urging her along the merchant's road just outside of the trader's town of Perth.

When they topped a hill, the red adobe houses inside the walls of Perth came into view, their small windows dark and foreboding.

Pieces of something seemed to drift from the buildings into the sky. The pieces began to converge over the rooftops, darkening the clouds as they swirled left and right in choreographed movements.

"Ravens," she hissed under her breath. A cold fist pressed against her sternum at the ominous sight.

Had the Devouring completely destroyed the city?

She shuddered imagining the Curse's effects on a large population such as the capitol city of Cromwell.

Surely if the nobles of Penryth had known the true extent of devastation inflicted by the Curse, they would have done more for the northern kingdoms . . .

The lie helped ease her guilt, but not by much.

Making the sign of the Goddess, she urged Lady Pearl into a gallop, not wanting to dwell on the thought of all these years living within the comfort of Penryth castle and the protection of the wall, while these people . . .

No, she wouldn't think about it.

The tracking rune glowed in the dark, making it easier to follow. They made good progress through the night as Haven fought off fatigue, yawning in the saddle and reciting an endless array of bladework maneuvers to stay awake.

Somewhere between an imagined feint attack and a parry, rolling hills of grass gave way to an endless canvas of sandy dunes.

By now, obviously convinced she would never trail him this far, the Sun Lord had stopped trying to hide his tracks.

Which is how she determined the Sun Lord met up with a group of others, the sand churned with their horses' hooves. His kind, by the large, unshod hoof print of their steeds.

Still, she pressed on, undeterred by a few more arrogant Solis.

Underestimating her was a mistake and worked to her

advantage. They wouldn't expect her. If she could just catch them taking a break, sleeping the few hours a day they did sleep, she might still retrieve the runestones.

Her opportunity came halfway into the night. The essence of the tracking rune thickened and began to sparkle, so bright it lit her path along the sand. The magickal trail wended up a small mountain range and disappeared.

Her feet didn't make a sound as they kissed the sand. Taking hold of Lady Pearl's halter, she walked the tired mare to the base of a large formation of rocky cliffs.

The Solis were close. Probably on the other side of the steep ridge.

After encouraging Lady Pearl to be a good girl and not make a sound, Haven approached the base of the mountain and began to climb. The wall of granite was pitted for climbing, but the steep slope made her progress slow and tiresome.

Halfway up, her fingers ached from being worked into the tiny cracks in the rock face. Pebbles littered the brim of her hat, and dust blurred her eyes. At one point, a rock the size of her fist dislodged, clattering down the granite.

She froze and waited until she was sure no one had heard.

As soon as she topped the peak and spotted the fire far below, on the other side of the mountain, she ducked, her chin pressed into the rocks.

She found the rune track, now orange, and trailed it. Down the craggy mountain face and around the fire—

A snarl loosened from her chest. *There!*

The thieving Sun lord rested on his back, arms settled behind his head, eyes lost in the stars like some idiot poet pondering the meaning of life. A dark cloak tangled around his legs, revealing a shirtless torso.

Her gaze caught on the moonlight dancing off the silver runes of his chest.

Any other time she might have marveled at the beautiful shimmering lines, the way they rose and swirled over the planes of his body, accentuating his wide shoulders and powerful physique.

She might have even yearned to sketch such a sight . . .

But tonight she was only interested in finding the runestones he stole from her, and she dragged her gaze from the pretty Sun Lord to assess the camp.

Two women, obviously Solis and probably royal Sun Queens by their height and their tall, exquisitely bred horses, huddled around the fire. A dark Solis in a blood-red cloak was hunched over a steaming pot simmering on the fire. He, too, had the powerful air of a Sun Lord.

She sighed, the sound dramatic even to her ears. *Wonderful.* There were probably four powerful Solis in this entire cursed kingdom and they all happened to be right here, guarding her runestones.

The chances of taking them back just kept getting smaller. Her hunger, on the other hand, was growing.

Haven's stomach ached as the cool breeze brought a savory smell to her nose. Some sort of stew.

With another bitter sigh, she flattened herself to the rocks and found a semi-comfortable position, prepared to rest atop the peak until they took their two hours of rest. The sticky bun in her pocket had grown stale, and she shoved the bland pastry joylessly into her mouth.

Then she waited.

The gritty rock was cool on her cheek as her breathing evened out and her eyelids drifted together . . .

Her eyes snapped open. Cold air whipped her cloak around her legs. She was shivering, her neck aching and kinked. A dull headache nipped at her temples.

Below, four Solis lay draped in blankets around the smoldering fire. A quick glance at the moon's path told her barely an hour had passed.

Lifting on her elbows, she skirted along the top of the mountain peak, careful not to kick more rocks down the sloping granite as she found a path and began her descent. At least this side of the mountain was fairly easy terrain to walk, requiring little climbing.

The closer she got to the sleeping Solis, the slower she approached, barely breathing, her movements slow and controlled. If caught, this would prove to be a really stupid idea.

Which was why she wouldn't be discovered. Problem solved.

Proud for not making a single sound, Haven padded across the thin grass, creeping around the campfire to where the tracking rune ended.

A satchel sat unprotected on a rock.

At her feet, Archeron slept on his back, wrapped in a dark sable cloak. A small triangle of the Sun Lord's handsome face peeked from his hood. The rise of the sleeping Solis's cheek was barely noticeable, glowing beneath the moonlight.

He looked young, almost boyish. His full lips—which she was used to seeing curved in bitterness—were relaxed and slightly parted. It gave him a guileless look . . .

Except he wasn't innocent. He was a swindler and a rogue. A thief of the very worst kind. He knew stealing her runestones meant she couldn't cross the Bane to rescue Bell.

He knew, and he did it anyway.

She gritted her teeth until her jaw popped. Punishing him now for his actions would be her death sentence, and yet . . . she couldn't swallow the idea of letting him escape justice entirely.

Perhaps she would cut the cinch of his saddle? Or replace

the water inside his canteen with gritty sand? Or dig for a sand scorpion and set it free inside his cloak . . .

Grinning, she reached for the runepurse—

An emerald eye flitted open. The black pupil enlarged as it focused on her. Then Archeron lifted to his elbows, yawned, and plucked her runepurse from the rock.

"Goddess Above," he growled through a yawn, "you are persistent, mortal. Don't you ever sleep?"

Rage blazed through Haven's veins, bitter and blinding. *He was the thief. Not her.*

In one smooth, deadly motion, she reached for her bow and nocked an arrow.

"Aw," a Sun Queen with storm-black hair cooed in Solissian, their native tongue, long arms stretching from her blanket. "Can we keep her? Please?"

Another Sun Queen, with sun-lightened hair pulled into braids all over her head, groaned and kicked off her blanket, not even glancing at Haven. "Surai, the mortal girl is not a pet. Nor is she tame, by the looks of her."

Haven snarled, her fingers over the butt of her arrow, itching to release the weapon. Runes! She was as good as dead if she released this arrow. Yet they were treating her like a child.

Deep laughter came from the other side of the fire, and the young man in the crimson cloak grinned, exposing bright-white teeth. Like Bell, this Sun Lord had dark skin, but his was the exquisite shade of the night sky.

"You're right on both counts," the Sun Lord said. "They are treating you like a child. And you will not survive if you try to fight us."

The bow wavered in Haven's hands. She'd heard of Solis who could read minds, but they were supposed to ask for permission.

Then again, Archeron hadn't asked either. "I didn't give you permission to go inside my head."

He laughed. "I don't need your permission to soulread, mortal."

She rested her fury on Archeron, who was picking at his nails, his face a mask of disinterest. "Those are my runestones. Give them back."

"No," he murmured without even looking up.

Swallowing the urge to sink her arrow into his neck anyway, she lowered the weapon and forced a polite smile. "I thought Sun Lords were supposed to be honorable."

"A mortal chiding me on honor? Hilarious."

She glided onto the rock, the runestones calling to her as she neared. The other Solis watched her with curious expressions, like she was some damned traveling monkey here for their entertainment. "I have honor. Now give it *back*."

Raising an eyebrow, he slid his gaze to her. "Or what?"

Haven's fingernails dug into her palms. This wasn't going the way she'd planned. *Ugh! Why was he so stubborn?*

The Sun Queen, Surai, marched close, hands on her hips, her long, sleek ponytail swinging back and forth as she chided Archeron in Solissian. "Don't be cruel, Archeron. Look at her manner of dress. She is obviously soft in the head."

Archeron chuckled, his intense gaze never leaving Haven's. "This mortal is a lot of things, but soft in the head isn't one of them." He shifted his attention to Surai. "Since when do you care for mortals?"

"Maybe she just knows when a serious transgression has transpired," Haven snapped.

Sighing, he stood, dusting flecks of dirt from his pants. "Don't be so sad, little mortal. I imagine the men you stole these stones from felt the same way, but they got over it. So will you."

"What do I need to do?" she hissed before forcing her voice to sound more submissive. "I mean, what can I do, oh pretty Sun Lord, to earn them back?"

"What do you want them for?" Archeron asked, his lips twisting into an amused smile that begged her to throttle him.

"I need them to cross from the Bane into the Ruinlands. You know that."

"Oh, now I remember." He ran two fingers over his jaw. "Hmm, are you useful?"

"Useful?"

"Yes. See, you could join us until we cross the Bane, but you'd have to be useful."

Motherless bastard! The Sun Lord was toying with her. He never planned to make a bargain; he just wanted her to look stupid. Her jaw clenched so hard her teeth ached, her anger over everything that had happened these last twenty-four hours exploding.

One second she was on the rock. The next, she was inches from Archeron, his sweet breath warm on her cheeks, and her dagger pressed into his throat.

"I'm quite useful when I want to be," she snarled, glaring up at him. The blonde Sun Queen was instantly two feet away, legs spread in anticipation of a fight, her hand on the hilt of her sword.

"Oh, I like her," Surai purred behind Haven. "We should definitely keep her."

A wry grin split Archeron's jaw, even as the other male Solis joined them, his body tight with tension. "If I wanted a shave, mortal," Archeron drawled, "I would've asked. But since you're here, I am curious as to why all of our interactions result in your blades at my throat?"

"I don't know, Sun Lord. Perhaps it's time for some introspection."

Archeron pressed two of his fingers into her blade and guided it away from his neck. But his silver-flecked emerald eyes were tight as they glided over her face, and his lips parted as if to say something—but then his gaze darted to the cliffs, and he growled a warning. "Shadowlings!"

In one smooth motion, he plucked his sword from a nearby rock and twirled the blade, the muscles of his arms clenching and writhing. The bright-orange runes traveling down the length of the steel blurred into a flickering flame.

He caught her stare. "Want to prove yourself, mortal? Now's your chance. And *murdering* me does not count."

The others also armed themselves, steel glittering the night air like stars. Surai held two curved katanas out low and ready. Other than three runes glowing over the steel of each weapon, they were plainly decorated and worn from use. Soldier's swords.

Compared to the other Sun Queen's whip, bejeweled to the hilt with rubies, or Archeron's enormous sword dripping with gold and emeralds, Surai's weapons were the common steel of a soldier.

Catching Haven's curious stare, she turned and winked.

Dark shapes scuttled along the tops of the cliffs, the air cooling a degree with each beat of Haven's heart. From the little she could see of the creatures, they were either gremwyrs or lorracks, and both could be easily downed with a poisoned blade.

She nocked her arrow, the raven's feather tickling her cheek, and cut her eyes at Archeron a few feet away, grinning at the beasts.

"Say it's a deal!" she snarled as something heavy landed close by in the sand. "I prove useful and you get me across the Bane to the Ruinlands."

Cracking his neck, the pretty Sun Lord flashed his eyes at her. "Deal. Now let's see what all those nights behind the wall taught you."

Haven didn't even have time to register her surprise as a dark shape shot from the woods at her.

FOURTEEN

If this was Haven's chance to prove herself useful, she had a long way to go.

The creatures were everywhere. As if the sky had literally opened up and spewed the monsters, a miasma of taloned-wings and daggerish claws more than capable of slicing through armor and bone.

"Good thing I'm not wearing any armor, then," Haven muttered, launching an arrow at one of the creatures as it arced through the air toward her.

Her arrow lodged in the closest creature's broad chest, sinking to the raven's fletching. With a screech, the beast fell at her feet in an explosion of dust and stench.

In the final throes of death, the beast dug its talons into the dirt and flapped its thin, membranous wings, blowing her cloak back. All at once, the beast stilled, its wings shrinking as they shriveled around its body.

"Gremwyrs," she hissed, ripping the arrow from its protruding sternum and nocking the quarrel just in time to take out another vile gremwyr rushing from behind.

They were everywhere: darkening the sky, bleeding down the cliffs, darting from the trees in black swarms.

The Solis moved among the sea of beasts, so fast her eyes could hardly track them.

Surai twirled and danced, her curved blades slicing through gremwyrs two at a time. Her movements were graceful and efficient, her face a mask of repose.

In contrast the blonde Sun Queen wore a feline grin as she cracked a whip, knocking the aberrations from the sky.

Abruptly, she dropped the whip, there was a flash of gold, and she transformed into a massive cat. Roaring, she plowed through a wall of gremwyrs, ripping them to shreds.

Stop gawking and be useful.

A rush of wind tickled her cheek. She rolled just in time to dodge the talons of the gremwyr above, landing on her back at the same moment she shot her arrow into the creature's black belly.

As the monster dropped to the sand beside her, the talons along its wings raked her hat, sending it to the sand, ruined beyond repair. She jumped to her feet and shot again, then again and again. Finding a rhythm in the chaos.

Exhale, shoot, retrieve. Repeat.

The screams of the creatures permeated the air. Her breathing became a cadence to ground her, a battle cry. Every breath meant she was still alive. She could still fight.

She could still be *useful.*

Screw you, Sun Lord.

A wave of gremwyrs rushed over her, the stench like being

engulfed inside a rotting carcass. Her eyes stung, and her lungs burned.

Before she could react, the gremwyrs were flung back by an invisible hand, crashing into the cliff with bone-shattering force.

Archeron stood casually in the middle of the chaos, flicking his hands and sending beasts surging back with the ease of a composer.

Pausing—as if he had all the time in the world—he glanced over his shoulder at her and . . . winked.

Winked, for Goddess's sake.

Infuriated, Haven vowed to shoot faster, dropping anything that moved. As soon as a gremwyr hit the ground, she had her arrow out of its flesh and sailing through the air again. Aiming was easy.

They were everywhere.

It was like a living nightmare. For every Shadowling Haven killed, two more popped up and took its place. At this rate, she would soon tire. And the others' magick would eventually drain.

How much longer could they last?

Happy thoughts, Ashwood.

But even with her hatred of Archeron, and her determination to prove him wrong, there was only so much that could do to fuel her.

At some point, she began to falter. Her muscles quivered and burned. Her lungs seemed to shrink.

With darkness nibbling the edges of her vision, she stumbled over a mound of gremwyr carcasses piled high in a circle. In the middle sat the red-cloaked Sun Lord, his eyes closed, a placid smile on his face. A gremwyr darted over the bodies of its friends and crumpled at the top, falling over dead.

Whatever magick this dark Sun Lord possessed, it was powerful.

Haven cried out as pain seared her upper back. The ground began to get smaller, her legs kicking air. Something had hold of her shoulders and was trying to fly away with her.

Growling, she traded her bow for Oathbearer. The razor-honed blade easily pierced the creature's leathery underbelly, raining viscous black goo over her.

Then she was falling. The ground rose to meet her with a painful thud. The air pelted from her lungs. Her sword was lost.

For a wild, airless moment, she was blind. She clawed at the ground, fingers tangling in clumps of bloody sand. Trying to force her senses to cooperate as her vision danced and spun. To force much needed air inside her lungs.

In her mad panic, a whisper rose from the darkness. *Use me,* it begged. *Show them how powerful you are. How useful.*

Like mud being wiped from a pane of glass, her mind cleared and she staggered to her feet, the eerie voice fading into nothing until she questioned it ever truly happened.

The creature's lifeblood coated her left cheek, sand clinging to the sticky mess.

She spied her bow a few feet away and managed to finish the injured beast with an arrow.

As soon as she reached for another arrow, another gremwyr charged, saliva dripping from its glittering fangs—

Suddenly it halted, tilting its humanoid head as if hearing something she could not.

Then it pumped its massive wings and flung itself into the air. The others did the same, funneling over the cliffs and into the sky the way bats swarmed from caves.

The way they responded was almost as if their master was calling them back . . .

The adrenaline drained from Haven's veins, her entire body

suddenly limp. Every ragged breath brought with it the smell of carnage. After the cacophony of battle, the screeches and flapping wings and Haven's labored breaths, the sudden silence felt surreal, a trick.

Inside that silence a voice whispered, too low to make out anything.

Shaking her head, she ran a hand over her arm, sticky with gremwyr blood.

She coughed.

Then she fell to her knees and vomited.

Pressing her palms into the sand, she stole a deep breath, forcing as much air as she could into her raw lungs. The others were carrying on as usual, cleaning their weapons and joking.

Embarrassed, Haven wiped the spittle from her lips. No one else puked. And she would bet no one else's arms trembled with exhaustion. Or lungs burned like they'd been ripped from their chest, turned inside out, and roasted over the fire.

More chilling, she assumed no one else had heard voices.

Surai walked over, her boots crunching softly in the sand, and clapped Haven's shoulder. "Carvendi."

It was the Solis word for *good job,* more or less.

"Umath, Sun Queen," she murmured, her throat raspy and raw. *You're welcome* in Solissian.

Surai laughed, a sound like tinkling porcelain, and said in Solissian, "Oh, this mortal, she makes me laugh. I am not a Sun Queen, but the others are royalty—and they won't let you forget, either." She held out her hand, a bracelet of seashells chiming around her delicate, olive-skinned wrist. "I am Surai of the Ashari."

Haven rose to her feet and dusted her palms off on her pants before taking Surai's hand. Solis custom was to kiss one another's forehead, so Surai was obviously making an effort for her. "Haven

Ashwood from . . . Penryth."

"A pleasure to meet you," she said perfectly in the mortal tongue. She nodded toward the large cat sitting at the base of the cliff and licking its enormous paws. "That's Rook, a princess from the Morgani Islands, and every bit the royal pain in the ass she appears. Although I'd wager she likes you, mostly, and"—her eyes flickered to Archeron—"that gorgeous bastard I think you already know: he's Effendi, which explains the arrogance. Then you have Bjorn from Asgard, our Seer. Don't talk poorly about his stew and you'll get along fine."

Haven cut a glance at Bjorn rolling up his blanket with quick, tidy movements. As if he could feel her stare, he turned his head.

"Are you reading her a book or making introductions, Surai?" he asked in a tone that made it hard to determine if he was teasing or not.

Surai made some gesture Haven assumed was vulgar in Solissian, but then her gaze returned to the Seer, Bjorn, and froze.

Her mouth parted, although she managed to keep her gasp inside her throat. His eyes were white as ivory, twin moons that stood out against his midnight skin like the first snowfall on a mountain peak.

Haven quickly averted her gaze, and Surai laughed again, her lavender, almond-shaped eyes crinkling at the corners. "Don't feel sorry for him. He may be blind, but he sees more than any of us."

For the second time in the last five minutes, embarrassment warmed Haven's cheeks. She hid it by checking her arrows for damage and cleaning them in the sand the best she could.

Later, in the daylight, she would clean them properly.

Surai eventually left to join the big cat, Rook, and Haven's curiosity drifted to the massive feline. If Rook was a shifter like she'd read about, why hadn't she turned back yet?

Don't get too curious, she scolded herself. *The less you know about them, the easier it is to walk away.*

The tingle of attention drew her gaze upward. Archeron stood a few feet in the distance, hardly a hair on his head ruffled to indicate the ferocious battle a few minutes earlier.

He looked her over, his lips bunched to the side.

"Do we have a deal?" she demanded.

Before he could answer, something behind him stole her attention. She lifted her bow on instinct.

Archeron's mouth fell open, his hand moving to stop her—

Her arrow whizzed past his cheek and into the gremwyr, its mouth yawning in a ragged scream. Archeron finished the creature with his sword.

Turning back to her, he lifted his eyebrows with a look that could be confused with respect.

"Told you I'm quite useful. When I want to be." She brushed by him, whispering into his ear in rough Solissian as she passed, "I think that solidifies our deal, no, pretty Sun Lord?"

Apparently, he'd never heard a mortal speak his language, because a flicker of surprise flashed inside his jeweled eyes, making her giddy from head to toe.

Grinning darkly, he murmured back, "It's a wonder that arrow didn't find my heart instead, mortal."

Glancing over her shoulder, she said, "Give it time."

Then, slowly, purposefully, she winked and turned back around, so quickly that she nearly missed the way his nostrils flared with outrage.

As she strolled away, her shoulder blades tingled, his fiery gaze practically branding holes into her flesh.

Now it was her turn to smile. *Don't be mad, Sun Lord. At least you've been warned.*

Not that her words would be taken as anything but bluster. He underestimated her, as he always would, and no amount of fighting to prove herself worthy would change his mind.

In his eyes, she was detestable simply for being mortal. She was beneath him. Not worthy of scrubbing his boots, much less fighting alongside him as an equal.

So she would use that against him. Against *all* of them. She would be the nice, weak little mortal they expected. She would smile and do everything they said, and the first moment their guard slipped, she would take back her runestones and leave them far behind.

FIFTEEN

Prince Bell wavered atop the cliff he had just been brutally dropped onto and debated throwing himself off. The lie he told himself as he hung from the beast's claws—that he was trapped inside one of his stories and it would end happily ever after—now seemed ridiculous, a childish wish.

If that were true, he wouldn't be torn at by icy winds and bathed in the cold shade of an obsidian castle. He wouldn't be a thousand miles from his home, the only escape a winding set of black, snow-capped stairs leading down to a crumbling bridge that stretched for an impossible length, disappearing into mist.

If that were true, there wouldn't be what he guessed were snowflakes dusting his clothes and melting over his cheeks.

Snowflakes. Wherever he was, it was far away from the sun-drenched lands of Penryth.

Gathering a lungful of courage, Bell grasped what was left of a stone banister filmed with ice and peered down—and down and down—the cliffs fading into mist.

Despite the cold, sweat drenched his palms, and he stumbled back, forcing down his runefeast threatening to return from that morning.

His gut clenched tighter as the beasts that brought him here swooped in long, lazy circles through the air, sending the mist swirling. They hardly paid him any attention. Maybe he could run?

As soon as the thought hit, he dismissed it. There was nowhere to run to. And even if he did, he would freeze to death in a matter of hours.

The Shade Lord stood a few feet away, grinning at him, dark wings folded together behind his back and his black raven's feather cloak rippling in the wind like a second pair of wings.

He was arrestingly beautiful . . . in the same way the giant predatory cats stuffed and tacked along the walls of the king's hunting lodge were beautiful. Except this glorious beast wasn't dead and stuffed with cotton.

No, he was very much alive and looking for all the world like he might devour Bell.

The pretty monster jerked his head toward the open door of the castle, and Bell flinched.

"Go ahead, Prince," the Shade Lord urged.

Bell swallowed. Goddess save him, he was petrified, unable to move or beg for help. His body had always locked up at the slightest hint of fear—something Renk had loved provoking whenever possible.

What would Haven do? No sooner did the thought come before he had his answer: Fight. She would have fought the entire way here, clawing and kicking.

But Bell . . . Bell had been too terrified of falling to move. Too terrified to scream or call out or hardly breathe.

Coward, a tiny voice whispered. It was Cressida's voice, and it was relentless. *Trembling, weak, unworthy coward.*

"Scared?" the Shade Lord inquired, but his voice lacked the mocking tone that was inside his head.

For a heartbeat, an emotion Bell almost took for empathy flickered inside the Shade Lord's strange eyes.

But then he flashed a lazy smile, his row of gleaming teeth quelling any delusions of kindness. "Follow me, little rabbit."

Bell shadowed the Shade Lord inside, grateful to escape the tall cliffs and whipping winds. But as soon as they entered, a blast of cold air ran over his body, nearly as frosty as the chill outside.

Shivers rippled through him as he crossed the smooth parquet floor, interlocking tiles creating a gorgeous mosaic of suns and mountains.

Haven would love this . . . No, he couldn't think about his best friend and protector.

Not yet. It hurt too much.

Their footsteps echoed inside the vast chamber, muffled by the howling wind. Shadows pooled in corners, and snowdrifts lined the marble baseboards. Furniture covered in white sheets rose from the floor like the icebergs from his books.

He glanced longingly at the murky sky peeking through giant cracks in the walls and had the misfortune of noticing the lacework of spider webs filling the cavernous space above.

When Bell shifted, he caught hundreds of dark shapes skittering across the delicate silver webs. Too big for any normal spider.

"Goddess Above," he whispered.

Heart in his throat, he searched for a burning candle or lantern. Something to light his way.

But other than the faint gray glow seeping in from outside, there was nothing to brighten the darkness. No fires to warm it, no torches to chase away the deep, insidious cloak of kohl that clung to the walls.

Terror shot through his veins. There was something ancient here, a primordial evil, and every step deeper into the chamber sent his heart into a tailspin and his skin crawling.

A wide set of onyx stairs rose at the center of the room, splitting off into two staircases. He followed the crooked steps with his gaze as they spiraled into the sky. Despite the frigid cold, sweat wet Bell's neck.

Perhaps once these stairs possessed handrails or railings, but not now.

The Shade Lord swept his arm out in a grand gesture. "Welcome to Spirefall, Prince Boteler. Your home for the rest of your short life."

Bell blinked, remembering the Shade Lord's presence. Then the Shade Lord was gone—just gone. Poof.

If his voice wasn't still ringing off the high ceilings, Bell would have thought he'd made him up entirely.

"No, wait!" Panic surged through him, and he shot to the entrance.

The heavy stone doors slammed shut in his face with a crack that reverberated through the castle and knocked him back on his heels. He grabbed for the metal door handle, but pain zinged into his fingers and up his arm.

He yanked his hand away. The door was warded.

Of course.

He spun around, his breath coming out in cloudy bursts. Bits of snow spiraled down from the wide rifts in the ceiling high, high above. This place could be another realm for all he knew. As his teeth chattered and his fingers curled with cold, fear gave way to resentment.

He'd never asked for magick, so why did it have to choose him?

But didn't you? a small, bitter voice demanded. His conversation with Haven replayed in his head. *Maybe my father would be proud of me if I did have magick.*

Well here he was, practically overflowing with stupid magick, and he imagined his father didn't even miss him.

Slipping his hand into his pocket, Bell rubbed his fingers over the runestone Haven gave him. If the Shade Queen were here, he'd need any protection he could get.

"Hello?" he called, his voice sounding small and scared as it reverberated over the towering walls. "Anyone here?"

The only noise was his rapid breaths and his throat swallowing repeatedly.

If Cressida were here, she would have reprimanded him for the nervous habit. Then he would switch to cracking his knuckles, which would infuriate her even more.

He swallowed again, a grim smile finding his face as he imagined never seeing his father's mistress again.

At least there was that silver lining.

For the next few minutes, Bell explored the lower level of the castle, his unease giving way to curiosity. Compared to Fenwick Castle, this place was enormous, filled with massive oil paintings of the old fables when winged Noctis ruled the lands.

The sumptuous colors splashed across the canvases were unlike anything in Penryth. Too bright. Too brazen. Too something.

And the poses. He blew out a breath and glanced away from the mostly naked figures, their muscled bodies contorted in acts that would've sent his father to the Netherworld with one glance.

A deep ache opened inside Bell's chest; Haven would've loved exploring this place.

Hopefully she was okay. He swallowed a bittersweet laugh—of

course she was okay; she was Haven. By now, she would've come up with some plan that involved more weapons than sense.

No, don't think about that. He extinguished any fleeting hope for rescue with a dose of reality.

Even Haven couldn't take on the Shade Queen and the Curse.

Pushing thoughts of his friend away, he began climbing the stairs. His new too-tight boots—his father made him wear the gift from Cressida even though they were the wrong size—squeaked against the dark stone.

Perhaps he was tired, but the climb seemed to take forever. His ears popped, his lungs ached. He stayed as close to the middle of the stairs as possible, terrified of one misstep sending him falling to his death.

As he neared the top, breathing hard, sounds trickled down.

Laughter. Whispering.

And strange, animalistic noises that froze the pittance of air in his chest.

Somehow, when he got to the top and saw what waited for him, he managed not to cry out. The room was massive, a drafty space filled with a few oversized couches and tables.

But it was the creatures in the room that turned Bell's veins to ice. Scaled, winged, fanged monsters of every size and shape. Shadowlings, like the one he'd killed with runemagick in the forest. Like the ones that brought him here.

Claws scraped the stone, wings fluttered the room, and teeth gnashed the air.

Bell took two steps and then vomited all over the granite floor. A man—no, a Noctis—turned at the sound of Bell's retching, his black, bat-like wings flickering behind him, a look of disgust twisting his marble face.

"Ah," he spat, curling his lips at Bell. "Another of Ravenna's sacrifices just unloaded his lunch all over the floor."

Now the Shadowlings were staring at him too. They had alert, predatory eyes and horrible snouts that sniffed the air. Terror tightened his throat and pitted low in his belly; he was sure the monsters could hear his fear, smell it.

He turned to flee back down the stairs—

Another Noctis with sunken cheeks and blood-red eyes landed on the second to top step, membranous wings flaring as he caught his balance. Four dull-gray talons curved over the rims of both wings.

While terrifying, the Shade Lord who collected Bell had also been stunningly handsome. These Noctis were ugly, animalistic. Their featherless wings, their pale, translucent skin and primordial eyes. The way they feasted on him with their intense, hungry gazes.

The monster grinned, his voice high-pitched and chittering. "Oh, Ravenna will like this one."

Bell felt the blood drain from his face as he backed away, searching frantically for a way out. All the times he looked at the pictures of Shadowlings and Noctis with curiosity inside his books now felt like a sick joke. This was a place of monsters and horrors; he could feel it in his bones.

I need to leave right now.

Faint hissing, like a barely audible whisper, grabbed his attention. The first Noctis had somehow gotten closer without Bell noticing. The beast was a few feet away, vile head tilted sideways.

The other one appeared in his periphery, moving closer without making a noise.

"I cannot smell his magick," he hissed. Then he was towering over Bell, reaching for him with long, hideous black claws.

Bell wanted to run. Instead he froze, paralyzed with fright, every muscle in his body rigid.

A roar split the air, waking Bell from his trance. He lunged back, falling to his rear and scuttling against a wall.

A massive figure covered in a black cloak circled the Noctis, snarling. "Leave him." The cloaked figure's voice was low, guttural, the voice of a beast trying to speak the language of man. "Return to the mortals Morgryth gave you."

The Noctis shrank back, baring their fangs before scuttling into the shadows. Growls rattled deep from the Shadowlings' chests as they watched the figure.

He was hunched, and except for the bulge protruding from the back of his cloak, shaped like a man, with arms and legs and a torso. Bell squirmed, trying to get a better look, but the shadow from his hood covered his face.

All at once, the air seemed to drop ten degrees. The cloaked figure looked past the Shadowlings and Noctis at someone who had just entered.

Bell blinked, and the Noctis was upon them.

Bell's breath fled his lungs in a whoosh. This Noctis stood taller than the others, with enormous wings larger than the rest, ice-blue eyes made for brutality, and chalky skin. He wore all of the fineries Bell was used to at court: polished leather boots up to the knees, a well-tailored black jacket, and a jewel-handled dagger at the waist.

Judging by the way the others cowered in front of this new Noctis, and by his finery, he was another powerful Shade Lord like the one that brought Bell here.

The Shade Lord made a flippant gesture at the cloaked figure that'd saved him. "Run along, Creature."

Bell had been at court long enough to recognize the cruel, haughty voice of someone used to getting their way.

"And you," the Shade Lord whispered, piercing Bell with a dead gaze. "My poor, dear sister has survived on the pithy magick of common mortals for years. How she will feast on you, Penrythian Prince. How she will savor your blood, your magick. If she has the time, she will crack your bones and suck out your sweet marrow. And when she tires of your screams, she will rip out your heart."

Bell jumped to his feet, finally ready to run, to fight. It was too late. The Shade Lord sunk his claws deep into Bell's arm, yanking him across the floor and deeper into the castle.

"No," he screamed.

He tried to escape the creature. Kicking, clawing and punching with his free arm, leaving scratches across the sleeve of the Shade Lord's velvet jacket.

But Bell was puny next to the powerful Noctis, and the more he fought, the higher the Shade Lord lifted him, a wicked sneer slashing his jaw until Bell dangled in the air by his arm and his shoulder burned.

Twisting, Bell peered beneath the leathery wings back at the cloaked figure. And Bell held onto the image until the shadows of the castle plunged him into glacial darkness.

SIXTEEN

If Haven could have killed with her thoughts, the smug Sun Lord would've died a thousand deaths by now.

She slammed her hands over her hips, pointing her elbows out like daggers. "Lady Pearl comes with us."

Archeron raised a sluggish eyebrow. The others waited in the distance, their horses prancing and nickering impatiently as a nectarine dawn whispered across the horizon. "Lady Pearl?"

"Yes. That's her name. And I refuse to leave her to die."

Archeron sighed. "She cannot keep up with our mounts."

"Then I'll find another way through the Bane without you."

The corners of Archeron's lips drifted downward. "By the Shadeling, you're like a child! You do realize that you're trading your prince for a common mortal horse?"

Haven's jaw ground so hard she was afraid it would lock up. "First, she is not common. And second, I will not betray her."

"Fine." Archeron leaned down until he was almost on her level.

"But what did you think would happen once you led her into the Ruinlands? Believe me, she has a better chance if you release her now than later."

A ragged breath hissed through her teeth. She hadn't thought about that. In fact, there were so many things she hadn't planned for.

She glanced at Lady Pearl as the mare nipped at a few sparse blades of grass, her beautiful tail swishing back and forth.

Could Haven really just leave her behind?

Her gaze collapsed to the ground. "Just give me a minute to say goodbye."

His lips parted as if ready to argue, but then he must have realized she was giving in, because his face softened and he nodded.

After he joined the others, she walked over to Lady Pearl and removed her saddle and reins.

"Thank you for being such a good horse," she whispered in the mare's gray-tinged ear. "If anyone can survive here, it's you."

If she had more time, she might cast a protection rune on Lady Pearl, except the Shadowlings roaming the land were attracted to light magick, and that would only draw more attention to her.

Still, Haven wished she could do more for the courageous friend who had gotten her through late night training and helped her pass the royal guard trials.

At the academy, the students were allowed to each pick their horse.

Naturally, as the only girl, Haven was given last choice.

All the other students chose flashy stallions and anxious geldings, impressed by their massive size and the muscle shivering beneath their shiny coats.

When it was Haven's turn, Lady Pearl was the only horse left. The other recruits snickered as Haven walked the mare out of her stall.

But Haven took one look at the calm, patient creature following behind her, Lady Pearl's intelligent eyes appraising the students and other horses like they were all fools, and smiled.

Now, leaving Lady Pearl felt like the worst kind of betrayal. Haven allowed herself one last brush of her lips against her loyal friend's velveteen muzzle.

"I'm sorry, old girl," Haven whispered.

Then she turned her back on her beloved horse.

As Haven marched toward the band of Solis, her face an emotionless mask, it took everything she had not to look back.

The only riderless horse was a sorrel-and-white dappled beast with apple-green eyes and dainty silver horns, but before Haven could mount it, Surai leapt from her horse to the dappled one.

As Surai managed to nestle her fluttery frame into the huge, olive saddle, she said, "Take mine instead."

Hers was a sleek charcoal beauty that reminded Haven of smoke and shadows. It had pale-blue eyes and beautiful onyx-banded silver horns smooth as marble.

A sleek treeless saddle rested on its back, which Haven preferred to the heavier saddles used by most mortals anyway.

As she slipped her left foot in the stirrup and swung her right leg over the dark horse, she couldn't help but wonder why Surai switched horses.

Or, more importantly, where Rook was.

"Our little Rook is ahead doing reconnaissance," Bjorn answered with a stony glance. "And she's very possessive of Aramaya, her horse. If you were wondering."

"I wasn't."

Surai laughed. "She's hunting too. I'm sure of it. The girl will have filled her belly with every creature in those forests by the time we change."

Haven tilted her head. "Change?"

For a heartbeat, Surai's lavender eyes seemed to dim to the color of dusk. Then she cleared her throat and urged Rook's horse to the front, the twin scabbards on either side of her hip jostling softly.

Usually Surai's reaction would've sent Haven searching for an answer, but now, bone-weary and starving as she was, Haven was more than happy to let Surai keep her secrets.

If she allowed herself to learn about these Solis, she might start caring—and she couldn't afford that.

Although there were little details she'd picked up that were helpful.

For instance, the Solis didn't seem to need much sustenance. Not in the way Haven did. And, even after missing their two hours of sleep last night, they appeared well rested.

But the most important detail so far was the discovery that, right before one of the Solis peeked into her mind, she felt a light tingle at the base of her skull.

Anytime the strange prickle began, she shut off all her thoughts. But constantly guarding her mind was tiring, and that plus hunger and fatigue wore on her.

As the morning crawled on, Haven lagged behind the band of Solis, the sun squirming beneath her eyelids and calling her to her dreams.

She fought her mortal tiredness, biting her cheeks and drawing the few nails she hadn't chewed to nubs across her chest to stay awake.

Only the Goddess Above knew what would happen if Haven fell asleep now. No, she had to stay awake in case the opportunity to steal the runestones presented itself.

Besides, if she rested, chances were she'd fall and break her neck.

She eyed the ground. At this height, she felt taller than the trees, and just as helpless as they were to the world. The beast of a horse she rode was missing reins, and when she tried to lean her body to direct it, she might as well have been a gnat fluttering her wings against its hindquarters for all the attention it gave her.

Growling, she dug her heels into the horse's side only to have it turn around and try to bite her.

Bjorn pulled up beside Haven, an amused half-grin revealing a row of shiny teeth. "Having trouble?"

She dodged another bite, her boot held high in case she needed to kick the beast. "How do I guide him?"

"He is a *she*. The larger Alpacian steeds are female, and the smaller ones are male."

"Small?" Haven hissed.

"Yes." His voice trembled with choked laughter. "And unfortunately for you, the only way to guide an Alpacian is with your mind. It's called soulbinding. That's a simple task for a Solis, at least with animals, but beyond the grasp of mortals, I'm afraid."

"Right. Thank you." She dug her knuckles into her thighs, swallowing down the sharp retort on the tip of her tongue.

Why did everything around the Solis end up pointing out how weak mortals were?

She exhaled. Let them believe what they wanted. They would part soon, anyway. Earlier than expected, if her plan went well.

After a spell, the rhythmic movements of her horse lulled her into a half-sleep, the world around her a wavering slit of rushing trees and parched blue sky.

Her body loosened; her breathing slowed. Gradually, the colors began to leech from the landscape, and her companions faded away as oily veins of black rivered the hills and woods, sunlight breaking off in pieces like shards of glass.

Ravens surged to fill the space, cawing, their wings battering her flesh and sending chills racing down her spine.

The Shade Lord purred, *Are you on your way to me, Little Beastie?*

It seemed to take minutes, hours to turn her face to the voice. She blinked against the darkness of this dying world, her eyes locking onto two glowing rings of yellow framing vertical pupils.

We like him, a voice whispered. *Yes, we do.*

Ravens poured from the Shade Lord as he grinned and suddenly reached for her—

A scream tore from her throat, shattering her vision.

It was a . . . nightmare.

Relief loosened the claws of dread wrapped around her spine. But her heart continued its onslaught against her sternum, pounding loud enough for the Solis' delicate ears to hear.

Speaking of the high-and-mighty immortals, they were all staring at her—Archeron in particular, as if she were here solely for his entertainment.

Grimacing, she rubbed her forearm over her sweaty forehead. "It was a . . . a nightmare."

She hoped they couldn't see through the lie to the horrible truth: She didn't know what that was, but it was too real, too vivid to be a mere dream.

A side effect of the Shade Lord's blood? Or perhaps it was a waking prophecy like the ones Odin had before Freya betrayed him?

Lucky for Haven, the others bored easily, and they went back to ignoring the odd mortal girl who needed more than two hours of sleep. Everyone except Bjorn, the seer.

For a moment, her insides burned as his sightless eyes engraved every inch of her with their unyielding stare.

Then he turned, spurring his mount forward, his red cloak rippling behind him like spurts of fresh blood.

A pent-up breath roared from her lips, and she bit her cheek until she chewed the inside raw, her mouth filling with a metallic tang.

Just the thought of falling asleep again and seeing the Noctis's demonic eyes twisted her gut into a knot.

What did he want? Revenge? To torture the mortal who got away?

Her jaw tensed. There had to be some rune to keep her from sleeping. As soon as the idea formed, she grabbed ahold of it, ignoring the obvious: A rune spell would alert anyone around to their presence.

Or, at least, anyone looking.

But if she didn't use the rune, the next face she might see could be the Shade Lord's.

Besides, the Shadowlings already knew they were here, and a tiny rune spell would hardly show up on their radar, if at all.

Do it, a voice whispered. It was the same voice from earlier. *Just a little spell,* it continued, whispering against her skull like coarse muslin against bare flesh, scratchy and faint. *What would be the harm?*

She shook her head in an effort to dislodge the auditory hallucination. Obviously a symptom of her fatigue.

Still, real or not, the voice was right. She had nothing to lose and everything to gain by casting the spell.

Her chance came midday when they stopped to water the horses at a cerulean, stream-fed pond, shaded on three sides by tall cedars. As the Solis dismounted and stretched their lithe bodies, Haven wandered off behind a crooked pine.

Glancing around to make sure she wasn't followed, she pulled out the small, gold-handled dagger she kept in her boot.

The runic arts were strictly forbidden to mortals.

It didn't matter that just like all common mortals, Haven possessed so little magick, the rune would hardly have any effect. If done correctly, she'd feel like she consumed ten cups of strong Drothian coffee, without the jitters.

Twirling the dagger between her fingers, she hesitated.

If Archeron caught her runecasting, he'd surely break off their deal and keep the stolen runestones for himself.

Which was why she would hide it from the big-headed idiot— from all of them—stealing the runestones while they finally slept.

Haven sucked in her bottom lip. Years had passed since she cast a rune, and her forehead wrinkled as she worked to focus on the process. Folding back the sleeves of her tunic, she pressed the tip of the dagger into her flesh and closed her eyes, running through the different runes she knew would keep her awake.

Fiery lines tangled behind her eyelids, crossing and curving and spiraling.

Each mark spoke to her. Called to her.

A smile twisted her lips as she came across an energy rune, a backward S with two dots and a slash.

She stole a deep breath, waiting until her heartbeat slowed and her mind cleared. Then she carved the rune into the flesh at the top of her forearm with soft, loose strokes, focusing on the small bit of energy that trilled through her.

If only she could harness the magick inside the Nihl . . . but she would have to be content with the traces of magick most common mortals possessed.

A hiss snaked from her lips as the magick broke through, followed by a gasp of fear.

Too much! The blistering magick sank down into her bones and burned its way through her marrow. The magick was supposed to only be a trickle, a drop, yet she could feel it raging through her like a fiery river. Uncontrolled, unending.

Let it in, the voice commanded. *All of it.*

For a ragged breath, the pain was so bad she thought her chest might crack open. Her knees hit the ground, pine needles gouging her palms as she clawed at the earth.

Make. It. Stop.

She switched from clawing the ground to gouging just above her heart, trying to rip out the magick that had taken hold of her.

It had never hurt like this, or lasted this long.

Something was wrong.

SEVENTEEN

Just when Haven thought she might die from the agony ripping through her body, the misery lifted. *What the Netherfire was that?*

Whatever it was, the pain had vanished. Haven released a heavy breath and assessed her body. Her flesh burned hot as the cooking stones Penrythians used sometimes in lieu of pans.

Otherwise, the only trace of magick left was the scent of cinnamon and roses prickling the tip of her tongue.

Burying her misgiving over the intensity of the spell, she scrambled to her feet and wrapped her forearm in a strip of cotton. Then she rolled down her sleeve and returned her knife to its sheath, in a hurry to get back before she was noticed.

The result hit her like a wave of fire. Energy zipped through her veins and lightened her body, her steps buoyed by an unseen force.

She felt amazing. Like she could jog a thousand miles. Fight a hundred beasts. She could climb a mountain, or grab Surai's horse and ride her to the ends of Eritrayia . . .

Perhaps the spell had been more powerful than planned, after all.

Despite itching to race and ride and climb everything in sight, Haven forced herself to appear normal. The immortal *droobs* would probably notice if she were to suddenly jog circles around the pond—which is exactly what her brain was telling her to do.

With a sigh, she retrieved her map and sketchpad from her mount's saddlebag and joined Bjorn on a grassy embankment. The only sign of her newfound energy was her foot jumping wildly over the muddy shore like a dying jackrabbit.

She kicked the errant appendage, happy when it finally quit its wild flailing and behaved.

A sultry chuckle filled the air to the left. But she forced her gaze onto Bjorn and away from the tempting water . . . and Archeron.

Still, from the corner of her eye, she could make out the fool stripping off his tunic and pants in one quick motion and diving in.

Surai followed, sending little tempting waves lapping at Haven's boots.

Just as she stole a quick glance at the scene, Archeron emerged, water gliding down his tawny skin. He shook the moisture from his shoulder-length locks like a dog would, a fleeting rainbow of droplets haloing him.

Then he slicked his honeyed hair back and laughed, the rhapsodic rise and fall of his voice both captivating and infuriating.

The silvery flicker of runes incandesced over his flesh, sunlight running down the intricate web of interlocking ley lines that mapped every inch of his body besides his face—or, at least, everything Haven could see.

Those were the runes the Solis were born with. The ones that formed the complex pattern sharpening the Solis's raw, natural energy into specific powers.

Every Solis's rune pattern was unique, like a fingerprint.

Feeling Bjorn's silent, curious gaze on her, Haven tore her eyes from the Sun Lord, ignoring the warm ache that spilled down her middle.

She refused to feel guilty for finding Archeron attractive. Any woman with two eyes would do the same.

That didn't mean she liked the arrogant fool.

Something stroked the base of her skull. She felt it, but too late.

Attractive? Bjorn's voice said, invading her head. *Absolutely. And arrogant to a fault. But never foolish.*

I. . she glared at the seer, struggling for an acceptable response. *I've seen prettier,* she lied.

Hmph. That must be why you keep staring at him.

She narrowed her eyes at him.

Don't be embarrassed, he added, not unkindly. *Beauty is one of Archeron's gifts. In our world, fairness is appreciated, not shied away from.*

Fire burned her cheeks. She pulled in a steadying breath and ran her gaze over the map in her lap, smoothing the curled edges with her fingers.

If the seer had access to her thoughts, then she would bore him with geography.

She focused on the continent of Eritrayia, ignoring the left side of the map, which consisted of the turquoise waters of the Glittering Sea and the Solis lands of Solissia.

Farther north, she pressed her fingertip into an empty spot between two curse-fallen mortal cities. Just above her chewed nail rested the border of the Bane.

Above that, the entire top half of Eritrayia, the Ruinlands, was scribbled in shadows. And beyond that was a blacked-out region where the Shade Queen and her Shade Lords ruled over all the Noctis.

The Shadow Kingdom.

Haven's chest tightened as she tried to imagine what she'd find there. No one knew, because no one had ever gone beyond the Ruinlands and returned.

"You want to know about the Ruinlands?" came a man's deep voice.

Haven turned to Bjorn as he oiled his axe, sunlight swimming over the runed blade. At least he was speaking aloud this time. "What do you know about it?"

A smile stretched lazily across his face, reminding her that he, too, was handsome. "It's a dark and magickal place, filled equally with horror and wonder."

"You've been there?" Haven flicked another glance over her map, half expecting him to say the Ruinlands was a made-up place. "I thought it was impossible to escape?"

"Nearly, but not impossible—though I did leave something very valuable behind."

"Your sight?"

Bjorn ran a finger over his dark neck as he nodded, a frown trembling his lips. "And more."

The haunted tone of his voice sent shivers down her spine. Whatever terrors they would face in the Ruinlands, it was enough to make even a hardened Solis warrior like Bjorn scared.

"So . . ." She toed the ground. "What's the plan from here?"

"Once inside the Bane, we travel to Lorwynfell in search of a scroll."

Her gut clenched. *Lorwynfell? As in, the haunted kingdom?* "What sort of scroll?"

His jaw tightened, and he looked out into the water. "The kind, mortal, that will tell us how to break the Curse."

Once Bjorn was gone, and she felt his mind leave hers, she

allowed herself to think about *her* plan.

And the glaring fact that it was woefully lacking.

Perhaps falling in with the Solis was fortuitous, after all. Perhaps she would wait until *after* they found the scroll to steal the runestones.

That made way more sense, even if putting up with Archeron for a few more days wasn't ideal.

Feeling much more confident, she blinked with rare contentment as sunlight refracted off the rippling surface of the water and danced along the sandy bottom.

Surai still hadn't emerged. Haven trailed the Solis girl beneath the clear water as she flitted back and forth like a fish.

A snarl tore from the embankment above. Dirt clots tumbled down the side as a shadow slipped over them. A second later, a golden cat splashed into the water after Surai.

Before Haven's scream could leave her lips, she realized who it was. Rook. The feline splashed after Surai, smacking the water with her paw and pouncing over and over, her black-tipped ears flattened to her skull. Under the full sun, the bronze spots in her tawny fur were visible.

All at once, the cat went rigid in the shallow water, sat back on its hindquarters, and transformed into Rook, the real Rook, with flaxen locks braided to her skull and a red band tattooed across her eyes.

Dark feathers hung from her braids, twirling in the light breeze. The same breeze carried the tang of magick, musky and coppery and undoubtedly dark.

Surai slipped out of the water to face Rook. Water pasted Surai's long curtain of hair over her slender back, her delicate shoulder blades poking out like tiny wings of marble. Wet, the sleek strands were the color of black Ashari pearls and just as lustrous.

For a heartbeat, the two girls just looked at each other in the way Haven imagined she would look at Bell when she found him. They were utterly still, their chests unmoving as they held their breath and took the other in.

The sudden intimacy made Haven want to tear her gaze away. At the same time, she was fixated on the raw emotion, the need in their eyes.

Haven found herself holding her breath as she watched Rook slide her arms around Surai's naked waist, draw her close, and crush her lips against the smaller girl's.

In that moment, Haven felt as if she were witnessing another type of magick. The rare, elusive kind that everyone wanted and few ever possessed.

Love—this was love in its most unapologetic form.

Without thinking, Haven fished her charcoals from her tin and began to draw the two Solis. Half her lip sucked in as her fingers flew over the page of her sketchpad, trying to capture what she was feeling.

She worked fast, the sound of the charcoal grazing the paper calming her. When she was finished, the tips of her fingers were black.

Frowning at the page, she wrinkled her forehead, unsatisfied with the result.

Something was missing.

She was about to crumple the paper and try again when a drop of water splattered over the sketch, streaking the head of Rook.

The Sun Lord stood over her, water dripping from his hair and glistening his body.

His *naked* body.

Goddess Above! She averted her gaze, her cheeks burning. "Put some clothes on!"

A chuckle. "You mortals and your chastity." There was the sound of leather pants being slid over wet skin. "Better?"

She cut her eyes at him, trying not to linger on the upper half of his torso, his wet golden skin and ridged abdomen that tensed and corded with every breath. The map of runes etched into his sleek flesh glimmered faintly beneath the sun.

Her cheeks pulsed with heat as she recalled how the runes traversed every inch of his naked body. "Yes."

"Get up."

She bristled at his demand, taking her time to arrange her map and notepad inside her saddlebag and dust off her legs before standing. She raised an eyebrow at him.

Stretching his arms behind his neck, he twisted lazily beneath the sun, his eyelids half-lowered and lips puckered at the corners. "Get your sword."

"My sword?"

"Yes, that thing you fantasize cutting my throat with. Get it so I can show you how to properly use it."

"I know how to properly use it."

"Debatable."

Her jaw locked, but she retrieved Oathbearer from its scabbard and twirled it inside her right hand.

A sense of purpose came over her as her fingers tightened around the hilt. The weapon was a present from Bell, customized specifically for her height and weight to be perfectly balanced. The guard of the hilt was a fancy circle of gold, inlaid with black diamonds and emeralds in the shape of dahlias. "You mean this old thing?"

"Precisely. That old thing."

Finding her stance, she raised her eyebrows at him. "Where's yours?"

"Is this not the moment you've been waiting for?" A taunting grin split his jaw. "Here is your chance, mortal. Draw a single drop of my blood and the runestones are yours."

Her heart quickened. Normally she wouldn't fight an unarmed opponent, and it was obviously a trick, but she didn't care.

She needed the runestones—and she didn't mind injuring the smug Sun Lord in the process.

"And"—she rolled her neck—"you won't use magick?"

"I will not need to use magick."

Scowling, she released a breath, drew the tip of her boot across the sand, and readied her mind for combat. The energy from the runemark pulsed through her core and surged upward to fill her chest.

Begging for release.

Archeron waited with his arms crossed over his chest, all ropy muscles and confidence. One honey-gold eyebrow quirked upward with impatience.

Her feint and lunge was textbook perfect. She'd used it to best a hundred mortal men in the Penrythian Royal Guard Academy. Sunlight glimmered off the sharp edge of her steel as it drove toward his bare chest, but just as the tip was about to pierce the triangle of flesh above his heart, he slipped sideways.

She stumbled, nearly falling into him.

Archeron clicked his tongue. "That might have worked for you in Penryth, but not here, mortal."

Snarling, she attacked again.

Again, he slipped from her blade's bite as easily as water through a sieve. His teeth gleamed behind a feline smile. "You telegraph your movements with your eyes."

She circled him, slowly this time, sizing him up. The bare flesh of his stomach and chest rippled with every breath, taunting her.

All she needed was to connect her steel to that perfect flesh and draw a drop of blood.

One single, little bitty drop of blood. How hard could it be?

This time, her attack was a brilliant double feint. She hardly breathed, hardly made a sound, her sword whistling as it sliced toward his hairless midsection with expert precision.

There was no way she was going to miss . . .

A fraction of a second later, her blade cleaved empty air. She whirled around and swung at him again, chopping away, letting her anger get the best of her.

Grunts spilled from her throat, marking her frustration.

A smooth chuckle from behind. "Stop ogling me and pay attention."

Once again, she pivoted to meet him, even as a part of her was beginning to understand it was pointless. A cruel game.

He was smoke and shadow, moving this way and that, filling space one second and gone the next. The faster she moved and the harder she tried, the easier he seemed to evade her. Until her shoulders burned, her lungs ached, and she thought she'd go mad with fury.

"Magick!" she hissed between labored breaths.

"Skill," he purred in a voice that could sweeten Penrythian coffee.

From her periphery, she saw the others had stopped to watch. Frustration crashed through her in unrelenting waves.

He was taunting her.

Sucking in a lungful of air, she glared at him. "Why are you doing this?"

For a moment, his eyes lost their amusement. "Because you need to realize that this fantasy of you rushing into the Ruinlands and saving your friend is just that. A fantasy."

"So what?" She kicked the dirt, wishing it were his head. "Why do you care?"

He blinked. "I don't."

"And why are you trying to break the Curse anyway? What's in it for you?" Her words came out in angry barks. "Wait, you need something, and you think the rumors about the wishes are true. You think if you break the Curse, you will be granted a wish."

She could tell by the way he froze she'd hit a nerve . . . that pushing any further was dangerous.

Her lips twitched. *Good.* Maybe her steel couldn't touch him, but her words might. "What will you wish for, Sun Lord? To be free of your bindings to a certain king, perhaps?"

A dark shadow flickered across his face, and she flinched as he suddenly prowled toward her.

Before she could scramble away, he was close enough to touch his nose to hers. His entire body radiating rage.

"Turn back," he growled. "You're about to enter a world full of dark magick and creatures that'll sniff out your mortal flesh from miles away. They'll stalk you while you sleep, and when they catch you, they'll feast on you while you still breathe." He paused, the anger seeping out of him like poison, and his lips twisted cruelly. "Besides, knowing Morgryth, your prince is already dead."

Dark rage burst inside her chest, her heart beating so fast it was like one giant, continuous explosion rattling her ribs.

That can't be true. He's still alive. He can't be . . . can't be . . .

"You bastard," she snarled, her words not her own. They seemed to come from someone else as she continued, "I hope you live your entire life bound to that horrible man."

Her hand trembled around her sword. She tried to force back her fury, but it was like trying to force burst water back into a dam.

All the pent-up anger from years watching Bell be humiliated, then watching his father do nothing while his son was taken . . . stolen . . . and now this haughty Sun Lord . . .

How dare they, the voice seethed, followed by the chilling words, *make them pay.*

Something inside her fractured. The rage was like an inferno sizzling through her body, demanding release.

With a snarl, she wrenched her blade into the air.

The moment the hilt left her hand, a bolt of energy pulsed down her arm like lightning. Flames shot from her fingers. Delicate tongues of red and orange licking the air.

My sword! She tilted her head back, searching the sky for Oathbearer. Impossibly, the blade was still in the air, at least ten stories high, tumbling end-over-end.

When the weapon reached so high she could hardly see it, the blade shattered with an explosive *crack.*

Please be okay please be okay—

Only, as shards of her beloved blade rained down around them, pattering against the earth, she knew Oathbearer was destroyed— and she only had herself to blame.

Tearing her gaze from the wreckage, she glanced at Archeron. Every single muscle in his body seemed to stiffen at once as he rested his furious scowl on her.

She released a ragged breath. Her forearm tingled and burned where the rune was carved, her fingers still warm from the fire.

What in the Netherfire just happened?

There was no way she could've thrown her sword that high. Besides, the blade was Asgardian, forged from runefire and infused with wyvern blood.

It was supposed to be *indestructible.*

The energy rune—no, she was a common mortal. The rune was

just a conduit. It couldn't create magick, and last she checked, her blood was barren.

Yet even as she ran through a list of reasons why what happened *couldn't* have happened, the truth was scattered around her feet, impossible to ignore.

Somehow, Haven had performed magick. Powerful magick.

Her lips parted, but as soon as she tried to speak, the energy drained from her body and she crumpled to the ground in a heap.

EIGHTEEN

A man shrouded by a crimson cloak was watching her. Steel-gray mist swirled around him. Even with his face hidden, she knew who he was.

"My rose," Damius whispered in that rasping voice. "It finally found you."

A nightmare—this was a nightmare. Except unlike the usual dreams of her old master, this one seemed real. She could feel his presence, the evil inside him prickling against her skin like electricity right before a thunderstorm.

Serpents of terror slipped between her ribs and curled around her heart.

"Who found me?" she asked.

With a sweep of his hand he flung his hood back. His face was a swirling pit of black, his eyes glowing red.

She turned to run, but not before she heard his reply. "The darkness. Now that it's discovered its prize, you can never escape."

Haven jerked out of the nightmare into a very different world. Where the Shadeling's shadow was she?

Fighting newfound panic, she took stock of her situation. Heat seared her backside, and sweat ran in rivulets down her neck and face, dripping onto the blood-red sand swaying below.

She was . . . upside down. Why was she upside down?

Her hair, more pink than gold in this strange light, had broken free from its bun and curtained either side of her face, restricting her periphery.

Groaning softly, she lifted her head a couple inches—only to be even more confused. The landscape had a similar bloody hue, as if the sun beat down through an arterial lens.

And when she inhaled, a metallic aroma hit her senses, almost like old blood warmed by the sun.

She shivered. Runes! They were already in the Bane. How long had she been out?

Her mind scrambled to understand. The last image ingrained indelibly in her mind was pieces of her beloved sword sticking from the grass.

Her heart ached at the memory.

Other things ached, too. Her ribs, for one. Her head also, pooled with blood from being upside down.

She tried to move, only to discover her hands were secured behind her back with something rough and itchy, like a frayed rope.

Oh—*oh*. A rope meant she was bound, which in turn meant something had gone very wrong. Other memories dredged to the surface. The pond. Archeron naked. Fighting Archeron half-naked while he scolded her . . .

And . . . Oh.

Magick.

Despite still feeling groggy and weak, she managed to angle her head to the side. As she took in the black swishing tail and large charcoal rump, indignation poured through her.

She was restrained and slung over a horse. Someone actually had the nerve to tie her up, physically lift her like a child, and then fling her on the animal like a sack of grain, all while she was passed out.

Not someone. She knew exactly who was responsible.

Voices speaking Solissian made her go still. The first voice sounded like Rook. ". . . absolutely sure this is the only way?"

"Afraid of a little old Curse, Rook?" Archeron's honey-smooth voice teased. "And I thought the Morgani incapable of fear."

"Shut up, you motherless fool."

Archeron chuckled. "My mother would have your head for that."

"Not before she has yours," Rook shot back. "Besides, I'll gladly die in battle any day. This is different. If we perish in the Ruinlands . . ." Her voice trailed away into silence, and Haven's interest was piqued. "That fate's worse than a thousand deaths."

"Then let us not die there."

Haven rolled her eyes at his smugness. *Let us not die there,* she mimicked inside her head. *Good one, Sun Lord.*

"I suppose it doesn't matter," Rook said. "We're sure to die at Lorwynfell anyway."

Goddess Above, the Solis were pessimistic creatures. Well, they could die all they wanted. She would live—once she figured out how to break free of her bindings.

A pause. When Archeron spoke again, his voice had changed. It was quieter, less cocky. "And Bjorn is positive the only scroll left on the Curseprice is inside the castle?"

"It's Bjorn, so who knows." Rook barked a sly laugh. "Why,

afraid of dying, Archeron?"

Archeron snarled some response Haven couldn't quite hear, followed by a pause. She froze as she felt the attention shift to her.

"Speaking of fear, Archeron," Rook purred. "Does the little mortal scare you so much you need to keep her tied?"

Exactly! If free, Haven would have hugged the Sun Queen. Haven held her breath as she strained to catch his response.

"The little *chinga* is nothing but trouble. She's unpredictable, a liability at best."

Chinga? She'd have to ask Surai what that meant later, but it couldn't be good. Even from a distance, the coldness in his voice was clear.

"Look at her." Rook clicked her tongue. "You're being paranoid."

Haven couldn't decide whether to be annoyed or grateful for that remark.

"And you've forgotten what the mortals did to us, Rook," he retorted. "She might be entertaining, but she's also human and cannot be trusted."

Entertaining? Untrustworthy?

Haven's blood boiled, and it took everything she had to pretend to be unconscious. *Trust?* He wanted to talk about trust when he was the one who stole from her and then tied her up against her will like a prisoner?

Rook sighed. "What do you say, Bjorn? Is the mortal a threat?"

Haven counted twelve beats of her heart as she awaited the seer's response.

Finally, she heard him chuckle from somewhere near the front. "I think the more interesting question is how does she have such powerful magick?"

Haven nodded in agreement. She would love to know the

answer to that.

"No!" Archeron growled, the ferocity in his tone making her flinch. "Not our problem. We get through this blasted land and wash our hands of her. The less we know, the better."

"You mean," Bjorn amended. "The less we know, the less we care."

Haven grinned; the sightless seer was definitely growing on her.

"I mean just what I said," Archeron said. "Not our problem. But if you insist on learning about her magick, Bjorn, ask her yourself. She's been eavesdropping for the last five minutes."

Rolling her eyes, Haven arched her back, lifting her head just enough to find the Sun Lord riding beside her. "Untie me."

A smug grin sliced his jaw. "No."

She twisted her head, pleading with the others, but they looked to Archeron. Apparently, he was some type of de facto leader.

Growling under her breath, she locked eyes with him. "I'll use magick if I have to."

"Go ahead. I'll wait."

She gritted her teeth and squeezed her eyes shut, forcing her indignation and anger into a ball of energy that zipped down her spine . . . and did nothing.

She tried again and again. Each time, nothing.

Archeron pulled out a knife and began to clean his fingernails. "Your magick is rough, raw. You cannot control it, and that makes you dangerous."

"Oh . . . *ascilum oscular!*" she snapped, using one of the insults the trader had taught her.

The immortals burst out laughing.

Archeron's eyes danced with mirth as he said, "You want to . . . wipe our asses with your lips?"

"No, I said kiss my . . ." Her words trailed away as Rook burst into shrieks of laughter. Apparently the trader's Solissian slang wasn't as good as he put on.

Time to switch tactics.

"Look." Her back muscles strained as she struggled to keep her head up. "Let me go, and I promise, no more magick."

"Somehow," Archeron said in a teasing voice that failed to veil his underlying contempt, "I don't believe you."

Runes, he was annoying. But his horse burst into a gallop before she could tell him as much.

She might have yelled after him anyway, insisting that she wasn't a liar and that she would find a way to repay that grave insult.

But her energy was spent.

With a growl, she flopped back down onto the saddle, shoulders throbbing and head dangling ridiculously. Blood pooled behind her eyeballs and gave her a headache.

She rested her cheek against her horse's smooth pelt and caught her breath, focusing on magick, any magick she could muster.

If only she could conjure it again, she would blast that glib look from his face.

Mid-thought, a small shadow flickered over the red sands. A shadow with wings. Something light landed on her back, just above her bound hands. Something with glorious blue-black feathers and a . . . beak.

Raven!

The word sent tendrils of panic crawling through her body, and she struggled against her bindings, trying to knock the ominous bird away.

She felt its little feet hop over her hands. *Why is no one doing anything?*

Sharp, biting pain speckled her wrists. *The beast is pecking me!*

A scream grew in her chest and inched toward her lips . . . until the rope binding her wrists moved.

Just a fraction, but still. Enough for understanding to dawn.

The raven wasn't trying to hurt her. It was freeing her.

NINETEEN

Haven's fear eased as little bird feet scrabbled over her back and her binds began to loosen.

The rope suddenly split, her arms springing free.

Shoulders burning, she brought her hands around, pressed her chest up, and swung a leg over the saddle. A beautiful, sleek raven perched on the delicate tip of the horse's left horn.

Lavender eyes peeked from its dark feathers, kind and inquisitive.

Recognition shot through Haven. "Surai?"

Cawing once, Surai cocked her head, ruffled her gorgeous onyx wings, and then lifted into the sky.

Haven watched the dark form disappear into the cloudy, blood-tinged skies, her wheels turning.

Rook was a large, wild cat for most of the morning and afternoon. Surai became a raven midday.

Two creatures that were natural born enemies.

Haven's gaze slid to the dark blue-black feathers dangling from Rook's braids. Trophies from the enemy. The *Noctis.*

Yet, somehow, they were partners. Lovers.

Haven let out a deep breath. *Not your concern. Focus on finding the scroll they keep mentioning, and then, once you're across the Bane, stealing the runestones.*

That would occupy her thoughts from now on.

Not the Solis.

Lifting her hood over her head, she glanced at the others. Thankfully, Archeron was still far ahead, and only Bjorn and Rook were there.

Bjorn grinned above the ax he was sharpening. "Told you Surai would free her, Rook. You owe me five powerrunes."

"Shadeling Below," Rook grumbled. "I should stop wagering with a seer."

Bjorn chuckled. "I could have told you that without my sight. Surai's heart leads her."

Rook's gaze drifted to her partner making lazy circles above. "For someone who once took out five of the Shade Queen's best Noctis, she can be so soft sometimes." She let out a sigh and glanced ahead at the murky form of Archeron, barely visible in the red haze that hung heavy over the Bane. "He won't like it."

Bjorn went back to honing his blade. "We'll have bigger worries soon."

Haven glanced over the sky, frowning at the veiled sun. The haze was getting thicker. They were already deep in the Bane, which meant she'd been out for a while.

She yanked her hood down her forehead, a dark shadow falling over her as she imagined the inevitable confrontation with her old master, Damius. To cross the bridge to the Ruinlands, they had to go through Damius and his band of Devourers.

With the Goddess's luck, Damius wouldn't see his favorite slave—just another nameless face headed to their doom over the bridge.

A shiver tore through her chest.

Soon, they would cross the runetowers of Lorwynfell, rendering her light magick useless, while the Devourers' dark magick grew stronger.

Her magick.

The word stuck in her throat, and she couldn't quite bring herself to say it, even as questions arose.

Like, how did someone like her, someone common, produce magick? Was it a fluke or something she could reproduce?

But the biggest question of all revolved around Bell. Because if she had magick, that meant it was possible she'd felled that Shadowling, not Bell.

Which meant . . . perhaps he didn't possess magick after all.

No. She shook her head to dispel the thought. Now was not the time to be distracted with pointless conjecture. Not when his life hung in the balance.

Her focus returned to the seer. He was supposed to know what happened next, so why didn't she just ask him?

Nudging and cajoling her horse, she somehow talked it into catching Bjorn's.

His sightless ivory eyes looked to her. "It's not that simple."

She sucked in her lower lip. "Excuse me?"

"The answer to your question: Can I see what happens next?"

Her lips tugged into a frown. She'd been too preoccupied in her own thoughts to notice Bjorn entering her mind. She had to be more careful.

"Well?" she said. "Can you?"

"It's complicated."

"I'm listening."

He went back to looking straight ahead. "But are you?" He paused for what seemed like hours, until she wasn't even sure he was awake. "Look ahead. Now imagine a deep, clear lake, and below the surface are a hawk and a snake bound together in struggle. What's happening?"

Her forehead bunched as she thought. "I'd say the hawk grabbed the snake, but the snake was too heavy and they fell into the water."

"Why did the hawk not let go?"

"It was hungry?" She sighed. "Who knows?"

"Exactly. Perhaps the hawk was injured and fell into the water, and the water snake took it for a meal. Perhaps the hawk and its meal were shot from the sky by a hunter's arrow. Perhaps it's a serpenfowl, part bird of prey, part snake."

"So, what? You see the picture, but it's hard to decipher?"

He chuckled, still staring straight ahead. "Mortal, I see a hundred pictures, a hundred possibilities, and they are constantly changing."

She growled as her lazy excuse for a horse started to fall back, trying to urge it forward with her thighs. "So, what do you see for us in the Bane?"

"An ever-changing array of pictures," he called over his shoulder. "And they all center around you."

"Wait! Just . . ." She dug her heels into her horse only to have it nearly buck her off. When the beast calmed enough she wasn't in jeopardy of falling to her death, she called to the seer. "Bjorn! What do you mean it all centers around me?"

But either he was too far ahead to hear—doubtful with the freakish Solis hearing—or, more likely, he was ignoring her. When his shoulders trembled with laughter, she knew it was the latter.

"Worthless *droob*," she muttered. Her horse's black ears swiveled back to Haven, and she grunted, "That was meant for you too, stubborn thing."

After Bjorn's cryptic words, Haven set to work preparing, sharpening her blades over a whetstone and tightening her bowstring. When that was done, she tackled her hair, twisting and knotting the long silky strands until they formed a messy ball, hidden at the base of her skull.

There. She felt better now that her hair was hidden. She finished the look with a gold scarf from her pack to cover the rest then pulled up her hood.

By the time she was done, she could hardly see three feet in front of her horse, the air choked with rust-colored haze that tasted gritty and metallic in her mouth.

If the stars were out, Haven couldn't tell. The haze wrapped them in a darkness even their lanterns couldn't pierce.

They traveled like that for hours in silence, except for the occasional sounds of horses nickering, their hooves sinking into the sand. Her skin prickled with the eyes she knew followed them, and she wrapped her cloak tighter around her body.

She ran her hand beneath her hood, toying with her knotted hair. She was Haven Ashwood now. If Damius saw anything beneath the deep hood of her ruby cloak, she would look nothing like the slave girl with the long mane of rose-gold hair he once tormented.

Besides, there was a silver lining in all of this. She could use her relationship with Damius to her advantage. She knew the bastard in a way the others didn't.

Which meant she knew he would never honor whatever agreement they came to.

Everything was planned out. Once the Solis brokered the deal, her old master would betray them, she was sure of it—in the same way she was sure a death adder would strike. While they fought, she would lift the runestones from Damius and cross the bridge.

By the time the Solis realized the mortal girl they teased and looked down on had gotten one over on them, she would be long gone. A shame, too.

She would love to see Archeron's face when he realized.

Light from the others' lanterns illuminated the weapons they held out and ready. She might have dozed off a couple times, but her senses were wired, alert for any noise, any feeling that would indicate it was time to fight.

Dark shapes appeared to the right. Her gut clenched, her horse skittering sideways, its slender black ears flattening against its skull.

The kingdom of Lorwynfell.

Tales of its fall were ingrained into Haven's memory. Next to Penryth, it had been the most powerful mortal kingdom, ruled by a half-mortal, half-Noctis Queen.

Bell devoured all the books he could find on Queen Avaline, which meant Haven knew everything about her too. The Queen who never married, who refused a thousand suitors because they could not best her in battle.

Instead of putting her interests in a husband, she doted on her kingdom, particularly other crossbreeds who were shunned by mortals and labeled evil by the priests.

Blinking against the dirty air, Haven tried to imagine the lands lush and rich for harvesting, like it once had been. Known for their peaches and dark-haired women, Lorwynfell had been the crown jewel of Eritrayia.

Hard to believe, now. Haven wrapped part of her cloak over her mouth, leaving a slit for her eyes, and strained to make out the once ivory towers of the castle.

But all she could see was a shadow through the haze, slender and ominous, like a king cobra drawn to its full height and moments away from attacking.

Despite Queen Avaline's Noctis heritage, she fought alongside the Solis against the Noctis during the Final War. Lorwynfell was the only mortal kingdom to refuse breaking alliance with the Solis at the end.

And they were crushed for it. Broken from battle and unable to flee, the Curse had taken Lorwynfell first, desiccating its lands and people.

Haven shivered remembering the stories of the undead still going about their business inside the castle, dancing and feasting.

A tale meant to scare children, surely.

Still, Haven kept close to Rook and Bjorn, her pulse drumbeating inside her skull. Archeron appeared, half his face covered in a gold-and-black scarf, emerald eyes sharp and alert.

Those eyes flitted to her, slid to her unbound wrists, back to her face, and held. Below his scarf she sensed a grin.

She sneered at him with a look he'd have no trouble reading. *Try to bind me again and I'll murder you.*

His eyes tightened, but he wheeled back into the haze.

Four runetowers standing guard over Lorwynfell's gates sprouted from the sands. Once used to keep the Shadowlings out, the Devourers had perverted them with the dark magick that stifled the Solis' lighter magick.

The others seemed to sense it, hunkering down into their mounts. For Haven, her body began to feel dull and heavy as the magick she only now knew she had drained from her.

It was a strange sensation, made even stranger by the prickling pangs along her bones. As if sharp claws clacked a tune over her skeleton.

Rook appeared beside Haven, her face almost covered by her deep-scarlet hood. The red band around her eyes matched the haze in the air and made her golden eyes seem brighter.

"Can you feel it?" Rook asked. "The runetowers are feeding off our powers."

Haven nodded, although she still doubted how much magick she possessed.

"Weapons out and eyes open, mortal." Rook cast a glance out at the haze. "We are being watched by Devourers. We make camp first, eat, and rest. Then we raid the castle. You up for it?"

A grin stretched Haven's face. "Did Odin love Freya? Of course I am."

Haven watched Rook disappear back into the haze. The charge that skimmed along her skin wasn't magick; it was anticipation of the fight. Because one was coming. That fact was as inevitable as the sands spreading across the horizon or the gibbous moon surely hidden above.

Strangely, she enjoyed all of it: the jagged beat of her heart, the dryness of her mouth, the fluttery feeling inside her stomach.

Aside from Bell, fighting was the only thing she loved. The only thing she was good at.

This was the ultimate test. Succeed and she was one step closer to breaking the Curse and saving Bell.

Fail and she would lose everything—including her life.

TWENTY

Bell jerked awake, blinking back the tormented dreams that still played across his vision. Wails pierced the air—his own ragged breaths, he realized, sputtering out like sobs.

He was leaned against a hard wall, his body stiff, achy, and near frozen. Countless heartbeats wracked his chest before he remembered where he was.

A cell—a tiny, windowless cell—deep in the Shade Queen's castle.

Not that he needed a proper window. Half the far wall had crumbled away, leaving a jagged hole of open sky. Blasts of wind howled through the room, sending snowflakes swirling across the obsidian floor, making his teeth clatter.

The cold pierced his heavy red cloak like it was gossamer instead of fine Arlavian velvet.

Sighing, he lifted the fur-lined hem with stiff, purple fingers, grimacing at the tattered edges and oily stains. Some of it undoubtedly his blood. It was a fine cloak too. Handsomely made, the murex dye—made from a rare type of snail—would only grow brighter as it aged.

A bitter laugh formed in his parched throat. *Fine time to mourn the state of your garments, Bellamy.*

His thinking only proved his absolute worthlessness in this situation. And a hopeless situation it was.

He winced as he touched his tender nose, recalling how after he was taken by the brutish Shade Lord, he was paraded through the castle like one of his father's prized horses.

After a few hours, the Noctis toying with Bell tired of his fighting back and broke his nose with a sharp backhand, leaving stars in his vision and his mouth full of blood.

And all the while, the strange beasts—the winged Noctis—they watched him with those greedy, primal eyes. Trailing him down the shadow-steeped corridors. Sniffing the air behind him.

If not for the larger Shade Lord, the other Noctis would have torn Bell to pieces.

He could feel their hungry stares even after the Shade Lord had thrown him into a cell. Even after the lock clicked and he faded into sleep. They were in his nightmares, in his head.

They wanted his magick.

Magick. The word clanged around his skull, worse than the dull headache throbbing behind his eyes. Prince Bellamy Boteler, first lightcasting noble in decades to grace the mortal realm. He'd finally gotten what he'd wanted. He was good at something. He was special.

"Special and doomed, you idiot," he muttered, glancing down at his very magick-less—and cold—fingers.

Where was that magick now? What good was it if he couldn't even make a meager flame to warm the blood back into his hands?

If he couldn't use magick to at least vanquish the nightmares that tormented him?

Teeth clattering, he drummed his head against the stone wall, *thud, thud,* a frosty breath shimmering the air as he tried to calm the tide of panic rushing over him, drowning him.

They wouldn't just leave him here like this. He was important to the Shade Queen's daughter, Ravenna.

They wouldn't let him freeze to death. They wouldn't.

Keep telling yourself that.

Who knew what the Noctis were capable of? They might not even need him alive. Especially if his magick proved to be a fluke, which seemed more and more likely by the hour.

Bitterness surged up his throat and threatened to choke him. He wasn't even good at magick. How his father would laugh. How the entire kingdom would.

Bell huffed out a breath, trying to remember what his books said about a new lightcaster's abilities, but instead his thoughts went to Haven. The mornings curled up in the library beneath dusty blankets, sipping tea, surrounded by tomes nearly too massive to lift.

She only half-listened to him when he read, but he loved watching her chew the end of her charcoal pencil as she frowned down at the sketch pad she carried everywhere. He loved that the hideous floppy hat she wore still had twigs and leaves from the night before, that she might not have thought to wash the grime from her face.

Most of all, he loved that even though she wasn't really listening to the stories he read, she always made a point to look up and nod so he thought she was.

Before Haven, no one had ever bothered with caring how he felt.

A noise startled him from his memories. Faint scraping. He turned his head, straining to listen over the howling wind as his heart crammed into his throat, pumping blood back into his aching fingers.

Again, the scraping. Only this time louder. Closer.

The noise was coming from outside. He stumbled to his feet, alarmed at how numb they were, and slowly edged across the black floor to the far wall. A dirty gray sky peeked from the opening, shrouded with dense fog and veiling what he imagined was a glorious half-moon.

Rocks clattered down the side of the crack, and Bell froze, hardly daring to breathe as something heavy rustled above the opening. Terrified as he was, the thought of a presence to quell his loneliness sparked hope inside his chest.

Silence followed, making him question his sanity.

Then the murky light disappeared as something huge blotted out the canvas of sky. The shape took up the entire opening, and it seemed to hesitate as it peered inside. At him.

Then it reached for him and he knew he'd been wrong, so very wrong.

Loneliness was far better than whatever monster had come to claim him.

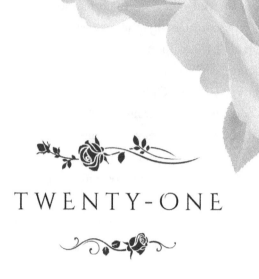

TWENTY-ONE

Darkness fell soon after they passed Lorwynfell. They skirted along the walls of the city, the bow Haven placed on her lap smooth inside her tight grip.

Haven stretched through a yawn. The haze had lifted, if only enough to see ten feet in front of them, and delicate moonlight broke through in places, silvery spotlights from the gods.

Trees suddenly sprouted from the landscape. Black, twisting, leafless spires that pierced the sky. By the height of the trees, she guessed the forest must have once been old and beautiful, but now . . .

Well, now it was hideous.

As they passed through the dead woods, Haven trailed a hand over the slick, clammy bark of one of the trees, slime sticking to her fingers. A rotten carcass perfumed the moist air.

Wrinkling her nose, Haven focused on the squelching of the horses' hooves as they sunk deep into the layer of moss, mud, and decomposing leaves.

They stopped where the forest met a grouping of boulders and greenish-gray limestone cliffs. The pitch-black mouth of a small cave yawned to their left. Haven sagged in the saddle, her tailbone bruised and body aching from riding.

How long had it been? A day? A week? She didn't know. Her mind was numb with a jumble of fear and adrenaline, her senses dulled by fatigue. Nothing would be clear until she rested.

But there was still work to be done before she could sleep.

After dismounting, she joined the others, where they silently set to making camp. The air was wet and cold and muffled, as if sound didn't quite carry here.

Once the horses were watered and a fire built, Bjorn began working over a giant, scuffed cauldron. Just as steam began to curl from the liquid inside his pot, Surai flew down from the trees, carrying some sort of rodent with a wiry tail in her beak.

Wings fluttering proudly, she dropped the disgusting creature at Bjorn's feet and darted into the woods.

Haven's stomach growled loud enough to make Archeron turn and look her over. His razor-sharp gaze never failed to unsettle her. Shifting on her feet, she found herself watching the pot in a dream-like haze.

Before she knew it, she was hovering over Bjorn.

"The stew will not cook any faster with you watching it," Bjorn said without turning around.

Haven took a seat on a rock, letting out a grievous sigh. "I'm starving."

"I imagine channeling all that magick made you hungry."

"Is it always like that?"

"Not if done properly, no." He turned, holding a steaming spoon to her mouth. "How much training have you had?"

She practically bit the spoon, slurping loudly. "None. It happened for the first time at the pond."

He raised a dark eyebrow. "And?"

"And that's all I know."

A smile twitched his lips. "No. The stew. Is it good?"

"Oh. Yes." Warm broth dribbled down her chin, and she wiped it with a sleeve. "Why did it make me pass out? The magick, not the stew."

Dipping the ladle into the pot, Bjorn filled a too-small clay bowl with the chunky stew and handed the steaming bowl to her. Then he settled onto a rock beside her as Surai, now in human form, flitted over and grabbed a bowl.

"Everything and everyone possesses magick," he began in an older voice at odds with his much younger face. "But for most common mortals, their magick was received at birth, and the door to the Nihl locked. So, when they are runemarked, the rune simply channels the little remnant of magick their bodies possess. Yet, when you carved that energy rune into your flesh, you took an unlocked door and flung it wide open. If you had been properly trained in the Runic Arts, you would have remembered to close it afterward."

Great. They knew about the rune. "Leaving it open drained my energy?"

Bjorn rubbed his hands over his knees. "Have you never heard of the magick price?"

"Oh . . ." Bell had read to her about it, hadn't he? Probably more than once, and she imagined him shaking his head at her now for not paying attention.

"Magick is not free, Mortal. It always takes something of equal value in return. But it is an ancient master, with a mind of its own and desires we can only begin to fathom. And that makes its price unpredictable, sometimes ruinous—particularly for mortal flesh. Be glad mortals cannot harness dark magick. That price you cannot pay."

Haven sunk a little into the rock. She had been rash and stupid for carving that rune.

Swallowing another mouthwatering morsel, she promised herself no more impulsive decisions.

That might have been okay at Penryth, but here, where there was so much she didn't understand—monsters, magick, and strange customs—Bell's life depended on her thinking before she acted.

Rook slunk down beside Surai, wrinkling her nose at the contents of her bowl.

"You should try it," Haven offered. "It's good."

Archeron's grating laugh came from somewhere behind her.

She whipped her head to face him. "What? It is."

Now they were all laughing, even Bjorn. She bristled and crammed a bite into her mouth. What was she, a little pet to entertain them? *Little Mortal, this. Little Mortal, that?*

As Haven's spoon scraped the bottom of her bowl, she noticed rune marks circling the inside rim. "Wait, what are these?"

They laughed even harder, Archeron's loud snicker the most infuriating.

"Did you think Bjorn managed to make the stew taste delicious with the foul beast Surai brought him?" Archeron said, biting back more chuckles.

Taste runes! She frowned. "But, I tasted the stew from the pot."

"Also runed." Archeron nodded to the simmering pot.

Haven didn't care. Whatever it was, it warmed her belly and made her sleepy. But she did mind being laughed at by a Sun Lord with a too-pretty face, and she vowed to wipe that smile from his expression someday.

All her joints seemed to crack and pop as she stood to stretch and glance at the cave.

"Go," Surai said, an understanding smile twisting her lips. "Sleep. As a mortal, you must be exhausted."

Haven took a step then paused. Rash, indeed. She hadn't even thought to pack a blanket. Something she now regretted immensely.

As if reading her mind, Surai got up and returned with something. Grinning, the Solis thrust a sand-colored blanket at Haven. Delicate, white lotus blossoms were embroidered over the thick fibers in exquisite detail.

Haven's hands yearned to take it. "I . . . can't."

Surai's face crumpled. "Refusing a gift in my culture is a grave insult."

"Oh." Haven plucked the blanket from her hands, holding it awkwardly in her arms. "I'm . . . I didn't know. Sorry."

A peal of laughter shot from Surai's lips. "I'm teasing you!"

Haven blushed. Once again, she was the butt of the joke.

"Don't take it personally, mortal." Rook slipped a muscled arm around Surai's lithe waist and shot a dark grin at Haven. "If she teases you, it means she likes you."

Haven shifted on her feet. She hated charity and was uncomfortable with spontaneous kindness—even the kind that came with ribbing. *Especially* the kind that came with ribbing. "Noted. Too bad that doesn't apply to Archeron."

The girls exchanged tense glances.

"He doesn't hate you," Surai offered gently. "But mortals are . . . hard for him to understand."

"Is that why he called me *chinga*?"

Surai's eyes widened, and Rook barely held in a laugh.

"What does it mean?" she persisted.

Rook chewed her lip, hesitating before she answered. "Chinga are invasive pests that inhabit parts of Effendier. They . . . burrow under your skin and eat their way through your flesh until they pierce your heart, lay eggs, and kill you."

"Lovely," Haven muttered.

"But I'm sure he doesn't mean it," Surai offered.

It took all of Haven's willpower to keep from rolling her eyes. She would never understand how they held Archeron in such high regard. "So . . . I'll keep it, then." She held up the blanket. "For tonight."

Surai gave a little bow, her midnight hair slipping over her forehead. "No trouble. I'll sleep in Rook's bag anyway."

Haven blushed again as she found a sheltered spot a few feet inside the cave. A cool draft funneled over her head, but any deeper inside and she wouldn't sleep.

She would take stars and open sky over warmth any night.

A pang of regret gnawed at her as she eyed the beautiful blanket. In a few days, she would betray the Solis and take back her runestones. They belonged to her. It was only right.

And yet, she couldn't quite shake the guilt she felt, made worse by Surai's gift.

What if she could trust the Solis? It would be easier to travel with them than alone.

No, she reminded herself, biting the inside of her lip to drive the message home. Archeron had already stolen from her once. And tied her to a horse. And mocked her mercilessly.

Truly, his transgressions were countless.

The Solis with the kind lavender eyes and ready smile might be nice, but if it came down to it, Surai would always choose the side of her people. And Haven and Archeron would always be enemies.

Best to only trust herself.

Right before wriggling under the covers, she peered out. Archeron stood at the edge of the trees, shoulders stiff, his face lost in something Haven couldn't see. He seemed to be staring in the direction of Lorwynfell. Other than the heaving of his chest, he was as still as the night.

Yet pain was written all over his face.

Sinking deep into Surai's wool blanket, which smelled of lotus, spice, and earth, Haven wondered what someone like the Sun Lord would have to worry about.

Maybe the humidity messed up his hair. The thought made her chuckle until she drifted off to sleep . . . and fell into a nightmare.

Darkness. She couldn't see. She felt the Shade Lord, close. Too close. His nose dragging over her neck, inhaling her, aching to drink her in. Suck her dry. She tasted his cinnamon scent, felt the cold, foreign prickle of his dark magick trying to penetrate her.

And part of her welcomed it. Yearned for the sinister power to rush through her veins . . .

For a heart-stopping moment, she was inside his mind, watching herself sleep. Even though this was a nightmare, and she was fully cognizant of that fact, somewhere deep down she knew it was really happening.

That was her right now, lying there. Unprotected. At his mercy.

It had been years since she'd really looked at herself. Now she was forced to see the way she was, the way she truly was. Vulnerable and small-looking, curled into a tight, anxious ball. Her head tilted to the side, her face tense even in sleep. Moonlight swam along her rose-gold hair, partially undone from its captivity beneath the scarf.

Hair that she used to wear thick and wavy, weighing more than a sack of flour. A treasure she cherished right up until the night it became a chain around her neck.

Wake up, Little Beastie.

Haven's eyes snapped open. Her heart was racing. Where was she? A quick sweep over the landscape jogged her memory.

Right. The Bane.

Running a sweaty palm through her hair, she slowed her ragged breathing, her eyes scouring the cave for the Shade Lord as they slowly adjusted.

Just a dream—a nightmare.

Still, she caught the dying whisper of a dark voice echoing through her skull, unintelligible . . . and yet terrifyingly *real.*

A horse nickered softly near the woods. Pressing up on her elbows, Haven glanced over the Solis sleeping in their bags. Surai's head rested on Rook's chest, her dark hair swept over her face and her cheek rising with Rook's slow breaths.

Both girls looked peaceful, she noticed with a twinge of jealousy, their dreams nice and gentle.

In contrast, Bjorn sat cross-legged at the lip of the cave, white eyes open and bright against the night.

Haven held her breath as she approached on silent feet. As soon as she got close, she could tell by his even breathing and slack gaze that he was sleeping . . . or something.

Scuttling down the rocks, she quietly slipped through the boulders until she caught sight of movement near the trees. Flashes of silver. The whiz of steel cleaving the air called to some deep part of her.

Archeron's eyes were closed. He held two swords, his lithe body carving through the darkness in an elaborate battle against an invisible opponent. The muscles of his arms and torso strained through his thin tunic.

Mesmerized by his graceful movements, she stopped to watch, hardly daring to breathe as he danced across the grass with bare feet that seemed to float.

The trance was broken as he froze, a sigh escaping his lips. "It's impolite to stare."

Grinning despite his stern tone, she strolled over to him. "What are you doing?"

He sighed again, a low, aggrieved sound, his swords scraping into the scabbards that hung from his trim waist. "If you must know, praying."

"Praying?"

"Is there an echo?"

"I've never seen anyone pray like that. Who to? Odin or Freya?"

"Why not both?"

"Both? At the same time?" She scoffed. "Lorwynfell must have you worried. Why?"

She didn't mean it to come out like that. Or, maybe she did. Archeron had been acting strange since they passed the castle, and if bringing it up knocked him off his game, then it would be easier to know his weaknesses when it came time to take back her runestones.

The corners of his eyes tightened. "Tell me, mortal, why is your prince so important to you?"

Her muscles jerked taut at the mention of Bell. "That's none of your business."

"Exactly." She blinked, and he was inches from her face. "You don't trust me, and I sure as the Netherworld don't trust you, which makes us not friends. And not-friends do not discuss their feelings. Not-friends do not pretend to care, when the first chance they get, they plan to steal my runestones."

"My runestones!" she snarled. "That you stole first!"

"A technicality, and beyond the point."

"No, that is the point! You snuck into my mind—"

"You allowed me inside," he objected. "You might as well have offered me an invitation with your meager defenses. Although, somehow you knew enough to kick me out after you realized."

"Why do you despise mortals?" The raw pain in her voice startled her. "What did we ever do to you?"

Other than a tendon trembling in his jaw, his face was a mask of apathy. "Perhaps I simply cannot stand your inferiority. Perhaps the plainness of your features insults me. Perhaps I find mortals duller than the mud beneath my boots."

Rage heated her cheeks. Rage and the resolve to leave this cocky Sun Lord behind at the first chance. She'd find a way without him. "And perhaps I find your face uglier than a gremwyr's ass, you *droob!*"

Infuriatingly, the corners of his lips twitched upward. "We both know that's not true."

Her chest heaved as she glared at Archeron, every curse under the Goddess boiling on the tip of her tongue. But before she could unleash her torrent of insults, tinkling laughter drew her attention back to the cave.

Rook was stretching her arms to the veiled stars and yawning. Beside her, Surai grinned as she twisted her sleek dark hair up in a bun. "Shadeling Below, your arguing could wake the Shade Queen's undead daughter."

The anger slowly drained from Haven as she helped pack up the camp, clanging pots and bowls while huffing. To think she'd considered giving the Solis a chance!

Not now. Not a chance in the Netherworld.

First moment the pretty-boy Solis let down his guard, the runestones were hers.

After a few minutes, her fury gave way to excitement. Her veins thrummed with the anticipation of the raid. The shadowy castle filled her mind, but instead of fear, she felt elation, her pulse clearing her mind for battle.

Archeron was the last to his horse. With sinuous grace, he mounted the beast and charged through the woods, branches snapping in his wake. Haven and the others followed, blazing a swift trail to the castle. Leafless trees became flat desert and a dead sky.

As they charged ever closer, the hood of Haven's cloak whipping back in the wind, she felt drawn to Archeron's saddlebag. The runebag was there; she knew it deep down in her bones, could feel them whispering to her.

Her curiosity flared. Why had the mention of Lorwynfell provoked him? She bit her lip, a tiny voice warning her not to push it.

To the Netherworld with that, she decided, rocking with the rhythm of her horse's steady gait. This could be her opportunity to steal back the runebag sooner than planned.

And if that opportunity came with the Sun Lord's secret, so be it.

She felt the pull of the runetowers first, as if something had taken hold of her soul and was gently tugging, nibbling.

The ominous shape of Lorwynfell rose ahead, blotting their path. Her skin prickled as the ruined kingdom rose from the darkness.

Passing through iron gates marked with intricate, long-dead runes and empty watchtowers that scraped the dark clouds, Haven muttered a prayer to both Odin and Freya—just in case.

They clattered over a broken wooden drawbridge, a brackish moat visible from missing boards, at least fifty feet below. The musty odor of stagnant water and carrion filled the air.

Her breath froze in her chest, and she didn't breathe again until they were past the spiked portcullis that hung above the arched gates.

As they spilled into the shadowy courtyard, Archeron's body went rigid, his face a tight, emotionless mask. The others glanced at him with worried frowns they tried to hide.

Curiosity raged through her. What was this place to him?

The others dismounted and tied their horses to the rotting beam of what once were probably stables. As she leapt to the cobblestones and did the same, cold fingers of dread scraped around her heart.

That's when she noticed the stillness, the marrow-curdling quiet of the courtyard. She could swear shadows flickered from the arrow loops carved high up in the towers, and strange bluish light spilled from the arched windows in the castle.

The hairs on her neck went rigid. Everything inside her screamed to run from this place. Run, and don't look back.

But she needed the Curseprice, and she needed the runestones. She wasn't about to let a few rumors and shadows scare her.

Bell was counting on her.

Haven took two steps, and then a huge shape suddenly charged across the courtyard.

TWENTY-TWO

Haven's spine went rigid and her breath caught in her throat as she readied her crossbow, prepared to send the beast to the Netherworld . . . until the shaggy, golden head of Rook appeared, her eyes glowing yellow.

She padded to them and rubbed her head across Surai's thigh, nearly knocking her over. Surai scratched behind her mate's ear, and then Archeron directed them inside the deep shadow of the castle wall. He led while they jogged single file toward the front door.

"Any idea what I should expect inside?" Haven whispered, proud at how steady her voice was, despite almost sending a quarrel through Rook.

Bjorn laughed, glancing back at her.

"What? Why is that funny?"

"Because your question depends on your actions. There are things inside these walls best left unseen, mortal."

Haven rolled her eyes. "Thanks for the cryptic answer, Seer. As always, your helpfulness knows no bounds."

But her sarcasm fell flat, dampened by the strong feeling they were being watched. Even in the low light, slinking in the shadow of the castle walls, her shoulder grinding the stone, she felt exposed.

Surely, the castle was empty. Surely, the rumors weren't true.

Ducking through an open door, she repeated these words as the faintest of voices trickled over the stone and into her ears. Haven tilted her head and strained to hear. But her heart pounded in her skull, drowning out anything she might have heard, and she pressed deeper into the castle.

As she flitted through the halls on silent feet behind the Solis, the metallic tang that hovered over the Bane swelled the air, settling low and heavy in her belly. Nausea roiled up her throat, her heart rattling faster with each step.

By the way Archeron confidently led them down corridor after corridor, he was no stranger to these halls. Rook was his shadow, her fur standing on end and her ears back as she readied to pounce on anything that moved.

Other than Haven's soft breaths, the crew were silent.

The meager moonlight pouring through the windows, already veiled by the haze, was lost as soon as they snaked down a winding set of steps. Cold, dank air washed over her. The smell of earth and something ancient stirred her marrow.

"Something's down here," Haven half-hissed, half-whispered.

"We know," Surai breathed. "Queen Avaline conjured a djinn from the Netherworld to guard her treasures. It's quite likely the scroll she protected is the only record of the Curseprice the Shade Queen hasn't destroyed. If she hasn't already discovered it."

Djinn.

The word bounced around Haven's brain as she tried to picture the beast from the book in Bell's library. But her nerves were getting to her, and all the images mixed together into one horrible creature.

"What's a djinn?"

"Oh, just a mindless demon from the Netherworld," Surai whispered, stroking the katana hilts on either side of her waist. "It starts out in spirit form, using the flesh of its victims to grow corporeal. It's really quite disgusting."

"Wonderful," Haven muttered. Just in case, she loaded the oleander-tipped arrow onto the middle slot of her crossbow. Whatever the demon lurking below was, it had the Solis worried—and something told her the arrows in her crossbow would only serve to piss it off.

Every step deeper into the bowels was an effort. Haven had to bury down deep the alarm sounding inside her, the one that had kept her alive all these years . . . until the stairs ended in a pitch-black chamber and she could hardly breathe, hardly think, the urge to run pulsing down her nerves.

A green light flickered then bloomed into a giant star inside Bjorn's open palm, reflecting against his pearlescent eyes. Muck slicked the chamber walls. A gamey scent permeated the moist air, along with the thick, cloying smell of roses. Magick.

Haven sighed. "It's warded."

Archeron flicked a tired glance her way. "We know. But the door will open for certain friends of Queen Avaline."

Friends? Haven loosed a tense breath, watching Archeron slowly approach the door. Runes shimmered over the hammered steel. Words written in Solissian burned brightly just below.

Haven struggled to read the text, but Surai beat her to it. "Only a pure heart can survive the evil beyond this door," Surai whispered. "Take what is not yours and live no more."

"What happens if you aren't on the friends list?"

Even though Archeron didn't turn, she could tell by his loosened shoulders that he was grinning, which was odd considering his answer. "The flames of the Netherworld will consume my flesh until I die a painful, gruesome death. You may want to step back."

Perhaps he was joking?

But no, the others backed up, watching him reach for the iron door handle, hardly blinking . . . or breathing.

She must have closed her eyes because when she looked again, his hand was on the door handle. No Netherworld fire. No gruesome death. His body relaxed as she heaved a sigh of relief.

Bjorn clapped Archeron's back. "Good to see you still alive, Archeron."

Archeron growled. "You saw that, didn't you?"

"I did. But I thought letting you sweat would lighten the mood."

The door popped open, and Haven felt the wards guarding the next chamber ease away. Cold, wet air washed over her. The overpowering odor of sulfur stung her eyes.

The sulfur tang grew stronger as they funneled inside to a large, cavernous chamber that seemed to go on without end. Bjorn's green light was nearly lost in the expansive darkness.

No matter, because blue light swirled around columns etched with runes, illuminating the middle chamber.

Turning in a circle, she made out six caverns beyond, steeped in oily darkness.

Something cracked beneath her boot. Bones. Chills clawed down her spine as she gazed over the mounds of scattered skeletons.

"Which cavern?" she murmured to no one in particular.

Surai grinned. "I vote for the one without the djinn. Bjorn?"

Bjorn shut his eyes for a second then turned and pointed to the cavern behind Haven. "That one holds the scroll. I can't see the djinn."

Haven followed the green light as it chased away the shadows inside the cavern—and froze. Her breath hissed out in a murky cloud.

Treasures sparkled beneath the delicate light, winking from the honeycombs along the wall like bits of fire. Gold trinkets and candlesticks; rubies and emeralds the size of quail eggs; sharp, jeweled crowns and necklaces weighted with diamonds and pearls.

Never in her life had she seen such wealth, enough to fill the great hall of Penryth and feed the entire castle for years. Runes, enough to buy a kingdom, or four.

Drawn to the baubles and shiny things, she forgot for a moment she had no need for them. She reached a hand out to touch an enormous crystalline-blue egg, scales etched into its pearlescent surface—

"Touch nothing," Bjorn commanded, and she bristled with injustice as his pale eyes fixed accusingly on her. "Only the scroll. We have one minute to read the scroll and replace it before the djinn appears . . . I think."

"Your decisiveness never disappoints, Seer," she muttered under her breath, taking a kernel of pleasure as his lips twitched in response.

Cobwebs hung from rolling ladders that reached all the way to the high ceiling. Picking the sturdiest looking ladder, Haven scaled to the middle of the catacombs and began searching.

Along with trinkets and jewelry, there were aged books slathered in sheets of dust and delicate vases decorated with foreign runes she didn't recognize.

She worked quickly, methodically, ticking off each dusty hole piled with treasure until she'd made it halfway across the wall.

Her eyes caught on something—a rolled-up paper tied with red twine. Her heart gave a wild kick. The paper was alone.

"Bjorn," she hissed. "Bring your light."

Bjorn's light ended up being a small, greenish runestone. As soon as he held the stone close and light shone over the paper, she could make out tiny runes over the twine.

Surai poked her head close and gasped. "That has to be it."

Haven reached to take the scroll, but Archeron's hand wrapped around her wrist. "Easy, Mortal. If I know Avaline, she will have warded it as an extra precaution from the Shade Queen."

She reclaimed her wrist, frowning at the intimate way he said the Queen's name. He must have known her. Another piece to the puzzle surrounding this wretched place. "So, what then?"

Bjorn slowly waved his hand over the scroll. "Intent runes. Only those who mean to use the information for good can open the scroll."

"That should be all of us," Surai remarked in a hesitant tone.

Haven tapped her foot on the ladder, impatient to see the Curseprice. "To the Netherworld with waiting," she breathed, snatching the scroll.

Shimmying down the ladder, the others watched as she slowly, slowly untied the twine. The scroll loosened in her hand.

For a moment, as the twine fell to the floor, she felt something sliding around her mind, assessing her. A cold, dark presence. Then the feeling was gone.

She released a ragged breath and started to open the scroll. But as she did, her gaze slipped to the pocket of Archeron's pants. And to the ribbon dangling from his pocket. Greedy excitement surged through her.

The runestones.

Quickly, she tore her gaze away, back to the half-opened scroll.

"Please," Bjorn said, "take your time."

"My hands are shaking. Here." She thrust the scroll at Archeron, praying he would think the anticipation on her face was for the scroll.

The ancient paper crinkled as Archeron pulled apart the edges of the scroll, holding it low so everyone could see. His lips parted slightly as the first part of the Curseprice appeared in the yellowed paper, etched in fiery letters. Haven could almost hear the Shade Queen's raspy voice as she read.

Forged in heartbreak, set in bone, cast in blood, carved in stone. A thousand years will my curse reign, unless I have these six things: The tears of a fairy from a wood so deep.

Searing the first sentence into her brain, Haven chanced another look at Archeron's pocket. Her hand just happened to move a bit closer to him as another demand appeared.

The fig of a vorgrath from his mate's keep.

Her hand was inches away, but she kept her eyes riveted to the scroll. Her heartbeat was rattling around inside her skull.

The scale of a selkie burnished gold.

The bone of a wood witch a century old.

She slipped her fingers an inch inside his pocket, slow and steady . . .

The midnight sliver of a Shade Queen's horn.

Gathering a breath, she turned slightly, preparing to hit as soon as the next demand flashed over the paper. No one made a sound as they breathlessly waited. The paper brightened as the next sentence began to form—

Now.

Her shoulder brushed Archeron's at the exact time the purse

slid from his pocket. But, if he felt it, his eyes stayed glued to the words on the paper.

She let out a soft breath. The runestones weighed down her pocket now. All she had to do was wait for the last demand to complete the Curseprice.

Sounds drowned her thoughts. Like something wet and heavy dragging over bone and stone, mixed with the sound of talons scratching the floor. Something reeking of rotting flesh and sulphur.

Haven turned around. They all did.

And the cavern burst into chaos.

TWENTY-THREE

Time stretched out and slowed until Haven could make out every detail of the djinn. The hulking mass of muscle and putrid flesh nearly touched the dank ceiling, pocked with black, festering sores. The red, red eyes of fire and too-wide mouth of horrors.

She could swear rotting chunks of flesh and bone splinters wedged between its jagged teeth.

"Why did it appear?" Surai demanded, glancing over at Archeron. "Our minute wasn't up."

Archeron's gaze wandered to Haven and caught as he growled, "Someone must have stolen something else."

Oh . . . She stifled the urge to tap her pocket with the runestones. *Oops.*

Faster than she could blink, the djinn swiped a long arm through the cavern, claws scraping off the stone.

Haven leapt back into the cave with the others before realizing her folly. Her best bet would be to fight past him to the door. Any farther back and she'd be trapped.

A howl ripped from the djinn's mouth, blasting hot, sulfurous air over them.

Biting back a gag, Haven lifted her crossbow.

The djinn swiped again, flinging her against the wall. Pain shot through her head as it cracked against the stone, rubies and diamonds showering her cheek and hair.

Another smoky roar brought her to her feet.

Raising her katanas into the air, Surai inched toward the djinn as Archeron slunk against the wall, his sword held low. Yellow runes flashed over both their steel.

The djinn shrieked twice, turning its huge, misshapen head from Archeron to Surai.

Haven raised her triple-loaded crossbow, aimed dead center on its fiery eye, and pulled the trigger with a twang.

The first quarrel sunk a few inches into its forehead.

The second missed.

But the third sunk to its fletching into its eye.

The djinn screamed with pain, its claws striking blindly. Treasure snowed around them in a furious din of shrieks and clangs.

Wonderful. I've just managed to piss it off.

"Run!" Haven yelled as a small opening between its legs appeared. She leapt and rolled. As she passed under the creature's body, slime and ick coated her face and left her gagging.

As soon as she popped out the other side, she sprinted, feeling for the runepurse as she did. *Still there.*

Take that, you droob! she thought. *This dull, plain, inferior mortal bested you, Sun Lord.*

Her feet tripped and slid over bones. Scuffing the slick stone floor. Slipping along small, gooey piles of regurgitated human parts.

Rook's feline snarl joined the sounds of the others fighting, but she refused to let the sound stop her.

The door appeared. She grabbed the handle, brimming with a thief's pride . . . and hesitated.

No. Do not turn around, Haven Ashwood. Do not—

Against her judgement, she turned. Something tugged at her as she watched the Solis battle the djinn. Surai and Rook side-by-side, the always bold Archeron circling the dumb creature, distracting it.

Show off.

Yet a part of Haven marveled at his willingness to court injury in an effort to help his friends.

Even Bjorn, she begrudgingly noticed, dove nimbly between its legs, slashing at its belly with his ax.

Nethergates, they were good together, as if tethered to one mind. She bit her cheek, torn. To be a part of that, to fight and bleed together . . .

Stop, she ordered. *These are not your friends.*

To them she was only a mortal who would get in the way if she stayed. They didn't need her.

Bell, however, did.

No sooner did his name appear in her mind, she was flinging open the door and sprinting up the steep stairs. Slipping on scummy stone, scrabbling down the pitch-black halls.

Fear and shame surged over her.

She left them.

"They'll be fine," she growled, slamming into a wall. Dull pain barreled up her shoulder.

She was the one who should be worried.

In her haste, she had taken a wrong turn somewhere. By now, she should see windows, but all around was cold, quiet darkness.

A cool draft pierced her flesh, but she didn't remember one before. And eerie, haunting music trickled inside her ears and scuttled along her bones. Simultaneously calling her and warning her away.

That was definitely not here before.

Turning around, she pounded back the other way, but somehow the music grew louder and more insistent until it began to pull at her as if tiny hooks had latched onto her flesh and were drawing her closer.

All at once, bright light filled her vision.

For a fraction of a heartbeat, she was blind. When she unscrunched her eyelids, a gasp escaped her lips.

A grand ballroom three times the size of Penryth's ballroom appeared, all gold and blue and shiny. Six sparkling crystal chandeliers dripped from mirrored ceilings, and mirrored walls encircled the yellow-and white-checkered parquet floor.

But it was the figures dancing over the polished squares that held her attention. Draped in swathes of the finest jewel-toned silks and velvets she had ever seen, the courtiers leapt and twirled. Chunky citrine and opal jewelry hung from them. Ceremonial weapons flickered softly from their waists.

They could have been royal courtiers attending a ball—except beneath the gorgeous clothing and jewels, all the flesh, muscles, and tendons had melted away, revealing yellowed bones.

She flung a hand over her mouth. Cadavers—no, not even that. Cadavers possessed bits of flesh and hair, pieces that spoke of humanity.

These were reanimated skeletons picked clean and then redressed in some horrible parody of normal life. Made to dance and celebrate even in death.

The wall of mirrors created multiple reflections, teasing the eyes and making the ballroom seem to stretch on forever. A sea of waltzing undead. An ocean of horrors.

And in the center of it all stood a skeleton inside a glorious midnight-black gown that pooled around her like shadows. Sapphires and garnets winked from the black crown perched atop her skull, bits of dark hair snaking down her back.

Two skeletal wings unfolded behind her, spreading seven feet on either side.

Queen Avaline.

It was then Haven felt the dark magick infesting the room, choking the air, poisoning everything inside.

Madness haunted these people. Madness and grief and something else, something unspeakable.

Haven blinked and suddenly she could see the oily-black tentacles that swirled around the bones and poked from eye-sockets, making them dance and twirl like puppets on a string.

Her heart shuddered inside her chest, the trance broke, and Haven turned to run—

And knocked over a small statue in the corner. As the moonstone girl with wings shattered, pieces skidding across the floor, Haven froze and forced herself to look back. Instead of curling into a ball and pretending to hide, which is what she wanted to do.

The dancers stopped dancing. The music ground to a halt. The slimy tentacles churned the air like a nest of enraged serpents.

Swiveling her skull, the Skeleton Queen locked onto Haven. Behind the dark pools inside her eye-sockets, Haven felt something primordial study her.

Haven stopped breathing, Bjorn's words from earlier clawing at her brain.

There are things inside these walls best-left unseen, mortal.

He hadn't meant the djinn.

The horrifying realization came a second before the Skeleton Queen pointed a bony finger at Haven and shrieked.

A panicky heartbeat passed, long enough for Haven to think perhaps she would be okay.

And then, as if the entire skeleton ballroom were acting with one mind, they leapt across the floor and spewed after her, their bones scraping and clacking together in a sickening symphony.

TWENTY-FOUR

If death had a sound, it would be this, Haven decided, slapping a hand over her ears to muffle the sickening crunch of bone grating against bone. Her legs churned and churned, but the macabre racket only grew louder.

Perhaps she was inside a nightmare. Despite her terror, her body couldn't seem to move fast enough. Her papery lungs couldn't suck in enough air.

All the while the creatures chasing her gained ground. Perhaps this was the dark magick's cruel trick: like a butterfly trapped in a spider's web, the more she struggled to get away, the more ensnared she became.

Finally, a trickle of silvery light cleaved the darkness.

Cold air stung her cheeks as she broke free of the castle, her crossbow freezing inside her palm. With the other hand, she lodged three quarrels onto the deck.

She pivoted just as two skeletons in bright-yellow tunics lunged.

Her quarrels released with a twang, smashing the two skulls into a mist of pale shards. The sound of bone splintering churned her stomach.

The now headless skeletons fell, writhing on the ground.

More followed. They swarmed from the castle impossibly fast, holding their bejeweled swords high in the air as they lumbered after her.

Haven sprinted, her heart thrashing in cadence with her legs. Near the front courtyard, the horses reared against their leads and whinnied, stamping the air with their front hooves.

Only twenty feet. She could make that.

Nearly there, she heard a *twang*. Something streaked by her cheek. An arrow. They came from the arrow loops above.

More whizzed by, darkening the sky and impaling the courtyard, petal-less flowers sprouting from the mud.

As the wave of arrows rained from above, the sound reminded her of a horde of angry hornets awakening from their nest.

If only they were, she thought bitterly, bracing beneath a fallen beam propped against the castle.

The Sun Lord appeared from seemingly nowhere, dodging arrows, his face enraged and his cloak streaming behind him. His murderous gaze locked on her.

Runes! Ignoring his infuriated look, Haven pulled out her scythes and flipped around, knocking more arrows from the air as she backed toward her horse.

One grazed her arm. She cried out, though she hardly felt the sting, warm blood trickling down the back of her arm.

The other Solis poured from the doorway. Surai's jade cloak fanned out as she spun around, katana blades flashing. Rook snarled from the doorway, her hackles raised and ears flattened on her head.

"Nice of you to join us," Archeron breathed into Haven's ear, his furious voice promising retribution.

Her lips parted, a snarky response forming on her tongue. But one look at Archeron, the quiet rage inside his eyes, and she decided against it.

A grunting moan drew her attention to the door just as the djinn burst into the courtyard, the stones around the doorway exploding in mortar and dust.

The Solis spread out, Archeron joining them.

With a sigh, Haven retrieved her crossbow and loaded the deck, wrinkling her nose at the creature's carrion odor.

"Aren't you pretty?" she growled, aiming the bead of her sight on its other eye.

The djinn's bulging head dropped just as she released her quarrels, and the bolts clattered uselessly against the wall.

Growling, she tried again, but her arrows were lost in the piles of loose flesh around its chest and shoulder. Other than a low snarl, the Netherworld demon hardly seemed fazed.

Nethergates! Drawing her scythes, she spun into the action, dancing around the beast's thick legs in quick movements that confused it.

In. Slash. Out.

Her boots slipped in the gore that slopped off the creature's body. A tangy, dead stench burned up her nose, and she nearly vomited.

They worked together to injure the demon until everything became a blur of teeth, claws, and wobbly, overripe flesh.

When Haven would draw back, a Solis would take her place, only staying in the djinn's range long enough to strike. This gruesome dance seemed to go on for an eternity.

Finally, Haven leapt back and folded over, braced on her knees as her heart hammered inside her skull. Her lungs burned, and her shoulders ached from swinging her blades. "How do we kill this thing?"

Surai lunged forward, quick as lightning, plunging her sword deep into the demon's side. Nothing. Not even a growl. "We can't—not without magick!"

"Then what are we doing?"

"Trying to slow it down so we can escape!"

Panting, Haven peered up at the djinn. That would take forever. There was too much flesh and not enough time.

An arrow whizzed by her head as a reminder. The djinn's arrival had slowed the arrows and the attacking skeleton army, but a quick glance back at the courtyard and the approaching skeletons told her they'd gotten over the surprise.

"We have a problem!" Haven yelled.

"Stop pointing out . . . the obvious," Archeron snarled between breaths, "and make . . . yourself useful."

She straightened, cracking her neck as she eyed the djinn. The scythes weren't working; that was clear. An ax would hardly make a dent. Her sword was shattered into a hundred pieces by magick. Her magick.

Magick that can't be accessed because of the runetowers.

Yet she still felt something. A tiny seed of energy buried deep in her core.

The more she thought about the pulse of power, the more she sensed it. As if her mind alone could make it grow. Could stretch out the dark threads she felt sprouting from its surface.

Black and spidery threads weaving through her insides . . .

As if it knew it had gotten her attention, she heard it whispering, calling to her, begging for life. For a purpose.

Wake me, it implored. *Use me. Be useful. Show them you are not inferior. Prove that you are more than just an ordinary, weak mortal.*

A roar startled Haven from her thoughts.

She looked in time to see the djinn rake Rook with its claws, sending her crashing into the wall.

Staggering to her paws, the injured cat stumbled then dropped to the cobblestones. Blood spurted from a gash on her chest.

More arrows rained to the ground, clattering off the stones.

They were out of time.

Be useful.

Focusing on the kernel of ice lodged in her core, Haven imagined it growing, pulsing outward. She nurtured it with the promise of release. The promise of demon blood.

Frost spread along her ribcage, giving form to her anger and hopelessness until a cold, hard fist of energy formed, fingers of ice shooting down her arms and into her hands.

Her fingertips tingled. Her flesh became numb. But her insides burned and burned with icy-fire.

We demand death, the voice whispered. *Give it to us.*

But a smaller, more rational voice inside her warned this magick was different. Colder. Darker. Twisted. Like the magick inside the castle. Like the kind inside the Shade Lord.

It wanted more, demanded more than she could ever give.

Yet, all it wanted was blood—the demon's blood. How could that be harmful?

Besides, in this moment, all she cared about was saving the Solis and eradicating the guilt that plagued her heart. She had left them. Had run from a fight like a coward.

Now she would make up for that betrayal.

For an eerie moment, the world seemed to pause and go silent. Electricity danced along her fingertips, lighting up the night. A bluish-black flame of power, of rage and darkness and unspeakable evil.

And then someone was coming at her. A voice demanding she stop.

Archeron.

But she hardly heard him. Her power roaring for release . . . for its promise of blood.

With an explosive crack, magick spewed from her fingers into the djinn. The demon howled, a screeching, gut-curdling noise. Its flesh bubbled and writhed, pouring outward, growing, as if all of its victims were trying to claw through its skin.

She turned away and said the word to close the door. "Paramatti."

The others jumped back, their gaze flicking to Haven, and she realized the bright-blue magick was still pouring from her fingers. Her chest felt as if an ice block was lodged beneath her sternum, so cold it burned.

More, the voice hissed. *We require more. Let us have the others.*

Bjorn grabbed her shoulder, shaking her, hard. "Repeat this now. Victari!"

Don't listen, it whispered. *They want to take your power.*

"Haven," Bjorn growled, his sharp voice cutting through the whisper. "Stop before it kills you."

"Vict—" Her throat shuddered as if the magick was trying to strangle her. Maybe it was. Curling her fingers into claws, she summoned all the energy she had left and gasped, "Victari!"

The blue lightning sputtered out with a *hiss.* Warmth washed over her body. She sagged into Bjorn's arms, head spinning, deep gasps escaping her throat as her vision blurred.

Why was the air suddenly thin and hard to breathe?

Archeron grabbed the other side of her, his fingers tight around her arm, and together they dragged her to the horses, her boots thumping over every cobblestone.

Without looking at the Sun Lord, she knew he was still furious by his stiff grasp and the callous way he dragged her.

She rolled her eyes up to look at Bjorn. "Why didn't the door close?"

Bjorn didn't even glance at her as he said, "Because that wasn't light magick, you fool. You opened a door to the Netherworld and conjured dark magick."

Her mouth fell open with shock.

"Stop blathering and walk faster," Archeron muttered, glancing over his shoulder at the djinn.

Haven did the same, her head wobbly and heavy on her neck. The djinn was ten times its original size and still growing. Swelling like a bloated corpse left out in the sun. Its waxy skin bubbled and stretched . . .

As she watched, a horrible splitting sound came from the djinn's body, like ripping flesh. And then . . . it exploded.

"Watch out!" But her cry did nothing to prevent the rain of putrid flesh and half-digested bones from covering them.

Globs of warm, gooey stuff stuck to Haven's face and neck. The filth was in her hair. It weighted down her fallen hood and coated her tunic and pants.

Acrid vomit splattered up her throat; she was going to be sick.

All at once, her body went boneless; she landed on her knees, bent over, and purged her stomach on Archeron's polished knee-high boots.

Once. Twice. Three times.

When her stomach finally calmed, she braved a glance up at Archeron, but his murderous scowl scared her gaze back to his boots—now covered in Bjorn's runed stew.

"Finished?"

One could slice apples on his sharp, angry voice. She wiped an arm over her mouth and nodded.

Without so much as an, *are you okay?* Archeron dragged her to her feet. This time he held her out at a distance, his scowl apparent in her periphery.

Nethergates! What did she have to do to prove herself worthy? Take out an army?

As soon as the thought entered her mind, she remembered the skeleton army that wanted them dead. Except the entire gruesome court had halted.

All at once, the skeletons froze and bowed low as the ghastly crowd parted. Only one figure came forward.

The Skeleton Queen.

TWENTY-FIVE

Even without flesh to soften her features, the queen was more regal than Haven could ever be.

She strode forward, all high, bony cheekbones and grace, shoulders back and chin held high. A gold chain circled her skull, a bright ruby flashing over her forehead. Onyx gemstones glinted over her bodice. The back of her midnight gown slithered over cobblestones like a silken shadow.

She stopped a few feet from them.

But her eyes—if one could call them that—were locked onto Archeron. He had gone completely still, except for the heaving of his chest.

His face—covered in gore—could have been chiseled from marble for all the emotions it displayed.

And yet, she knew buried pain when she saw it. The quiver of his jaw. His curled fists. The way he didn't blink, his gaze never leaving the queen.

That's when Haven noticed the smaller necklace around the queen's bony neck. A teardrop-shaped glass vial hung from a fine gold chain, and it rested just above her sternum.

The delicate glass held a tiny red flower, similar to Archeron's cerulean bloom.

As Avaline slowly closed the gap between them, the two pendants lifted in the air and were drawn together, radiating red-and-blue tendrils that tangled together to form a purple swirl of light.

What in the Netherworld?

Bjorn, apparently reading her questioning thoughts, leaned into her ear. "The Heart Oath. Your people have a ring, I believe?"

She wiped at a lump of something vomit-worthy sliding down her neck, resolving to keep her walls up. "Archeron and the queen are engaged?"

"More like bound by magick."

"What do you mean?"

"When a Solis is born, we're given a sacred heart flower. Once you choose someone to spend your life with, your sacred flowers are bound together in magick."

She shifted on her feet. "And, if the oath is unbound?"

A grim smile. "There is no way to unbind the Heart Oath. It may be severed, but at great cost."

That sounded a lot like marriage, she thought.

But her snappy response died in her throat as the Skeleton Queen turned her dark gaze on Haven. Bony fingers scraped tight around the jeweled hilt of her longsword. The dark pools inside her eye sockets assessed Haven with the intensity of a hungry feline.

"She's not the enemy, Avaline," the Sun Lord said in a hushed, soothing tone, the way you would speak to a confused lover. "That battle is over. Remember?"

The Skeleton Queen was close enough Haven could count the sapphires inside her black crown and see the dark cuts in her ribcage—battle scars from another time.

There was a rush of air as her skeletal wings spread behind her, the ancient, twisted bones that once held flesh cracking.

Archeron took a step closer to the cursed queen. "Look at me, Ava. Your war is over. You don't need to hurt this mortal girl— foolish and annoying as she may be."

Haven bristled at his slight but kept still, her breathing shallow.

Avaline's neck bones creaked as she looked from Archeron to Haven, slowly, so very slowly. Despite the queen having no eyes and no lips, she was obviously assessing Haven the way a queen might appraise an adversary.

Snapping her wings closed, Avaline turned and glided back to her ghoulish court. As she led them inside the castle, a hundred bones rattling the night, the tension in Haven's shoulders and back melted away, leaving her weak and tired. So tired. But also, ecstatic they had survived.

And that she might have played a small part in that.

Her horse was warm, and the second she slid across the saddle, he darted for the gate along with the others. It took her a moment to realize she was inside the horse's mind, controlling him.

Her lungs expanded, sucking in greedy chunks of air. Free, she was free!

Grinning, she forced the gelding into a gallop, cold air washing over her face, riding him hard until she noticed the others had slowed.

Only then did she relax her grip on his mind and allow him a break. They both needed it. Her body felt weighted down with sand; just lifting her head was a chore.

Shadeling Below, what she wouldn't give for a bath and a

feather bed right about now.

Still, her lips stretched into a proud grin as she joined the Solis. She had just done two things she wasn't supposed to do as a lowly mortal. Magick, and soulbinding an animal.

And both felt glorious.

As she flicked a weary gaze to Archeron, ignoring the vomit drying on his boots, she expected him to be impressed.

She had, after all, saved them.

Except his face didn't look impressed. Not in the slightest. His golden cheeks were tight with barely suppressed rage, his cupid's-bow lips puckered. A vein popped in his forehead.

He wheeled his horse in circles around her, his eyes unblinking as they carved into her. "Do you know what you've done, Mortal?"

Her jaw hung open. He was impossible to please! "I don't know. Saved us?"

Growling, he forced his horse faster and faster around her, churning the sand, the poor beast rearing and pawing the air as if he could feel the Sun Lord's rage.

Haven popped out her chin and stretched. Could he be any more dramatic?

Finally, he ground his mare to a halt and faced Haven, his hands clenching and unclenching at his sides. "Was it worth it?"

Haven's mind went to the runestones in her pocket. She nearly played dumb—yet something about his quiet, dangerous tone, the way Rook limped beside them and Surai avoided Haven's gaze—made her tell the truth.

"No." She tried to swallow, but her throat clenched tight. "I didn't mean for Rook to get hurt."

"No? What did you think would happen when you stole the runestones and woke the djinn, then left us to deal with it?"

She rubbed a thumb over her temple, shrinking beneath his

glower. The plan seemed better in hindsight. "I didn't think that would wake the demon."

"You don't think. That's the problem!" He raked his fingers through his slimed hair. "I said 'Don't use magick,' and you used magick. I said, 'Don't steal the runestones,' and you stole the runestones."

"You never said not to steal them," she pointed out, unable to resist. "Only that you thought I might."

For a moment, she thought he would jump from his horse and murder her. His eyes were stretched wide with rage, the vein throbbing across his forehead and temple like a snake.

His voice doubled her fears as he growled low and soft-like, "It was *implied*."

"I'm sorry, okay?" Haven glanced over at Surai. She hated this feeling, this guilt. Yet no matter how hard she pushed it down, it came back up like a bubble beneath the surface of a lake. "It won't happen again. You can even"—she gritted her teeth—"you can have the runestones back."

She swore she could hear his teeth grinding as his emerald eyes bored into her. "Perhaps where you come from, Mortal, a couple magick stones can make up for hurting someone's family. But not in mine."

It took all her energy not to roll her eyes. Goddess Above, it seemed there was no slaking his anger! "Just get me through the Bane, and you will never see me again."

He shook his head. "You still have no idea what you've done, do you?"

Dread snaked down her spine, making her joke when all she wanted to do was hide. "What? Is inadvertently covering a Solis in demon-guts a crime?"

"You are the most selfish, stubborn creature I have ever met!

Shadeling Below, you're worse than a chinga." He waved his hand in a dismissive gesture. "The Devourers can have you."

A sinking feeling swirled around her belly. "Devourers? Why would they. . ."

"Want you? You are a mortal with both dark and light magick, and since you felt compelled to use your magick, again, after I explicitly told you not to, now they know it, and they will absolutely demand you as the price of our crossing."

All the breath had been sucked from her lungs. *Damius.* She tried to protest, to form the words that would change his mind, but someone had her arms and they were forcing them into binds.

No! She couldn't go back to him! She wouldn't!

She struggled, shoulders straining and popping with effort, but she was weak from using magick, and Bjorn was stronger.

Her mind raced as she tried to once again conjure magick, but there was nothing to use. And even if there was, she had no idea how to call it or bend it to her will.

When Bjorn was done, he gave her a sad smile. "You can try all you want to use dark magick now, but the runed willow vines that bind you make it impossible."

Bound, pissed, starving, and covered in demon-slime, Haven writhed and bucked and kicked against her restraints like a wild animal.

She tumbled face first off her horse into the sand more than a few times.

Each time, one of the Solis would calmly stop and chuck her back on her horse as she wiggled, bit, and whatever else she thought might help her escape.

She cursed them, all of them. She called Archeron every foul name in existence. She promised to rain Netherfire and death on their heads.

All to no avail.

As the morning wore on, the sun burned her cheeks and her starvation became nearly unbearable, one thought pulsed inside her skull, a song of survival.

She had to fight back. To escape. If she let the Devourers have her, she would be dead in a day—or worse. There was always worse.

After all, her old master, Damius, wasn't one to forgive.

TWENTY-SIX

Bell shrank back against the cold stone wall of his cell, every muscle in his body corded with panic. The hunched figure prowling through the hole toward him filled half the room with his massive girth, blocking the steady howl of the wind as he dumped snow from his cloak onto the floor.

Bell's gaze darted over the figure. Where were his wings?

But there was only a bulge in the back of his cloak, too low to be wings, and the dark fabric was shabby, rips torn into the silk, as if a great beast had once clawed down his side.

Recognition shot through him. This was the man who fought back against the other Noctis.

No, not man. The Shade Lord had called him creature, so he was something else.

The creature paused. Deep shadows from his hood veiled his face, and yet, Bell could feel the thing studying him. A deep breath hissed from the creature, almost like a sigh, and it held out its arm, exposing worn black gloves stretched over a massive hand.

"Come," it said, less a word than a commanding growl.

Bell swallowed. Seconds ago, he would have done nearly anything to leave this frozen room. But now, fear flowed through his veins instead of ice, and his shivers had turned to spasms of terror.

What if this . . . this thing was trying to trick him? What if it wanted his magick like the others?

The creature thrust out its arm again, sending Bell flat against the wall. "Come." When Bell hesitated, it made a frustrated grunt that bounced off the stone walls. "Or would you rather stay here and freeze to death?"

Bell watched his breath plume out in a frosty cloud, wondering what it would feel like to die in such a way. Would it be painful? Or would his organs simply shut down one by one, a quiet, painless death?

"The Shade Queen wouldn't let me die," he insisted, pushing away his morbid thoughts. "At least, not before . . . you know."

A guttural laugh tore the air. "It would not be the first time." The creature watched Bell a moment more and then went to leave. "Fine. Freeze to death. What do I care?"

"Wait," Bell said, despising the fear in his voice. "Don't leave me."

The creature paused as Bell forced himself to take a step forward, then another, until he was within a foot of the beast. His heart was ramming his sternum, but if the creature was going to steal his magick and drain his blood, it would have already done so.

"I . . . I'll go."

Bell realized he hadn't even asked where they were going—not that it mattered. Anything was better than this icy tomb. And once they were outside the castle walls, he could escape.

The creature was the first through the crack. Cold blasts of wind slammed Bell's cheeks as he started after it . . . and froze. He thought there would be handholds, a ledge, something, anything to hold onto.

Instead, his gaze slid over midnight-black obsidian covered in a sheet of ice gleaming under the strange moonlight.

With an impatient snarl, the creature leaned down from the spire of the roof and grasped Bell by his collar. A gasp hissed from his throat as he was plucked from his perch and tucked against the creature's enormous shoulder.

And then the creature was leaping across turrets and spires, stone shingles crumbling beneath his feet and disappearing into the misty void.

Bell's belly churned; he was going to be sick.

Don't look down.

But he did, despite the fear making breathing impossible.

Maybe, just maybe, there was something below that would help him escape. A bridge from the castle he hadn't noticed. A surrounding kingdom close by.

But there was nothing save mist. Lots of it. The dirty gray shroud covered everything, swelling the lower stretches of roof and submerging the bottom half of the dark castle.

So he shut his eyes and focused on the sounds of the creature's grunting pants instead.

Real brave, Bellamy, he scolded himself, taking stock of his situation. He imagined the creature slipping. Imagined the absolutely idiotic look on his own face as he fell to his death, cradled by this monstrous *thing*.

Maybe the king's painters would commemorate his absurd death with a painting titled *The Cowardly Prince Bellamy's Ignominious Death.*

Finally, when the jolting stopped, Bell allowed his eyes to

open. A long roofline stretched out beneath them. This section of the castle was in ruins, a giant chasm where once there were chambers and life.

From here, the only way to get to the last section of the castle was by a thin extension of stone, the only remaining wall left holding the two wings of the castle together.

On the other side, dim firelight trickled from the collapsed corner, reminding Bell he was bone-cold, his fingers numb and tingling. He watched his breath crystalize over the creature's shoulder and disappear into the night.

The wall ended. A misty, too-big hole gaped between here and the fire-lit chambers on the other side. Without pause, the creature leapt over the expanse, sending Bell's heart into his stomach.

They landed with a thud on the lip of the dwelling, and Bell tumbled from the beast's arms in a heap of frozen limbs.

Without even glancing down to see if Bell was injured, the brutish creature began prowling through the house. Steadying his numb legs, Bell managed to get to his feet.

Then he watched opened-mouthed as the beast summoned fires inside the hearths. But his awe was replaced by gratefulness as blessed warmth crept over him, and he rushed to the closest fireplace, slumping onto the soot-stained ledge.

Now that—that was magick. He thrust his hands as close as he could to the fire, uncurling his fingers to let the heat catch them. Smokeless flames of red and gold sent sparks spiraling to the ceiling.

"Are you paying attention?" he muttered to his hands. "That's what you're supposed to do. It's called magick."

Metal clanging came from somewhere down the hall. But Bell was only half paying attention.

While the creature pounded up and down the hallways, snarling and huffing, Bell took in what he assumed was its home.

Snowflakes drifted in from the crumbled wall in the corner, but the rest of the abode looked intact, a stark difference from the dark, eerie castle on the other side. Faded damask wallpaper curled from the walls, an enormous chandelier dripped crystals and cobwebs, and beige sheets draped over all the furniture, covered in years' worth of dust.

Running his reanimated fingers through his curls, which were damp with melted snowflakes, he whistled in appreciation. This place must have once been gorgeous. Even the fireplace spoke of wealth, the grimy moonstone tiles veined with amber and flecked with gold.

Above the fireplace, a jeweled rose glittered beneath a veil of cobwebs. With a little cleaning, he could see himself here in front of the fire, reading books with Haven.

Too bad he would leave soon . . . tonight, even. If the creature left him alone long enough to flee.

"Take this."

Bell spun around at the gruff voice, nearly falling into the fire. The creature held out a silver-gilt tureen on a tray, roses cresting the lid.

It was cold against Bell's fingertips, and empty, he discovered once he lifted the lid. He opened his mouth to ask, but a quick nod from the creature and the bowl filled with steaming yellow broth.

Heat from the broth bled through the delicate bowl into Bell's fingertips, and he looked from the bowl to the creature, flicking up an eyebrow. "How do I eat this?"

From behind the dark shadows over his face came a grunt. The creature held his gloved hands palms up, as if a bowl rested in them, and brought the imaginary bowl to what Bell assumed was a mouth.

"Right." Tilting the tureen, he took a scalding sip, cringing at the desperate way he gulped down the searing liquid.

If only his father could see him now. Beaten and filthy. Chugging magickal broth from a polished tureen like a grateful dog, happy to warm himself with magick fire beside a faceless creature.

Dog—one of many insults the creatively challenged Renk came up with. *Haven's dog. Haven's pet. Woof. Woof.*

Bell quickly finished the bowl, the warmth thawing the last bits of frost clinging to his bones.

"It should be freezing in here," he said, glancing over at the wall of stars in the corner. "How does it stay warm?"

"Spells and runes," the creature said, waving his arm as if it was nothing. He shifted on his feet. "So, you're warm. You're fed. There are rooms in the back; choose any one you like. You may stay here until they summon you."

"Thank you," Bell said, his hopes rising. A room meant privacy. And privacy meant escape. "But won't the Shade Queen come looking for me?"

"She doesn't need to," the creature said, his voice like two rocks grinding together. "There are no unguarded entries or exits to Spirefall, except by air. And even if you somehow managed to sprout wings, the Queen has already claimed you with magick. She can track you anywhere. There's no way for you to escape your fate."

Bell snorted a bitter laugh. "Fate? So that's what this is? Because I was thinking it was just my really shitty luck."

The creature stared at him from behind a shadowy mask, an unsympathetic statue, and Bell suddenly wanted to break down his barriers and make him talk to him.

"You should know that about me. I'm quite possibly the unluckiest mortal alive."

Nothing. The creature didn't even blink in response.

"What?" Bell snapped, gasping for air. "No reply?"

"I'm not here to entertain you, Prince."

"Entertain? Oh, that's . . . that's funny." Bell's voice had gone two octaves higher. "All I require from you is answers. Please. I've—I've seen the curse-sick. I know what happens when all your magick is drained. I . . ."

He sucked in a breath. Blasted room was too hot. And too small. His chest too tight to breathe.

The creature retreated a step, sending Bell's heart into a tailspin. The thought of being left alone, even by this cold *thing*, was terrifying.

He wrenched at his collar, gasping. "Please. Don't go. Just tell me. What will they do to me? When will it happen?"

For a stretched-out second, the creature said nothing. Then he spun around and strode down the hall, his heavy footfalls shaking the room.

Right before he disappeared, he paused, growling, "I don't like to be disturbed. Please, keep to this end. And if you must cry, keep it quiet."

Bell's hands clenched around the empty tureen as he stared after the creature, his panting breaths in time with his racing heart. The room spun and spun.

His body hiccupped and jerked, as if he couldn't decide whether to laugh or sob. He had traded one prison for another. This prison may have food and warm fires, but the end result was the same.

At some unspecified time, he would be dragged in front of the

Noctis, and the Shade Queen's daughter, Ravenna, would drain the magick from his body.

Then, according to legend and Magewick, she would rip out his heart.

Goddess Above. His *heart*.

Bell stumbled. The muscles of his stomach clenched, curling his spine into a sharp C. The bowl slipped from his fingers and clanged across the stone, but it sounded so very far away as he dropped to his knees, every bit of broth in his stomach spewing onto the floor.

TWENTY-SEVEN

Tied atop her horse, Haven settled into the injustice of her situation with dramatic flourish. Once again she was a prisoner. Stripped of her dignity and honor. Forced to kneel and obey the Sun Lord's sadistic whims.

She kept busy by biting her cheeks to stay awake as the afternoon sun filtered through the grimy haze and scorched her cheeks.

Terrified they would hand her over to Damius while she slept, she focused on channeling her fury at the pretty Sun Lord's swaying back to keep her mind occupied on other, more pleasurable things.

Like revenge.

Yet, no matter how many times in her mind his exquisite linen tunic burst into flames, or his thick golden hair turned into angry vipers, nothing happened.

As if he felt her savage stare, he would glance back, sweat beading his pale hairline and emerald eyes glittering.

Sometimes, he even dared lob her a feline smile.

Motherless bastard! His posture was indulgent, his smooth golden fingers resting on his thighs, the relaxed shoulders and back of a man not bound to his horse and occasionally gagged.

Gagged, for rune sake.

The indignant thought turned her murderous, and she poked her tongue around her mouth, still dry and bruised from the gorgeous silk scarf Archeron had forced into her mouth.

She had called him the motherless son of a coward, blah, blah, blah, and worse, even. But the final insult was the gentle way he wedged it between her teeth.

It made the act seem somehow less invasive, less murder-worthy.

In between her fiery fantasies, Haven slipped from reality to daydreams. Unwelcome snippets from her past. A past she considered all but buried inside her nightmares until this morning.

She would blink, when suddenly russet blood mountains would grow from the sand, hulking monstrosities veined red and black, and the nightmare that plagued her every night for years was right in front of her.

Just the colors of the Northern Bane, the heavy reds and foul blacks, the endless granite mountains and choking haze, made her feel like she was six all over again. A slave in a strange, horrible place.

"Where have all the colors gone?" Those were the first words she ever said to Damius Rathbone, in Solissian because he didn't understand her native tongue, and everyone understood Solissian.

They were inside a huge tent etched with runes to protect them from the Curse, the harsh Bane winds battering the thin fabric and sending her heart racing.

Cloaked in scarlet linen, his mouth and nose covered in the

Devourer's black mask, Damius looked like a demon risen from the bloody sands.

Like most of the crossbreeds in the camp that touted Noctis blood, what she assumed were disfigured wings mounded beneath his kaftan, making him appear slightly hunch-backed.

He knelt before her. She was drawn to the color of his eyes. Pale, filmy blue. Streaked red, like the sand. The sun had shriveled his skin to old, dried out leather, but it was still pale as the moon.

"Who are you, little rose girl?" His voice was a rasping whisper that wedged deep into her bones. "Why does the Sun Lord who sold you to me think you are worth thirty runestones?"

Tears sprang to her eyes as she struggled to answer correctly. Something inside her, the same thing that had allowed her to survive up to then, said it was important. That she should appease him. "I don't . . . I don't know."

He blinked with unreadable eyes, but she could already tell somehow she had answered wrong.

"Thirty runestones. That's what you owe me." He reached for her, and she flinched as his fingers twined intimately through her long mane of rose-gold hair. "Until I have all thirty stones, you belong to me, Rose."

Haven had never understood the true meaning of slavery until then. Of being owned, being told your name, when to speak, when to eat, when to cry, when to breathe.

When Damius asked, she crawled through the blistering sands. And he did ask. Often.

When he called her new name, Rose, she ran. When he spoke, she flinched and listened with sweaty palms and a churning belly.

When he invaded her mind, peeling her insides apart, she gave in to him.

When he ordered, she obeyed.

Damius taught Haven many things. Survival. Negotiating. The runic arts.

But the most important lesson he ever taught her was that she'd rather die than be a slave to anyone ever again.

Haven came back to reality with a gasp. Her skin was clammy and cold, ridged with gooseflesh despite the heat from the desert sun. Her gut clenched, and she swallowed down a wave of nausea as panic surged through her chest.

I can't return to Damius.

Straining against her bindings, she drank in the landscape. They were traveling on the side of a mountain. Rocks kicked loose from the horses' hooves clattered down the cliff at least a hundred feet below.

Haven's head grew dizzy as she followed them down, down, *down,* to the city of Manassas, a sprawling haze of ruddy adobe buildings that spread to the horizon.

And in the distance rose the Bloodbone Mountains, exactly as imposing and horrible as she remembered.

Suddenly, her lungs seemed too small, her throat too tight. A bridge spanning a fathomless chasm between the Bane and the Ruinlands was just beyond. That was where the trade would happen. Where they would cross the crack in the realm that released monsters from the Netherworld below.

The Devourers controlled the bridge. Anyone brave enough to cross it had to pay the toll, usually in the form of runestones.

Today, I'm the toll.

Nethergates! She wiggled her wrists, grimacing as the willow vine rubbed her tender flesh, but she was bound too tight.

A growl rose deep in her chest. Scowling, she flicked a glance over her companions. Rook rode a few feet ahead, hunched over Aramaya, arms loose and head lolling to the side. A sickly greenish-white tint colored her clammy, sweat-slick skin.

Surai sat behind Rook, arms clasped tightly around her waist to keep her lover from falling.

A flicker of guilt found Haven. The djinn wouldn't have attacked if Haven hadn't stolen the runestones. Surai hadn't said as much—she was too kind—but that didn't make it any less true.

Shaking her head, she pushed the feeling aside.

Bell—she needed to focus on Bell. Nothing else was her concern.

When the city was behind them and they felt the cool shadow of the bluffs, Archeron let them rest. Haven eyed the leather flasks of water they drank from with envy, her parched throat shuddering.

Adding to her mistreatment, they left her on her horse, bound, back aching and butt sore, while they stretched their legs.

Netherworld take them. She was Haven Ashwood. She could get off her own damn horse.

Blinking grit from her eyes, she swung a leg over and slid to the ground. As soon as her boots hit the sand, Archeron calmly strolled over, picked her up by the waist, and hauled her back onto her horse.

"Stay." Emerald eyes cut to her, bright against the dullness of the Bane. They held an unmistakable warning.

"No." She slid back to the ground, landing with a grunt.

A honey-gold lock of hair slid over his forehead as he pinned her against the horse. "Stay," he ordered through gritted teeth, his warm breath fluttering her eyelashes. "Or I will tie you to the saddle like an elk carcass."

From her periphery, Haven noticed the others watching with curious faces.

"No," she spat. "Here, I'll say it in your language to make it clearer. Niat. Niat. Niat. Niat!"

"Stubborn creature!" His hands pinched around her waist as he started to lift her—

With a quick thrust, she jammed her forehead into his jaw, sending him sprawling back. Then she exploded after him, ramming her body into his torso, screaming like a wild animal.

Goddess Above, it was like slamming into a slab of rock. They tumbled to the sand in a hot, muscly heap.

For a breath, she lay there, arms throbbing as they twisted behind her back, cheek flat against his heaving chest.

Then she leapt to her feet and darted across the sand.

TWENTY-EIGHT

Two feet—Haven made it two whole Nether-frigging-feet before Archeron caught her from behind.

Her head snapped back as he tackled her, forcing her to the ground. Rolling, she tried to kick him, but he secured her legs beneath his armpit and then turned her back onto her face.

Hot sand wedged in her mouth, nose, and eyes. She coughed, spitting more sand and blood than saliva.

Sand crunched as he leaned down by her face. Soft breath warmed her cheek and ear. "Shadeling help me," he seethed in a breathy growl, "if Rook dies before we can trade you to the Devourers for the cure and safe passage, I will hold you personally responsible."

She cringed from his anger, adrenaline scorching her veins. "Motherless pig! I'm not a bag of runestones you can trade!"

"Watch me!" He marched away then spun around. A vein throbbed in his forehead, his bottom lip dripping blood. "You . . ." His fists curled by his slender hips, the muscles in his forearms cording. "You . . ."

A growl ripped from his throat as he stalked away, too furious to even finish his thought.

Haven's jaw hung open as she stumbled to her feet, adding sand to the grime coating her flesh. The others immediately turned around, ignoring Archeron as he stomped dust into the air and paced.

Tears of fury and frustration stung Haven's eyes. *Could Rook really be that ill? Could she . . . die?*

One look at Rook slumped against Surai's shoulder, refusing Surai's attempts to make her drink, told Haven she could.

A sick feeling came over her.

The djinn's claws must hold some sort of poison. Even now, she could see the red, festering flesh streaking Rook's collarbone and slithering up her neck.

Runes. Haven despised regret. It was a useless emotion, serving no purpose but to make one weak. And yet—she couldn't deny the deep sense of regret that filled her chest and tore at her mind.

She would force it down, and it would pop back up, stronger, heavier, until she couldn't deny that part of her knew the decision to steal the runestones and break the deal had been wrong.

In her turmoil, she hadn't noticed Surai until she was a few steps away. Haven stiffened, searching the Solis girl's face for anger or hatred.

Inexplicably, Haven cared what Surai thought of her. More so, she wanted them to be friends.

After quietly appraising Haven, Surai lifted her flask and pressed the rim to Haven's lips.

"Drink," Surai ordered softly in Solissian.

Haven gulped greedy swallows, despite the shame that pinched her insides, her raw throat cooling as the water slid over it.

When she was done, water wet her chin and dribbled down her neck. "Thank you."

"Umath." Surai tucked a black strand behind her ear as her worried gaze drifted to Rook.

"I'm sorry about Rook." As soon as the words left her lips, Haven felt the truth of her statement. The horrible, stupid truth. "Is it true the Devourers hold a cure?"

"Possibly," Surai said, without taking her eyes from her lover. "The only known cure for a djinn's poison is vorgrath venom."

Haven's eyebrows knitted together. Every living creature had a poison and an antidote. The Devourers relied on raven's blood for the Solis, but Noctis poison was rare in the Bane.

Even with Damius's established trade routes, flowers and their essence were hard to come by here, and most was useless. By the time the flowers traveled this far north, the dark magick of the Curse destroyed whatever light magick they possessed.

Instead, the Devourers relied on vorgrath's venom, which was enough to incapacitate anything breathing long enough to finish the job, even the Noctis.

The venom was rare and incredibly precious, but Damius always had a small supply on hand.

"Surai, listen to me. The Devourers have vorgrath venom, that's true. But Damius . . . the Devourers will take one look at Rook and realize how desperately you need it. They will ask for both me and the runestones and will only offer the venom in return."

Surai's hand fluttered over her throat. "You do not know Archeron—"

"But I know the Devourers. They worship the Shade Queen, and they hate the Solis for helping banish her to the Netherworld. You might save Rook, but you will not buy safe passage across the bridge."

Surai chewed her lip as she slowly twisted the cap back on her flask. "Why are you telling me this?"

"Because, if you help me escape, I promise on the Goddess Above I will cross the bridge and get you your venom."

A laugh escaped her lips. "You have never met a vorgrath."

"I came close. In Penryth, I tracked one for weeks until I found the fig tree it was guarding."

Her beautiful eyes, angled at the corners and rimmed in dark lashes, widened, lips parting. "Impressive, Haven. But you never actually caught it. If you had, you wouldn't be here today. They are as cunning as they are lethal."

"I will. Set me free and use the runestones to cross, and I swear Rook will have the venom by dawn."

Haven's chest shuddered as she waited for Surai to agree.

Instead, Surai shook her head. "I do not agree with Archeron's decision, but I refuse to go against him."

"Why? He's a boar! A . . . a tyrannical, puffed up pretty-boy."

Two lines appeared between Surai's thick charcoal eyebrows as she appraised Haven. "For all your skills, Mortal, you know so little. The Sun Lord you see is not Archeron; he is the shattered reflection of my dearest friend, the tortured soul of someone who has lost nearly everything. I will never betray him, but Shadeling help me, I will fight to the death anyone who does."

"Does that include me?"

Surai didn't even hesitate before she said, "That remains to be seen," and strode away.

Nethergates! Haven's hands curled into fists below the vine. She would have to try a different tactic.

Clenching her jaw, she followed Surai to the others, ignoring Archeron's savage stare. "I have to pee."

While the rest ignored her—a now infuriatingly calm

Archeron picking his fingernails with his dagger—Bjorn raised a dark eyebrow. "If you try to sever your binds on a rock, the vine will twist around your arms until your shoulders pop from the sockets. Still need to go?"

"No." She deflated, slumping into her ribcage, her bottom lip poking out. "Surely you see how foolish trading me to the Devourers is?"

Tenting his fingers together, Bjorn closed his eyes for a moment. "The only positive outcome I see is with you bound as we encounter the Devourers' camp. And fire, I see you surrounded by hungry flames of dark magick."

That sounded about as promising as a roomful of Shadowlings. She dumped her body onto a rock beside him, grimacing as her bruised ass came in contact with the sharp granite. "Look, why don't I just use my . . . whatever magick to heal her?"

Bjorn rolled his ivory eyes, somehow making the act look dignified. "This is why you are bound. You know nothing about the powers you somehow possess."

"Speaking of my"—she cleared her throat—"my powers. Any theories on why I have them? I mean, isn't it odd that both Bell and I have magick?"

"Odd, indeed, if the prince truly does possess magick."

"What do you mean?" she demanded, even as the horrifying suspicion she'd been trying to ignore reared its ugly head. "I was there. I saw his powers."

Bjorn ran a thumb over his dark jaw. "And was this before or after you gave him a protection runestone?"

Her heart wedged in her throat. "That doesn't mean anything. The stone couldn't have given him that kind of magick. It only harnesses the magick—you know that."

"Describe the mark."

The quiet tone of his voice crawled beneath her skin. "Two, um . . . two crosses, overlapping, and a spiral through the middle."

His lips pulled into a knowing smile. "That particular rune, besides being outlawed for mortals, protects its owner by drawing magick from the surroundings. Usually, the magick comes from nature. A copse of alders. A few woodland creatures."

Understanding hit her like a punch to the gut. "He channeled my magick?"

"I am sorry."

She released a ragged breath. Bell was locked away, waiting for the Shade Queen to cut out his heart to put inside her daughter, but it was Haven who should have been there. Her who should have been taken. Not Bell.

All the more reason to get out of her binds and break the Curse. "Why? Just tell me why I can't use my magick on Rook? I can save her, then you can let me go, and you'll never see me again."

"There's only one rune mark that would work," Bjorn said. "And you'd surely kill her with your inexperience."

She went to get up, but her gaze was drawn to the mark he was carving in the sand. He didn't look at her, didn't say a word. Just carved the three intertwined circles, dotting the centers with quick stabs of his pointer finger.

When he was done, he swept the mark away.

Why show her a mark she couldn't use? Still, she engraved it into her memory just in case.

As she traipsed back to the horses, arms numb from being bound, she fought to bury the panic burning through her.

There had to be a way to escape her situation. She refused to give up. To go back to being a slave and watching Damius's horrid grin stretch his jaw as he tortured her day by day. Trying to break her. To mold her to his wicked will. To forge her into a weapon.

She lived that future once, and it had nearly killed her.

Now, one way or another, she was going to fight back—
Netherworld take anyone who tried to stop her.

TWENTY-NINE

The Devouring hit when they were halfway down the mountainside, a raging sea of silvery fog spewing from the pits of the Netherworld. As it crashed over the Devourers' camp, obliterating four rows of sand-colored tents, a slight tremble started in Haven's chest until her entire body quietly shook.

Why now? The Devouring always came at night, and the last time she checked, the sun still blazed behind a curtain of filthy haze.

Something's wrong here.

A moment later, they were immersed in freezing clouds of gray. Haven watched her frosty breath plume out, the startling Curse smell of bergamot, cinnamon, and blood watering her eyes.

All at once, the breeze died.

With the fog came the silence. Broken only by their horses' hooves clacking over rock and the occasional pebbles clattering down the steep shale. She strained to pick out other noises that would warn of Shadowlings lurking, her mind racing to orient herself without her vision.

Closing her eyes, she pulled in a ragged breath and reconstructed her surroundings from memory. Tents rose against the darkness of her eyelids, cobbled together with all patterns of colorful fabric, some long and elaborate, others small and circular. Most had been bleached by the sun and stained brownish red from the haze.

Damius's pavilion rose in the center, by far the largest. Set away from the camp—along the chasm separating the Ruinlands from the Bane—were the trading tents, gambling dens, and the last little pavilion, a slouched purple tent where Damius kept the whoring slaves.

An invisible vice squeezed her chest as she remembered all the times he threatened to send her there.

Goddess Above, the women inside the tent were pitiful. Covered head-to-toe in red sheets, only their eyes showed. Empty eyes, devoid of life. Unable to leave the ratty little tent, they lived off buckets of filthy water and the men's slop.

Most days they starved.

Her eyes snapped open. She tried to swallow, but her throat was raw and papery, each icy breath like swallowing a horde of hornets.

The tents rose from the murk; she could feel the eyes peering from the small spy holes cut into the canvas, between the exotic Shadowling pelts lining the walls, all scales and musty black fur.

Runechimes clanged from somewhere in the camp, startling their already skittish horses who blew out nervous, milky breaths and hopped at every little noise.

The Devourers would be lurking behind their runed canvas walls. Watching the band of Solis.

Watching her.

Poking her chin high, she stared right back, surprised that her terror didn't claw its way to her face.

Still, as soon as Damius spotted her, she knew he would see through her brave façade. He would pull her apart, sifting through her insides with dark magick until he found her weaknesses. Her fears—

A wave of nausea slammed into her throat, and she doubled over, yanking her binds as panic threatened to consume her. No! Forcing her body to straighten and pushing her shoulders back, she heaved out a breath.

She was a child when Damius bought her. A lonely, confused girl.

If Damius thought he was getting that girl back, he was wrong.

"I'm not afraid anymore, Master," she growled, and as soon as the words left her lips, they became true.

This girl had escaped him. This girl had survived the Bane, survived imprisonment by a Penrythian King, and scraped her way to the position of Royal Companion Guard.

This girl could soulbind animals. This girl had magick flowing through her veins.

That was what Damius wanted all along. The reason he beat her, tortured her, humiliated her, tried to break her. All for the rare magick he thought she possessed. She'd thought he was crazy. No amount of beating her flesh or breaking her mind had produced anything close to powers.

But maybe her magick had simply waited for the right time.

Now, she had it, but she wouldn't let Damius have *her*.

Grinding her teeth, she twisted her wrists, grunting as the vine wrapped even tighter and she swore she felt her skin split open. The pain shot all the way up her shoulders, eliciting curses for the Sun Lord responsible.

To have a fighting chance, she had to free her wrists, fast. They would be near the bridge soon, where Damius met all travelers to trade for passage.

If Damius got her back, Bell would die horribly at the Shade Queen's hands, and Haven would wish she were dead.

She sighed and whittled her way into her horse's mind. One second she was on the outside, the next, she felt his defenses crumple.

As she slipped in, he neighed, startled, and reared before she felt their minds meld into one. It took all her effort to stay locked on, but after a few heartbeats, her horse relaxed, and she was able to force him close to Archeron.

The Sun Lord had one hand on the runesword at his hip, the other on a sleeve partially hiding five silver throwing daggers. Two longsword hilts made an X behind his head, where they were strapped flat between his shoulder blades.

Every inch of steel shimmered with runes, as did his flesh, the pale silver lines and curves faintly metallic.

Even without his powers, he was imposing. His gaze was cold and hard as it sifted through the fog, and his lips pulled into a feline grin, as if he enjoyed the tension, the whisper of bloodshed.

Fool! At least his bottom lip still bore the mark of her forehead.

As her gelding brushed shoulders with Archeron's mare, he let loose an aggrieved sigh. "Yes?"

"Set me free." Clearing her voice, she gazed down at her saddle pommel and tried to manipulate her voice to sound contrite. "You don't know what Damius will do to me."

"No."

The lazy, arrogant tone of his voice had her imagining violence, and she dug her fingernails into her palms. "Please."

"Hmm . . . no."

A dark shadow darted over Haven's horse, and Surai landed on Archeron's saddle, flapping her wings and cawing. Archeron shooed her away with a dark curse.

Even Rook, shivering and sheened with sweat, a thick, black cloak draped over her shoulders, pleaded with Archeron. "This feels wrong." Her voice was weak and raspy, like paper shredding, panting breaths punctuating each word. "A cure . . . is not worth . . . this . . . darkness."

Archeron's hard mask softened as he glanced at her, his knuckles kneading his thighs. "I will not let you die for her mistakes, Rook."

"She's . . . young, Archeron. Like we used . . . to be." Her dry, chalky lips split in a pained grin. "Remember?"

Without a word, Archeron clicked his tongue and spurred his horse forward into the fog.

Panic was setting in, but Haven refused to believe he would give her over to a monster like Damius if Archeron knew their history. Somehow, she had to make him understand.

Runes and shadowfangs! If only she could soulbind him like her horse!

She straightened her spine. Wait. If he could invade her mind, could she send him her thoughts? Her memories?

Whatever she sent him, it would have to be quick. Already she could see the tall runetotems that circled the trading tents.

She released a breath and searched her memories, digging deep down to the ones she buried. The ones that left her a ragged shell.

Then she shut her eyes and focused on Archeron. His face. His eyes. His arrogant lips. But nothing connected to him, not until she imagined him in the water, laughing a real laugh, his runemarks flashing in the sunlight. She pushed further, deeper, searching for that person beneath the layers of pride and disdain.

All at once, she connected to his mind. There was a spark of surprise, followed by curiosity. When she felt certain Archeron was paying attention, she dragged forward her memory from the recesses of her mind and flung it at him like a weapon.

The memory replayed inside her head too. She'd been locked inside the tiny hut for countless days for an infraction she couldn't remember. She was seven, maybe eight. Her throat was gritted nearly shut, her dry lips splitting open every time they moved. The sharp ache of hunger had long ago become an intense, burning need for water.

When Damius came for her, he dragged her to the edge of the crevasse between the Bane and the Ruinlands, where she'd seen the monsters come from.

The chain constricting her neck jingled with each cruel jerk of his hand.

Vision blurring, she dropped to her knees. The ground ended less than a foot where she crumpled. One look over the edge, down, down into the infinite abyss, the rolling mist and deep dark nothing, turned her stomach to jelly, even as she longed to throw herself into it.

Somewhere in those hellish depths were the two wyvern soulbound to Damius.

And beyond, the Netherworld.

Wailing. Haven's head whipped around to the slave-girl Damius gripped by her long red hair. Cyra. Wide brown eyes stared at Haven, each blink a silent plea. Freckles smattered her delicate cheeks. She was barely older than Haven.

A small cry slipped from Haven's lips, despite her resolve not to let Damius see her squirm. He must have seen her slinking into the pitiful hovel where he kept the rest of the female slaves. Must have known she was sneaking them bits of food and medicine.

Still, she couldn't let him punish Cyra. She was the closest person Haven had to a friend.

"Please," Haven pleaded. "Damius. Don't . . . don't hurt her."

"That is up to you, Rose." Haven recoiled at the new name spoken in Damius's serpentine tongue. "Show me the magick inside you. Just a little taste."

Haven scrunched her eyes tight, the knots in her stomach tightening into a tangled mass. She tried to find it. The magick he swore she had. But she was so weak, so thirsty, her mind swirling like the mist in the chasm below.

Nothing came. She was barren. A failure.

Damius began whistling the tune that haunted her sleep, the one meaning he was displeased, and her heart shoved into her throat. "Wait, please! I can keep trying!"

But he slid his gaze over her, disgust twisting his leathery face, and then he shoved Cyra over the edge of the chasm.

The girl's scream shredded the air and wormed into Haven's eardrums. She went numb. She hardly felt anything when Damius yanked her back to her cell by her hair.

Hardly felt it when he tore through her mind, shredding and digging, growing more agitated as he searched.

Days, weeks passed that way. With Damius desecrating her mind and Cyra's scream ravaging her heart.

Haven gasped back to reality, the memory fading. Did Archeron see it too? Reliving her dark past had stolen some of her calm from earlier, and she worked to steady her breathing.

But it wouldn't have helped much anyway, for as soon as she focused on their surroundings, she saw the Devourers, a circle of nine figures draped in the flowing blood robes worn by all their followers.

The air around them crackled and hissed with dark magick, the smell of blood and cinnamon overpowering. They waited inside the runetotems that would further drain the Solis' light magick, making their powers useless.

Her gaze darted behind them. Hidden by the fog just beyond was the rift where Cyra had disappeared along with so many others, the rift that split the earth when the Curse was cast, setting the Noctis free from the Netherworld below.

A flood of emotions swept over Haven as they crossed the invisible boundary into the circle. Just being back here was enough to drag up old demons, but being on the exact ground where she witnessed horrible, dark, twisted magick sent rivers of adrenaline roaring through her veins.

A warm, coppery taste wet her mouth—blood. She was chewing her cheeks raw.

Her hands twisted behind her, numb from her restraints. *Release me, Sun Lord!*

But if Archeron heard her, he made no outward indications.

Instead, he faced the nine Devourers head on with an arrogant expression that made him seem older than he looked. With his cloak streaming behind him and the haughty tilt of his head, he was every bit a lord.

Circling his horse around the Devourers, he sneered down at them. Even without his powers, his eyes said, *I'm not afraid of you.*

The Solis loathed the Devourers for their demented use of dark magick; the Devourers were cultishly loyal to the Shade Queen and despised the Solis for her banishment to the Netherworld over five hundred years ago.

Haven didn't care about any of that. Right now, all that mattered was her old master, Damius.

Where was he?

Archeron bent down and began arguing in Solissian with one of the Devourers, the tallest. Bjorn sat beside him, but his sightless eyes stared into the direction of the chasm.

Rook was on the other side, slouched over her horse. One pale hand fisted around Aramaya's mane. The other trembled around the hilt of her sword.

Haven strained to listen to Archeron's negotiations, but the men were too far away.

Besides, her heart drum-beating inside her skull drowned out almost everything else. She itched to make a plan. To hold a sword, a dagger, anything.

All at once, the Devourers looked up at the sky, their hoods falling back as they did. A shadow streaked the mist. An impossibly huge shadow. Haven's arms shook behind her back as the whooshing of wings hit her, great whirls of fog and sand flying around them. A screech rattled the air.

One name clanged against her skull. Wyvern.

Run!

Consumed with fear, Haven shot into her gelding's mind— and hit a steel wall. She tried again, concentrating on slipping past his guard. Once again, something flung her back. The other horses, too, were frozen, seemingly controlled by something else.

Someone else. Someone that kept them calm when they should have been fleeing.

A sudden rush of air blew back Haven's hood as something enormous hit the sand. Waves of fog rolled toward them. In the murk beyond, a beast snorted, talons churning the sand. Close. Too close.

The wyvern was coming. And so was Damius.

THIRTY

Bell woke to the sour tang of fresh bread. He was curled near the fireplace on one of the larger couches, the sheet that once covered it wrapped around his legs. The fire burned as if it had been fed recently—or magick kept it burning indefinitely.

Either way, he didn't care, as long as he was warm.

He stretched to a stand and followed the smells to a lavish dining room. Although the room itself wasn't very big, the table was huge, longer than the oak table in Penryth's banquet room. Heavy cobalt curtains draped over dirty windows, sealing out most of the natural light.

Once he had them open, faint silvery starlight brightened the room.

A single white plate rested at the head of the table, beside a carefully folded linen napkin. Delicate roses were engraved in the silverware that rested atop the napkin. Bread, butter, and two links of sausage covered the plate.

Bell's stomach growled as he sat and ate, but he hardly tasted the food.

He was thinking of Haven. For seven years, he spent every morning with her in the library. When they got older and early morning duties called—tutors and attending his father's many, *many* boring meetings, and training at the royal academy for her—they made time to meet for lunch at a meadow west of the garden.

Bell clinked his fork down on the plate, his appetite gone. Somehow, the idea of eating alone for the next week was worse than having his nose broken. Worse, even, then being locked inside a freezing cell hundreds of feet in the air.

For the first time since he arrived at this miserable place, he understood how alone he really was.

His chair grated against the floor as he stood, glancing determinedly through the open double doors to the hallway where the creature disappeared last night.

Bell refused to eat alone. Here, he might not be a prince, but he was still a guest, and the manners of this creature needed adjusting. Wiping his mouth with a napkin, Bell marched out the doors and down the hall to find his host.

Bell explored his side of the castle first, peeking inside rooms and listening for noises of occupancy.

After countless minutes with only his footsteps to rattle the quiet, Bell found an iron door with the same rose carving as the fireplace engraved into the top panel.

A frustrated breath left his lips as he grabbed for the door handle. Not sure why he bothered since it was obviously locked—

A brief shock tingled his hand, and the door clicked open.

Well then.

Not one to question good luck, he forced himself to slink down the dark corridors. Cold, drafty air slipped beneath his clothes and evoked gooseflesh across his skin.

Now if only magick would light the torches on the walls.

This side of the castle was a labyrinth of forgotten chambers and sitting rooms, and an hour passed before he discovered a small door behind the wide, spiraling staircase.

Twice he'd been near this area and never noticed anything behind it.

The third time, a strange silver door swirled in the dim light.

Once again, his fingers tingled when he turned the handle. As soon as the door cracked open, bright light swamped his vision, moist heat blasting his face.

Shielding his eyes, he slipped inside.

His mouth unhinged as a sea-blue sky swam across his vision, the blazing sun a breath of fire on his cheeks. He whipped around, but instead of a castle behind him, there was a marble fountain spewing crystalline water from a water nymph.

Past that, what looked to be miles and miles of hedges, flowers, and trees.

Alarmed, he tore at the nearest hedge, searching for the door, even as his brain told him it was impossible. He knew what waited on the other side of the castle walls. Snow and ice and darkness.

But here, there was a pale-blue sky swollen with light. Here, there was birdsong, and the lazy buzz of bees over flowers, a garden full of them sprouting from rich black dirt and vining along ancient stone walls.

There were vibrant pink blooms, white ones, every shade of purple imaginable.

If Haven were around, she could name them all. To her they were weapons. Poison for the monsters who had taken him.

Goddess Nature's last defense.

But to him they were simply the most beautiful sight he'd

seen in ages, and he didn't need names to know they smelled incredible, an exquisite perfume that dizzied his head and drew his lips into a smile.

The sounds and scents pulled him in. He ran his hand over a row of crimson rose bushes as he walked—he knew roses, at least—the bold colors perking up his mood.

For a moment, he wasn't in Morgryth's castle, being kept by a strange beast, but back in the Penrythian gardens. He could almost see Haven running around the hedge, the rose-gold hair she kept covered flashing against the vibrant green.

Then something in his periphery shifted, and he froze, the dream shattered.

The creature was hunched over a tangle of puffy orange flowers, his cloak, covered in dirt and leaves, trailing behind him.

Bell gasped, and the creature's head snapped up. A growl ripped through the garden.

Bell turned to flee, but the creature was quicker, leaping to block Bell's path.

Behind the dark hood covering most of his face, Bell thought he caught a glance of a smooth cheekbone, perhaps the soft curve of a boy's lips. The sight sent a shock through his core.

He had imagined something . . . more creature-like. But, then why did he insist on covering his face?

"How did you get here?" The creature's voice shook the glass and dragged Bell from his thoughts.

Bell trembled, but he forced his shoulders back and his voice steady. "I'm the Prince of Penryth and your guest. How dare you treat me this way!"

"Guest?" the creature demanded. "You're a prisoner, just as I am. Now"—the beast bent down—"how did you enter? Are you a spy for Morgryth? Did she send you?"

"Spy? For the Shade Queen?" Bell laughed, even as his stomach tightened beneath the creature's glare. "Why would she care about a bunch of flowers, anyway?"

Behind the shadows, Bell could feel the creature assessing the truth of what he said.

Finally, the creature let out a rasping breath and straightened. "How did you get inside the doors? They only open for my magick."

Bell shifted his gaze to his hands. "Only the Goddess knows. My magick, if you can call it that, hasn't worked since I was taken."

The creature grunted. "You were told to stay on your side of the castle."

Bell planted his hands on his hips. "I don't know who you are, but from the grandeur hiding beneath the cobwebs of this estate, I imagine it was once filled with guests? I wonder, did you treat them as poorly as you have me?"

The creature's cloak slid along the soil-strewn stone pavers as he turned to face a trellis of climbing roses. "You speak of things you do not understand."

"Sure. I wouldn't understand rules of nobility," Bell said, his voice thick with sarcasm. That might have been the only thing he excelled at. Knowing which lord to bow to first, whose hand to kiss, whose ego to stroke.

"If you must stay, Prince, then you will work. Something I imagine a noble of your standing knows nothing about." With that, the creature went back to the blooms he had been tending, leaving Bell alone to sit there feeling foolish.

The creature was right; Bell knew nothing of laboring beneath a hot sun. But sweat dampened his temples at the thought of going back alone, so he joined the creature, bending down in dewy grass to begin collecting fallen pink rose petals.

All the petals went into a burlap sack. When they finished, the creature handed Bell a bag.

He inhaled the sweet fragrance. "Why are we collecting these?"

A grumble rattled from the creature's throat. "No questions." He batted away a giant bumblebee and then tramped between two thick edges toward the door—if that's what it was.

Bell caught up near the fountain, watching the tall row of hollies to see if the silver door appeared—which it did.

"What sort of magick is this?" Bell asked.

"It's a portal," the creature said tightly.

"To where?"

Suddenly, the creature's head shot up and he stiffened, sniffing the air. "They're here!"

Before Bell could ask who, the creature flung his sack far from the door and ripped Bell's from his grasp. Then the creature heaved Bell through the portal.

Bell's feet barely hit the stone on the other side before he was being dragged through the halls toward his side of the castle. Urgency poured from the creature's body, torches flickering to life as they ran.

Just before they could reach the iron door separating the two sides of the castle, the door burst open, and a cold blast filled the room. The creature's hands tightened on Bell's shoulders as the Noctis who took Bell the last time appeared, flanked by gremwyrs.

"You're early, Magewick," the creature growled. "The moon is not yet full."

The Noctis, Magewick, grinned. "What do you care, creature?"

Bell felt the creature's grip loosen. An irrational part of Bell wanted to press into the beast and away from Magewick.

Stupid. One was a beast. The other a monster. There was no safe place to hide. "It's okay," Bell said about as evenly as he could. "I'll go without a fight."

Even though he couldn't see the creature's reaction, Bell felt a measure of respect form between them. The creature's hands on his shoulders squeezed once, softly. So that he might have imagined the tiny nudge of encouragement.

Then he was walking toward his doom like an idiot.

The gremwyrs turned their heads to watch him pass, taking deep pulls of his scent through their flat snouts, wings limp against their scaly bodies. Their putrid stench tightened his stomach, and he swallowed back a gag.

As soon as Magewick focused his intense gaze on him, his blue eyes reflecting green orbs in the dimness like a cat, Bell's entire body went rigid.

"The Shade Queen has some questions for you," Magewick said.

Bell tried to swallow the lump in his throat, but it lodged there, making him choke out every word. "About . . . what?"

A sinister grin split Magewick's face. "About a mortal girl with rose-gold hair."

THIRTY-ONE

The others had their weapons out, but Haven was riveted to the approaching wyvern. Its footfalls shook the earth. Its whining snarls split the quiet, permeating the air with the stench of smoke and ash.

Shadow. The creature from her nightmares . . .

Her spine went rigid. How many nights had she lay awake, expecting Damius to follow through on his promise and feed her to his dark pet?

How many times had she watched Shadow feast on Damius's enemies and imagined its teeth crunching her bones? Its deft talons plucking out her entrails while she lay alive. Screaming.

A shiver wracked her body as she dared to take in the beast. First the snout, covered in iridescent green-and-black scales shimmering like molten jewels. Golden ridges jutted from its serpentine neck and back, each one sharp enough to impale a man. They'd been filed down for its rider.

Black eyes studied her behind an opaque film, meaning the creature was completely soulbound. A pink forked tongue flickered between two curved fangs.

Last she saw the creature it was barely bigger than the Sun Lord's mare. It had felt huge then, colossal. An unbeatable monster.

Now, though, Shadow was even larger, dwarfing Damius's pavilion, the creature's wingspan blotting out the sky.

As if Shadow felt her studying it, the beast's membranous golden wings flapped twice in the air and then folded into its ridged back.

A man leapt to the ground, and even before he threw his hood back, Haven knew who it was. He'd already begun probing her mind, stroking here and there, searching for entry.

The invasive act felt like hundreds of tiny spiders slipping into hairline cracks along her skull, their long, delicate legs tickling her brain as they tried to squirm inside.

Forgetting all about the wyvern, she focused on the predator before her—the true predator—as her world shrank to him.

Only him, and nothing else.

Damius.

As soon as his eyes met hers, something foul and slimy wormed beneath her ribcage and into her heart.

She fought the urge to puke. To shrink into herself until she was a little girl again. *His* little girl, a terrified, meek slave begging for a sliver of mercy.

His irises, once the palest of blue, were ink-black, the whites of his eyes swollen with blood. Dark veins rivered below his bone-white skin, spreading down his neck and into his chest like a nest of angry vipers.

My sweet Rose. His voice slipped inside her head, a razor-thin blade gliding deeper as he stalked toward her. *Did you miss me?*

What about Shadow? He certainly missed you.

The wyvern shrieked, its serpent head snapping the air.

Knocked from her trance, she tore her gaze from Damius. Archeron was off his horse and standing between her and the Devourer.

Whether meant to be protective or not, the act worked to calm her. The Sun Lord towered over her former tormentor. Even stripped of his powers by the runetotems, his hair, skin, and tunic still covered in crusty djinn flesh, Archeron made Damius look small and unimpressive.

For once, she was thankful for the Sun Lord's bravado. Even if it felt much like a petulant little boy waving a stick at a hungry bear.

Damius held up a hand, the long sleeves of his robe pooling around his elbow and reminding her of blood. Clawing the sand with its talons, the wyvern responded to the command and shot into the sky, its wings eddying the mist around them.

If the Solis thought the beast's departure made them safer, they were wrong.

Shadow now had an aerial advantage. If commanded, he would rain down fire and death from the skies.

Haven had seen it happen more than once, and the resulting devastation was enough to fuel her nightmares for an eternity.

"How much do you want for her?" Damius asked Archeron in a tone that said she was already his.

Haven's heart thundered in her chest as she silently pleaded to Archeron. *Tell him I'm not for sale!*

Rubbing two fingers over his chin, Archeron stole a glance back at her, as if assessing her worth. "What will you do with the mortal?"

A flicker of impatience flashed across Damius's ghastly face. "Whatever I wish, Solis. She's my property, bought and paid for from your kind years ago. For returning her, I will give you the cure for your dying Sun Queen over there." His lips spread wide, revealing blackened teeth sharpened to needlepoints. "More than generous, yes?"

"And passage to the Ruinlands?" Archeron asked, his tone surprisingly calm.

"Oh, I would say the runestones in your pocket would suffice, even though those also once belonged to me." A laugh like ground glass shuddered from his throat. "Unfortunately, Queen Morgryth would rather you not enter, and I'm but her servant."

"Would she, now?" Archeron raised a honey-gold eyebrow, his stillness more terrifying than if he had exploded with temper. "I suppose we will accept your first offer. But I'd like my horse back."

Before she could protest, Archeron had his arms around her waist and lifted her from the saddle. She locked her jaw, ready to fight as he slid her slowly to the ground—

All at once, the vine released her wrists. Her boots settled unsteadily on the sand. Her thighs and back ached.

As blood flowed back into her hands, tiny pricks of pain shooting down her fingers, she felt the cold steel pressed into her palm.

"Don't make me regret this," he breathed into her ear.

But she hardly heard him. Now that she wasn't helpless anymore, now that she had means to slake her rage, it came surging forth from some long buried well inside her, bubbling up and up and up.

One by one the horrible, unspeakable crimes Damius had inflicted upon her came back. Those now-freed memories fed her fury and steeled her for the task at hand, every molecule of her being focused on plunging her dagger into Damius's black heart.

Time slowed to an aching crawl as Archeron seemed to regard

her for a heartbeat. Perhaps stunned by the change in her expression. Then he spun around, clearing space for her weapon.

With a vengeful yell borne of three years of agony and nine years of nightmares, Haven lunged. As the blade left her fingers and streaked toward him, she felt as if she were removing a shard of darkness buried deep inside her heart.

Finally, the demon from her past would be silenced.

A flash of red filled her vision. It took a second to realize another Devourer had leapt in front of Damius, taking the hit.

The dagger buried into the folds of the other man's robe, and he crumpled.

"No," she whispered, her voice a broken, ragged thing.

The other Devourers converged.

Grinning, Damius shot straight for her.

Nethergates! She grabbed for her weapons before realizing she had none.

While Archeron let loose a volley of knives, she found her bow and quiver full of arrows, along with her scythes and baldric, all neatly stored inside her satchel.

From her periphery, Rook slashed her sword alongside Bjorn and his axe, the two forming an impressive force. An appreciative whistle left her lips. Even half-dead, the Morgani Sun Queen was more of a warrior than any mortal Haven knew.

Determined to show the same amount of courage, Haven rolled beneath her horse and then popped to her feet. A second later and she might have been trampled. The poor creatures reared and scattered in a mess of horseflesh, mist, and steel.

This is it. She slipped through the chaos, slashing at anything red. *The fight you've prepared half your life for.*

Fight? came Damius's serpentine voice. *You've been away too long, Rose. You've forgotten what I do to those who challenge me.*

Her head whipped left to right as she searched through the mist for him.

He laughed, the sound coming from everywhere and nowhere. *I can smell your fear.*

Flung through the air so fast her belly churned, Haven went weightless. She slammed sideways into a runetotem. Pain ricocheted around her skull, darkening her vision. Warm sand gritted her cheek.

She got to one knee before she was again yanked into the air and hurled against the hard wood. Red, blinding pain. A brief flicker of darkness.

When she came to, blood burned her throat and slippery laughter wiggled around in her mind.

My Rose. I have missed our time together.

She crawled to her feet, spitting blood. The ground swayed beneath her. Maybe it was the hit to her head, but the fog seemed denser, colder; she could hardly see what was happening.

She blinked at the bow in her hands. The arrow quivered against the string.

Closing one eye, she searched the milky air, looking for targets. A noise—panting, or robes rustling—caught her attention.

She pivoted, swung the bow around. A blur of red rushed at her.

Devourer. No sooner had the thought hit than the red blur disappeared.

For a too-long moment, silence enveloped her. As if she were cut off from the entire world. Then something screeched above. The Devourer slammed into the earth by her feet, his robe shredded and guts exposed.

The Shadowlings finally joined the party, although it was yet to be seen if that was a good thing or a bad thing.

Haven swung her bow in a circle, her breath ragged as she

searched for gremwyrs. When none came, she left the runetotems, inching toward the trade tents.

Thick fog drowned the air. Thankfully, countless hours mapping the camp in her mind let her see what the others couldn't. She stumbled over more dead Devourers, but no Shadowlings.

A tiny voice broke through the adrenaline. Why would they kill the Devourers? Their pact with the Shade Queen made them off limits to the monsters.

Before she could follow the thought, her boot snagged on a stake. The rope led through the mist to a canopy. Invisible talons of ice scraped down her spine. The sun had bleached the purple fabric to a drab gray, and the skull chimes were new.

Still, Haven recognized the women's whoring tent.

The bridge would be twenty steps to the east and four to the south. She turned to go, then hesitated.

All those women—no, she didn't have time!

Still, her body refused to move. She could hear the battle moving closer, steel clanging and creatures snarling. If she freed the female slaves, they could slip away in the confusion.

They could have a fighting chance.

She released a breath, shouldered her bow, and then dropped to her knees. As soon as she touched the stained canvas door, a shock sent her reeling back.

It was runed.

Fumbling for her scythes, she stabbed into the canvas and yanked the blade down. The wall split open. The women spilled from the hole a few heartbeats later. Years of beatings taught them to be quiet. They didn't make a peep as their gazes—their eyes the only part visible on their faces—darted over the landscape.

"Go!" Haven hissed, shoving them away from the chasm. The women fled silently into the mist. As soon as she was sure they wouldn't fall to their death, she sprinted toward the bridge, counting her steps.

. . . 5, 6, 7, 8—

Whooshing air. She ducked just as a rock the size of a wolfhound barreled over her head. The giant stone sank into the abyss. A Devourer had his hands raised. Inky-black wisps swirled around his robes, growing larger.

She grabbed her bow, nocked an arrow, and drew back, but one flick of his hand shattered the arrow. The other hand pried huge chunks of rock from beneath the sand with lazy twists of its fingers.

Her heart lurched as the boulders twirled over her, raining sand and pebbles. Then he dropped his hand, and the rocks crashed down.

She dove to her right but was too slow. One of the rocks caught her foot. Fiery pain exploded through her ankle.

Adrenaline dulled the agony to an angry throb.

A scream tore from her throat as she pulled on her leg, but the boulder pinned her to the earth.

Her yell was more frustration than pain. She needed magick! Just a whisper of power, enough to lift this rock, would turn the tables.

She scoured her insides, but all she found was raging panic.

The Devourer bared his sharp teeth at her in a taunting grin.

Snarling back, she swung her bow like a club at his legs. His thigh shattered with a painful crack.

The Devourer stumbled but kept smiling.

Goddess Above. Dark magick was annoying.

With a final kick, she yanked free and spun around him, ignoring the throb in her ankle as she worked to gain a few seconds to draw another arrow.

She barely had the quarrel in her hand when she was flung backward with such force her chin snapped against her sternum. The ground punched the air from her lungs.

Wheezing, she grabbed for her bow, but her fingers sunk into warm sand.

The Devourer's staff thwacked right where her head was, but she managed to roll to the left—

The ground was gone. Air swirled around her windmilling arms as her stomach flip-flopped.

The rift! She was falling.

Scrabbling for a handhold, Haven clawed back over the side of the chasm, chunks of dirt raining over her face. Her heart was wedged into her throat.

The sharp end of the staff came down. Again. Again. Breaking her fingers. Cracking her cheeks. Her world became blinding waves of pain. He caught her with a blow to the spine that made her feet go numb.

Gasping, Haven paused to look up at the Devourer. The sky spun in erratic circles. His cruel black eyes pinned her there for a heartbeat.

Then, he lifted his staff.

THIRTY-TWO

Just as the Devourer's staff came rushing down on Haven's head, a furious cawing split the air. They both looked up at the churning feathers. Surai! Haven had never been happier to see a bird in her life.

The little raven's talons scraped across his face, drawing beads of blood; her curved black beak pecked his hideous eyes. He roared and batted at her.

Now! As the Devourer stumbled back, still fighting Surai, Haven lunged at him, ignoring the pain screaming from her bones. Their bodies collided.

For a heartbeat, his eyes locked onto her.

Then he careened silently over the cliff.

"Not smiling now . . . are . . . you?" she panted.

Surai circled Haven twice, cawing.

Get the cure, the raven seemed to be pleading. *Fulfill your promise.*

Dizzy from adrenaline and fatigue, fingers throbbing, Haven dropped to her knees and crawled along the sand until she felt the ground fall away. Sweat dribbled down her shoulder blades as she crept to the left, feeling for the bridge.

Something splintery and hard scraped her hand. She grabbed the pole on reflex and pulled herself to a stand.

From this height, the fog was thinner, and she could see the gray wooden slats of the bridge suspended by thick spirals of rope. Her mouth went dry, the breath shriveling in her chest as she placed her foot on the first plank.

She had seen a handful of people cross this bridge, but that was years ago. The rope could be frayed, the wood rotten.

Stealing a breath, she clenched the thick rope on either side, the braided strands prickling her palms, and took another step. The plank wobbled beneath her boot but held.

Cold wind blasted her from below. One look at the dark chasm between the cracks sent knives of adrenaline slicing through her veins.

Haven increased her pace, every step a little steadier. As long as she didn't look down, she could pretend the ground was a few feet below. That one misstep wouldn't send her plummeting to the Netherworld.

She was almost running now, grunting, hands sweaty as they slid over the rope. Splinters embedded in her palms, her broken fingers throbbing, but the pain was masked with adrenaline. Butterflies squirmed in her belly and jammed her throat.

The farther she got, the more the bridge swayed, sloshing around what little she had in her stomach. A wall of mist rose to divide the Bane and the Ruinlands, hiding what lay on the other side.

Her chest tightened. Perhaps there was nothing waiting behind that dark, churning veil but an abyss that would swallow her whole. Perhaps the Shade Queen and her monsters lingered.

Perhaps death.

Either way, anything was better than what raged behind her. With one last glance back, she lunged—and stopped dead in her tracks.

Something squeezed her throat. She tried to suck in air, tried to pry the invisible fingers away, but already her mind was fading. Her stomach churned as the bridge swayed wildly. The more she struggled, the more it careened.

Air. She needed air or she would die.

You are mine, the voice hissed inside her head. *Mine*.

The hands around her throat lifted, and air exploded into her lungs. She fell to her knees and glanced back, coughing, hardly surprised to see Damius's blood-red cloak bright against the haze at the end of the bridge. Alabaster skin peeked beneath the bright fabric.

Damius's body might be under that cloak, but his spirit was on the bridge with her. Only powerful soulwalkers could physically touch something. Damius had gotten even more powerful while she was gone.

Rubbing her neck, Haven searched the grimy air for any sign of him.

Come back to me.

She spun around, panic thrumming her body as she searched. "Never! I'd rather die."

As you choose, my Rose Girl.

A soft wind blew over her, and then Damius's body went rigid as he re-entered it. Even from here, she could see the cruel grin as his face reanimated. The hate seeping from his eyes.

Something stirred below.

A split second later, the mists swelling the chasm became a

raging sea as the wyvern barreled up toward the bridge. Haven bounded into a sprint, but it was too late.

The wyvern burst from below with an ear-splitting shriek that reverberated off the cliffs and inside her chest.

As the beast carved a sharp path toward her, its molten-red eyes burning like hot coals and massive wings sending bursts of wind blowing back her hood, the only thing that came to mind was Bell.

She would die. She would *fail* him.

The scaled beast landed on the middle of the bridge, its black talons shredding boards and rope. The impact flung her sideways. Grabbing for the ropes, she hung precariously to the side.

They locked eyes, and she could swear she was looking at Damius. Could swear that as it yawned its jaws wide, she heard the name Rose roll off its pink, forked tongue.

Orange fire spewed from its jaws. She threw up her arms as the bridge erupted in a whoosh, a wave of heat crashing over her.

"No!" Her voice was lost in the wind. Tongues of flame raced along the ropes and turned the wooden planks to ash. Smoke haunted the air.

Damius had destroyed the only bridge that could get them to the Shadow Kingdom to break the Curse. Dazed, she watched the wyvern take to the sky.

Her gaze tore from the dying bridge to Damius. He held out his hand as if he expected her to come running.

She hated how much she wanted to. How terrified she was of the other option.

But she had to get away from Damius just long enough to make this right.

The bridge shuddered and groaned beneath her feet. The ropes began to splinter and fray. Her heart hammered against her skull.

Rose. His voice was a plea, a desperate whisper. A command. *Rose, come to me.*

"Like I said before," she screamed. "I'd rather die!"

She lunged forward before he could soulwalk to stop her. The bridge sagged. Fire scorched her hands and face. Just as the fire felt as if it would melt away her skin, the planks beneath her feet started to buckle, and she leapt.

Hot, blistering flames engulfed her. Pain skipped over her flesh and dug into her bones.

Below, as if in slow motion, she could see the bridge give way, the fiery inferno receding. Her hands grasped for something—anything—to hold onto. But there was just *air, air, air* as she plummeted, the scream on her lips lost.

Something golden flashed through the fog. She latched onto the charred rope end. A heartbeat later, she slammed into the other side of the cliffs. Pain wracked her body. Pain from falling. Pain from the fire. Pain from her bones being beaten with the cane.

Hold on! Her injured, sweaty hands slipped and clawed over the rope until she found a smoldering plank to grab. Pain from her fingers bolted up her arm.

Her lungs heaved for breath, the rock face cool against her shoulder. Bile crept up her throat as her feet kicked empty space. A shrill screech split the air below and echoed off the dark cliffs.

Damius was coming for her. There was only one way this ended. But first, she had to give the others a chance to cross the chasm and end the Curse.

The only time in her life she ever truly prayed was the night she escaped Damius. Today would make the second time.

Goddess Above, if you have ever loved me, help me wield this dark magick raging inside me. I may not be worth saving, but Bell is.

A laugh bubbled up her throat.

How Bell would shake his head and scold her for praying to the Goddess for dark magick. But she needed it to repair the bridge, and light magick wouldn't work here.

Of course, once she runecast, she would no longer be strong enough to hold on.

Yet, dying for Bell to have a chance at life was worth a thousand horrible deaths.

Countless runemarks danced in her head. A hundred different marks to heal something. A hundred marks to repair it.

But only one mark kept coming back to her. Three intertwining circles carved into the sand. The one Bjorn showed her right before they came here.

He must have seen this happen already.

Sweat rolled down her temples as she shut her eyes. Focused. At first, she felt nothing but the ache in her muscles and bone, the searing pain from burned flesh she couldn't bring herself to look at.

But she concentrated on the hum of blood whooshing through her arteries. The air hissing from her lungs. A strange calm washed over her until she was numb. Until she was nothing but particles and dust.

The tingle started in her chest and surged outward, filling her bones. Throbbing inside her fingertips. She ran a finger over her cheek, gathering her blood. Then she made the mark over the charred, warped wood, ignoring the pulse of surprise at seeing the burned skin on the back of her hand.

Sweat stung her eyes. Her left hand knotted and cramped, barely able to hold on.

Right as she finished the mark, the fog below exploded with a screech. The wyvern's wings, thin and near translucent, seemed to span the entire chasm as they beat the air toward her.

"Too late, Damius," she whispered, hoping beyond hope it was true.

The runemark began to glow. The board tingled beneath her fingers as the drifting ashes disappeared, the wood panels repairing themselves, the frayed ends of the rope growing back, lifting in the air—

All the energy drained from her body at once. She lost her grip. Then she was falling, streaking through the bottomless pit, serenaded by the wyvern's furious roars and the sound of her own screams.

THIRTY-THREE

Rook was going to die.

Never one to hide from the truth, Surai came to this terrifying realization hours ago, not long after they escaped the Devourers. They managed to cross the bridge, thanks to Haven. Now they regrouped on high ground.

Rook's head was heavy and limp where it rested in Surai's lap, her flesh hot as Netherfire and braids damp with sweat. Moonlight filtered through the canopy of trees above, coloring her waxen skin a sickening whitish-gray, the shade of the long Asharian winter skies.

The smell of her ruined body poisoned the air.

Not for the first time, Surai leaned over and vomited into the mossy earth.

"Stop." Rook's raspy voice drew Surai's attention back to her mate. "I would rather . . . not die . . . with your vomit crusting my—my hair."

Surai blinked back her tears. Rook would consider them an affront, and Surai loved her too much to dishonor her in that way.

The tears her Morgani mate thought would soil her warrior soul could come after. After they buried her in the cursed earth of the Ruinlands. After the Morgani prayers sent her soul to the Goddess.

After—the word sickened Surai. There was no after without Rook. No future and no hope.

"Surai." Even near death, Rook managed to sound chiding. "I can feel you already mourning me. But I'm not dead just yet, darling."

Wiping her sleeve over Rook's forehead, Surai gently laid her mate's head on the mossy ground and stood.

As soon as she did, Rook's golden eyes closed in sleep. She was forcing herself to stay awake for Surai. This was their sacred hour when both girls were in their true forms.

And Rook knew it could be the last chance to say goodbye.

"Sleep, Princess," Surai murmured.

It was a title Rook refused. Technically, when she fled her arranged marriage and severed her Heart Oath, that title had been stripped from her.

Surai glared to the west, as if she could see past the mortal lands to the Morgani Islands, and snarled under her breath, "She's still a princess."

A faint rustling sounded from behind a copse of alders. Archeron prowled from the shadows, breathing heavily, his longsword held loosely in his left hand. Blood darkened the edges, half-dried.

Surai tried not to look too eager as she approached. "Did you get—"

But her plea shriveled in her throat at the sight of Archeron's grim face and downcast eyes.

"I'm sorry, Surai." His gaze flicked past her to the tree where Rook rested, but he refused to come into camp. "How is she?"

"Sleeping now." Surai slipped her hand over Archeron's forearm, corded with muscles and hard bone, and urged him to the fire. Moonlight danced over the iridescent runes mapping his forearm. "Come, let's feed you."

"I'm not hungry," he insisted.

But he followed, his steps measured and slow, shoulders curved inward. She didn't let up until the fire flickered inside his weary eyes. Plucking the sword from his grip, she wiped the blade across a patch of grass and then sheathed it into the long scabbard at his waist.

Hopefully, the purr of buried steel would be a hint for him to rest.

Steam trickled from the tin cup of moonberry tea she handed him. When he hesitated, she said, "Drink, stubborn fool."

He peered into the cup. "I found vorgrath tracks deep in the woods, but its mate doubled up behind me, and when I finally shook her off, the tracks were just . . . gone."

"And this?" Surai asked, running a finger over three long gashes damaging his tunic. The scratches beneath appeared superficial and had already begun to heal. "The mate or something else?"

He tilted his head back and downed a swig of his tea. "Gremwyrs near some bluffs. I'm fine, but they're not."

"And your face?" she asked, wagging her eyebrows at the red scrapes marring his golden flesh.

"Thorns." He gulped down more tea. "I swear to the goddess, Surai, this forest is trying to kill us. The trees move, the bushes slash and cut, and creatures . . ."

His words trailed away. The tea had done its job, easing the tension from his shoulders, the pain from his face. Still, she cringed at the shadows darkening his gaze.

"And what about the mortal girl?" Surai prodded carefully, watching for any sign he wasn't ready to talk about her.

"She's gone." She thought she caught his lips tremble as he said the words, but his face remained hard.

"Are you sure?"

A ragged breath parted his mouth, and he flicked his gaze to the woods. "I scoured the rift until the Devourers nearly discovered me. She's gone."

"Archeron," she said in a near-whisper, "stop punishing yourself for Rook's condition and the mortal's death."

A sneer twisted his mouth, but it was directed inward. "Then who should I blame? I let the mortal wake the djinn. And all I had to do to save Rook was hand her over. Instead, I put the girl over one of our own. A *mortal*, Surai."

"A mortal girl who died to ensure we could still cross the bridge." Her throat welled. "She could have used her magick to save herself, but she didn't. I think that's more than enough to earn redemption."

He shook his head, anguish in his eyes. "The worst part is, I don't know why I set her free. It makes no sense."

"You're right. Things might have been different had you handed her over. But we all saw her memory, Archeron. Not just you. Turning her over would have made us as much a monster as the Devourers." She dug the toe of her boot into the earth, wondering how to approach the next topic. "Besides, you were only following your heart."

"My heart?" he said, forcing a hollow laugh. "What does my heart have to do with this?"

Surai filled his cup again. She needed to tread carefully.

"After Remurian died and you were condemned to Penryth,"

she began, "I thought you were lost to us forever. That the soul-brother I knew, the soul-brother I loved, would die."

"If only I could have," Archeron remarked, bitterness tainting every word.

"But now," she continued, courageously pressing on despite his deepening scowl and the lethal warning in his eyes, "I see that there was someone there who lightened the shadows darkening your spirit. A mortal girl, perhaps?"

Archeron flung his tea to the ground with a snarl. "Have you lost your mind, Surai? Her? A mortal?" His hand flew to the amulet around his neck. "And what about Avaline? The Heart Oath? Do you think I would bring such dishonor on her name?"

"In this situation, there's no dishonor to court another. You know that."

"Another Solis. And even then . . ." He shoved a hand through his hair. "But courting a mortal, after what happened to Avaline's brother? To us? She hates them as much as I do."

Surai hesitated. That subject had been touchy even before Avaline was cursed and Archeron sent to Penryth as servant to the King. Archeron lost all reason when it came to matters of honor.

Time to change tactics. "Brother, when I met Rook, daughter of the Morgani Islands' Warrior Queen, she was engaged to an Effendier prince, and I was an Ashari scout."

Archeron growled and shook his head. "I know your story, Surai. If I remember correctly, I wagered a few runestones you would fall for the princess, and you still owe me for helping you two escape across the Glittering Sea. What I do not grasp is the point of it currently."

"The point is, your brain may choose one thing—it may even convince you that choice is honorable, and right, and the only way—but your heart will follow its own path. That path may not be logical, it may not even make sense, but the heart does not care."

Anger flared inside his eyes, and he roared, "Enough with my heart!"

There was rustling, and Bjorn leapt down from the tree by the fire, landing with a cat-like grace that always startled her.

He glowered at them. "How am I to see anything when you two are yelling like savage mortals?"

"Tell her, Seer!" Archeron grumbled, pacing around the fire, his fists clenching and unclenching. He threw a dark look her way. "Her mate's injury has filled her with nonsense."

A cryptic smile widened Bjorn's jaw, and he waited until Archeron stopped pacing before he said, "The heart does what it wants, I'm afraid."

Archeron's eyes widened with shock, and he looked from Bjorn to Surai as if they were colluding against him. "What does any of this matter? The girl is dead, claimed by the wyvern or the Netherworld, I care not."

Then he growled and stomped around camp, shoving fresh arrows into the quiver on his back. "I'm going to find a vorgrath. If I survive, I expect both of you to keep your mouths shut with regard to my heart."

Archeron stalked into the woods. Even after he disappeared from sight, the sound of his angry steps drummed against the quiet night air.

Bjorn sighed as he ambled to the fire to fill himself a cup of moonberry tea. "We should not tease him about that."

"No?" Surai said. "I think that's exactly what he needs right now."

Even though she knew his eyes were sightless, they stared at her above the steaming rim of his cup. "The Morgani Queen is not the Sun Sovereign of Effendier, Little Bird. Rook may have given up her kingdom for you, but Archeron will never have that luxury. He's a bastard, a Halfbane, and he will not throw away Effendier for anyone. Besides, I have not yet seen if the girl is even alive."

"But you have not seen her dead," Surai reminded him, jutting out her pointed chin. "Surely that's something?"

Yet even as the words tumbled from her lips, her mind told her no one could have survived that fall, or the wyvern waiting in the shadows, least of all a mortal girl.

THIRTY-FOUR

One second Haven was tumbling through the chasm, free falling.

The next, she was floating, caught inside a sinewy cage of flesh and bone.

Thinking it the wyvern, she struggled against the creature. Kicking and flailing until the last dregs of her energy left her.

"Stop struggling," a velvety voice commanded.

When had the wyvern learned to speak?

She managed to open her eyes. Alabaster skin. Slashed pupils that dilated when she stared into them. Opaline irises ringed in fire. Their color changed as she watched, from silvery-moonstone to the palest blue. Her wild gaze fixed on the onyx wings spreading over her until they blotted out the world.

As they began to dive deep into the rift, she tried to claw once more at whatever beast held her. But its arms tightened around hers in warning, and strangely, instead of terror, she felt an odd sense of refuge with the creature.

Whoever had her, they saved her from the wyvern. She had to believe whatever fate awaited her was better than Damius.

They spiraled down down down. Her mind wandered, her eyelids drifted closer together. She was hardly aware of the breeze on her cheeks, the sound of huge wings buffering the air as they descended deep into the earth. Her body was numb, yet a part of her knew her injuries were bad.

The wyvern's snarls dimmed until they sounded as if they trickled from the end of a long tunnel.

Away, away, she tried to whisper. *Away.*

At the realization that she was passing out, she struggled to open her eyes, to orient herself. But it was too dark, her body too tired, and she rested her head against the cool, firm flesh around her, surrendering to the sea of nothingness.

Dreams shattered her shadowy refuge, tendrils of memory and fear tangling into knots of terror. Bell, after he rescued her from the slavers' market. The feel of the silky cloak he gave her, soft on her gritty skin, stirring the emotions she had hidden for so long. Hot, sloppy tears washing the grime from her cheeks as she tried to understand his Penrythian tongue. "Haven," she begged the wide-eyed boy with the crystal-blue eyes, the only Penrythian word she knew. "Haven. I need . . . Haven."

Except, now, Bell was the one saying the word, her name, over and over as he shrunk beneath a dark, bent shadow.

Haven. Haven. Haven.

Help me, Haven.

Massive black horns curled from the shadow, a jagged sable crown winking at their base. Haven's lips parted to scream, but a raven poured into her mouth and slipped down her throat.

And she was forced to watch as the Shade Queen laughed and ripped out Bell's heart.

A scream burst from Haven's lips. Pain tore through her, blistering beneath her skin. She moaned. All at once, calm descended like a cool, wet sheet, numbing her pain, her terror, and she drifted off.

More nightmares and half-lucid dreams. Countless times, she awoke to the throbbing agony and was again comforted, lulled into a dreamless sleep. Over and over, until her world blurred into a canvas of days, weeks, years . . .

When she awoke again, fingers clenched in silk sheets, there was no more pain. Watery light streamed in from somewhere. She snapped up in bed, mind racing to put together where she was as she took in the tall-ceilinged chamber of glittering onyx.

A sluggish breeze entered through the three walls of open-air windows, gossamer drapes wobbling lazily. Ivory tapers burned on the walls. More guttered softly from an iron chandelier above. Their light burned pale blue, flickering off the dark feathers of the ravens perched along the chandelier's arms.

She could swear the grim birds were watching her.

She released a choppy breath, put off by the nearly imperceptible humming seeming to come from everything. The stone, the creamy marble footboard of the bed, the strange bluish-black flames sputtering in the half-dead candles. Even the air.

No—not humming, exactly. Quivering, or vibrating. Like the tingle she felt on her arms during a thunderstorm. The air was charged with something.

And every second she was awake, it became more noticeable, until all the cells inside her body shivered and itched, and she had to move.

She flung off her ivory sheets, cool air rippling over her bare legs and teasing gooseflesh across her skin, and bounded for the windows. A too-tight nightgown clung to her chest and thighs, and she yanked the silk hem as low as it would go—barely past her bottom.

Outside the open-air windows lay a strange, vibrant world veiled in a silver hue. Metallic-gray skies soared above forests colored more blue than green, steely mountains rising in the distance.

A crystalline lake the color of diamonds glittered from its nest of towering trees to the south, the strange white-blue sun reflecting on its brilliant surface. And farther back, an ominous shadow of black clouds haunted the horizon.

Something dark and leathery dove close to the window—a gremwyr. When it got three feet from her, curved black talons shredding the air, it screeched and shot back into the sky. More gremwyrs circled the clouds.

Am I dead? she wondered, less worried than she should have been at the prospect.

"Not quite," an amused male voice purred. "Though, you are the first mortal to come to the Netherworld alive."

She pivoted, reaching for her weapons, but they were gone— along with her clothes.

Stolas studied her silently from his position leaned against the door by her bed, his sharp chin propped on one hand. An ashen smudge of an eyebrow quirked above a bored smile. His white hair was tousled to crest his head and fall behind his ears.

A raven larger than the others perched on his shoulder.

But his languid stance couldn't mask the feral spark inside his feline eyes, the way he was drawn to her panic, like a cat tracking its prey. His wings, pulled tightly behind him, flared with her every movement, causing the raven on his shoulder to stir.

Her chest heaved as she flicked a glance over the room. Weapons—she needed at least one.

"Beastie," he drawled without blinking, his rasping voice sending shivers up her arms, "a thousand weapons would not help you now."

Her fists clenched painfully by her sides. For once, she wished she had nails to rake against his porcelain flesh, instead of her chewed-up nubs. The use of that word—Beastie—dredged up memories of the gremwyrs dragging Bell away. His terrified face—

With a wild yell, she charged at the Shade Lord, ready to gouge out his eyes—and was flung backward onto the bed. Hard enough to knock the breath from her lungs with an *oof*.

Again, she tried.

Again, she found herself dumped onto the bed. Brushing off the indignity, she lifted off her back onto her elbows and snarled at him, bare feet readied in the air like weapons.

A smile twitched his lips as he appraised first her half-exposed nether regions before moving his attention to her calloused feet, worn from years of ill-fitted men's boots and walking barefoot whenever possible. "Hmm. Those are . . . terrifying."

She kicked—and missed. The raven on his shoulder lifted into the air, pecking at her toes. She tried for him too. All too aware of how silly she looked.

"We could do this, well, forever, I suppose." He studied the pale half-moons on his neat fingernails. "But I, for one, am already bored."

Raking her hands over the mattress, she clambered to her knees, growling as the nightgown tugged uncomfortably against her thighs. "You kidnapped Prince Bellamy."

"Yes."

"You took him to the Shade Queen."

"Yes."

The stone was cold on her bare feet as she slid to the floor in front of him. "It should have been me."

He studied her quietly, the flesh of his neck and cheeks the color of snow, even beneath the golden light of dawn. "Again, yes."

Her heart stuttered. "That's . . . that's why I'm here? To replace him?"

"No."

Even though his voice was clear, his smooth lips enunciating the words perfectly, she refused to understand. "But I'm the one with magick. I'm the one. Me. Take me, not Bell." She was embarrassed by how her voice wavered. "Please, he's innocent."

Stolas's strange irises flickered buttery-gold before fading back to opal. "I'm sorry, but I cannot. Innocence means nothing here."

She blinked, and he was closer, just like Archeron. Another blink and he was inches from her, his cinnamon breath cooling her cheeks. The air around him prickled with energy. *Magick.*

A shadow seemed to pass over his face, his expression turning solemn. "I need you to break the Curse."

THIRTY-FIVE

She lurched backward, startled, the hard edge of the bed digging into the back of her knees. "But you're . . . you're—"

"Ravenna's husband?" His sour tone at the mention of the Shade Queen's daughter matched the disgusted curl of his lips. "Perhaps I grow weary of only seeing my wife on a full moon, after she's feasted on some poor mortal's heart."

If the stories about Ravenna were true, she was as cruel and twisted as the Shade Queen. Worse, even, if that were possible. "And the Shade Queen, how does she feel about breaking the Curse?"

His jaw tightened. "I would take care, speaking about Morgryth. Her spies are busy little birdies."

"Even here? In the . . . Netherworld?" She felt the need to whisper the last part.

Years of listening to her lady's maid promise she would end up exactly here, in the afterlife for the wicked, had left her with some issues regarding this place.

Shifting his gaze to the windows, as if Morgryth lingered just outside, he ran a thumb over the dark lapels of his jacket. "Inside these walls is the only place she cannot see or hear."

"But outside the walls she can? I thought you were the ruler of the Netherworld. Is this not your domain?"

His lips twitched into a sneer. "Your curiosity is tiresome."

"Well, so is your evasiveness."

"Evasiveness? I am the Lord of the Netherworld," he snarled, "and I've lived lifetimes you couldn't fathom. I don't answer to you."

"Which is why I don't trust you. The Curse is about to give your kind everything you ever wanted. The Mortal kingdoms are months away from falling. Why would you want to help us?"

His features sharpened. For a terrifying second, his gaze roved over her, predatory and lethal.

But then he schooled his expression into one of impatient exasperation, the way adults usually did with annoying children. "My reasons are not important. What's important is that you have a grasp on your magick."

"Light magick can't be used in the cursed lands."

"No. But dark magick can."

Her lips parted. How in the Nethergates did he know?

"The same magick you feel rooting around your marrow and surging through your veins. That you feel in the room. In the air. In everything here. Begging you to release it, to set it free."

She tried to speak, but her throat clenched tight around the words.

He prowled closer, the air vibrating between them. "And that magick will come out one way or another, Beastie," he added, softly, quietly, his velveteen voice caressing her spine. "Either you learn to be its master, or it will be yours."

Fury overwhelmed her. She would be no one's slave ever again. "How?"

"I will train you. Normally, the Noctis start learning how to use dark magick after their one-hundredth name day." She raised an eyebrow, and he elaborated, "Our bodies mature slower than yours. Every twenty years of your life equals one of ours. A century-old Noctis child would still be that, a child."

The moisture fled her mouth. A century. One hundred years old and still a child, equivalent to a mortal at five summers? It sounded impossible.

"Why would you train me?" she demanded, rocking forward on her toes. The Solis punishment for a common mortal with magick was severe, so she assumed the Noctis had a similar rule. "Why the risk?"

"We already went over this," he explained behind a tight grin. Two dark slashes of eyebrows drew together above his eyes, now tinged dusky around the vertical pupil. "I would like you to break the Curse that plagues your lands. The one that will claim your friend soon."

"Not good enough." She crossed her arms, feeling ridiculous in her frilly, ill-fitted nightgown. "I want to know why."

He blinked at her with those strange eyes. Once. Twice. Lazy blinks that riled her blood. Beneath his eyelashes—thick and dark as the feathers blanketing his wings—his eyes had turned a furious yellow. "No."

"Fine. Then I'll find another way." She turned, only to feel his cold fingers slip around her arm as he spun her back around.

His voice was steel as he said, "I could just as easily soulbind you into submission."

Her gaze flicked down to his pale, elegant fingers wrapped

around her bicep. Ice shot from his grip and into her flesh. Into her bones. Dark, purring magick.

Then she remembered the day in the Muirwood forest when he ordered her to scream. She had wanted to, had nearly obeyed, but somehow, she resisted.

"You can't soulbind me, can you?" she said, half-question, half-boast. "You tried in the woods, but it didn't work."

Another blink, this time less arrogant. "I knew you were different, but I needed to know how different."

Knew? Is that why he let her go? "You let me cut you!"

He crooked a jagged eyebrow, the act almost making him appear boyish. "Was there any doubt?"

Goddess Above! She had consumed his blood. Was that in the plan as well? The earthy, cinnamon taste tingled on the very tip of her tongue, and she cringed at the ache that gripped her throat.

She ran the back of her hand over her lips. "Is that why this is happening? Because I—I had a drop of your blood?"

He didn't say a word as he watched her struggle to understand, but she knew he must have watched her for days. Must have seen her clench her dagger between her teeth each time she climbed the wall.

"Why?" she hissed. "Just tell me why. Why are you, the Shade Queen's second, Lord of the Netherworld, helping me?"

For a heartbeat, a shadow flickered over Stolas's face, his eyes darkening to the color of thunderclouds. His wings shuddered as if he were trying to keep them from spreading.

Then his gaze fell to his fingers wrapped around her arm, the curved, steel-gray talons sprouting from them and dimpling her flesh. He dropped his hand, red marks staining her skin in the shape of his fingers.

When his eyes lifted to her face, they had returned to their opaline color. "I will train you how to use your dark magick. In return, you break the Curse, something we both want very much for different reasons. End of discussion."

He broke away suddenly and stalked across the room to the open windows, taking his magickal charge with him. As if they had a mind of their own, his wings flared and stretched behind him, nearly smacking a dark vase off a table.

His raven's cloak trailed along the stone floor—although she was startled to notice the feathers were too large to be taken from ravens.

They were, however, the same size as his own striking plumes. And if not for having already seen the silver brooch that held the cape together around his neck, she would think the cape an extension of his wings.

"You have one minute to decide," Stolas said without looking at her.

Her lips parted—to argue or question him further—and hesitated.

What did it matter his reasoning? He could have let her fall into the rift to die. He could have killed her a hundred times over without even ruffling a feather, if that was his goal.

Who cared *why* he wanted the curse broken.

All that mattered was saving Bell. And if she could find a way to use her dark magick to do that, everything else was irrelevant.

She padded across the smooth stone, ignoring the urge to touch one of the stunning, iridescent feathers refracting indigo and magenta inside its jet-black plumage. The softness was in deep contrast to the rest of the Noctis, who was all angles, sharp planes, and sinewy muscle.

In fact, the only thing that seemed to have any curve at all were the horns atop his head. Although those, too, were much prettier up close, the material not actually black but the darkest midnight blue, banded with slivers of onyx and even silver.

"Done with your assessment?" he asked darkly, still staring at some invisible point in the sky.

"You can train me." She picked at a piece of crumbling stone along the open window ledge. Below, a lush carpet of alders and oaks spread out, steeped in the shadow of the mountain. "How long will it take?"

"How long?" A muscle feathered in his sharp jaw. "The Noctis train for centuries. Most of their lifetime, actually."

"I don't have a lifetime. In fact, I don't even know how long Bell has."

"The next full moon," he murmured.

A fresh crop of sweat moistened her neck and palms. That soon? "Okay. So, what is that? Five days? Six? I can't take time out to train with you." Guilt washed over her as she remembered Rook. The cure. "Actually, I should probably leave."

"Fine."

"Fine? I thought—when will we train?"

His eyes glinted as they looked at her. Eyes that could petrify with a glance. Wild, predatory eyes. "Why, in your dreams, Beastie. But first, I need a lock of your strange hair."

Some deep, primal part of her hesitated.

Her dreams were personal, private. The only time she was defenseless. To let him in would be madness . . .

But her qualms only lasted for a moment. Because, even if inviting a Shade Lord into her dreams was an invasion of privacy, even if the thought of Stolas present during her most vulnerable moments filled her with nausea, the idea made sense.

Break the curse during the day; learn how to use her dark magick at night while she slept.

Save Bell from her mistake. Whatever the cost.

Stolas's eyes widened slightly as she nicked the curved dagger at his waist and severed a single rose-gold strand from the crown of her head.

Then she dropped the glistening hair into his waiting palm. "There. It's all yours. But I keep the dagger."

His lips twitched. "You *borrow* the dagger until the task is done."

"It's special to you, is it?" She held the weapon up close to appraise. "Next you'll tell me it has a name."

"She," he amended. "And her name is Vengeance. She was a gift from someone I care about deeply. Do take care of her."

"What makes *her* so special?"

"The magick inside the blade allows her to cut through anything without the victim ever feeling pain."

Haven twirled the dagger in her hand, reveling in the magick she felt pulsing inside its jeweled hilt.

As she watched the gremwyrs streak across the sky, swooping and diving like bats, an unsettling mixture of anticipation and fear pooled just below her sternum. She pressed her fist into her stomach, fighting off a feeling of sinking dread, as if she had done something she could never take back.

Hopefully, she wouldn't live to regret this.

THIRTY-SIX

It had taken all of a day for Bell to forget the horrors of Spirefall, and all of one second to remember. As he trailed along behind Magewick, cold seeping into his bones, fear took hold of him. Every footfall was an effort. He had to force his legs to function, to take each step deeper into the castle.

Quite possibly, to his death.

The corridors were a blur of granite and shadows, distant shrieks reverberating off the walls. A giant cavern opened in front of them, wide enough to fit his father's summer palace inside, and at least twice as tall.

Catacombs lined the walls, filled with monsters and the Noctis—if there was a difference.

And on a dais at the very bottom sat a dark female figure atop an alabaster throne. A tremor wracked his body as he took in the black, bat-like wings spread behind her, crooked bones twisting inside thin, almost translucent skin that reached twice the length of most Noctis wings.

Magewick twisted his lips in amusement. "After you, brave Prince of Penryth."

Bell thought he had been prepared to meet whatever awaited him, but the moment he saw the Shade Queen, Morgryth, fear and adrenaline slammed into him. He took two steps before he was turning to run.

Magewick landed a blow to Bell's stomach, and he doubled over, unable to breathe. Shrieks of excitement echoed across the chamber from the creatures inside the catacombs.

"Courage need a bit of bolstering, does it?" Magewick taunted. "Shall I fly you down to meet her? Or can you walk? I would rather not keep her waiting."

Still folded over, Bell cradled his stomach as he forced his legs to take each step, one after the other, fighting the nausea that burned his throat. He thought he'd outgrown the illness that connected his emotions to his gut when he was thirteen, yet here he was, about to puke again.

He clenched his fists. If his father were here, he would gladly hand Bell over to the Shade Queen now.

Barfamy was Renk's nickname for him, or one of them. *Prince of vomit and fear.* Bell was a disappointment to his father, and a shadow of the prince his brother had been. If only Remy hadn't died, Bell's life would have been so different.

When Bell was ten feet from the Shade Queen, Magewick grasped Bell's neck. The Shade Lord's icy fingers wrapped all the way around Bell's throat, forcing him to his hands and knees on the hard stone. "Kneel for Queen Morgryth Malythean, Goddess of Shadows, Cursebringer, Ruler of Darkness and Death."

The room erupted in animalistic howls. Bell's head was pushed down, but he could see the shadows darting over the obsidian floor as Shadowlings and Noctis took flight in the cavern, the soft rush of their wings stirring the air.

Magewick removed his frigid grasp, freeing Bell's head.

Slowly, he lifted his focus to the throne where Morgryth sat. Dread flooded his body the second his gaze landed on the queen.

She was hideous, an apparition of death. Dark shadows pooled around storm-gray eyes, her skin like bleached, dried leather pulled too tight contrasted with the black, lustrous armor of scales that covered her body. Onyx horns curved over her head, the sharp ends nearly touching the spikes on her shoulder-plates.

A dark, jagged crown rested atop her head.

But her throne is what drew his focus. Pale in the torchlight, the macabre creation stood taller than any man and was constructed entirely of bone. Shin bones. Arm bones. Spines lined the edges of the throne, each vertebra tipped with black jewels. Finger joints and other small bones formed intricate runes Bell had never seen.

He could swear some of the pieces still bore jewelry. The glint of rings and bangles over dull bone making the scene somehow even more macabre.

Two small skulls grinned at him—so small, in fact, they had to come from children—one capping each throne arm.

As if Morgryth knew what he was thinking, she drummed her long fingers over the skulls. Her head tilted and creaked, her primordial gaze scraping over him.

He felt naked, as bare and exposed as the bleached bones she sat on.

"So this is a Penrythian prince?" Her voice was the perfume of a poisonous flower, alluring and terrifying, and her words slid through his mind and snaked down his spine so that he wasn't entirely sure if she was speaking aloud or inside his head. "So weak. Such delicate bones."

Despite the hundreds of creatures and Noctis in the chamber, the room was quiet, as if not a single soul dared to breathe while she spoke.

Bell's dry throat shuddered. He managed to swallow, the sound like a thunderclap in the silence.

"I wonder," she mused in that terrible, lovely voice, her fingers circling the eye orbits of the small skulls, "how your collarbones will look atop my throne after Ravenna takes your heart. They are exquisite."

Bile surged up Bell's throat, and he swallowed again, his world shrinking to the throne and the monster who inhabited it.

The Shade Queen slid to her feet, her wings snapping to their full length, and strolled toward him. He ducked his head, but she clicked her tongue in disapproval, slipping a bony finger beneath his chin and lifting his face.

Her eyes were mesmerizing, lulling, and a strange calm washed over him, even as his heart punched his ribcage and his lungs shriveled.

"Who is the mortal girl, Prince?" she whispered. "The one that wandered into my lands looking for you?"

Haven. As soon as her name flashed across his mind, he felt something squirm inside his head, pushing into his thoughts, an invasive tendril searching, breaking past his guard . . .

The runestone in his pocket pulsed hot against his hip, and then the tendril was pushed out of his mind.

A dark shadow flickered across the Shade Queen's face, and her head canted a half-inch to the side as she studied him with suddenly interested eyes.

Blood-red lips stretched into a tight smile. "Who is the girl, Prince? *Tell me.*"

Calm flooded him, easing the tension from his muscles, and

Haven's name worked itself onto his tongue. He could trust this queen. He could tell her about Haven—

The calm shattered, and he sucked in a breath as he was ripped from whatever trance the Shade Queen put him under.

Shadeling Below, he'd almost betrayed his friend.

Chewing his cheek and focusing on the pain, he said, "I don't know who she is."

The Shade Queen blinked at him, but something had changed. As if a veil had fallen from her face, exposing the nightmare beneath. Beetles and centipedes and other night-creatures squirmed inside her bones. A dark-green serpent watched him from its perch tangled inside her ribcage, its pink tongue hissing out. A slug writhed from her eye socket and plopped to the floor.

A gasp of horror escaped his throat, and she dug a fingernail into his chin, forcing his face closer to hers.

Her breath was like a cold burst of death on his cheeks as she whispered, "We shall see, Penrythian."

Her armor creaked softly as she stood, leaving him on his knees while she crossed the dais, the ends of a black cape slithering behind her.

He shuddered. Now that he saw her true self, he realized the cloak was no longer made of fabric, but a mass of scorpions and centipedes and spiders all writhing together.

It was utterly disgusting; *she* was utterly disgusting.

When the monster reached her throne, her gaze slanted back to him, a cruel smile parting her lips.

"If she is not your friend," the Shade Queen said, "then this will be of no consequence to you."

With a wave of her hand, she summoned darkness, an inky cloud that churned around her. Inside the shadows, an image formed of what looked like a battle inside swirling mist, seen from above.

Figures he didn't know fought against men in red, but a girl sprinting across a bridge drew Bell's attention.

Cold dread wrapped around Bell's heart; he recognized the ruby-red cloak and rose-gold hair of Haven. As the jeers and screeches came from all around him, he watched a wyvern land on the bridge and breathe fire over it.

Where was she? There was only one wyvern in all of Eritrayia, and that was the Netherworld beast Haven's old master had tamed, the one he used to terrify and bend Haven to his will. She hardly ever spoke about the beast or the man, but her nightmares were a different story.

Why would she return there, the one place she swore she'd rather die than revisit?

To save you, idiot, he snapped to himself.

Haven seemed to hesitate, glancing back at a man watching her from the edge of the rift.

Then his best friend leapt over the flaming bridge as it collapsed, and Bell watched her disappear into the mists below.

If he wasn't already on his knees, he would have fallen. His vision shrunk to that image of mist and fire. Even as the Shade Queen's magick faded and the battle scene evanesced, he replayed Haven falling on a loop inside his head as guilt and grief threatened to drown him.

The only person he ever loved was dead because of him.

"Take this Penrythian prince back to the creature," the Shade Queen ordered in an amused voice. "The full moon will brighten our skies soon. Let him reflect on the tragic loss of the girl who is *not* his friend until then."

Bell hardly noticed as Magewick began to drag him up the steps of the chamber. He was lost to himself, forced to watch as Haven fell again and again, the sound of the Shade Queen's wicked laugh reverberating through his skull in an endless ballad of misery.

THIRTY-SEVEN

As Haven followed the Shade Lord down an empty corridor, frigid drafts of air piercing her flimsy nightgown, she was painfully aware he could be leading her to her death. Even though he had saved her, and he could technically have killed her already, more than once, perhaps he was toying with her.

She shivered as another icy wave hit. Maybe the cold came from Stolas, the dark magick inside him drawing energy from everything he touched, everything he passed. Possibly even her.

She tangled her arms across her chest. "Where are we going, Shade Lord?"

"Stolas is fine," he said without glancing back. The raven on his shoulder, however, watched her closely.

She struggled to keep up. She felt like a child padding behind him. Had he always been so tall? "Just Stolas? No last name?"

"Do you always ask so many questions?"

She rolled her eyes, annoyed that he couldn't see her. "Do you always lack civility, or is it only with me?"

His wings fluttered before tucking against his back. "Civility? I plucked you from death's jaws, brought you to my home, cleaned the god-awful layer of foulness that encased you, abstained from feeding off your magick—though I am still considering it—and now I am taking you to eat before releasing you. What more could you desire?"

She tugged at the hem of her nightgown. "Bigger clothes, for a start. This would fit a child."

He waved a hand as he walked—or prowled, more like it. Stolas had probably never walked anywhere in his life. "It was available, and all you mortals are rather . . . small."

Scampering to catch up, Haven twisted between his large body and the carved mountain wall, her eyes catching on the blood-red streaks veining the stone. "What about magick? Can't I just conjure new clothes?"

He paused and glanced down, his gaze raking over every inch of her before settling over her eyes. The whisper of a smile twitched his lips. "I don't know. Can you?"

A challenge, then.

Strange, silvery light trickled down the hall—sunlight. Only this light seemed to be filtered through a metallic shroud.

Still, light was light, and Haven found herself walking faster toward the glow. She hadn't realized how much she craved the sun until they entered the courtyard and delicate sunlight seeped over her skin.

She took in the surroundings. Steely mountains flanked the courtyard on either side. Below, dense forests snaked along the valleys, their foliage nearly gray. Beyond, more jagged mountain peaks rose to the horizon.

Her shoulders tensed as she took in the Shadowlings roaming

the courtyard. Monsters of every kind. Some large and menacing, others small and crooked and bizarre. The two Shadowlings that tried to knock her from her tree outside the runewall in Penryth appeared across the lawn, chasing each other like puppies.

As she forced her chin up, unafraid, and continued walking, she caught Stolas's look of approval in her periphery.

Ravens circled the air above them, following Stolas like a giant shadow constantly reworking its shape. Their caws echoed off the mountains and formed an eerie song.

And everywhere, *everywhere*, she felt the cold prickle of dark magick. Lurking inside the white roses crawling over the marble barrier that rimmed the cliff. In the pale-silver grass beneath her feet and the cold, metallic air that smelled of cinnamon and blood.

"I thought the Netherworld would be . . ." Her words faltered as she glanced at him.

"Horrible?"

"Well . . . yes."

"It is for some." The muscle below his temple jumped, and his gaze fell to the shady valleys below. "The truly awful beings that come here suffer greatly."

"How?" She shouldn't have continued, but she was curious. After all, if her lady's maid, Demelza, was to be believed, someday Haven might be sent here for real.

"How do you think?" His voice was soft and lethal, and he was every bit the Netherworld Lord as he pinned her with an unapologetic stare. "I find them and I terrify them. Would you like to know more details, Beastie? Like how even the bravest mortals scream and cry out for their mothers? How they try to bargain with me? How my monsters tear them to bits over and over?"

A chill nestled between her shoulder blades as she shook her head, scolding herself for asking such a stupid question.

Of course horrible things happened here, but the Netherworld's beauty had made her almost forget it was hell.

"You think it's beautiful?" Stolas asked suddenly, his eyebrows arched.

Before her fury for having her thoughts read overcame her, before she convinced herself she could never find it anything but hideous here in this faded mirror-world, a part of her thought this place might be the most strange and beautiful realm she'd ever encountered.

But then the thought was gone and she realized the opposite was true. "No, I just . . . it looks so much like the mortal realm."

He blinked, and she thought she caught disappointment in his eyes. "What you see is a mirror image of your world, the living world. Only instead of woodland creatures we have monsters, and instead of light magick living inside the trees and the animals and the air, we have dark magick. It thrives off the light magick of the souls trapped here."

She shivered. That explained her reaction to this place and the deep, bone-penetrating chill.

Once more, she glanced over the faded landscape. Except faded wasn't the right word. Sure, the colors were less vibrant, but the silvery hues were rich, glossy, and complex, each one seemingly woven from a thousand different shades of silver.

Take the metallic sky. Even if she tried for years, she'd never be able to capture the way the clouds pooled together like strands of melted Ashari pearls floating atop a rippled pool of mercury.

"So," she began, tearing her gaze from the strange landscape. "If this is a mirror image of my world, there's a Penryth somewhere out there?"

"Yes."

"And . . . an Effendier?"

"Also yes."

"Filled with poor souls unlucky enough to be sent here?"

"Again," he growled, his voice dripping with impatience. "Yes."

"Then which part of the world are we mirroring now?"

"The Ruinlands." He flicked his dark gaze over the valleys. "Once, mortal cities stretched across these lands as far as the eye could see. But the moment the Curse hit, everything from here to the Bane was destroyed. The Netherworld gained a lot of mortal souls that day."

She shuddered as she imagined those cities and their people decimated by the Curse. "And the mortal realm gained the Shade Queen and her monsters."

He let out a dark chuckle. "Morgryth and my wife always despised it here."

"Why?"

"Not enough light magick to feast on. Not enough mortals to terrify." He shrugged.

"That's horrible."

"No," he clarified. "Destroying the Noctis lands was horrible. You cannot take away one's homeland and expect them to not take it personally."

Haven's history wasn't great, but because of Bell's obsession with the Nine Mortal Histories, she had an inkling of what the Shade Lord was referring to.

During the time of the first descendants of the Nine, when the Noctis were defeated by a mortal and the Solis army, then banished to the Netherworld, the Island Kingdom of Shadoria had been stripped from the Noctis and given to the Nine.

They named the lands the Court of Nine, a place where members of the Nine ruled together over the mortal kingdoms.

When the Curse broke open the Netherworld and let out Morgryth, the Effendier Sun Empress had destroyed Shadoria with magick rather than let the Noctis reclaim their kingdom.

"And what happens when the Curse finally destroys all of Eritreyia?" Haven asked.

He lifted a shoulder. "Then all of your world and mine will be like the Shadow Kingdom"—he nodded toward the inky clouds in the distance—"a cold and desolate place without sunlight or life."

"And that doesn't bother you?"

A bitter smile curved his jaw. "What do I care for sunlight and greenery? I am a creature of wintery, midnight skies rife with stars and shadows. Darkness feels to me what the sunlight on your skin feels to you."

And yet there was something in the way his voice wavered near the end, or perhaps the way his smile was a bit too forced, that made her question his words.

"Come," Stolas ordered. "Enough talk. Let us discover what you know about magick."

Haven swallowed, afraid Stolas's mercurial temper would flare at how little she actually knew. But there was no way around it, so she followed him across the grounds, a tangle of dread working into a knot inside her belly.

THIRTY-EIGHT

Stolas gestured impatiently toward a wrought-iron table near the cliff's edge, and they sat, gusts of wind lapping at them.

Turning his hand palm up, Stolas waved his fingers over the table and a silver platter appeared. "First, you must feast, before your mortal flesh withers off your bones."

His dramatic description of human hunger would have made her laugh, if her stomach wasn't so busy growling at the dazzling mound of food. Figs and candied walnuts, poached pears, green olives, pickled beets.

Another tray appeared, sunlight glistening off the braided wreaths of steaming bread. A third tray crowded the others, filled with every color of cheese imaginable.

But her appetite was tempered by the tales of flesh and blood travelers falling into the Netherworld and becoming trapped forever after eating from the Shade Lord's table.

Lifting her chin, she clamped her mouth shut.

"Not going to eat?" he demanded.

She shook her head, even as her stomach rumbled. "Not if it binds me to you."

One side of his lips quirked. "Ah, even now I cannot fathom who invented that foolish rumor. No, eating from my table will not bind you here, nor will a sliver of my horn give you power. And wearing one of my feathers around your neck will not make you immortal. Satisfied?"

Not nearly, but as Haven let her gaze fall on the delicious offerings once more, her need overwhelmed her good sense.

She reached for the food and promptly forgot about Bell. Forgot about Rook.

For a selfish moment, the only thing on her mind was the warmth of the bread against her tongue and the startling tang of the goat cheese that followed.

She couldn't chew fast enough to satisfy her body, could hardly catch a breath between her greedy bites, and soon, the strange murky glare of the sun reflected in the bottom of the half-eaten trays.

Stolas drummed his fingers over the table as he watched her gorge.

She lifted an unapologetic eyebrow, cheeks aching with food. "Wh . . . at?"

Sighing, he steepled his hands together and waited. A few minutes later, she groaned and leaned over the table, the ornate iron pressing into her cheek.

"Done?" he drawled, dark brows pulled into sharp peaks of judgment.

"For now."

"Good. We have time for a brief lesson. Two things: One, I want you to recreate the clothes you were wearing."

She opened her mouth to suggest he just give them back—

"I burned them."

Runes. She lifted up and cracked her neck, running a finger over the tiny streams of rust marring the table.

"Are you listening, Beastie?"

She rolled her eyes. "Yes!"

"Good. Two: I want you to soulbind me to your will at some point before you leave."

Her lips puckered to the side. "Wouldn't that be dangerous for you?"

"No." His dismissive tone scraped along her bones. "And if you order me to do something silly, like jump off this cliff, I will ignore you."

"But if you're soulbound, how can you refuse my request?"

"This is . . . practice. If your soulbinding is good, I will *voluntarily* allow my will to be bound. Now, clothes please."

A tiny shiver of excitement raced through her at the thought of soulbinding a Shade Lord, even if the idea reminded her of Damius and his wyvern.

"Focus." Stolas's voice was cold, commanding.

"I *am*."

He scoffed. "I've seen more focus from Ravius."

The bird on his shoulder stirred, fluffing its feathers.

"You named your raven the word 'raven' in Solissian?" She barely kept the mirth from her voice, despite his now murderous stare.

"Poor Prince Bellamy. If only you were as interested in saving him as you were devouring those succulent pears."

The insult drove away any lingering humor from her mood. Her jaw locked, and she flexed her fingers, pinning him with a savage glare.

"Better. Now, close your eyes and produce your shabby little clothes."

She did as told, even though all her instincts screamed not to lose sight of the predator a few feet in front of her.

With her eyes closed, she swore she could feel his knife-like gaze raking over her flesh. Studying her the way one might study a fine rack of lamb or perfectly golden-crusted peach cobbler.

"Now imagine your leather pants sliding over your thighs. Imagine the places you sweat with them on. Perhaps beneath the familiar aroma of animal hide, they carry a faint whiff of your sweet scent. Can you smell them? See them stretch against your legs?"

Slowly, the scuffed leather pants she'd stolen from Bell's closet emerged in the backdrop of her mind. She pictured their details. The rip in the right knee. The fine silver threading along the waist. Imagined slipping them on over her flesh, tugging to get them up her thighs—

A loud crack split the air, as if two rocks were hurled together. Her eyes snapped open, her nose wrinkling at the charred smell.

Strewn over the half-eaten trays, one leg missing, were her pants. Flames sizzled and hissed down the other leg.

She growled under her breath and tried again. This time, the supple leather turned to ash as soon as she touched the pants. The next, they were perfect—if she were the size of a doll.

Again and again and again, she tried. And each time, it was wrong. Too big. Too small. Too burnt. Too something.

Finally, she slumped back in the chair, dusting bits of ash and leather from her bare thighs. "It's impossible."

Hooded, lazy eyes watched her, his power evident with every unimpressed blink. "Think. You must have liked those pants, because you kept them, despite their horrid condition." She ignored the condescension coating his voice. "Why?"

She remembered the first time she wore the pants. The way the eyes of the male courtiers and servants who used to watch her changed from interest to indifference. As if she went from something that could be bought and owned to nothing. An anomaly, at best.

Putting on those pants had given her a certain independence that a dress never could.

She closed her eyes and thought of that feeling. Almost like being free.

Unlike the other times, there was no noise. No feeling. Her eyes snapped open. "Nothing ha—"

Her favorite russet-brown leather pants were folded neatly on the table. Her lips parted. She ran a finger over the top of the pants. The leather was exactly the same. The soft, pliable, brain-tanned leather made especially for Penrythian royals.

Stolas fixed her with a stern stare. "Why are you grinning?"

And she was, she realized. Because the pants reminded her of Penryth, of Bell.

Gathering all her willpower, she sucked in her bottom lip and focused on the tunic. That only took her five tries.

Again, she smiled. Again, he scolded her.

"Must you grin like a curse-sick mortal every time?" Stolas drawled. His fingers toyed with his golden cufflinks, his gaze traveling a lazy route between her and the pants.

In one word, he looked unimpressed.

"I must."

Her floppy hat came next. At the sight of her sweat-stained, beaten up old friend, she beamed—annoying Stolas to the point he growled, low and deep.

Ignoring him, she focused on the last item, her cloak. It took the longest to invoke.

She nearly gave up, and would have . . . if Stolas hadn't been watching with furrowed brows and a challenging gaze.

The expensive cloak was another present from Bell on his twelfth birthday. That was the first year he made it a tradition to celebrate her birthday the same day as his, since hers had long been forgotten.

As soon as she thought about that day and pictured the emerald ribbon tied around the ivory box the cloak came in, the invocation worked.

The sight of the ruby-red satin atop her clothes, fluttering in the wind, tightened an invisible cord inside her chest until she could hardly breathe.

Shadeling's shadow, she missed Bell.

"What's the matter?" Stolas growled, obviously alarmed that instead of smiling, she was close to tears.

"Nothing you would understand," she said, gathering up her clothes. She kept her face angled away from him to hide her anguish.

She could feel him watching her, and there was something different in his gaze now. But she didn't dare delude herself into thinking there was concern there, or the slightest sliver of empathy for her sadness.

Everyone knew monsters like Stolas weren't capable of such human emotions.

THIRTY-NINE

Haven was stunned at how heavy her conjured garments were, how very real they felt. She glanced down at the white silk straining against her hips.

Real or not, they were better than whatever the Netherworld Stolas had her wearing.

Pressing the clothes to her chest, she said, "I need to go change."

"Go ahead," he said.

"In private."

With a dark chuckle, he led her inside, through the gloom of the corridors and into a long, cavernous bathroom.

The ravens shadowed Stolas, the soft flutter of wings brushing stone as they followed him soon replaced by the burble of running water.

Centered in the room was a rectangular pool, water steaming and bubbling for at least thirty feet. Sunlight poured from several skylights above, painting everything silver as it danced along the gilded rim of the water. Four ebony columns rose from the floor, marking the four corners of the pool, etched with creatures she could only guess at.

If the secret got out that the Netherworld had such amenities, hell would soon be overcrowded.

After checking to make sure she was alone, she ripped off the nightgown and slipped slowly into the scalding water.

A breath hissed from her lungs as the heat worked out the knots in her muscles.

Goddess Above, she never thought she would miss Penryth and its many luxuries. Living there had made her soft, weak. She massaged her hands over her bruised thighs, corded with lean muscle from mornings spent training and nights spent crouched in trees.

If the purple color was any indication, she had been here no more than a day. Not long enough for her broken bones and burns to heal.

She would ask the Shade Lord about her injuries before she left, she decided, reluctantly slipping from the water and burying herself in one of the plush white towels near the marble vanity.

No way would she owe Stolas for anything else.

The clothes fit exactly like before. She found a tall mirror set into the stone and checked her reflection, frowning at the bruises darkening her cheeks. Her focus slid to her hair. It had been so long since she allowed herself to see it uncovered.

Now, draped in two sleek rows on either side of her chest and darkened by water to a dusty rose, it cut a bright contrast against her fair skin.

She tugged on a strand. Why couldn't the Goddess have given her normal hair?

Twisting her hair back, she tied it into a loose, wet knot. Then she covered it with her floppy hat, grinning as the flimsy brim drooped to cover one amber eye.

She was nearly out of the room before a silver flash drew her attention. A small horsehair brush laid bristles up on a short ledge. Closer inspection revealed ravens engraved in the sleek silver handle and long, silvery-white hairs tangled in the bristles.

Was there another woman here? Nothing else in the sparse bathroom pointed to any visitors, much less a female with beautiful hair. Her gaze found the nightgown pooled along the stone steps.

Someone had worn that before her, and it probably wasn't Stolas.

Stolas slipped from the shadows as soon as she entered the cold hallway, wolfish, with a restless energy that put her on edge. Even with his wings tucked close to his body, he barely fit inside the tight corridor.

While it took her eyes a few seconds to adjust, his had no such problem—evidenced by their golden glow.

"Would you like me to heal your bruises?" he asked quietly.

Her fingers fluttered over her cheek. "I'm fine."

"Fine?" His gaze ran up and down her body. "You look as if you have battled a wyvern."

She couldn't decide if there was sarcasm in his voice or not. "The last thing I want is to be bound to you."

He lifted an eyebrow.

"I know you healed my burns."

"And?"

She chewed her bottom lip. "I'd rather not owe you for that too."

"Beastie, you already owe me for saving your life, and not killing you in the forest. In fact, I'm fairly certain you cannot owe me more than you already do."

"But using magick is binding. You didn't use magick to save me from falling."

"A true blood debt is owed only if both parties agree before the use of the magick. Besides"—his sensual lips twisted to the side—"it wasn't magick that healed your burns."

"What was it?"

He leaned down, a lock of pale hair eclipsing one of his silver eyes. His nose brushed her cheek. "My blood."

With a feline grin, Stolas turned and glided down the hall.

Nausea rolled over her. She shivered, missing the warmth of the humid bath chamber as she trailed after him, cloak wrapped tight around her body, down a winding stairwell and through a cozy dining room rimmed with oversized benches and snowy cushions.

Her bare feet slipped across the freezing stone. She would need to invoke her boots once she was back in the forest.

At least one good thing had come from her visit here—although she still hadn't tried to soulbind him.

That gave her an idea. She rushed to the Shade Lord. His back stiffened in response before she ever touched him, but it was when her hands slipped around his right forearm that he froze.

His flesh was like ice, hard and cold and smooth. She circled to the front, slowly, carefully, as if cornering a snared Shadowling.

Still holding his arm, she rested the back of her hand against his frosty cheek. The tiniest of shudders rippled across his body, his eyes locked onto hers, slashed pupils dilating. The magickal charge between them electrified the air.

She had no clue what to do, how to reach someone's soul to bind to it, but she remembered when Damius had tried to soulbind her. The way he stared into her eyes.

She did the same now with Stolas, focusing on the dagger-ish pupils, the fiery ring of gold bleeding into his irises. Asking silent questions, searching for vulnerabilities, a shared emotion.

For ten rabid beats of her heart, his face was an icy mask beneath her hand. Then something—a flicker, a ragged breath—told her there was an opening.

Pushing off on her tiptoes, she whispered, "Stolas, you want to tell me . . ."

A connection was forming between them. Growing. Two frayed ends of a rope tangling together, twining and knotting. Their heartbeats were aligning, their breaths mingling. His pupils enlarged, his head pushed gently against her hand, and a silvery lock of his hair tickled her knuckles.

"Tell me," she continued softly, "whose brush is in the bath chamber?"

His feral eyes went wide, and a wall slammed shut between them. She gasped as the connection was severed.

"Did I say something wrong?" she demanded.

With a snarl, he shoved past her, prowling into the darkness.

She ran after him, desperate to reach that connection again. Desperate, despite the warnings flashing through her body, to succeed. Silver light trickled around the corner. Squares of sunlight stretched across the floor.

They were nearly to the circular slab of balcony when she called out, "Stop."

His long strides paused, but he refused to turn around.

"At least tell me what I did wrong." His silence spurred her on. "You can't offer to heal my bruises one second and then get angry at me the next. That's not how . . . this works."

"This?"

She should have heeded the warning in his voice. "Yes, that's not how a partnership works."

317

For a single breath, he said nothing. Tension crammed the air until she could hardly breathe.

Then he spun to face her.

Her heart rammed into her throat at the sight of him. His eyes were pools of the deepest night. His lips curled over white, glistening incisors.

She gasped as his wings fanned out, blocking the sun, the sky. He was both impressive and terrible to behold, a beautiful winged demon.

His voice was like stone against stone as he growled, "Since you seem to have forgotten what I am, let me remind you. I am the Father of Shadows, Lord of Darkness. I claim dominion over the entire Netherworld, and you—you're a mortal who any other day I would drain of life and not think twice about. We are not partners, and we are certainly not friends. Do you understand?"

She should have fled, but instead, she was rooted into place, her furious breaths the only sound. What had changed between them? Did she say something wrong?

But he was right. After successfully unlocking her jaw, she muttered, "I won't forget, Monster."

She thought he might have flinched at that. Then again, perhaps his wings simply flared with pleasure at her obvious discomfort.

But whatever that display was for, to scare her or put her in her place, it had done the opposite. It reminded her to be on guard at all times around him. A lesson she wouldn't forget again.

He handed her a red silk scarf. "Put this over your eyes." When she hesitated, he said, "I cannot properly soulbind you to forget where this place is, so you will have to be blindfolded."

"Why must I forget?"

"Because," he growled, making his impatience with her constant questions clear, "this place is hidden from everyone, even the Shade Queen. And I'd like to keep it that way."

She jutted her jaw to convey her unhappiness as she slid the silk around her eyes. She hoped, perhaps, the fabric would allow enough light to make out something. But all she could see was dark red.

Having her sight taken from her was more unsettling than she'd imagined. Her heart raced, and when Stolas drew up behind her to tighten the knot, a gasp slipped from her lips.

"Where will you take me?" she said, her voice sounding hollow and small.

"Where do you need to go?" Stolas asked.

"Wherever vorgraths are."

"The mortal Kingdom of Verdure then." His breath was an icy gust of wind shivering down her neck. "The middle of Penumbra Forest."

Before she could reply, he added, "To save time we'll take a portal."

"A wh—?"

Somehow, she managed to hold down her scream as the ground wrenched from her feet. Every muscle in her body went taut.

She was encased in ice, falling through the air, her stomach doing somersaults. One freezing hand was pinned against her left shoulder; the other hand pressed into her lower abdomen.

Just when she was sure they would smash into the ground, she felt Stolas's arms tighten around her, and they shot forward. She lost herself in the red and the cold, the foreign weightlessness, the wild vulnerability of not knowing what was happening as they glided for what could have been minutes—or hours.

Her heart drummed against her ribcage—not from anger or fear, but from elation. A part of her actually enjoyed this, she realized, her abdominal muscles tightening at the feel of soaring through the air like a hawk.

At being weightless, being free.

"A little advice"—Stolas's frozen lips fluttered over the delicate shell of her ear—"don't kill the vorgrath, unless you want its mate to hunt you to the ends of the earth."

"Thanks." She was suddenly aware of his body intimately pressed against hers. The way his hand pressed low against her belly, creating a flare of warmth despite his flesh being cold.

"If you need me," he added softly, "say my name three times. But only if it is an absolute emergency." A pause, followed by, "Don't let me down, Beastie."

And then the song of the forest—birds singing, leaves rustling— trickled into her ears, the ground pressed against her bare feet, and gravity took hold.

Her nose filled with the sweet aroma of the mortal world, moist earth and rotting wood and life. Warmth spread across her flesh.

She ripped the blindfold off and whipped around—

Alone—she was alone. Surrounded by massive, sinuous oaks and sycamores that devoured the sky. Bluish shafts of light trickled from the ceiling of foliage, revealing a green world of gnarled branches, hanging vines thicker than her arm, and dripping curtains of moss. Gray fungi larger than her crept up the thick trunks.

The air was swollen with moisture and the buzz of strange insects, and something else.

Something ancient.

Despite the warm, humid air, an undercurrent of dark magick ran through the woods. As if, beneath the perfume of moss and dirt came a whiff of something long dead.

Maybe it was the Curse wending through the landscape, slowly sating itself on the light magick. Or perhaps it was the monsters that inhabited the woods. She wasn't sure which option was worse.

A shiver pulsed through her, and she quickly set to work invoking the rest of what she would need—first on that list being weapons.

FORTY

Surai glanced wearily up at the tree where Bjorn stretched out, still and sanguine as a lizard sunning itself.

She was leaned against a hard rock watching Rook, now in her cursed animal form, resting quietly in the tree's spotty shade. Dappled sunlight danced across her golden ribcage with every ragged breath she panted.

She stopped opening her golden eyes hours ago.

Helpless terror wound its way around Surai's heart, and she ground her teeth, glancing back at Bjorn. If she were to climb those thick branches, his eyes would be ivory slits, his gaze far, far away from this world and its miseries.

How nice it would be to escape from her heartache, even for a moment.

Where Bjorn traveled when he was in the midst of his visions was a mystery to them all, probably even Bjorn. She often wondered what he had been like before the Shade Queen imprisoned him.

Out of all of them, he was the youngest.

And, yet, he seemed so much older.

Bjorn was cryptic about his years in Spirefall under the Shade Queen's shadow, but it was there, she knew, where his gift had been honed. There, where he learned to travel to the other realm, to see the many strands of possibilities their world held. There, where his spirit had been broken by Morgryth's untold cruelties.

All for the very skill Bjorn was hopefully performing now. Surai tried not to think about the price. His eyes, among other horrors he refused to speak of.

Goddess Above, when she and Rook found him, half-dead along the border, they assumed he would die in a day. His bones were broken, his side had been gouged by some type of Shadowling, and his feet . . . runes, his feet had been bloodied and swollen from walking miles over mountainous terrain with no shoes.

Rook nursed him back to life along with the help of Archeron and his best friend, Remurian. Between their healing runes and Rook's stubbornness, Bjorn escaped the Shadeling's shadow.

Still, it had taken four months before Bjorn uttered a single word. Rook doted on him. She swore he must have been a noble before he was taken, a fact Bjorn never confirmed nor denied. They all just assumed he was a Sun Lord because of his power and regal manner.

For a time, Surai was actually jealous of Rook's devotion to Bjorn—until Surai remembered Rook had been found much the same way after her mother discovered Rook was breaking off her engagement to the sniveling Effendier Prince she was promised to.

Not beaten and near death, like Bjorn. No, the Morgani Queen knew her daughter well enough that a thousand beatings would have done nothing to change her mind after she fled on her wedding day.

Instead, Rook's mother exiled her from her homeland and stripped away her title of Morgani Princess.

Rook must have seen part of herself in Bjorn. A wanderer, without family, home, or title. But Surai never felt such a closeness to the seer. Thirty mortal years passed, and yet, she still felt as if she hardly knew Bjorn at all.

Throwing an impatient glance at Rook, Surai sighed and stood, ready to try and wake the seer. But in that same instant, he dropped from the tree and landed on his feet, eyes wide and chest heaving.

"Archeron!" he cried, blinking and clawing at phantom shadows. Sweat glistened over his ebony skin, his ageless features cracked and twisted.

Surai rushed to his side, touching his face to calm him. "Bjorn, it's me, Surai. You just came out of a vision."

Gasping, he brushed her hand away. "Where is Archeron? It may already be too late!"

Her head pounded—from fear or frustration, she didn't know. "Take some air. Settle yourself."

His cheeks puffed as he blew out three hard breaths. She had never seen him so unnerved. "The mortal, I saw her. Somehow she is still alive. But I see her paths splitting. I see—I see . . ."

Surai pressed her palm against Bjorn's cheek, forcing back the urge to drag the information out of him. The muscles below his jaw flexed, jumping wildly.

The first few minutes out of his visions, Bjorn was disoriented, and the information could easily become mixed up if he was not gently eased back into this realm.

"Bjorn, I'm here," she cooed, trying to coax him with her voice. "It will be okay; just take your time."

"She has no more time," he gasped. "Her strands are too tangled around the shadow of death, and I cannot find a way to separate them. She must kill the vorgrath to survive. I also see an arrow plunged deep in the vorgrath's chest, and her death soon to follow."

"Perhaps there is—"

Before Surai could finish her thought, Bjorn grasped onto the collar of her cloak, his white eyes looking through her to something she could not see. "Everything—all of our fates—rest on this one mortal girl. She must not die. She cannot! The vorgrath is the key! Archeron—Archeron must find her and make another strand. He must not let her kill the vorgrath!"

Bjorn's eyes rolled back in his head, and Surai grabbed him before he could fall, easing him into the soft earth. Once she had him situated, she warmed some moonberry tea over the smoldering fire.

Her hands trembled as she forced him to drink, her mind whirring to make sense of everything he had said.

But no matter how many times she replayed his words, how many ways she construed their meaning, one thing was certain: All their lives depended on a mortal girl surviving a dangerous, wicked land that had slaughtered entire kingdoms in a day.

Closing her eyes, Surai sent a silent plea to the Goddess—although she wasn't entirely convinced that even she could help them now.

Still, something close to hope stirred inside Surai's chest, warming the cold shadows of despair that had taken hold. Haven wasn't like any mortal she'd ever met. Nor any Solis for that matter.

She was something else entirely. Brave beyond reason. Kind when it mattered. Fierce and loyal and deceptively strong.

But it was the inner light practically bursting from Haven that Surai clung to. The one that had broken through Archeron's wounded exterior—not that he'd ever admit as much—and made Rook trust her, even after what mortals did to them.

The one that made Surai call Haven a friend.

Maybe to kill a curse, it wasn't strength or skill that mattered— but heart. Maybe the light inside Haven could lift the darkness plaguing their world.

It was an irrational thought, and the others would have laughed at Surai for thinking it. But she was tired of accepting the scraps fate deigned to give them.

They'd already lost so much, and she refused to give any more.

Even if it meant being crushed by disappointment, even if it was all a desperate lie, she was betting everything on the mortal with the rose-gold hair.

"Everything rests on you now, little mortal," Surai whispered, praying to the Goddess to carry the words to Haven, wherever she was. "Don't let us down."

A faint breeze stirred the trees, and Surai thought she heard a distant voice rustle the air before it was gone.

FORTY-ONE

An array of weapons glinted in the marshy grasses at Haven's feet. She'd tried to invoke Oathbearer, but her sword appeared in its final resting state, a scattered mess of fragmented steel.

No matter. She had enough steel here to fell a small battalion. One side of her mouth lifted in a grin. Now that she knew how to invoke, she might have gotten carried away.

A far-off cry pierced the forest, reminding Haven she didn't have much time. She needed to arm herself and then get downwind before the many creatures inside this place smelled her—if they hadn't already.

Tightening her cloak around her chest, she glanced over the steel below. The light that reflected off the blades soothed the unease nipping at her spine.

After a brief inspection, she claimed her scythes, a gorgeous longbow made of birch, an unadorned short sword, and several smaller daggers. The arrows that went into her back quiver had been invoked last, and she was grateful for every single one.

She would have invoked other things, like the dried lamb ch'arki that hung from the trader tents in Penryth, but her power had faded to a hollow, inept tingle. Her hands frustratingly empty of the beautiful orange-and-blue flames of magick she'd grown so fond of.

Either drained by the Curse or inexperience—or both.

Her ignorance about magick highlighted how unequipped she was for the task at hand, not that she would openly admit as much. But standing alone in a forest a thousand miles from home, with nothing but a few handy bits of steel and the promise of training later in her dreams—if she made it till tonight—her usual confidence faltered.

She was one mortal girl. Her magick fleeting and unpredictable. How in the world could she track a vorgrath, siphon its venom and steal one of its precious figs, and then survive to make it back to Rook in time?

It came to her that she had no idea how to find the band of Solis after she accomplished the dangerous task. It came to her how very stupid and impossible this mission was. It came to her that she would probably die before nightfall.

Standing beneath the delicate shafts of light from the afternoon sun, she contemplated escaping this forest of nightmares and going home. To Penryth.

Or farther . . .

But the second she imagined fleeing, something inside riled at the thought. She was no coward. How could she even think about leaving Bell?

Any lingering ideas of abandoning Bell or Rook evanesced as Haven gritted her teeth and finished strapping on her weapons.

The oaths she made blazed bright in her mind. Four oaths bound in honor.

One to protect Bell.

One to break the curse and free him.

One to bring the vorgrath venom back to Rook.

And one to train with the Lord of the Netherworld.

Now those promises filled her with strength. Haven was a lot of things, but not an oath breaker. She would keep her oaths or die trying, to the Netherworld with anyone who tried to stop her.

Grinning, she plunged into the shadows of the forest, her mind on Bell and the time they had in Penryth. Unsolicited, the band of Solis entered her memories to keep her company. She wasn't quite sure who they were to her yet, but she felt bonded to them in a way she had never connected with anyone but Bell.

The cryptic seer and his awful stews. The fierce, brave Rook. The noble and kind Surai. Even the arrogant, infuriating Archeron found a place in her heart, his smug grin making her laugh out loud.

"Don't worry," she muttered. "I'll save you all."

The trees suddenly danced around her in a strange breeze that whispered voices and magick, and she closed her eyes.

For a fleeting moment, she thought she heard Surai talking. Her voice so close, so real, Haven almost believed the graceful Solis warrior was strolling beside her, katanas swinging in their scabbards.

Perhaps Rook was there in her feline form, chasing the shadows, her tail twitching with delight. And Bjorn, Bjorn smiled at Haven from somewhere close by, his blind eyes seeing deep into her heart.

Archeron was there, of course, frowning at Haven as he prowled on silent feet, doing his best to annoy her with insults and his ungodly good looks.

Even the Shade Lord, Stolas, appeared, his form shimmering and ever changing, his glorious feathers catching beneath the sun as he watched her beneath a scowl, his intentions as unclear as ever.

And Bell. Always Bell. With his gentle smile and dancing eyes. He was safe, unharmed. Happy.

Whatever this was, Haven didn't question it. Sometimes the best magick was the kind one couldn't control or understand, the kind that came unexpectedly from the inside. She wasn't sure how long the vision would last, or even if she would live past the night.

All Haven knew for sure was, for a fleeting moment, she wasn't so alone after all.

FORTY-TWO

The sun's rays were dusky silver as they bled into the treetops, whispers of nightfall in their slow decline. Stolas's ravens shifted with discontent on their perches high above, making the pearl-gray tree branches look alive.

They felt his restlessness, though he hardly noticed them.

His gaze was fixed on a small form as she penetrated deeper into the forest, her strange hat shadowing most of her face so that only her lips were visible. Upturned lips—not quite smiling, but amused.

What did Haven have to be amused about?

Snarling, he leapt from tree to tree above, tracking just over her shoulder. *The fool should be terrified, not half-grinning at the shadows as if they didn't hold monsters.*

The dark forest was alive with creatures, all of which feasted on mortals like her. Himself included.

Occasionally, as if she felt his presence, or perhaps his scorn, she glanced back.

Impossible. No one but he could pierce the mortal realm's veil to see the mirror world beyond. Still, he found himself taking care to be quiet, and holding his breath when she wandered too near.

Which was hard considering he wanted to give her a good tongue-lashing. The idiot mortal was lost, the day nearly gone. By nightfall, her fate would be sealed.

"Why do you put any faith in her at all?" a familiar voice called behind him.

Stolas wasn't surprised she had followed him. Even so, his wings shivered at the intrusion, erupting into nearly their full span. Branches snapped and his ravens scattered, a gust of wind blowing back her snowy hair.

"Do not go near her," he snarled. Pressure swelled in his fingertips, and then his talons released.

Only halfway, but the warning was clear.

She laughed, a deceptively innocent sound. "I could have drained her while she bathed, if I wanted." The limb he perched on bowed with her weight as she joined him. "Do you know how weak mortal's bodies are? They have no wings, no fangs, not even claws to protect them."

"I am well aware."

"Yet she is free and I am not."

"You are not ready."

"And the mortal girl is?" she hissed. "Look at her! She won't even accept her dark magick."

"Then," he said, a gruff edge to his voice, "it will kill her."

"Why do you put so much faith in her?" she continued, achieving a tone both curious and resentful. "You say I'm impetuous, but she is worse. You say my powers aren't honed enough, yet she can barely invoke a tunic."

The Lord of the Netherworld followed Haven with his gaze. The truth was he did not know. And that angered him. "She is a tool, one to wield to our advantage. Nothing more."

"Is that why you saved her?"

His chest rumbled with a growl.

"I've never seen you let anyone talk to you the way she did. Not even me. Not even Ravenna . . ."

A snarl tore from his throat. "Enough."

She backed away, her small, dark wings fluttering the air in alarm. Even Ravius, perched lightly on his shoulder, was startled by the sound and took to the air.

Cocking her head, she turned to study Haven as the mortal whacked wildly at brambles that had snagged her cloak. "I suppose it doesn't matter. She won't survive the night. Then she will be trapped in the Netherworld for us to play with for an eternity."

A muscle in his jaw twitched.

"Care to wager on it?" she pressed.

"And what are we wagering?" he mused.

It was a game they'd played since they were imprisoned in the Netherworld. Betting on which mortal would break first, which way they would try to run. What they would offer in return for their escape back to the mortal realm.

Now, though, it did not feel like a game.

"If she survives till daybreak, I promise to behave for a . . . whole year."

"A decade," he amended. "Not a day less. And if she doesn't?"

"Then I'm free from my prison for a day," she grinned, "to do whatever I like and drink whomever I like. But you cannot intervene to save her."

He felt his lips tug into a frown, and he once again rested his stare on the mortal girl. Through the mirrored veil, the faint shimmer of her warring powers was visible, swirling around her form, dark tendrils of bluish light twining with pale-gold fire.

If he lived another five centuries, he would never see such a sight. Dark and light magick fused together. As they flickered over her flesh, they formed rare runes of ancient origin, the meaning unknown to even him.

If only she could find a way to harness such a power . . .

But the shadowy roots of her dark magick writhed in desperation, trying to find entrance into her being as they fought against the lighter strands. Both looking for a stronghold to lay root.

Both vying to claim her.

His gaze fell to her face. Just like her magick, she was a study in contrasts. Strong yet weak. Fierce yet kind. Hard yet surprisingly vulnerable.

And, common, in the way of all mortals. Yet also strangely . . . alluring. With her vibrant hair and too-big eyes the color of tarnished gold, flecked with silver and bright with purpose.

As he took in the curve of her neck, the frailness of her human body contrasted against the jut of determination in her jaw, something inside him stirred.

Not protectiveness, exactly, nor affection—but certainly an emotion too human for his liking.

Would he try to preserve her life in the mortal realm again if it came to that?

The answer made him uneasy, and he snarled again before promising, "I will not change her fate this time. It's up to her now to live or die."

Spreading his wings, he took to the sky, leaving a wake of broken limbs raining down on the forest floor below. His ravens filled the air with their cries as they trailed after their master.

Gathering the birds to him, he wielded their black bodies into a cloak of slippery shadows until he was masked in their darkness.

Haven Ashwood might hold the future of the realm in her clumsy mortal hands, but he could only do so much.

It was time she proved herself to be who he thought she was.

One way or another, they would meet again. Either in her dreams—if she somehow survived the vorgrath—or in the Netherworld, her soul bound to him to torment for an eternity.

THE END

BOOK TWO

Curse Breaker

ONE

For the first time in years, Haven was lost. The vorgrath tracks she'd spotted hours ago now seemed an illusion, the musky scent the creature used to mark its territory a figment of her mind.

And yet, she could still smell the foul odor on her finger, swiped from a mossy tree not too far from here.

She spun around, her boots slipping against mud, breath loud in her ears as she searched the treetops for a break in the heavy foliage that veiled the sky. If only she could see the sun's position, she could determine what direction she was heading.

Usually the woods gave her answers. The side of a boulder the moss grew on. The direction the clouds were moving. Even where the spider hung its web could tell her north from south.

But the dark magick in these woods turned everything she knew about the forest on its head. Massive silver webs of arachnids she prayed never to meet shimmered from high branches on both sides. Moss carpeted everything.

Shifting her newly invoked pack across her shoulder, she ducked under the roots of a huge oak, grimacing as pearl-white larvae dropped onto her head.

She crouched beneath the same tree an hour ago, she was sure of it. Only now, instead of one fallen tree blocking her path, three twisting alders sprouted from the ground.

If she truly walked here before, there were no tracks. Either the forest was constantly changing, or she was losing her mind.

Oh, Bell. You would love to study this place. She could hear him prattling on about the magickal properties, see him studiously writing it all down. *Goddess Above, I miss you.*

Now that she was alone, without the band of Solis constantly distracting her, she had time to realize the hole her best friend left with his absence. His beaming smile, his teasing laugh.

He's why you're doing all of this, she reminded herself. *Don't let him down.*

Thinking about the Penrythian prince made her redouble her efforts to find the vorgrath. Not only did she need a fig from its keep to satisfy the Curseprice, but if she didn't somehow collect a few drops of venom from one of its famously long incisors, the Sun Queen Rook would die.

"No pressure," she muttered, stomping through the brackish waters of a swamp. Mud clung to her boots and made her legs feel heavy, the stench of rancid water filling her nose.

Fighting the urge to wretch, she wiped her forehead, collecting sweat and depositing moss and mud over her skin.

Blasted water! She'd never hated it more. It dampened the air and filled her lungs, making every inhalation a chore.

Her eyes strained from searching the boggy soil for the triangular, three-toed tracks left by the vorgrath. As she looked, her mind replayed the second piece of the Curseprice.

The fig of a vorgrath from its mate's keep.

Experience taught her that male vorgraths were never very far from their mate's keeps, guarding the fig trees day and night for their partner. The male vorgraths would kill any creature that came too close, especially during mating season.

Last summer, when she nearly snared the vorgrath terrorizing the Muirwood, she'd counted almost fifty woodland creatures slaughtered within a half mile radius from its keep.

Most of the victims were nocturnal animals, which told her the vorgrath was probably less active during the day. Perhaps it even slept for a few hours—if she were lucky.

By the time she'd found the vorgrath's treasure, a young fig tree hidden near a ravine, orange rays of dusk filled the Muirwood, and she decided to leave and come back in daylight.

When she returned the following day, the fig tree had been stripped of its fruit, and the male vorgrath lay dead on the ground. Killed by its mate, probably after the female smelled Haven's scent so close to her keep.

Whatever happened now, she couldn't forget that even if she somehow got the fig from a vorgrath's keep, and somehow collected its venom without dying, and *somehow* got away, the female would be close.

Haven discovered more vorgrath tracks near a bog. The day was fading, steeping the woods in deep shadows, a few coral rays of light retreating with every crushing throb of her heart. Here and there, bare patches mottled the trees where something had rubbed away the bark.

Strange, high-pitched shrieks pierced the heavy air, along with exotic noises she couldn't place, from creatures she would rather not encounter. But the further west she walked, the quieter the forest became.

Most people thought silence in the woods was a good thing, but Haven knew better.

She was now officially in vorgrath territory.

She crept through the latticework of tree-roots and vines, careful to avoid the water-filled footprint she followed. By the deepness of the track and the length of the toes, this vorgrath was much larger and older than the one from the Muirwood.

And cleverer—it tracked through streams and doubled back more than once.

Wonderful. Just her luck she found a mature, established vorgrath, which meant it would be large and overly protective of its lair. How was she not supposed to kill it?

But, according to Stolas, killing it would doom her. "Don't kill the vorgrath," she mocked, making her voice low and taunting to sound like the Shade Lord's, "unless you want its mate to hunt you to the ends of the earth."

Kicking the worm-eaten stump of a tree, she rolled her eyes. "How does that help me if I'm dead?"

For a breath, the forest stirred, and she could swear an annoyed chuckle trickled from above.

Shadeling's shadow, this place was getting to her. If only Surai were here to complain to. She imagined Rook scoffing as the two tried to find their way through the tangle of woods, Archeron stalking ahead, annoyed at something Haven said or did—like breathing or simply existing.

Still—she missed them. *All* of them.

She would have never admitted such a thing a few hours earlier . . . but it was true. The Solis had grown on her. Even if they made fun of her and treated her like a pet, even if Archeron had a habit of restraining and taunting her, being around them felt normal. Safe.

Growing soft, Ashwood.

Pushing thoughts of the Solis away, she pressed deeper into the overgrowth, growling under her breath as the shadows between the trees seemed to elongate and darken before her eyes.

Tension danced over her sweaty skin, drawing gooseflesh over her arms. She slipped out the dagger generously loaned to her from the Shade Lord.

The weapon was heavier than she preferred, weighted down with an intricate gold handle, the onyx hilt a set of raven's wings. Rubies and black diamonds swirled around the handle, hard beneath her palm.

"Vengeance, huh?" Haven muttered, calling the dagger the name Stolas used earlier. "You don't look like much, beyond a fancy paperweight."

She could have sworn the dagger flickered in anger, a pulse of magick piercing her palm, and the urge to chuck the dagger surged through her.

Still, vorgraths were stealthy creatures. By the time she noticed one upon her, her bow would be useless. And she held out the far-flung hope that she would catch this vorgrath sleeping—surely they did that—and be able to somehow incapacitate it without it noticing.

So heavy, magickal dagger named Vengeance it was.

The vines and foliage became denser, strangling the light even more. She quietly hacked a path, twigs and thorns gouging her cheeks, ducking and slipping through vegetation that seemed to tighten around her.

Undoubtedly if Stolas saw how she misused his favored dagger he would be pissed, but she was beyond caring.

The foliage thickened until she was caught inside the thick mess of brambles and vines. Panic weighed her down, and she forgot to be quiet. Forgot she was supposed to be calm. Hacking wildly, she clawed her way forward, gasping for breath, for light, for—

A hole opened up, and she tumbled forward.

Blinking against the watery darkness, tinged red by the last bit of sun, she straightened her hat and took in the scene. An enormous tree rose thirty feet in the distance. The massive, gnarled thing was centered inside the hollow of vegetation something had carefully built, a giant nest of vines, branches, and bones glued together with dried mud.

Immense roots swarmed the base of the tree, angry gray serpents half-buried in the earth. The branches were low, thick, and wide-set. And along the smallest branches hung dark, teardrop fruits.

The vorgrath's fig tree.

Haven froze, the breath dying in her throat. Adrenaline narrowed her vision, and her gaze darted around the tree, sifting through the shadows. There were no forest noises inside the vorgrath's nest, no whispering breeze or insects.

Nothing but her ragged, terrified breath and the low *thump thump* of her heart. A perfume of decay and overripe figs filled her nose and made her head spin.

Her hand tightened around the Shade Lord's dagger as she approached the tree. Sweat trickled down her shoulder blades. Her soggy clothes made her feel heavy and slow. Hunger and adrenaline and fatigue messed with her vision, making things seem close and then far away. Creating movement where there was none.

As she carefully stepped over the tall, winding roots near the base of the tree, her gaze fell over what looked at first like large eggs. But then, for a blessed moment, her eyesight sharpened.

Not eggs—human skulls.

Pale cracked skulls atop mounds of rusted armor and bone. Fear scraped down her spine as she catalogued the informal graveyard. Human accoutrements were everywhere. A muddy boot here. A mildewed travelers purse there.

Her breath caught as she spied a closed brass helmet on its side, vines and other vegetation growing through the visor. The Boteler standard, a black dahlia x, was visible on its side.

Twelve. Thirteen. Fourteen. Her mind automatically counted the skulls . . . only to stop when she realized what she was doing.

Goddess Above, two grape-sized puncture wounds marred most of the skulls, undoubtedly left by vorgrath fangs. Some had been shattered into hundreds of pieces, and an unwelcome image of the vorgrath smashing a human's skull into the tree trunk flashed inside her mind.

A few had been stacked one on top of the other to form gruesome pillars. A warning to stay away or die.

Good thing she never listened to reason or she would have fled on the spot.

Instead she said a silent prayer to the Goddess and toed between the skulls, muscles tense as she waited for her boots to crunch bone and wake the vorgrath.

Clever, she admitted, eyeing the macabre alarm system of bones, even as nausea tingled the back of her throat.

How many fools desperate to break the Curse had stepped where she did now, seconds before the vorgrath butchered them?

Deep, deep scrapes were carved into the pale gray trunk of the tree. A last warning made by talons longer than her fingers.

Runes, she wanted to take the warning and flee. Out of this nest of death. Out of the dark, ruined forest. All the way to Penryth.

Except, there was no Penryth without Bell. And if she succumbed to her fear, she could run to the ends of the realm and still never escape the guilt and grief for letting Bell die for her magick and Rook die for her stupidity.

Clamping the dagger blade between her teeth, she began to creep up the tree. She moved slowly, meticulously, aware of every scrape of her boot, every explosion of breath from her lips.

Her heartbeat was a furious drum reverberating inside her skull and drowning out all other sounds.

If the vorgrath caught her now, she would be helpless.

She pulled herself onto a two-foot wide branch and froze, straining to listen. The silence crawled beneath her skin, shivering across her bones.

What if the vorgrath was awake, waiting for her in the upper branches? What if it was biding its time, incisors already drawn and ready to puncture her skull?

Happy thoughts, Ashwood. She held her breath and scaled to a higher branch. Then another. Each time scouring every limb, every glistening leaf for a fig to steal. But it wasn't until midway up the tree that she found two plump figs hanging at the bottom of a cluster of leaves.

One fruit was still green and hard to the touch. But the other was a deep crimson color, firm yet pliable. It fell away with one cut from Stolas's dagger. As soon as the ripe fig was safely inside her pocket, the urge to leave overwhelmed her.

Releasing a silent breath, she glanced down to freedom. To survival. If she fled with the fig, Bell's chances were a hundred times better. But if she scurried higher, if she met the vorgrath and tried to extract his venom, she would probably die, taking Bell's chances to the grave.

A soft, gurgling rattle trickled from above. Like something

rousing from sleep. The dagger shook in her hand.

Run, Run, Run!

She did no such thing. With a heavy sigh—and her promise to Surai ringing in her mind—she shoved the dagger between her teeth and crept higher, her body numb with a potent cocktail of adrenaline and fear.

Netherworld take her, she couldn't break a promise. She wouldn't. Even if this was about the stupidest thing she'd ever done.

A wall of stench slammed into her, like rancid meat cocooned in wet dog fur. The odor stung her eyes. The wide branch above dipped low as something stirred, something heavy and large, a hideous melody of guttural grunts and clacking talons clawing her eardrums.

The vorgrath was awake.

Sniffing—it was slowly drawing in the air, tasting it. Tasting *her.*

The inhalations paused, and she went dead still, a statue of nerves and panic. For an anxious heartbeat, deadly quiet strangled the air, and her muscles contracted, prepared to fight even as her mind howled with blinding terror.

The branch dipped and lifted, leaves rustling and sending her heart into a tailspin as the vorgrath jumped high up in the tree.

Panting, Haven craned her neck to the tallest branches. Where was it?

A flash, then more rustling leaves. She replaced her dagger with her bow and nocked a poison-tipped arrow, following the shimmer of moving leaves.

But it moved too fast for a good shot. A blur of gray, a rustle of leaves, and by the time she swiveled her arrow-tip in that direction, it had moved again.

It was trying to confuse her. To knock her off balance.

The tree was shaking violently. Knees bent, Haven focused on stabilizing her core as the vorgrath moved faster and faster.

Again and again it jumped.

Again and again she switched her aim.

All at once, the tree branches froze. The noise stopped. Silence rippled over her, intensifying the frantic drumming of her heart.

Where are you?

She felt the limb she crouched on waver before she heard the vorgrath's claws click over the soft wood behind her.

On instinct, she swung around while simultaneously releasing her arrow.

The vorgrath was a hideous collection of shriveled, scaly gray skin pulled taut over spindly bones, two twisted and gnarled horns rising from its skeletal head and curling along the spinal ridges of its hunched back. Cadaverous arms, made for swinging across trees and slashing prey, reached nearly to its feet. Black talons longer than her dagger sprouted from its lank fingers.

But it was its eyes that shriveled the air in her chest. Wide, whitish-red eyes, like blood swirled in milk. There was no pupil, nothing in those eerie orbs to speak of humanity or connect with.

The vorgrath clawed at the arrow embedded into its gaunt chest, talons clacking. A high-pitched scream turned her bowels to jelly.

She'd hit just above where she guessed was its heart.

She nocked another arrow, only to remember Stolas's warning. Along with the pesky fact that she needed the creature alive to retrieve the venom.

Nethergates! Everything inside her screamed to put the monstrous predator down. But a promise was a promise.

So the dagger replaced the bow, and she inched forward as the vorgrath screeched at her, revealing jagged teeth that could shred

Penrythian armor and sever bone. Drops of poison glistened from the end of two long, curved fangs.

It was said the male vorgrath used its poison to incapacitate the intruder to present, still alive, to its mate. The thought was enough to send bile lapping at the back of her throat.

The vorgrath glanced up at the high branches.

"No!" she yelled, causing the creature to hiss. "Don't you dare jump, you hideous thing."

How did one go about soulbinding a vorgrath?

Its hate-filled eyes dropped to her dagger, and it hissed louder. The webbing over its protracted ribcage vibrated with a warning rattle. Grayish-black goo seeped from its wound.

"Shh," she cooed, stealing another step closer, mirroring the vorgrath's body posture. "Be a good little vorgrath."

The rattle became a staccato of deep growls that curdled her blood. All the delicacies she had scarfed at the Shade Lord's home threatened to come up as she slid closer.

She could do this. She had nearly soulbound a Shade lord. Surely, she could soulbind this terrible, ugly creature.

She was close enough now, one leap and its fangs would penetrate her neck, or her skull. The vorgrath's head clicked to the side. Two translucent membranes shuttered over its hideous eyes as they studied her.

Goddess Above, it was ugly.

Her breathing was in line with its chest; she blinked when it blinked. The beginnings of a tentative connection formed between them. The bond felt strange, alien, the vorgrath's mind a savage landscape of greed and rage and primal urges, but she grasped onto the one commonality they shared—devotion.

His devotion to his mate became a door to slip through. The vorgrath fought her at first, the tether between them fraying, low snarls churning the air.

But after a few heartbeats, the creature calmed, and she knew he was hers to command.

Still, she approached carefully, slowly. One hand on the glass vial she kept for poisons, the other on her dagger. As she soothed the jagged terrain of its consciousness, gagging on the vorgrath's desiccating odor, she struggled to keep him docile and control her overriding fear.

The dying light glimmered off dead-fish scales riding up the vorgrath's sinewy neck. She held up the vial, slipping the edge just beneath the curved five-inch fangs peeking from its upper lip.

Its gray mouth parted.

It was panting in time with her heartbeat, and up close she realized it did have pupils—tiny vertical red slivers inside a sea of white.

"Good," she whispered, hardly daring to breathe as an iridescent, silvery drop of venom slid to the bottom of the jar. Just one more drop . . .

Clack. Clack. She glanced down to the vorgrath's long talons clicking together. The connection was slipping.

All at once, the vorgrath's murky-white membranes began blinking over its eyes, its bony rib cage heaving faster and faster.

Nethergates! She just managed to squeeze out one more drop of venom and slip the vial into her satchel before the connection snapped.

A snarl spewed from the vorgrath, as if it was surprised she was there. Its primordial gaze flicked to the arrow still buried deep in its chest, back to her, and it dropped into a crouch, muscles rippling inside bulging thighs.

Dagger in hand, Haven backed away until she wedged against the tree trunk. In one smooth motion, she traded the dagger for her bow and had an arrow nocked.

"Don't even think about it, dummy," she warned.

That stopped the ugly thing. It tilted its head side to side, quick, animalistic motions, then screamed at the arrow, raking its claws against the tree limb.

But it didn't follow as she hopped to the next limb, then the next, never taking the iron arrow-tip off its chest.

Although killing the ugly thing was tempting, she didn't want to risk the wrath of the vorgrath's mate if she didn't have to.

Perhaps an arrow in its bony shoulder might slow it a bit. Or piss it off—not that she imagined the fury raging inside its dead eyes could burn much brighter.

When she hit the ground, arrow still dead center on the vorgrath's chest, it crouched low and began to creep from branch to branch after her, never taking its gaze off her arrow. By the time she made it to the nest's entrance, walking backwards, it watched her from the lowest branch.

Just like that, the last trickle of light dried up, and night came.

Her hand around the bow was trembling and slippery with sweat.

Inside the vorgrath's nest, buried beneath a canopy of vines and leaves and bones, the faint light of the stars and moon couldn't enter, steeping her world in absolute darkness. The only light came from the vorgrath's red eyes, two windows into the Netherworld.

Apparently in the darkness they glowed bright as Netherfire—which wasn't creepy or terrifying at all.

And then, those fiery orbs blinked out, and she turned and ran.

GLOSSARY

- **The Bane** – The central region of Eritrayia and a barren wasteland, it acts as the buffer between the Ruinlands destroyed by the Curse and the untouched southern kingdoms protected by the runewall

- **Curseprice** – The items that must be collected and presented to the Shade Queen to break the Curse

- **Dark magick** – Derived from the Netherworld, it cannot be created, only channeled from its source, and is only available to Noctis. Dark magick feeds off light magick.

- **Darkcaster** – One who wields dark magick

- **Devourers** – Mortals with Noctis blood who practice demented dark magick and worship the Shade Queen; live in the bane and guard the rift/crossing into the Ruinlands

- **The Devouring** – The dark magick-laden mist that descends when the Curse hits and causes curse-sickness and death in mortals

- **Donatus Atrea** – All-Giver, or runetree of life where all light magick springs from

- **Eritrayia** – Mortal realm

- **Fleshrunes** – Runes Solis are born with; the markings tattoo a

Solis's flesh and channel their many magickal gifts

• **The Goddess** – Freya, mother of both Solis and Noctis, she is a powerful and divine being who gifted mortals with magick and fought on their side during the Shadow War.

• **Heart Oath** – Oath given before an engagement to marry. Can only be broken if two parties agree to sever the oath and at great cost

• **House of Nine** – Descendants of the nine mortals given runeflowers from the Tree of Life

• **Houserune** – Rune given to each of the Nine Houses and passed down from generation to generation

• **Light Magick** – Derived from the Nihl, it cannot be created, only channeled from its source, and is only available to Solis and royal mortals from the House Nine.

• **Lightcaster** – One who wields light magick

• **Mortalrune** – Runes mortals from the House Nine are allowed to possess/use

• **Netherworld** – Hell, where immoral souls go, ruled over by the Lord of the Netherworld

• **Nihl** – Heaven, ruled over by the Goddess Freya

• **Noctis** – Race of immortals native to Shadoria and the Netherworld who possess dark magic, they have pale skin, dark wings, and frequently horns

• **Powerrune** – Powerful type of rune forbidden to mortals

- **The Rift** – Chasm in the continent of Eritrayia caused by the Curse that leads to the Netherworld and allowed the Shade Queen and her people to escape

- **Ruinlands** – Northern half of Eritreyia, these lands are enchanted with dark magick and ruled by the Shade Queen

- **Runeday** – The eighteenth birthday of a royal child of the Nine Houses, where he or she receives their house runestone and potentially come into magick.

- **Runemagick** – Magick channeled precisely through ancient runes

- **Runestone** – Stones carved with a single rune—usually—and imbued with magick

- **Runetotem** – Tall poles carved with runes, they are used to nullify certain types of magick while enhancing others

- **Runewall** – A magickal wall that protects the last remaining southern kingdoms from the Curse

- **Sacred Heart Flower** – Given to the Solis at birth, this sacred bud is kept inside a glass vial and worn around the neck of one's intended mate

- **Shade Lord** – A powerful Noctis male, second only to the Shade Queen

- **The Shadeling** – Odin, father of both Solis and Noctis, he once loved Freya but became dark and twisted after fighting against his lover in the Shadow War. He now resides in the deepest pits of the Netherworld, a terrifying monster even the Noctis refuse to unchain.

• **The Shadow War** – War between the three races (mortals, Noctis, Solis,) sparked by the Goddess Freya giving mortals magick

• **Shadowlings** – Monsters from the Netherworld, under the control of the Lord of the Netherworld and the Shade Queen

• **Solis** – Race of immortals native to Solissia who possess light magick, they are more mortal-like in their appearance, with fair eyes and hair

• **Solissia** – Realm of the immortals

• **Soulread** – To read someone's mind

• **Soulwalk** – To send one's soul outside their body

• **Soulbind** – To bind another's will to yours/take over their body

• **Sun Lord** – A powerful Solis male who enjoys special position in the Effendier Royal Sun Court under the Effendier Sun Sovereign

• **Sun Queen** – A powerful Solis female who enjoys special position in the Effendier Royal Sun Court under the Effendier Sun Sovereign

SOLISSIAN WORDS AND PHRASES

- **Ascilum Oscular** – Kiss my ass (maybe)
- **Carvendi** – Good job (more or less)
- **Droob** – Knob/idiot
- **Paramatti** – Close the door to the Nihl, used during a light magick spell
- **Rump Falia** – Butt-face
- **Umath** – You're welcome
- **Victari** – Close the door to the Netherworld, used during a dark magick spell

THE NINE MORTAL HOUSES

- **Barrington** (Shadow Kingdom, formerly Kingdom of Maldovia)
- **Bolevick** (Kingdom of Verdure)
- **Boteler** (Kingdom of Penryth)
- **Courtenay** (Drothian)
- **Coventry** (Veserack)
- **Halvorshyrd** (unknown location)
- **Renfyre** (Lorwynfell)
- **Thendryft** (Dune)
- **Volantis** (Skyfall Island)

KINGDOM OF RUNES PLAYERS

Mortal Players

- **Haven Ashwood** – orphan
- **Damius Black** – Leader of the Devourers
- **Prince Bellamy (Bell) Boteler** – House Boteler, crown prince, second and only surviving heir to the king of Penryth
- **King Horace Boteler** – House Boteler, ruler of Penryth
- **Cressida Craven** – King Horace Boteler's mistress
- **Renk Craven** – half-brother to Bell, bastard son of Cressida and the King of Penryth
- **Eleeza Thendryft** – Princess of House Thendryft of the Kingdom of Dune, House Thendryft
- **Lord Thendryft** – House Thendryft of Dune Kingdom
- **Demelza Thurgood** – Haven Ashwood's Lady's Maid

Noctis Players

- **Stolas Darkshade** – Lord of the Underworld, husband to Ravenna, son of the last true Noctis Queen
- **Avaline Kallor** – Skeleton Queen, Ruler of Lorwynfell, half Noctis half mortal, promised to Archeron Halfbane
- **Remurian Kallor** – Half Noctis half mortal, brother of Amandine, died in the last war
- **Malachi K'rul** – Shade Lord, Shade Queen's underling

- **Morgryth Malythean** – Shade Queen, Cursemaker, queen of darkness, ruler of the Noctis
- **Ravenna Malythean** – Daughter of the Shade Queen, undead

Solis Players

- **Bjorn** – Sun Lord of mysterious origins
- **Archeron Halfbane** – Sun Lord and bastard son of the Effendier Sun Sovereign
- **Surai Nakamura** – Ashari warrior
- **Brienne "Rook" Wenfyre** – Sun Queen, outcast princess, daughter of the Morgani Warrior Queen

GODS

- Freya – the Goddess, ruler of the Nihl, mother of both Noctis and Solis
- Odin – the Shadeling, imprisoned in the Netherworld pits, father of both Noctis and Solis

ANIMALS

- Aramaya – Rook's temperamental horse
- Lady Pearl – Haven's loyal horse
- Ravius – Stolas's raven
- Shadow – Damius's wyvern

WEAPONS

- Haven's Sword – Oathbearer
- Stolas's Dagger – Vengeance

ABOUT THE AUTHOR

AUDREY GREY lives in the charming state of Oklahoma surrounded by animals, books, and little people. You can usually find Audrey hiding out in her office, downing copious amounts of caffeine while dreaming of tacos and holding entire conversations with her friends using gifs. Audrey considers her ability to travel to fantastical worlds a superpower and loves nothing more than bringing her readers with her.

Find her online at:

WWW.AUDREYGREY.COM